Just When We Are Safest

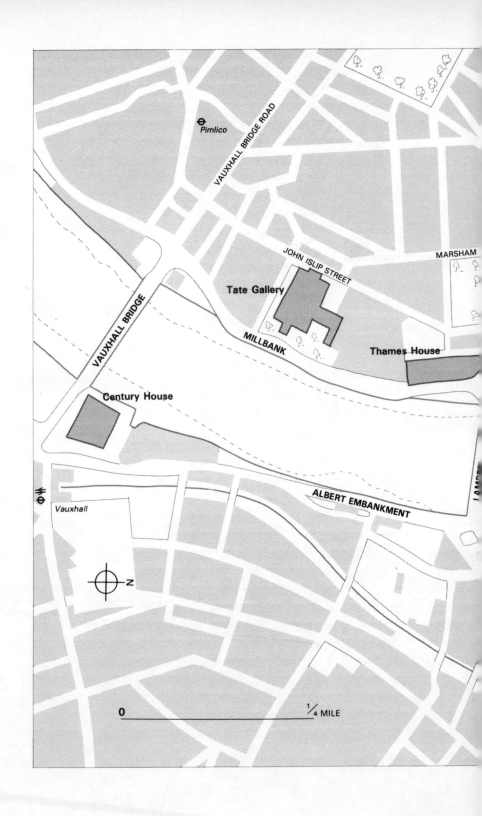

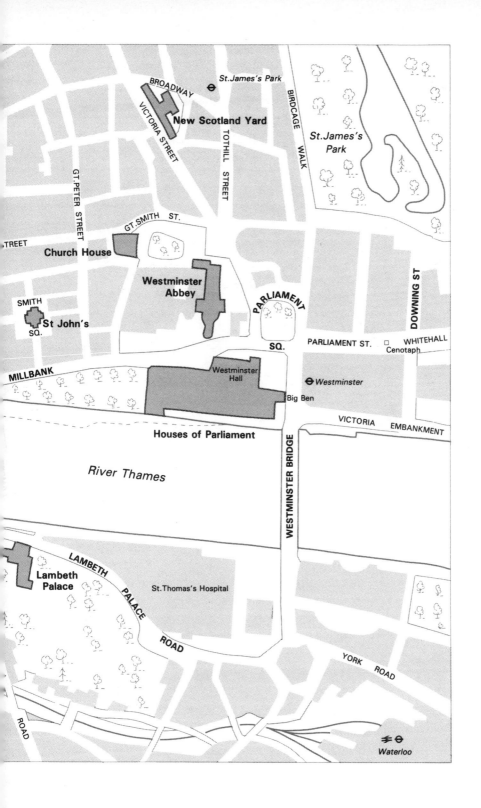

by the same author

DRAWN BLANC
SOMEWHERE IN ENGLAND
SEDUCTION OF A TALL MAN
SOMETHING WORTH FIGHTING FOR
THE LAST HOURS BEFORE DAWN
THE CHAMPAGNE MARXIST
NIGHTSHADE

Just When We Are Safest

REG GADNEY

Just when we are safest, there's a sunset-touch,
A fancy from a flower-bell, some one's death.

Robert Browning, *Bishop Blougram's Apology*

faber and faber
LONDON · BOSTON

For Fay with love

First published in 1995
by Faber and Faber Limited
3 Queen Square London WC1N 3AU

Phototypeset by Parker Typesetting Service, Leicester
Printed in England by Clays Ltd, St Ives plc

© Reg Gadney, 1995

Reg Gadney is hereby identified as author of this work
in accordance with Section 77 of the Copyright,
Designs and Patents Act 1988

A CIP record for this book
is available from the British Library

ISBN 0–571–17382–9

2 4 6 8 10 9 7 5 3 1

MI5 will change my life tonight.
Inspector Mary R. Walker (Metropolitan Police),
unpublished diary

WINTER

Monday 20 December

2 inches of snow covers London. Visibility almost zero. Temperature 2 degrees below freezing.

Today is R + 302. That equals 302 days I've spent with the love of my life. My only love. My wry, private, funny and lovable Senior Investigation Officer from HM Customs & Excise, the one and only – ALAN ROSSLYN. I'd like to thank the following people who are important to my life: the Cat – because you are feline, gangly, sleek, quiet, all those things, and my greatest listener. The Hot Tin Roof Man. The Basement Man. My Secret Lover. All of you are the same man, Alan Rosslyn.

You gave me the idea of sorting out my thoughts on paper, alone, in secret. Answer your own questions in writing, you said.

Now I ask myself: What do I tell the spooks in their new headquarters at Thames House, Millbank, SW1?

MI5 will change my life tonight. My two-hour interview with them will start at 6 p.m. and finish around 8 p.m. Then they will give me their verdict. Either they will say – we're pleased to offer you the appointment, there's a place for you on the basic training course near Portsmouth. Join the family. Welcome to your future with the domestic security service. Subject to the outcome of the medical inspection, you're in, if you'll be good enough to sign here. The acceptance form will be next to a copy of the Official Secrets Act. Would you care for a dry sherry, or perhaps something a little stronger? That's how it will go if they say 'Yes' to me.

Or, if they say 'No', they will take an age to get to the rejection point. Sorry, Inspector Walker, all things being equal, no offence meant, it isn't personal. They will damn me with faint praise: Your record is outstanding. Actually it's brilliant.

But, your future is with the Metropolitan Police. We think we don't entirely suit you. It is your interest we have in mind. So much enjoyed meeting you. Thank you so much for coming to see us on such a pissing awful night. Your record's fantastic, really . . .

They are terribly careful not to cause offence to the people they reject, in case we failures spread the news: MI5 are a bunch of arseholes. They don't set out to make more enemies than they have already.

My life could actually go either way tonight. Here I am, at 29, sitting in my office at the Yard, a very smart police officer who gets the respect she deserves. Maybe I won't be here much longer. It depends on MI5. Must make a list of things to take.

From the wall: most important. Note: the Proficiency in Handling Firearms Certificate that proves I handle guns as well as I've dealt with bank robbers bearing weapons; crack dealers, crazed beyond belief; rapists, paedophiles, cocaine-snorting members of the House of Lords. I can. I have. I know I am one of the best women police officers in the United Kingdom. No one can deny it. Except me – and I do, because I'm totally unsure of where I'm going. I am a question-mark. ? The only other person in the world who knows of this deep uncertainty about myself is Alan.

So – what do I tell them?

I hear him say, 'The truth, the whole truth, nothing but the truth.'

Why?

'Because they know it already.'

Well, they don't. What they don't know is that my life's untidy. And I can't bring myself to tell it to them – not to MI5, not to Alan, and not to THUG who still wants me in his bed.

THUG, old lover, who cannot stand the failure of rejection. THUG, a copper too, old enough to be my father, the possessive lover with a wife at home he doesn't love. THUG who is plonked behind his desk four floors above me as I write. THUG who's just phoned to wish me good luck tonight. He's certain MI5 will sign me on. MI5, he says, don't issue invitations unless they are sure they'll get accepted. My record's great, he says. You're not a member of Greenpeace, CND, Friends of the Earth, the Animal Liberation Front or the Workers' Revolutionary Party. You'll walk it. Then, like Alan, he says: 'Tell them the truth, love. Any chance I can have a date? Go on, love, please.' 'No,' I say, 'that's that. Let's stay friends.' He puts the phone down.

Do I say to MI5: I've got a husband, X, who's queer? I've got a lover who is not a queer, Alan, who's crazy for me and vice versa? Do I say my secret life's untidy?

I suspect they know. They've interviewed my mother, my superior officers, even THUG and he's very superior, and the bloody bank manager who isn't. This is the big question: What do they know about my past? It frightens me: my fear. My past.

2

Do I tell them the IRA scare me?

Thinking about these questions I can't find a way to handle them. If I tell the truth, MI5 will say 'Piss off out of here, don't come back, inspector.' A confidential note will follow my return to duty at the Yard, disciplinary action and then the inevitable suspension. They'll say 'You've forced us to say no because you've said yes to far too many men. Promiscuity = unreliability = the woman who cannot trust herself. Get lost.'

What about my future here at the Yard?

God knows we've been over that one enough. The police is male domi-nated. The higher up the tree the women climb, the easier it is for the men to see up our skirts. Mary Walker of the Yard? Don't make me laugh.

But MI5 – that's another story. There's a woman director general in the treetops up-river at Thames House. In the beginning I know I impress the women interviewers from MI5. They can tell I have the gift of getting right inside a villain's mind. Villains tend not to scare me. It's me, Mary, who scares herself. Only, I suppose, let's face it, the IRA are different.

They asked at the first meeting if the IRA scare me. 'No. Not the slightest,' I lied.

'Think ahead,' they said. 'Suppose you are a terrorist, hell-bent on a spectacular, the big bang, going for the jugular. What targets would you select?'

I said: 'The banking district in the City of London. Or the headquarters of MI5. Or the new headquarters of MI6 at Vauxhall Cross.'

My answer seemed to strike a chord.

'But the headquarters of the security services are bloody well protected,' the women said.

Well, that's what they have to say, isn't it?

I will stick to my little theory when I go to see them later. I'll expand on it a bit.

This is what I'd do as a terrorist.

Plan long-term infiltration. Get an informer in place. The sympathetic weasel. Get the geography of the MI5 headquarters right. Then I'd find a disaffected soul who needs the cash. Some government scientist with lethal knowledge. Not of bombs. Forget the bombs. Too old-fashioned. I'd up the stakes. Use chemicals to poison the water, poison the air, fuck up the air-conditioning. Gas the spooks. Wipe out the lot of them in one fell swoop.

Far-fetched? Not at all. Still with me?

'See,' as Alan says, 'we have the gift of telepathy. We know what people are thinking even before they realize they're thinking it.'

3

Now, my guess is this – the selection people at MI5 know I have the Gift. More than that, there's proof I have. The IRA, no less, proved it for me. They bombed Bishopsgate. They killed one, injured 46, scored around £500 million of damage. QED.

Soon afterwards, this woman showed up here in my office unannounced to say MI5 is 'very keen' on me. When I asked what exactly they had in mind for me to do, she said, 'Surveillance to begin with. We won't rush things. We'll assess your special aptitudes with a view to you going undercover. You'll be armed. Meanwhile we'll be checking on your past. You'll be invited to a crucial interview. Things are looking very good.'

I wonder if they are.

The crucial interview is set for tonight.
The time: start 18.00 hours. End 20.00 hours.
The place: Thames House, Millbank, SW1.
Dress: uniform.

I am trying to imagine what sort of interview they've planned. I asked the woman what to expect. She said something like, 'It'll be plain sailing for you. You'll be asked about straightforward matters. The ability to kill if necessary. The future of terrorism. All you have to do is tell the truth about yourself – your personal relationships, your hopes, your fears. It's best to be open with us. Don't forget, your interviewers will know even more about you than you know about yourself.'

Christ, that's all I need.

Or should we live our dream? Start a new life way out west on some small plantation in the Caribbean. Leave England. Start afresh. Make babies in the sun. Alan says no. Give it your best shot, he says. Put the dream on hold. Go for it, Mary. Win – stuff like that.

What I am doing scares me. But it's too late now. I can't go back. These words stare at me from the page. There are so many ways of describing how it feels to be trapped. None I know can describe what it feels like, what it is, to be completely free.

I'll settle for saying I'm doing this for Alan – to prove to him I've got the strength of mind.

This morning we were in the shower together. 'Jingle Bells' was coming from the radio. It's a lousy tune. Like 'White Christmas'. I hate the snow.

When I reached my office this morning I found two postcards waiting on my desk from Alan. He's sent them to boost my confidence. One is The Kiss

by Rodin; the other, The Kiss *by Klimt. He's written on the Rodin card,*
'You win, Mary', and on the Klimt he says, 'Tonight you'll know the best'.

I've never had a more thoughtful lover.

He's the one man who's always put me *first, who really makes me* feel
first. That I matter more than anyone else on earth. He's rare.

*Whereas I have to write everything down to remember it, he hoards facts
inside his brain. Like, for example: I sent him identical cards 213 days ago.
That was 89 days after we met.*

Now it's R + 302.

*Alan promises to wait for me tonight at eight on Lambeth Bridge. When
it's all over, he'll be there.*

*I want to see him standing, in his black coat, in the snow, his tall and
catlike figure hunched beneath the streetlight like a gangster in a black and
white B movie, looking good.*

*That's what I think. But Alan doesn't. He underestimates himself and
how much I love him. Always have, always will.*

End of interview with self. New Scotland Yard. R + 302.

1

Alan Rosslyn kept his promise to wait for her on Lambeth Bridge. With the tide turning, the Thames was black. Downriver, the Houses of Parliament were a luminous blur. Snow on the wind gusted in his face and melted in his hair. Passing traffic sprayed slush and grit across the pavement forcing him to stay close to the parapet. He checked his watch against the muffled chimes of Big Ben.

Mary's interview in Thames House, the new headquarters of MI5, was running late; a good sign, he thought; if she'd got here before him it would probably have spelled rejection.

Thames House rose up on Millbank through the driving snow. The grey and massive building was a last echo of an imperial style of architecture. In one of its hundreds of barred and lighted windows he saw lights from a solitary Christmas tree: garish red, a sickly green, then acid yellow. They flickered and flashed like some coded signal.

He turned up the collar of his coat. It was a poor defence against the snow. The coat was an early Christmas present from Mary, a bargain of sorts from a charity sale in a Pimlico church hall. A label on its lining showed the coat had once belonged to a Baptist minister, formerly of Antigua and North Kensington. Rosslyn had found the provenance appropriate. It encouraged his secret dream of a future life in the Caribbean: fantasies of sun, sand and palm trees tossed by sea winds a thousand miles from the misery of the London winter.

The only other person he had shared his dream with was Mary Walker.

They had first met as students on the basic course run by the Metropolitan Police Firearms Training Branch at Lippitts Hill in Essex. From the beginning of the course, on which there were some ten students in all, Rosslyn and Mary had been marked out as outsiders. Mary was the only woman and Rosslyn, as a senior investigation officer in Customs & Excise, was the only non-police officer. For two weeks they were fully trained in weapons handling. Their instructor continuously assessed and monitored thirteen different categories of students' ability and aptitude, from Physical Attributes, Emotional Strength, Teamwork and Co-operation, to Decision Making under Pressure, Impact and Assertiveness, and Interpersonal Sensitivity. Each category was marked out of four by the instructor and entered on the individual Tutorial/Progress Report form. The maximum possible score was fifty-two points. The chief instructor had introduced an innovation to the course that Rosslyn and Mary joined. By way of encouraging a spirit of competitive teamwork he assigned each trainee a partner. To the extrovert Mary, who he called Mary-Get-Your-Gun, he had assigned Rosslyn, Mr Duty Free, and the competitiveness between the two of them had been intense. From the outset Mary had the edge on her partner.

When they had enrolled on the first Friday their pulse rates, rested, were about eighty beats a minute. For holding handguns steady the rate needed to be some fifty-five beats. To reduce their pulse rates they trained together in the gym with weights, holding them out at arm's length as if they were handguns. They exercised to strengthen muscles in their shoulders, arms, wrists and fingers: timing each other with stop-watches until the pain became unbearable; timing each other holding their breath, faces turning from white to red to purple, feeling their lungs reach bursting point. After all that, with running and swimming to develop heart and lungs, Mary got her pulse rate down to the required fifty-five beats. And she achieved it some days before Rosslyn.

Competition between the two of them during live training on the ranges was equally intense. In dark blue training overalls, they stood side by side, their ears protected by ear mufflers from the incessant cracks of the guns; Mr Duty Free firing his shots, Mary-Get-Your-Gun firing hers to better his scores; mastering the art and science of firing the Smith & Wesson Model 10 revolvers, Glock pistols and Heckler & Koch MP5 carbines: weapons manufactured in Germany by Obendorf, a firm owned by British Aerospace and assembled by Royal Ordnance. Such details the students were required to know.

The intensity of their competitiveness at Lippitts Hill continued in what is called the Judgement Room. This small interior training range uses special film and video projection equipment imported from the United States. It requires the students to react immediately under conditions of extreme stress. They use live ammunition in their handguns and, in the dark, on the paper screen, they are confronted with moving life-size clips of armed murderers, terrorists and maniacs coming at them with every kind of knife, blade, gun, grenade and explosive device. You react before the figure on the screen. If you fire second you're dead meat. Some of your assailants may, of course, be carrying imitation firearms, or maybe nothing. They may behave just as if they're armed. And if and when you kill an unarmed assailant, well, eventually the jury may find you guilty of manslaughter. You have a split second in which to decide to do the right thing or to do the wrong thing. To kill or be killed.

Mary never hesitated in the Judgement Room. She scored full marks; whereas Rosslyn, who twice reacted too slowly, scored low points for his hesitations. Thus, at the end of the first week, Mary was ahead of him on points.

During week two, the gap between their scores began to narrow, mainly the result of Rosslyn scoring top marks during the seminar run by a visiting officer from the National Criminal Intelligence Service. This seminar was another innovation introduced by the chief instructor 'as a mark of the new spirit of co-operation between the services fighting organized and enterprise crime in the United Kingdom'. The main questions in the written paper included: 'The number of shooting incidents in London has decreased during the last ten years. True or False? Discuss.' (Surprisingly, according to the Metropolitan Police Firearms Laboratory, the correct answer is True.)

Rosslyn elaborated upon 'the general consensus that corrupt firearms dealers and thefts from firearms certificate holders provide the majority of criminally held firearms. With the January 1993 removal of customs barriers between European Community states, the way is open for United Kingdom criminals to obtain weapons on the near Continent with little risk of detection. In Belgium and France it is possible for a United Kingdom citizen to purchase pump-action shotguns on production of a passport. Ownership of firearms in Belgium is one of the highest in the world.'

9

He went on to show how 'it is possible for anyone with the right Belgian connections to obtain an almost unlimited number of high-powered weapons.' And he argued how very easy it is 'to obtain weapons, explosives and explosive devices in the countries of the old Soviet Bloc, especially from the Czech Republic which has the largest armaments industry in the world and from German centres such as Dresden.'

He warmed to his theme and scored top marks. He also succeeded, towards the end of that second week, in scoring higher marks than Mary in the categories of Planning Tactics, Restraint and Control, Information Assimilation, Alertness and Conscientious Application.

At the end of the course each student was required to read the instructor's written assessment, then sign the two-sided form to show that they agreed its contents, and finally make a confidential comment on their performance. Mary wrote: 'I know it's true that women police officers generally make the best shots or the worst shots. I want to be in the first group. It's a myth that women are no good with guns.' She had made her point. She had the edge and in every kind of weapon training she had come out ahead of Rosslyn with a very high score of 45. The woman on top. The man one step behind. The score sheets told the story: she'd got the better of his 36 by far. Even at the end of course party she still felt the need to remind him that she was the winner by trying to drink him under the table in the pub, the Owl, at the entrance to Lippitts Hill and again, afterwards, when the successful students went on to an Indian restaurant in Loughton.

Looking at her slim and boyish figure Rosslyn wondered aloud how the so-called experts could claim that women's body weight meant they would get drunk more quickly than men.

'Do you always say the first thing that comes into your head?' she asked. 'Is that how you show Restraint and Control?'

'If I think it's true,' he countered, 'yes. I say what I think.'

'You're not going to get far with that attitude. You didn't do too well with Interpersonal Sensitivity either, did you?'

'Your policy's dishonesty, is it?' he asked.

Something in Rosslyn's face stopped her short. He seemed tense. The dark eyes, his broken nose, the thick hair combed back severely hinted at a reservoir of controlled violence. 'What's eating you?' she said. 'Aren't you used to finishing second, or is it because I'm a woman?'

The party over, the other students were leaving. 'I'll tell you what's on my mind,' he said. 'If you must know.'

Like most skilled interrogators he was a good storyteller. Over another cheap brandy he told her what was bothering him.

A Customs & Excise investigation team had caught the scent of an IRA ring smuggling arms and explosives into the United Kingdom. Working undercover he had personally targeted an Irish woman, one Deirdre 'Dee' Patricia McKeague. His surveillance officers believed she was a major storeman using rented lock-up garages in West London. Rosslyn had wanted to make a quick arrest. But he had been restrained from taking her off the streets by his superiors, on orders from some faceless interservice committee of advisers from the Met and MI5. They hoped to use McKeague as bait to catch even bigger poison fish. They had wanted him out of the way. So they had sent him on the Lippitts Hill course to play cowboys with the coppers. He wasn't prepared to divulge any operational details to her.

To change the subject, she asked him about his family.

'My father was army. Engineers in Germany in the sixties. Not officer class. A warrant officer. Too clever to be an officer. He knew everything about building bridges and stuff like that. A brilliant mind. Brilliant.' She smiled at the note of pride in his voice. 'I was farmed out to my aunts in Bournemouth. Not much fun really. Just pets for company. Mice and a hamster. Then the cat turned nasty. No more mice. And the hamster got run over by a mail van. I saw it.'

'Is it always that violent in Bournemouth?'

He smiled. 'Most of the time.'

'Where was your mother then?'

'She ran off with some German. I never saw her again. She could be dead for all I know. My father died in Dortmund. When the army returned his personal effects I got a whole batch of my mother's letters to him. I never realized how much they hated each other. Beyond that, what do you say? There's no point digging up the past. Maybe I shouldn't have read my mother's letters to Dad. Sometimes I wonder why he kept them.'

Mary turned aside for a moment. Then she gave him a look of concern. 'If it's painful, don't talk about it.'

'It could have been worse. Anyhow, it didn't stop me going to university.'

'What was your subject?'

'Zoology.'

'How did you end up in Customs then?'

'Just answered an ad.'

The proprietor of the Indian restaurant was fiddling with the door to the street, impatient to close up for the night. Their conversation was at an end.

By the time they next met in London, Dee McKeague, the IRA's storeman, had been arrested under the Prevention of Terrorism Act. Rosslyn invited Mary to celebrate the catch with a night in the West End. He told her he was now being welcomed at New Scotland Yard and had even been offered observer status on the very interservice body which had once wanted him out of the way. He was on first name terms with junior detectives in the anti-terrorist branch and had been bought the odd half-pint of real ale by gung-ho types from MI5 in the pubs they frequented around Westminster.

That night, outside Victoria Station, Mary told him that, even though she didn't wear a wedding ring, she was married. She refused to talk about her husband. He saw her on to the last train and she seemed reluctant to go and unusually tense. The train's departure was delayed. Her reluctance to discuss her husband aroused his curiosity. He was tempted to press the matter further but finally decided against it. Instead, he reminded her what their instructor at Lippitts Hill had said: 'Start worrying after you've fired your last shot! Switch off. Slow down. Relax!' He reminded her of the instructor's technique for relaxation. 'Imagine a place of escape. Mine's in the Caribbean. Sand. Palm trees in the wind. The sea. The sun.'

As the train pulled out she kissed him.

If afterwards someone had asked him when he first realized that he was falling in love with her he would have said it was at that moment.

On Lambeth Bridge he stamped his feet. The cold was biting. Beyond the Horseferry Road roundabout he saw three police officers examining a mound of blankets. One of the officers shoved a boot into the shapeless pile. Another lifted a steaming figure to his feet: a derelict in a Santa outfit with a cider bottle in his hand. *You'd think they'd find better things to do*, Rosslyn thought: *even Santa's entitled to get pissed for Christmas*. The police officers were laughing, caught in the glare of headlights from a Royal Mail van. They were waving at another figure standing at the corner of Thames House.

It was Mary and she was waving at him. She's got in, he thought, they want her. She's in. He crossed the road, unsteadily, the feeling returning to his frozen feet.

They embraced beneath a streetlight.

'I've done it,' she said. 'They want me, Alan.'

'I knew they would.'

'I couldn't have done it without you.'

'Nothing to do with me.' He kissed her mouth.

'It's an offence to make love to a uniformed police officer in public,' she said. 'Christ, not here.'

'Who cares? Let's go home.' He peered along the embankment for a cab. 'I'm frozen.'

She was looking up to the windows in Thames House. 'Shit, I've forgotten my bloody shoulder bag. Wait here, OK? Five minutes. I'm sorry. Don't go.'

Holding on to her policewoman's hat, she ran off into the snow. Once she stopped to adjust her skirt. And, turning, as though with second thoughts, she shouted: 'I love you.'

He waved back to her. Then she was gone.

He crossed the street to a doorway, thinking he should have sheltered here before. He'd take her to a restaurant to celebrate her secret triumph. He was thinking of the one she liked the most when he suddenly saw her next. He was baffled at the sight of her. She was standing alone, a few yards from a high security gate, in a pool of floodlight.

She seemed dazzled, frozen, her eyes fixed in a stare like a frightened child.

Suddenly she shouted: 'Get back, Alan!'

Then he saw her glance in a new direction, at a dark blue police van parked not far down the street. Slowly, as if drawn to danger, she walked step by step towards it.

Ahead of her, beyond the police van, he saw the three uniformed police officers running down Horseferry Road. There was now no sign of Santa Claus.

Warning shouts, high pitched and frantic, erupted overhead. Then they were obliterated in an outburst of klaxon hooters, a siren and warning bells.

From rooftops, beyond the car park at the rear of the building, a bank of arc lights pierced the snow.

Mary seemed to be looking up at the windows above, at the faces peering into the brilliant light. She screamed: 'Get back from the windows!' Then she continued, even more slowly than before, towards the police van.

A man's voice yelled through a bullhorn: 'You! Move yourself. This way!'

Rosslyn assumed he was shouting at Mary, until the voice added: 'You in the black coat!' and he realized he was the one they were shouting at. 'Raise your hands above your head.'

He did as he was told and turned to see who was barking at him. With the fierce light in his eyes it was impossible to tell. There were running footsteps behind him.

'DON'T MOVE!'

A hand grabbed his coat so violently that he overbalanced. He was dragged into a doorway and pushed down hard to his knees. 'What *is* this?' His arm was jerked up behind his back. The crushing weight of the police officers forced him downwards.

He kept his eyes on Mary. He thought: *She seems to know what's going on. She's in control.* Then he heard the gunshots.

The first one struck her in the chest and stomach. It seemed to lift her backwards as if her body was being dragged away in bits by an invisible wire.

The others hit her head. One moment it was a red and watery blur as if drenched in spray from the nozzle of a giant hose; then there was nothing there, only a hideous mound of clothing, steaming like the derelict Santa Claus the police had disturbed less than fifteen minutes earlier, and a stream of blood spreading through the snow.

2

Some thirty minutes after Mary's death he was examined cursorily by a woman doctor in Thames House and given a mug of hot sweet tea. Then three officers from Special Branch questioned him in a windowless room. A Christmas tree stood in the corner. It flashed red, then green, then yellow. Someone said that the tree was one of several given to Thames House by 10 Downing Street. The colours made strange patterns on the wall.

Immediately after the shooting he had used tremendous force to break free from the grip of the police officers whose combined strength had forced him to his knees in the doorway. He had kicked one of the policemen in the groin, butted the second with his head and pushed him backwards against the third. Then he ran to where Mary had fallen. Her head and face had disintegrated. He had grovelled in the slush, his hands smeared with her blood. Police officers led him away from the scene to Thames House, to the room where he was sitting opposite the Special Branch.

Mary's blood was drying on his coat which was ripped at the shoulder from the struggle. He gave his answers in a monotone, without emotion, describing his version of Mary's death mechanically. Sometimes his voice seemed to belong to someone else. He heard himself speaking from a distance, saying 'Yes' and 'No' and 'I don't remember'.

The atrocity was something they could all agree upon, like his personal details: 'My full name is Alan Hutton Rosslyn, thirty years old, senior investigation officer, HM Customs & Excise.' He gave them the address of his flat in Pimlico. The questions struck him as meaningless as an opinion pollster's.

Everyone had seen the killing. What was the point in him adding to the story? He knew what he wanted. He wanted Mary.

From somewhere a technician had produced a video system. They sat through the replay of Mary's death as seen by the surveillance cameras. Every moment of the murder had been recorded. The main protagonist, the person who had fired the rifle, could not be identified. Mary's killer had fired from a position high in scaffolding hidden by tarpaulins. The failure of the surveillance cameras to reveal the killer's identity seemed to be taken almost as a personal insult by the Special Branch officers. The killing had taken place under the very noses of the Security Service, right on the doorstep of its new headquarters.

The Special Branch officers thanked Rosslyn for his help. They said MI5 would talk to him shortly and left him alone in the bare white room with the flashing Christmas tree.

To begin with, he felt no grief. His immediate reaction was physical. He couldn't stop the shaking in the muscles of his arms and legs. His clothes were covered in Mary's blood. So were his hands. He remembered the rush of people clambering up the scaffold; then the voices bawling, panic-stricken, shouting for people to take cover.

Someone had draped a blanket over Mary. Someone else removed it. The whole scene seemed alive with anger. Men and women ran around like hyperactive children. It was incomprehensible.

His breathing was uneven and irregular; his sight grew blurred. He felt almost disembodied, as if the whole thing was some horrific *déjà vu*, and he was the victim of a violent and disjointed nightmare. When two women came into the room behind him he was feeling so faint he was unaware of them for several moments. Then a voice said: 'I'm Frances Monro. This is Serena Watson.'

He turned to see a woman, a redhead in a dark blue suit. 'My assistant,' she added self-importantly. Rosslyn wondered whether the names were genuine. 'I know this is a bad time for you, but I have to ask you one or two questions.'

'Go ahead,' Rosslyn said, distantly.

'Some things don't quite add up,' she began. 'For example, what exactly were you doing outside here this evening?'

Rosslyn noticed she wore a gold earring in her left ear. He said: 'I'd have thought you knew Mary was my fiancée.'

Her face had a look of infinite superiority. 'We know about Inspector Walker. My question is directed at you, Mr Rosslyn.'

'I'm aware of that, Miss Monro. If Mary had never met you people she would still be alive.'

'If I am guilty of a solecism, Mr Rosslyn, forgive me. Nevertheless, how did you know she had an appointment with me?'

Rosslyn felt the resentment rising in his chest. 'I didn't know who she'd come to see,' he said. 'She never told me who exactly was going to interview her.'

'She never mentioned my name?'

'No, she didn't.'

'Or my rank and grade in the Security Service?'

'No. And I don't know them either,' Rosslyn said. 'And I have to say they don't make much difference to me anyway.'

Still that knowing smile. The awful bright eyes that never left his face. Her smugness was unbearable.

'We intended to recruit Inspector Walker,' Ms Monro continued.

'I know that. It turned out to be a god-awful mistake, didn't it?'

'You are very angry.'

'Right.'

'And violent too?'

'Only when I need to be.'

She gave him her best headmistress look. 'Our personal records appear to show that she was married. How do you explain that she was your fiancée?'

'Because she was divorcing her husband. There's no bloody law against asking a woman to marry you even if she's married already.'

'I suppose there isn't. Forgive me, I never noticed an engagement ring.'

'Because I hadn't given her one.'

'That makes sense.'

'I think so too.'

'What was the basis of this divorce action of Inspector Walker's?'

'Incompatibility,' Rosslyn said. 'Her husband's gay.'

'There's no law against that either,' Monro observed, smiling at her assistant who was staring at the carpet tiles on the floor.

Rosslyn noticed the colour rising up Ms Watson's neck. The woman had the look of a gym instructress, with short fair hair. She must have seen Rosslyn notice her blush. She buttoned the collar of her white shirt with studied casualness.

Monro must have noticed it too, for she suddenly changed the subject. 'You're a senior investigation officer in Customs & Excise.'

'Right.'

'Your immediate superior is?'

'Richard Gaynor. Customs A, Group D, Branch Six Head-quarters.'

'Weren't you the one who arrested Deirdre McKeague, the IRA storeman?'

If you know this, why ask? he thought. He wasn't about to deny his greatest professional achievement. Dee McKeague was being held in custody in a maximum security cell at this very moment. The two women must know it. After a long pause he said: 'Yes.'

'You have direct contact with terrorists?'

'With informers. We were tipped off about Dee McKeague.' They must know that too.

'So you know the importance of security. You realize that loitering in the area of a prohibited place within the meaning of the Official Secrets Act is a punishable offence.'

'I'm aware of that,' Rosslyn snapped. 'Neither Inspector Walker nor I were committing an offence. What the hell are you driving at?'

Monro tensed, and her assistant chimed in: 'I know this is a difficult time for you. But we need to confirm that you are covered by the act.'

'Of course I am.'

'Then would you describe what you were doing during the twelve or so hours before Inspector Walker died,' Monro said.

'I was working in my office.'

'You presumably have witnesses who can substantiate that?'

'Of course.'

'What time did you leave your office?'

'Some time around seven.'

'And you came straight here presumably.'

'Yes.'

'Is there anything else you'd like to tell us?'

He leaned forward, sweating, beneath the stark light. His mouth was very dry. 'Look, I've had enough of this.' His anger must have communicated itself to Monro who flinched. 'I saw Mary murdered in cold blood. I saw her die. You didn't. I've already spoken to Special Branch. And if I do remember anything of use I'll tell it to them first.'

'I find you very hostile, Mr Rosslyn. We can't allow our feelings to get the better of us. Can you remember anything else about the moment you saw Inspector Walker hit by the gunfire?'

'I remember the sound. And some stupid radio inside this place playing "Jingle Bells".' He felt his tears were not far off. 'If you two are so interested, Mary and I sang it together in the shower this morning. She said it was sentimental crap.'

Monro closed her notebook. 'You'll be taken from this place to a hospital' – it sounded like a death sentence – 'where you'll be kept for the time being. Simply for reasons of security. We don't want you put at risk.'

The women got to their feet. 'Thank you. You've been very helpful, Mr Rosslyn. We'll arrange an escort for you. No doubt we'll meet again.'

Not if I can help it, Rosslyn thought. He felt an overwhelming tiredness, the need to be left alone.

The hospital was the King Edward VII Hospital for Officers in Beaumont Street. In the corridor outside his single room there were armed police officers from the protection unit of the Special Branch. They changed shifts every eight hours. After a day or two the security routine had relaxed. The door to his room was left ajar so the officers could share in the banality of BBC TV's Christmas offerings. When Rosslyn wanted to use the bathroom his guards reminded him to leave the door open. They apologized for this invasion of his privacy. 'Rules are rules,' they said. The guards wanted to be his friends. 'We're all in the same boat,' they said, 'once the shooting starts.'

During the Queen's Christmas message Rosslyn was joined by a jovial black SB officer. 'Everywhere man is in chains,' said the officer, with no apparent interest in Her Majesty's anxious mood. He explained to Rosslyn that he was 'pursuing' a correspondence course in 'the religions of the world. With an eye to my future in active local politics in the Caribbean.' Rosslyn remembered his dream of sun-kissed paradise and realized it had lost its magic.

The nurses treated him with a more practical kind of sympathy. They seemed to know why he was being guarded there, out of sight, away from the prying eyes of those who might wish to see him dead.

It was several days before he received the visit from Commander Thomas Harding. Harding was the man who had been the public face of Scotland Yard for six years in the war against the terrorists. After each outrage he appeared on the nation's TV screens like a messenger of death, offering solemn comment and expressing his sympathy for the families of the victims. He was, by now, something of a celebrity, the expert and regular visitor in the living room, almost as familiar to the viewing millions as the eccentric TV weatherman. You would see him turn aside from the latest scene of devastation, careful not to block the images of destruction, and stride purposefully to the camera. Then he would suck his teeth with a frown conveying anger, sadness and disapproval, and deliver another appeal for public vigilance. There were only a limited number of ways to say the same old thing. But the audience was fed up with his failure to halt the violence. The nation had put up with misery and frustration for long enough.

Rumour had it Commander Harding was being poorly treated by the politicians. Not surprising, when you felt each successive bomb blast in the streets signalled the government's failure. Their failure, made the more public by Harding's TV appearances, became Harding's failure. Like it or not, it looked personal. He became the focus of armchair politicians. Bad news stuck to him, criticism of him seemed justified. This spear carrier in the war against the terrorists wielded a weapon as feeble as the hero's in some cheap pantomime. It's the fault of his kind, people said, that the United Kingdom's no longer united; never mind the Kingdom looks daily more like a poor variety show with the royals in the leading roles. Some said you couldn't blame the bloke. They weren't *his* bombs. Unfortunately, that's how it began to look. People knew his face; they recognized him in the street. They wouldn't recognize a terrorist if they saw one with a lighted fuse.

When Harding eventually turned up, dressed in a grey suit, more like a consultant surgeon than a veteran cop, he offered his condolences. 'We've little doubt Mary was a victim of the IRA,' he said.

'Have they claimed responsibility?'

'No. But I can explain.'

'Then you mean,' Rosslyn interrupted, 'you've had a tip-off?'

'No.'

'What makes you so sure it was the IRA, have you found the murder weapon?'

'Not yet. But the National Firearms Lab at Huntingdon has tested the bullets removed from the scene of the shooting and two removed from Mary's body. The NFL ballistics experts have matched them with a Kalashnikov. The number of grooves on the bullets match. So does the direction of spin.' He spread his strong hands on the bed rail.

'There's been a very careful post-mortem. I was there.'

'You watched the post-mortem?'

'I'm afraid so. I know what you'll be feeling, Alan.'

'I want to know everything.'

'But you won't want to hear the details. All I can tell you is that Mary walked straight into the beginnings of a spectacular aimed straight at MI5.'

'No tip-off.'

'No.'

'No suspects?'

'Not yet.'

'Not one?'

'No. We have to be patient. There's nothing like the murder of a woman police officer to excite the Met. Her killer can hide, but not for ever. The number of escape routes is finite. Forensic have been over the whole area two or three times. Take it from me, our people are listening in bars and clubs from Camden to Liverpool, Glasgow to Southampton.'

'What else are you doing?'

'It's a full-scale investigation.'

'I want to know what you're doing.'

'I can only tell you what my colleagues are telling me. On a need-to-know basis.'

'That's not much comfort, is it?'

'I know. But we can, maybe, take some heart from the fact that, well, you could say she didn't die in vain.'

'You think that?' Rosslyn asked bitterly. He remembered the chaos around Thames House. The shouting. Being jumped on and held down for his own safety.

'You were there, Alan.' Harding was saying. 'Mary saw a police van. Immediately, sixth sense, innate suspicion, call it what you want, anyway something told her the van was suss. And it was. It was packed with high explosive. It was intended to cause massive damage to MI5, to their people, their building. Think of the propaganda value in that. Thames House blown up. The very heart of the Security Service damaged to the tune of millions. The UK made the laughing stock of the whole world.'

There was a long pause.

'It didn't happen though,' Rosslyn said, choking back his feelings.

They got Mary. 'And I don't understand why Mary let herself stand out there, so exposed.'

'Who knows what she was thinking?' Harding took a deep breath and turned his head aside. 'We'll never know.'

'I've gone over it endlessly,' Rosslyn said. 'Apart from everything else, I don't see, for one, why the bomber hung around instead of just getting the hell away?'

'I can't say,' Harding said. 'What I've been told is that the van had been parked there by a single driver. Remember, it was a police van. That's why it stayed there unchecked.'

'Not for very long.'

'Long enough for the driver to leave through the building site opposite.'

'Where to?'

'To a neighbouring street presumably. Within walking distance.'

'Then what?'

Harding paused. 'Then disappear.' He was choosing his words carefully. Either he genuinely had not reconstructed the killer's movements or, for his own reasons if he had, he was not going to reveal all the details. He went on: 'If you consider the geography of the area, it is most probably that when the killer saw Mary in uniform walking towards the police van the thought struck home that "Christ, that policewoman is going to take a look at the van. There are only so many minutes left until it explodes. Suppose she looks inside the van and finds the HE? The bomb squad will get here pronto and disarm my bomb. People inside Thames House will be evacuated. I have failed." You see, I have to think myself into the terrorist's situation. The killer has a sixth sense too. The adrenalin's really pumping. It's the same on both sides. For Mary too. You don't necessarily think clearly. You imagine the worst. After all of this planning, you think, my luck is seriously out. Or I can just walk away hoping the policewoman hasn't noticed anything suss.'

'Or,' Rosslyn said, 'you create a diversion?'

'Is that what you think happened?' Harding asked.

'Don't you? You shoot the policewoman. You hope, in the ensuing confusion, the van gets ignored. I mean, Jesus, I saw it, you have to admit all eyes were on Mary. It was obvious she suspected the van.'

'Exactly,' Harding said. 'That's how we got there in time to disarm the bomb inside it. You're familiar with high explosive technology, I suppose?'

Rosslyn nodded. He had caught Dee McKeague in possession of a lethal quantity.

'The van contained fifty pounds of Gelamex, Cordtex, an alarm clock, terminal and battery. The whole thing was packed tight with nitrobenzine and sodium cholate. A vast quantity. To say it was lethal would be an understatement. The effects of its force would have been horrific. We disarmed it.'

'Why didn't they evacuate Thames House?'

'Because it's bomb proof. The order was to disarm it straight-away. No alarm. No public attention. To allow the enemy no propaganda value. But, bomb proof or not, you remember Mary shouted at the faces in the windows of Thames House?'

Rosslyn thought of Mary and her warning shout.

'Those people would have been cut to bits by flying glass,' Harding said. 'Away from the windows they were safe. They owe Mary more than perhaps they realize.'

'They didn't save her, did they?'

'I'm sorry. I know. All I can say to you is that if Mary hadn't been so courageous there could have been terrible injuries. Even loss of life.'

There was silence. The explanations seemed so unsatisfactory. Eventually, Rosslyn said, 'To me it seems just like that. A terrible loss of life. Mary's loss.'

'I'm sorry I can't tell you anything else. I can understand your pain. I know how great Mary's loss is to you, to me, to her family. That's why I'll be attending her funeral in person. We have to carry on, Alan. You know. H.O.P.E. Humour. Optimism. Patience. Energy.' He paused. 'You did very well. Especially, so I hear, with MI5.' He smiled. 'You have H.O.P.E. I listened to the tape of their interview with you. It's made my Christmas.' He straightened his tie. Stretched his neck.

'I didn't know they recorded it.'

'They record everything,' Harding said. 'It's their job.'

Everything, Rosslyn was going to add, except the identity of Mary's killer who must already be a long way ahead of the police hunt. There seemed little point in wiping the confident smile from

Harding's face by saying so. Instead, he thanked him for the visit and wished him 'Happy Christmas'.

'Happy Christmas,' Harding said.

3

They scattered Mary's ashes on the Yorkshire moors in the January snow. The landscape was white and black; the low sky, iron grey. Her mother had arranged the ceremony 'according', so she told Rosslyn, 'to my daughter's wishes'.

He guessed the ceremony had more probably been the brainchild of Mary's husband, a fey man with a shaven head who insisted upon being called 'Mr Walker'. A priest in billowing robes asked the group of mourners to form a semicircle in the snow.

They shifted about uncomfortably in the cold, their shoes crunching the frozen heather. A sheep moved by a high stone wall like the phantom of a disturbed rock. It stared at the group of strangers in the barren moorland with a look of disbelief.

Beyond a broad gate, broken from its hinges, down a track of footprints in the snow, he saw the unmarked police cars. Police officers stamped their feet, as impatient as Rosslyn for the ceremony to end.

'If you would,' the priest said to Mary's mother. A kind of pass the parcel game ensued. The undertaker handed a small cardboard box to Mary's mother, to Walker, then to the priest: none of them seemed very willing to be caught holding it. Rosslyn closed his eyes, unable to watch.

The priest said: 'We commit the mortal remains of Mary Walker to the snow and earth of her beloved Yorkshire birthplace. May Almighty God the Father, the Son and the Holy Ghost, preserve her soul. For now and evermore. Amen.'

When he opened his eyes Rosslyn saw the grey patch of bone dust on the snow. A little of it must have stuck to the hem of the priest's robes for he was dusting himself between his legs, embarrassed, as if he had suffered some accident of a personal nature. *Mary*, he thought, *would have seen the funny side of it*. But the momentary spark of humour was soon gone. His eyes were hot and he could no longer hold back his tears.

There was mulled wine and a glutinous cheese fondue in the upstairs private room of the pub in Skipton. A log fire burned in the grate. Beside it stood a Christmas tree surrounded by grinning plastic figures of Santa Claus raising flagons of beer: cheery statuettes advertising an Australian lager. The room was crowded with strangers: Mary's relatives, some local journalists and police officers. Her mother and Mary's husband, now with his sullen man-friend, stuck close to the priest and his saturnine verger. On the mantelpiece, above the smoking fire, was a colour photograph of Mary in uniform with a card printed in fluorescent red saying *In Memoriam.*

He saw Harding offering condolences to the mourners. Then, with a kind of solid dignity, Harding asked for silence. 'I want to say a few words about the last chapter of a young life extinguished by men of evil for a base cause. About a death without meaning. Mary Walker. Another name on the lengthening roll of servicemen and police officers murdered by an unseen enemy.'

He sipped a glass of water. 'Mary served the best years of her young life in the police *service*, not the police *force*,' the commander emphasized. 'The *service*. She lived her life for you and me. She died for you and me. She worked for a brief period in my department, SO 13, our anti-terrorist branch. She had been singled out to me as a police officer of great promise. She was high-spirited, of great humour, physically fit and of exceptional intelligence. She was much loved by all who knew her. There are those here, not only from the Metropolitan Police, but from Customs & Excise no less, who will testify to her skills.'

Don't say my name, Rosslyn begged in silence. His eyes met Harding's. He looked down at the row of Santa Claus statuettes.

Harding went on: 'A close colleague, a male colleague from Customs, a born marksman, was on our weapons training course at Lippitts Hill in Epping Forest. He's a young man whose work has directly led to the discovery of a major arms store and the arrest of a woman terrorist.'

Eyes looked around the room. None seemed to focus on Rosslyn.

'When I interviewed her confidentially, it was the last time we met.'

You can say that again. She never let on to me she'd ever been interviewed by you.

'She told me something of her hopes and fears. She made an unusual admission. Namely, that she hoped one day to secure the conviction of a terrorist, no matter what the risk to her personal safety; no matter that she might well be marked out as a potential target. When I asked her why, she told me it was because she wanted to put a stop to the murder of children. Especially the children.'

Someone standing behind Rosslyn in the doorway began to sob.

'Mary was a young woman who put others first. That's what she did that night at Millbank. Some intuition told her something was wrong about the fake police vehicle. And she tried, she tried, as the last act of her young life, to protect the lives of others. So it is important we never think of Mary in connection with what some historians may come to regard as an operational failure. She sacrificed her life, remember. Let us observe one minute's silence to reflect upon a young woman. Her laughter. Her playful smile. And the light she carried in living a decent life. For I promise you this. The light of Mary Walker's life will never dim.'

Rosslyn watched Harding bow his head in silence. From below, from the jukebox in the public bar, he heard the awful tune: 'Oh jingle bells, jingle bells, jingle all the way.'

He had never realized it was possible to hate Christmas quite so much. And this was New Year, when Christmas had long since passed its sell-by date. The cheap tune chirruped over the sobs.

'Thank you,' Harding said.

The minute's silence was over. The mourners offered the commander muted thanks. Most of them were in tears.

Time to go, to find the cab driver who said he would drive him to Leeds for the London train.

'Alan?' It was Commander Harding's voice behind him. 'How are you getting back to London?'

'Train from Leeds.'

'Forget that. We'll take you back in the helicopter with us.' Harding turned aside to say 'No comment' to a journalist.

There was a tap on Rosslyn's shoulder. 'Alan.'

Mary's mother, red-eyed and agitated, was holding out two brown paper parcels tied with Christmas string. She looked quickly across the room to where Walker was in conversation with his

26

man-friend and the priest. 'Mary gave these to me for safe keeping,' she said hurriedly. 'You must have them now. Don't open them here. Your letters to her are inside the larger parcel. The other one contains her diary. She kept them in her office at Scotland Yard with instructions they be sent to me if anything happened. I'd like you to have them.' She began to weep. 'I knew she loved you. Just, well, Alan, I never realized how much. Whatever you do in the future, please, never forget her.' For a moment she gripped his hand. Then she turned away leaving Rosslyn with the parcels.

Harding was waiting for him by the door.

The white moors tilted and dropped away. In the south-west the afternoon sun was a dull blur.

Rosslyn looked down at the miles of snow, the patterns of the black stone walls, a patch of forest, disused wool mills in the dead industrial valley towns.

Somewhere down there were Mary's remains. He wondered what it would feel like to be with them, alone in the frozen waste, with only the noise of the police helicopter droning away towards the disappearing sun.

'Must have pleased you to get a major woman storeman,' said Harding from the next seat. 'We could do with more of Dee McKeague's sort in the bag.' Harding turned to mutter something to a police officer in the seat behind, who passed over a flask of coffee. Harding filled two paper cups.

'Mary was much loved at the Yard,' he said. 'Sort of a lucky mascot. I wish I'd known her better. She told me a lot about you. At Lippitts Hill. I heard you two were friends. She told me they call you the basement man. You live in a basement, interrogate in the basement at Paddington Green. You're not one of the crowd, so to speak. That's what Mary said about you. The basement man.'

'You two seem to have discussed me a lot.'

'You were very important to her,' Harding said. 'By the way, when did you two get things together?'

'She asked me for some advice. She says: "This colleague's husband has run off with this bloke. He's gay. As a man, what would you tell her to do with a gay husband?" Something like that, I think. I said strange things happen in marriages. I'm not an expert. Suddenly, she begins to cry. Of course, all along she'd been talking about herself. Then she came to live with me. And that was that.'

'You liked Lippitts Hill?'

'Yes. They were great days. Do you know we hit the man-sized targets, what, several hundred yards away? We fired at the moving pictures in the Judgement Room. Men threatening us with axes. Armed men in masks. I'd never seen her so happy. We both loved Lippitts Hill. They were the best days. What happens now, I don't know. I wonder sometimes if my heart's still in it.'

Harding looked out of the window. 'If you want to chuck it in, I'd sympathize with that.'

'Losing her is terrible, terrible. I'd like to get the chance, just once, to face her murderer, you know, person to person, eye to eye.'

Harding turned back from the window to look at him. 'I think you'd hesitate a fraction too long,' he said, 'before you squeezed that trigger.'

Perhaps he's seen my Tutorial/Progress Report.

Harding paused. 'You say you'd like the chance to face them. What will you do when you're face to face with the one who did it?'

'If I know it's the one who murdered Mary I won't hesitate.'

'Even though her killer's most likely the same age as you? More intelligent than people think. A few, like you, are well educated, middle class, from decent hard-working families, trained in firearms. They're not wondering, like you, if their hearts are in it. I'm talking about people with unimaginable dedication, right now underground. Cold bastards. Very cold indeed.'

Rosslyn looked down on the miles of white and grey landscape turning blue-black and darker towards nightfall.

The pilot waved to Harding to attach his earphones.

'Fifteen minutes till we land,' he said. 'Don't let the bitterness eat your guts out.' He sifted through the papers in his briefcase, turning the pages of a pamphlet. Rosslyn noticed the title of the House of Commons Home Affairs Committee's Report: *Accountability of the Security Service.*

The helicopter lowered over huts in sight of a high communications mast. Here was the Metropolitan Police heliport which, by awful coincidence, was Lippitts Hill. He remembered it had been a German prisoner of war camp. Now it looked bleak, more like the place of its original purpose than a training centre. *And this was where we met?* A strange circle seemed to be enclosing him. Drawn by fate, by Harding, by the memory of Mary? He was not sure which.

He walked from the helicopter with the brown paper parcels beneath his coat. The driving sleet was whipped in his eyes by the spinning helicopter blades. He could just make out the red lettering of the illuminated warning sign: DANGER. HELICOPTER OPERATING AREA. A.S.U. PERSONNEL ONLY. He realized that here, in the middle of Epping Forest, not far from London, the thaw was beginning. He hated the prospect of returning home alone.

4

His basement flat in Pimlico rarely saw the daylight.

A damp stairwell separated it from the street. The window in the front room was high in the wall behind heavy iron bars set into the brickwork. It was impossible to open it more than a few inches. Even then dust and litter were tossed into the stairwell from the pavement. His landlord had made a vague attempt to revamp the flat in the high-tech style of the previous decade. The central heating pipes had been painted industrial grey, the floor was covered in rubber tiles and the shelving would have been better suited to a wholesale warehouse. Someone had painted it blue and red and black.

The intrusive modernity had by now grown stale: the peeling paint, cracked tiles and garish colour seemed more appropriate to an inner-city community centre. Rosslyn had covered the ugly shelves with cotton sheets and the repulsive flooring with North African rugs. There was nothing he could do to stem the rising damp. His letters to the landlords, a celebrated firm of experimental architects, went unanswered except for a misspelt circular justifying increases in rent with a request that he cough up by direct debit to save the architectural practice 'unreasonable costs'. Mary had urged him to tell the landlords to get stuffed. He might have done just that had she been alive. Without her he saw his flat for what it was: a tip.

At night he often dreamed of her. Once he saw her standing on Lambeth Bridge. She smiled at him, then very slowly turned away and walked through the sleet towards Thames House. He called out to her. But she didn't turn. Big Ben chimed the hour. It went on clanging out the time, well past twelve, until it struck twenty-nine. Her age. He woke up certain that he had been screaming in his sleep.

It was after this dream, when sleep eluded him in the early hours, that he decided to face the contents of the parcels given to him by Mary's mother. He opened them carefully in his kitchen.

She had kept every letter, postcard and scrap of paper he had written to her. He was astonished to see he had written something almost every day. Sometimes he had written to her twice, even three times, in a day. She had kept his letters in chronological order, wrapped in cellophane. Turning through them, each one addressed to her c/o The Landlord of a pub near Victoria Station, he felt he was peering at a dead man's secret, at his own life, not Mary's. The sensation was unbearably painful.

Her diary was even worse.

He found she had avoided entering days and dates of the month. Instead, she had used a rather obvious code: R for the first day they met; then R + 1 and so on, right up to the day of her death: R + 302 – almost ten months, the time of their life together. The police officer's record of times, places and observations.

He looked up R + 14 – the day they became lovers. Mary's entry read:

Couldn't stand seeing X in the morning knowing he'd been making love to Y all last evening. The thought of what they do in bed together disgusts me. X comes in all breezy smelling of whisky around 2 a.m. 'I went to see my friends,' he says. 'I can't stand being trapped.' So I say: 'Why did you agree to marry me?' He laughs like a spoiled child with a secret. 'I don't know,' he says. 'Probably because no one else ever asked me. Anyway, I didn't know I was gay, did I? You can't blame me, Mary. We all have a cross to bear. If you were more generous you'd help me carry mine.' He stoops over me to kiss my cheek. I can smell Y's expensive aftershave on him. I shout: 'Don't touch me!' and he gives me that awful knowing smile, creeps away and makes a ridiculous show of closing the door, very slowly, until the latch clicks into place. I lie awake a long time thinking of R. I've never wanted another man quite so much. I don't want to stay here in my bed. I want to sleep in his.

Next to his body which looks hard and spare like a marathon runner's. There's a used look about his face, sometimes a sadness, a distance in his greyish eyes which suddenly vanishes when he smiles and he becomes animated, gesturing with his long fine hands. Sometimes he smiles with his mouth closed, with one eyebrow raised, and he has the look of a sceptic who enjoys his sense of doubt. He looks the sort of man whose features will improve still more with age, at peace with himself, because he doesn't give a shit and trusts his feelings.

In the morning, a few hours later, I leave for the Yard. When I get there I realize I've forgotten to take a change of clothes. I'll have to show up at R's place in uniform. Perhaps I should call him to see if he minds. I so badly want to hear his voice.

Then, around noon, he calls me. I start to apologize for the memory lapse. Does he mind me turning up in uniform? He's so gentle, his voice full of smiles, so flirty, so happy, that I start crying like a kid. 'Listen, why don't you say you're feeling lousy and come over now? Tell me what the real problem is.' I'm totally confused. I think he's at his office. Turns out he's not. He's taken the day off to clean his flat, make me supper. 'I can't leave,' I say. He tells me to do whatever makes me happy. So I say, 'OK, I'm coming.' I tell the boss I've got a problem with my period. And that's it.

He seems nervous when I arrive. He's made lunch of smoked salmon and strawberries. There's a bottle of champagne and even Calvados, my favourite.

His flat's a basement.

The pits.

I volunteer to clean it up, get rid of the terrible design, hide the pipes. It's like a boiler room. He asks – Would I like to go away this weekend, somewhere I've never been? I say I've never been to Italy, Spain, Germany. Only, actually, Dieppe for a night with X.

'Yes or no?'

'Yes.'

During the strawberries I tell him about X and he listens in silence. I say I feel so unwanted.

Then he says it isn't true. 'I want you.'

I say: 'I want you.' I think I say something stupid like 'Have you ever undressed a policewoman in uniform?'

'Have you?' he asks.

'No,' I say. 'Now's your chance.'

So he takes me into his bedroom. I notice he's put clean sheets on the bed. He had it in mind. Must have.

He takes off my uniform. I take off his clothes. He's wonderful with his hands. I can feel all his fingers doing different things exactly where I want.

I want to please him and I hold him, full and very hard in one hand and squeeze his softness with my other.

Then he's inside me. His hands run down my spine. I've never been so wet.

He shouts out when he comes. His face looks so serious, so pained. His eyes are smiling. The sweat runs down his face. So I lick it and hold him very close.

Later on, I ask him where we'll go this weekend.

'It's a secret,' he says. 'Somewhere you've never been.'

He sleeps for a time.

Here I am in the basement, playing hooky with the basement man. Asleep he doesn't look frightening – more like a little boy. Content and very happy. I want to tell him I'm so fond of him. But if I tell him I love him so much it may scare him off. There's something broken inside him and I want to mend it very much.

After this we:

1. Shower.

2. He goes out to buy me a set of clothes for the evening. Comes back.

3. Go for a walk in Hyde Park.

4. Have champagne at the Dorchester.

5. Have dinner at Bibendum – Christ, the cost. I'll have to investigate where he gets the money.

6. Champagne at Le Suquet. More inquiries.

7. Go back to the basement.

8. Make love.

9. And I tell him I love him.

To my surprise, well almost, he says the same to me.

Mary's diary held a kind of repellent fascination. He would cradle it tenderly, cherishing it as an object; sometimes pressing it close to his face, longing to discover a trace of her scent. But, shocked by the unexpected force of his grief, he was unable to read on. He could not bear the thought of getting to the end. He had to spin it out.

His colleagues at work seemed to be avoiding him. His past successes offered no consolation. A sense of bereavement gripped him. He feared he was growing into the sort of person Harding had described. Wasn't it anyway Mary's view? *The basement man.*

Now the basement man was losing touch.

'See the doctor,' Richard Gaynor, his immediate superior, advised. 'I know a shrink.'

Gaynor, the old school duty man, bearded like the portrait of a sea captain on a tobacco tin, a moody man whose temperament often altered from calms to storms in a single hour. He could instil the fear of God in suspects and subordinates alike.

Rosslyn watched him prowl round his desk. The captain on his bridge. A big man, Gaynor moved in a stoop with caution. His language was at odds with his passion for the novels of Conrad which he collected in their first editions by mail order from Hawthorn Books of Bristol. His Polish grandmother, originally a Korzeniowska, was said to be a cousin of the writer. He was also said to be a fine ballroom dancer, a compensation for an incapacity for a full relationship with women. This was Gaynor, the safe pair of hands, who played things according to the book, whose nervous energy found an outlet in his work. He stood beside his desk, feet apart, swaying like a golfer concentrating on his shot, staring at his polished shoes. His slim black leather freemason's suitcase was next to the waste-paper basket. It was hard to imagine the sceptic Gaynor in an apron with a trouser leg rolled up above his knee.

When Rosslyn evaded the suggestion he should visit a psychiatrist Gaynor settled for the direct approach. 'Look, I'm going to be up front with you, as a friend.'

Rosslyn thought: *Duty men don't have friends.*

'I'm worried about your state of mind, Alan. That's why we haven't given you too big a workload for the last three months. Class B importation and possession, soft drugs, soft stuff, odds and sods. It isn't the most exciting old routine, is it? Drugs in Farringdon, tea chests from Nigeria. We haven't stretched you, Alan, have we? We have to think of our colleagues, don't we? I mean, we can't go on like this indefinitely, can we?' His voice grew harsher. 'Look, just come off the ropes and start punching your weight, will you?'

'Who am I fighting then?'

'For Christ's sake, Alan. Listen. Dee McKeague. Everybody wants to be the one to get her to grass on her nasty friends. And she hasn't cracked, Alan, has she?'

'What are you saying to me?'

'You make my point. Listen. I want you to be the one who breaks her. To get back on track. Be the hard man. Or do you really want to let others show her the rougher side of justice. Well. Do you? Of course, even if the cow never talks, the record shows you were the officer who first traced the arms and explosives to her shitty house and the garage in West London.'

It's out of my hands, Rosslyn thought. *Maybe McKeague will be tossed to the likes of Miss Monro and Miss Watson.*

'Just a thought, Alan. The CIO has called a secret meeting for the twenty-fifth of March. Top level, Alan. Be here.' His voice was heavy with sarcasm. 'Second floor, Alan, here at Custom House, headquarters, Alan, Lower Thames Street. And why are you to attend? Because of your involvement in McKeague's arrest. Be here. And just get a grip on yourself, will you, or is your patron saint Saint Inertia?'

What was there to say to Gaynor? The big man, who was telling him of yet another secret meeting which would surely be as futile as any other, paper shuffling, a substitute for doing anything as positive as actually catching somebody – like, for instance, Mary's killers.

But he decided to keep these opinions to himself.

On 25 March, Rosslyn waited in the corridor to be called in to the chief investigation officer's secret meeting.

The black coffee he got from the drinks machine was weak and tepid. On a chair beside the machine he took up a discarded copy of the Customs & Excise staff newspaper *Portcullis*. He turned to the letters page. The correspondence was divided between the disaffected and the ambitious in about equal measure. A junior officer seconded to Shoreham Customs had made a stab at humour at the expense of SIS's acronyms: 'As indicated by the local PMU,' he wrote, 'my PI and DPA may be restricted by the PRA signing himself c/o SIS (Somewhere in the South).' Elsewhere among the Letters to the Editor a correspondent offered suggestions for the improvement of promotion boards. In the small ads someone called Tom William Putt offered to buy 'Your Unwanted Scalextric track and "bits"' and gave an address in Tunbridge Wells. The voice of the CIO's secretary interrupted his reading. 'Would you come in now, Mr Rosslyn, please.' He followed her into the CIO's office.

The CIO, a large bald man with a ruddy face, looked up from a stack of files at the end of the long polished table. 'Didn't mind the wait, Alan, I hope,' he said quickly. Usually the CIO conducted meetings from behind his massive desk. He liked to separate himself from his juniors. He'd begin genially with a comment about the view of the river and HMS *Belfast* and some comment on the ship's history. He prided himself on being something of a naval history buff and HMS *Belfast* in particular. Not today though. Rosslyn noticed an uncharacteristic note of steel and impatience in his voice.

'We're running late,' the CIO said. 'You know everyone, I think,' he added with an airy wave at the others round the table.

Rosslyn glanced at Gaynor, the five deputy chief investigation officers, and the others there, unfamiliar faces.

'Except of course,' the CIO continued, 'observers from the Intelligence Committee, the National Criminal Intelligence Service, our newer friends from the Met. Pull up a chair, Alan.' The voice was much brusquer than usual. It seemed that the CIO was in a hurry to be finished with the meeting.

Rosslyn sat at one end of the table on a green leather chair distanced from the others like an interviewee. The highly polished surface of the table reflected the glare of the sunlight from the high windows facing the river.

'We're reviewing a basket of proposals, Alan,' the CIO said, 'with a view to submitting a secret report to a working party of the Task Co-ordinating Committee made up, in turn, of senior officers from military intelligence, MI5 and the Special Branch. We're to make recommendations as to how, I quote "Customs & Excise high-grade intelligence gleaned from undercover surveillance officers will most efficiently serve the war against the terrorists". Unquote. As chairman of this particular working group, committee, working party, whatever we want to call ourselves, I've been asked to get general views on the subject from at least one senior investigation officer with first-hand recent experience in the field. And that's you.' Rosslyn watched the CIO loosen his tie. 'I'd like you to read this.' He passed a single sheet of paper to his secretary who walked round the table to give it to Rosslyn. 'Once we've finished our coffee break we'd like to hear your view. Like a cup of coffee?'

'Thanks.'

The sheet of paper Rosslyn read contained a diagram of staggering complexity.

'What do you make of it, Alan?'

'Do you want my honest view?' Rosslyn said. 'Or my polite one?'

'Just tell the meeting what you think.'

Rosslyn thought fast: What did the chief want to hear? Was he dumping the dirty job on to him? *Is he asking me to say what is palpably obvious to a moron, namely: this is another exercise in bureaucracy? Why me? Have the others gone along with it?* There was no telling from their

TOP SECRET

The Prime Minister

Cabinet Secretary

Cabinet Office Committee on Defence and Overseas Policy (OPD)
(Intelligence, Security, Defence and Counter-terrorism Policy)

Prime Minister	Foreign Secretary	Chancellor	President Board of Trade	Attorney General	Defence Secretary

Cabinet Office Committee on Intelligence Services (IS)
(Intelligence and Security Services, Review Policy)

Prime Minister	Foreign Secretary	Defence Secretary	Home Secretary	Chancellor of the Duchy of Lancaster

Cabinet Office Sub-committee on Terrorism (OPDT)
(Reviews counter-terrorism planning, terrorist attacks. Reports to Cabinet Office Committee on Defence and Overseas Policy)

Home Secretary   Foreign Secretary   Defence Secretary
President of Board of Trade   Transport Secretary   N. Ireland Secretary
Attorney General   Scottish Secretary

Home Office   Foreign Office   Ministry of Defence   Police

MI5:   *IRA Intelligence Co-ordination in Britain & N. Ireland.*
COBRA: *Active on major terrorism outbreak. Deployment of SAS.*
MI6:   *SIS Overseas Intelligence Co-ordination. Active against IRA in Republic of Ireland.*
GCHQ: *Government Communications HQ, Cheltenham. Satellite & Broadcast Intelligence retrieval.*
DIS: *Defence Intelligence Staff. Intelligence retrieval on IRA attack against military targets.*
AIC: *Army Intelligence Corps. Undercover operations against the IRA in N. Ireland.*

Joint Intelligence Committee   RUC
Senior officers of MI5, MI6, DIS and GCHQ   Met. anti-terrorist branch (SO 13)
                                            Met. Special Branch (SO 12)
                                            All other police forces

HM Customs & Excise, Investigation Division

expressionless faces where the truth lay. These were veterans of countless meetings of this kind. Theirs was the waiting game; they were content to let others make the running. They were the survivors covering their arses, sitting out their time until they received some honour appropriate to their rank. He felt a deep contempt for them. *The diagram is complete crap. Top heavy. And where was Customs & Excise?* He glanced at its position. *Right down there – at the bottom of the awful heap. What the hell does the Chancellor of the Duchy of Lancaster have to do with it when he's at home?* He wanted to shout at them: *Look! There are thirty to forty terrorists on active service in the United Kingdom. At this minute. If Paddy could see this thing now he'd jump for joy. And you people sit here asking me to tell you what to think about a diagram. In eleven years more than twenty atrocities, over three dozen murdered, getting on for 600 maimed and injured, damage costing billions. And how many IRA terrorists convicted? Three! Three lousy Paddies with names not one of you remember.*

So he was surprised when he heard the apparent calm of his own voice saying: 'With great respect, I'm not sure I have anything very helpful to say.' He had led off with a low card. He waited for the others to follow suit. They watched him in silence. 'I don't understand quite where this gets us.'

'What is it you don't understand, Alan?' the CIO asked.

'I don't understand' – he pointed to the diagram on the table – 'how this helps anyone. What does it say? "Most efficiently serve the war against the terrorists".'

'We're looking at who uses the intelligence and how they use it, Alan. Think of the diagram there as a kind of filter, a conduit, a hierarchy of responsibility.'

'Don't you think, with respect,' Rosslyn asked, 'it's clogged up?'

'Alan. We're asking *you*. Is that your view?'

'I can only hold a view about the evidence you've shown me. I think anyone seeing this would think "Who are all these people? What do they *do*? Day in, day out?"'

Here one of the nameless observers chimed in: 'You're a very experienced senior investigation officer. You must be familiar with the hierarchy of command.'

'I can't say I am,' Rosslyn said.

'You seem to have a critical view of it nevertheless,' the nameless observer said.

'Don't you?'

'Yes and no,' the man said. 'We're engaged in a very complex war, aren't we? Therefore, of course, command structures are frightfully hard to get right. If I may ask, through you, Mr Chairman, why doesn't Mr Rosslyn give us chapter and verse? He prefaces his views with the phrase "with great respect". I rather think Mr Rosslyn is not offering *respect*.'

Rosslyn looked down at the diagram. 'It may seem so to you,' he said. 'I have more respect than most people for the terrorists. Their success. The brilliant way they evade arrest and conviction. The timing of their attacks. Their efficiency. The way they've preserved the loyalty of their own side, even in the United States where their propagandists are allowed free rein. How many of our people, people in your diagram, have visited the US and promoted our cause? Not too many. And those that have seem not to have been very effective. All I think, all I'm saying, is that Customs have been effective. Our intelligence gathering has been better than anyone else's. What I'm suggesting is that if the high-grade material we get is passed through this thing, this sieve or conduit or whatever you choose to call it, if it's to become part of the internecine warfare among our own agencies and forces, well, it'll get lost in the wash.'

Suddenly several voices were raised at once, mostly hostile. Rosslyn lifted his hands, feigning mild surprise at the antagonism he'd aroused. 'May I add something?' he asked quietly. Then louder: 'A last word about misunderstanding?'

'Go ahead, Alan,' said the CIO.

'This diagram is headed TOP SECRET. It may well be that's what Whitehall thinks. The only trouble is that one very much like it has already appeared in the *Sunday Times*.'

There was an embarrassed silence.

It was broken by the CIO. 'Thank you anyway for coming, Alan.'

In turn he was interrupted by his secretary who had moved unnoticed to the head of the table behind him. She was holding a ellow slip of paper. The CIO took it without looking round. Once he'd glanced at it, he turned to Rosslyn. 'Come outside with me a moment, Alan.'

In the corridor the CIO spoke close to Rosslyn's face. 'Thanks for what you said. I couldn't have put it better. But I wouldn't have brought up the *Sunday Times*. It isn't Scotland Yard's favourite newspaper at the moment.'

He pushed the slip of yellow paper into Rosslyn's hand. The message on it was brief: the prisoner, Dee McKeague, insisted upon seeing him, as soon as possible, alone and in strict confidence. The superintendent of Paddington Green police station would arrange for the interview to be recorded in whatever way Mr Rosslyn suggested. The interview might need to be kept off the record. Afterwards, Mr Rosslyn could take possession of the tape. 'It seems appropriate,' the superintendent concluded, with a rare display of insight, 'that Mr Rosslyn be the relevant officer to gain the information which may be on offer.'

It was the superintendent's considered view that Dee McKeague intended to reveal the identity of Mary's killer.

5

Rosslyn showed his ID to the custody officer at Paddington Green police station and was directed to the basement cells.

The change in Dee McKeague's appearance since the time of her arrest on charges under the Prevention of Terrorism Act astonished him. At her last remand the magistrate had directed that, in the absence of available Category A accommodation, she should be held at Paddington Green police station. The overcrowded British prison system was at the point of collapse.

McKeague was sitting at a table in the airless interview room. Her swollen hands were shaking. He wondered whose boots had stamped on them. There were bloodstains on the white paper overalls the police had given her. Like the overalls, the regulation slippers on her feet were too small. Rosslyn noticed she had trodden down the heels.

He slipped a tape into a recorder fixed to the wall.

'Paddington Green police station. Interview Room. Present SIO Rosslyn, Customs & Excise. Deirdre McKeague. No solicitor present. Interview commences eleven-fifteen a.m. Friday the twenty-fifth of March.'

He handed her a cigarette and lit it for her. Then he began: 'You have to understand, I'm a Customs & Excise officer. We don't do deals, McKeague. You're looking at forty years at least. You'll be an old woman by the time you get out.'

'You're a hard man, Mr Rosslyn.' The West Belfast accent was harsh. She squinted at him through puffy eyes. 'I want to do a deal with you.'

'I've told you. No deals.'

'Why are you here then?' she said.

'Because you asked to see me. You don't seem to understand. My job deals with the illegal importation of arms and explosives. It's true, I have powers of search and arrest. But your lawyer must have told you I don't have the power to do deals.'

'I haven't spoken to him about it.'

'Why not?'

She sank lower on her chair with a look of hopelessness. 'I can't hear you properly.'

'I said: I can't do a deal. You should be talking to the police, or the security services. Not me.'

'You must be joking. I don't trust any of them.'

'They don't trust you either. Nor do I.'

'But I can do a deal with you,' she said.

'You're not listening to what I'm saying, McKeague. You were under twenty-four-hour surveillance for weeks. You imported forty kilos of Semtex. Enough to kill hundreds. You had ten Kalashnikovs and ammunition. For Christ's sake. You even had a Smith & Wesson tucked in your belt when you were arrested. I can't do a deal. You're looking at forty years. Forty.'

'I was stitched up.'

She was making the old excuse. It was always someone else's fault. It was time to put her straight. 'Then why haven't you said so before?' he said reasonably. 'The anti-terrorist branch was there at the time of your arrest. SO 13 would have listened. You could have spoken to them at any time, if you'd wanted to. You'll get every chance to complain to the court. Look, let's face it – you were banged to rights.' He pointed to the paper mug of coffee on the table. 'Sip some of that.'

She lifted the cup to her bruised lips with difficulty.

'Who beat you up then, McKeague?'

'Who do you think?'

'I'm asking you.'

'Police. Your sadist friends in the security services. Fat bastards. People should be told about the animals who did this to me.'

'You can lodge a complaint, if you wish.'

'And you think there's any use in that? I don't.'

One of her hands twitched like a broken claw. He had seen a dozen others like her: killers and skilled liars born to terrorism in Ireland and the Middle East, with long experience in the art of concealment. McKeague was no different. Only he had never seen a prisoner who had been so ferociously beaten up. Nevertheless, he doubted she was about to reveal any of her confederates' names. Let alone the identity of Mary's killer. Few of her kind grassed on their comrades. Those who did soon fell victim to appalling acts of retribution from fellow inmates in some maximum security wing. Unseen hands wielded the broken razor blade, the sharpened screwdriver, or drew the cutting wire tight around the throat. Supergrasses, once identified, were sooner or later left to die alone in their own blood as a warning. Some of them, unable to face the nightmare of such execution by their fellows, committed suicide. A very few caved in and whispered names to the Security Service officers who monitored the prisoners for useful signs of weakness and collapse.

McKeague's hands were shaking. 'I want to talk about MI5.'

'I'm not going to comment on operational matters,' Rosslyn warned her.

'I'm not asking you to,' she said. 'I'm *telling* you. MI5 planted a serious HE device on me.'

'That's shit, McKeague.'

'Listen to me. They brought it along with them when I was arrested.'

'What did they bring along, McKeague?' he asked, incredulously.

'An explosive device from Dresden, or Brussels, or somewhere like that. A serious piece of new technology.'

'And they planted it on you? Along with the Semtex and the Kalashnikovs? They didn't need to *plant* anything extra on you. The evidence was staring us in the face.'

'Then they took it away.'

He shook his head. 'You are seriously telling me, let's get it right, they brought this HE device with them when you were arrested?'

'Right.'

'Then they planted it somewhere?'

'Right. Along with the rest.'

'Then they took it away?'

There was a brief silence.

'I'm telling you the truth,' she said.

'Why would they have taken the device away?'

'Ask yourself,' she said.

'I am asking myself, McKeague. And I don't have an answer, do you?'

'Yes.'

'What is it?' he asked.

'They want a legitimate reason to get a serious bomb. Look at what I'm saying. Use your brain, Mr Rosslyn. They're making their own work look good. Better than the anti-terrorist branch. Better even than your lot. They're planting evidence. They explode a few minor devices, right? Potboilers. A lot of aggro. No casualties. Then they make out a case against people like me. Piece of cake. Then everyone says: "They're doing just great."' The wheezing in her chest continued. 'If I get the maximum for importation, what am I looking at? Seven years? And there's a big bloody difference between seven and forty with no remission. Thirty-three bloody years.' She made an effort to raise her hands. 'What's their game? You tell me. They're desperate. So are the police. So are you. So is the British public, Christ. They're bloody desperate, that's why. You're all at war with each other. You think we're filth. That's why you're using filth to fight us. Well, you're failing. You always will. You're caught in a private war you can't win. If it stays private you'll lose. The big difference between you and me is that I'm in here. And you're not. You can walk out of here any time you want. You don't even have to sit here listening to me. But I have to bloody well listen to you. And I have to take beatings from bastards that even you can't believe. You don't want to know. Because you don't want to know your friends are evil bastards. Animals. Am I right?'

Rosslyn watched her touch a patch of dried blood on her damaged ear. She seemed possessed of some demonic courage. Certainly, there was a germ of truth in her manic theorizing. That absurd diagram proved the point.

'If you want me to believe you,' he insisted, 'give me names.'

She considered his offer. Then like someone offering up a vow, she said: 'I will.' There was a pause. 'In one or two days,' she went on, 'there's going to be a really serious bomb, I can tell you. In north London, if you want to know. And it will be down to MI5. Give us another cigarette.'

He lit one and handed it to her.

'Some weeks back,' she continued, 'I was approached by someone to do a hit job. This person offers me a quarter of a million pounds, or thereabouts, to get rid of two MI5 personnel.'

'Who was this person then? Who asked you?'

'No comment,' she said acidly.

'Then who was this person working for? Give us a name –'

'I reckon they were working on their own. And this person tells me there's quarter of a million in it for me. This person offers to provide the bomb. I ask about it. I'm told it's the type I saw planted on me when I got arrested. I say: "I don't want to know. Good luck and good night." You know why I say no to them? I say no to them because it's as clear as daylight to me the offer is a fit-up. They must be thinking here's some thick as pigshit Irish woman who's too greedy for her own good. Well, they're wrong. It smells. Here's someone who knows the business top to bottom. You know when the penny dropped?' She raised her swollen fingers to her battered face. 'It was when they did this to me. I knew I'd been approached then, from inside MI5, by someone who knew the whole of the surveillance operation against me. They'd tried to get me to do their dirty work for them. I'd be the one to carry the can. I said to myself: "No thanks, Dee McKeague."'

Rosslyn watched her with a half-smile that said: *Go on, McKeague. I'm waiting.*

She smiled back as if to say: *There you are. Now have it on a plate. Give me a deal. Then, down the line, I'll show you the world.*

Rosslyn thought: *But what are you offering? Some cock and bull story of conspiracy to murder within MI5? Or, what I really want, namely, the identity of Mary's killer?*

They sat there, facing each other across the table, silent, with fixed smiles, like chess players. Rosslyn waited. To let silence hang, like now, was an old ploy, a useful interrogation tool if you're confronted by a loser. *Sure enough,* he thought, *your composure is beginning to crack.*

She was frowning, staring at her fingernails. She took a deep breath. 'I can give you a name.'

You are cracking.

'That's not enough,' Rosslyn insisted.

She waited for a moment. 'An address, then.'

'You expect me to believe they gave you an address?'

'They didn't give it to me, for Christ's sake. I followed them. I got it for myself.'

'A name, an address,' he said. 'They won't be enough, McKeague.'

'Then Mr Rosslyn, for God's sake, you tell me what else you want.'

'The name of the person who killed Mary Walker.'

'Sure. I can give that to you.'

'WHO WAS IT?'

'It's the same person, who will use the device I told you about to do the north London killings. Think of it, Mr Rosslyn, aren't I the best thing that's happened to you? You want the name of Mary Walker's killer. We're talking of a professional. Someone who loves the work, who gets a kick out of it that's bigger than anything you could know.'

She was talking faster now, the adrenalin rising, with no apparent thought for the pain her injuries must be giving her. 'You're looking at an individual who specializes in high-profile targets. Remember the list? Grand Hotel in Brighton '84. The Carlton Club in June '90? The murder of Ian Gow, the next month. Twenty-five rounds from the AK-47 assault rifle pumped into the former Governor of Gibraltar, September '90. Didn't Gow say: "We will never, never surrender to people like this." Once he'd opened his mouth he was as good as dead already. Forget Manchester, and Warrington, and the City of London. The five homemade mortars at Heathrow. Better than the mortar attack on Downing Street that was. Look at the fucking chaos at Terminal One. And that was on the day your fucking MPs voted to renew the Prevention of Terrorism Act, right? The night before the London Anglo-Irish conference.'

'Come on, McKeague, you're wasting time. Let's get back to the attempt on Thames House.'

'The big peach? The woman police officer?'

'I'm waiting, McKeague.'

'The delivery men get away. But the timing of the peach, the plan, the mechanics. They were something else, weren't they? Right? There could've been more than a thousand MI5 people blown to bits. To do that one you have to be really good. You're not looking at your average IRA veteran. You're looking at a new breed altogether. Very big money. The best explosives. Maximum spectacular. Death on a new scale. Christ, you haven't seen anything yet, Mr Rosslyn.' She paused. 'Do I convince you? Remember, so far, in ten years or more, what's your score? Three convictions. So who's winning? You don't need me to tell you the answer. If I were you, I'd think very carefully about your deal with me.'

'I don't do deals.'

'What, even with someone offering you full and frank co-operation? Don't we need each other? You know, when I talked about that sow Walker I thought, somehow, you were seeing the light. You sort of flinched. Let me tell you something, Mr Rosslyn. If I'm right, it won't be me that's going down for forty years. You're looking at MI5 bastards. They'll go down for a bloody sight longer than the forty years I get.'

Rosslyn was watching her impassively. 'Tell you what I can do, McKeague. I can think about what you've said for a couple of days. Maybe talk it over with someone. See what we can do for you.'

'You realize the risk I'm taking. The maximum sentence with no appeal?'

'That's your problem.' Alone in a secure wing, he hoped. Down for the duration.

'And when I come out?'

'If we do a deal you get a new life. In Canada. New Zealand even. A new identity. Plastic surgery. The usual. The more you give us, the more we give you.' He thought: *MI5 won't attach a shred of truth to what you've told me.* 'Unless you're lying about the bomb in north London.'

'You think I'm lying?'

'Yes,' he said. 'I do.'

'Why would I waste your time?'

'That's a question you have to answer yourself.'

'And when it goes off, Mr Rosslyn, a whole lot more people will be killed and injured, including two MI5 bastards. You'll have yourself to blame for wasting two days making up your mind.'

'Then why don't you tell me right now who's planned it?'

'Because I'm not that stupid.'

'You don't trust me to come back with your deal?'

'No, I don't. You won't be needing me any more.'

'Listen, McKeague. I've never needed you.'

'But you've got a duty to listen to me.'

Rosslyn got to his feet. 'When I need lessons in duty, you can be sure of one thing. I won't come in here to some sodding terrorist to learn them.'

'Mr Rosslyn, with respect–'

'I don't want your respect either.' He gave the signal through the observation slit to the police officer to return the prisoner to her cell. He spoke close to the microphone: 'Interview ends eleven fifty-five a.m.'

He removed the tape and took it with him.

6

Chaos in the streets forced him to take a circuitous route back to his office in Lower Thames Street.

Another bomb scare blocked the Westway's elevated section near the Paddington Green police station. Further on, in Marylebone, a gas explosion felled one whole side of an Edwardian mansion block.

Elsewhere, an intruder was discovered in the gardens of Kensington Palace. Near naked, he gave his name as Moses Moses, a man sent by God Almighty to punish royal fornication. The police bundled the raving lunatic into a blue van to drive him, with a motorcycle escort, to a mental hospital in north London. Thus, Moses succeeded in blocking off most of the main streets in the Royal Borough.

Further to the east, suspicious packages were found outside Charing Cross and Liverpool Street Stations. So they were evacuated and the travellers poured out into the streets sullen and bearing grudges.

Rosslyn gained this picture of events over his short-wave car radio.

Stuck in traffic on the Embankment, his instinct told him McKeague was a time-waster. An inventor of baloney. True, she had a few theories halfway right, about the discord in the forces fighting the terrorists. You could see the signs of that failure and frustration in the physical battering the interrogation officers had inflicted on the prisoner. You could see it in the CIO's byzantine diagram of responsibility.

Her prediction of the imminent bomb attack? The vision of the new-breed terrorist behind Mary's murder? Well, the odds were on the bomb. They had been for years. Look into any police officer's eyes on any street and you'll see the suspicion and the fear. No one needs warning that London is in the bombers' grip. You had to be philosophical. Rosslyn was not about to telephone Scotland Yard and say 'Get ready. Be prepared.' The vision of the new breed owed more to fantasy than the real world at war. No. McKeague was bluffing.

When Gaynor had finished listening to the recorded interview Rosslyn asked him, 'Think she's the real thing?'

'I think she's as evil as she sounds,' Gaynor said. 'It would be dangerous to be sympathetic towards her. This device from Dresden, for example, from Brussels, Czech Republic or wherever, in her garage, in her garden. You didn't miss it, Alan, did you? The CIO won't like that. It could sound like a serious oversight.'

Christ, he's making out I'm incompetent. 'I'm sure, I never saw it. And the new breed of terrorist. Is this a serious view?'

'She's not the sort to give us a serious name, let alone a serious view. There's no new breed. Who'll support her evidence? There's no corroboration. Terrorists are terrorists. She's crazy if she imagines MI5's stitched her up. Christ, she sounds as insane as that loony Moses.' He laughed. 'Did you hear about Moses?'

'I heard about Moses. But McKeague. I wish I knew why she asked to see me, by name, alone.'

'Because she's read the papers. You don't have to be some corrupted Irish terrorist to know everyone's competing for convictions. Given a choice McKeague must be hoping we're the easier touch. If I were in her shoes that's what I'd be hoping.'

He handed the tape across the desk. 'This doesn't, in my view, constitute high-grade intelligence. All it proves is this: she's suffering from high-grade paranoid delusions. Same as all the rest. You can hear it in the voice. She's puffed up with the sense of her own importance. She thinks she's a bloody heroine.' He lifted his large frame out of his chair. The dark suit was crumpled, at odds with the new shirt and black tie. 'We'll pass this on to SO 13,' he said. 'Let them worry about McKeague's paranoia. Take it from me, she's deluded.'

'You don't want me to see her again?'

Gaynor toyed with the dark blue Investigation Division's *Annual Report.* 'SO 13 will sort her out. No problem. She'll get worse treatment from MI5.'

'You don't have to tell me. Someone's already given her a terrible hiding.'

'Nothing to do with us. She's no different from the rest. She deserves everything she gets. You did very well, Alan. Everyone agrees.' He handed Rosslyn the draft report to the Task Co-ordinating Committee. 'Read this. I'd like your comments. And please, no more outbursts like this morning's. For Christ's sake, think of taking some well-earned leave.' He fingered his beard.

Then, as an afterthought, he added gloomily, 'Let's look at the bright side.'

To be looking at the bright side seemed almost an affront to Mary's memory. He wanted, more than ever, to stare her murderer in the face. Yet, as he took stock of things, he began to wonder whether the secrecy surrounding his unknown enemy would not prove to be impenetrable.

Back in his office he made a few cursory notes on the draft report. The secret bureaucracies would go on wrangling, ineffective and out of touch. What he could tell them would convince none of them of the need for reform to end the muddle and confusion. His disillusionment was turning into disgust.

He examined the nuggets of intelligence McKeague had hinted she might offer. He dismissed the idea she could have been set up by MI5. True, they could easily have had an opportunity to place some device in the house when she was arrested. But for what possible motive?

He could understand, even sympathize, with the logic of her seeking a deal for leniency. She would know Customs & Excise officers have a clean record of non-violent interrogation. The idea of a deal itself was entirely plausible. Her nightmare vision of forty years in jail was real enough. You couldn't blame her for trying.

Next, he listed the problems of the predicted bomb attack.

McKeague's kind frequently tried this ruse to ingratiate them-selves with their captors, to waste time and to set the police off on wild goose chases across the capital and major cities.

The story that she had been approached by an unknown commis-sioning agent to assassinate two MI5 officers for a quarter of a million pounds sounded like the typical invention of a criminal fantasist. And with the very bomb planted at the time of her arrest?

He dwelt on the story through his lunch hour in the canteen, staring at his shorthand notes whilst his silent colleagues pored over the crosswords in *The Times* and *Telegraph*. He thought himself into her shoes. He told himself that he too would have turned down the offer, no matter how great the fee proposed. It had to be, surely, a trap.

He turned to a different clue on the list of McKeague's potential revelations. She had offered, though of course hadn't given, the name of Mary's killer. The extent of the injuries she had suffered at the hands of interrogators showed that they must believe she possessed intelligence of high quality. Otherwise they would not have pursued her with such violence. Yet he couldn't tell whether she might cave in to them; in all probability, he felt not. He reck-oned she had passed through some significant threshold of pain; the moment when she might have named Mary's killer had gone.

He spent a whole afternoon with secret interservice files. The reports told him nothing new; the pages of his notes reminded him he could only wait, passively, for the bomb to go off somewhere in north London. Or not. It was the one lead which might tie up the threads of evidence to prove conclusively the value of what McKeague was offering.

He assumed the anti-terrorist forces must be waiting, as he was, for the bomb to explode.

SPRING

It is IRA successes that demoralize the British and undermine their case.

IRA Code of Conduct, The Green Book

The steel frame of Thames House is faced with Portland stone, rising from a base of polished grey granite. The roofs are steeply pitched and covered with slabs of faience. The great archway which spans Page Street connects the north and south blocks at the third and fourth floor levels, and the frieze contains sculptured panels, representing the Arms of Westminster, London and the Port of London. The key-stone is carved with a presentment of justice.

Architectural Review, November 1931

Prolifération

Since the Gulf War Western governments have been increasingly concerned at the proliferation of weapons of mass destruction, both nuclear, and chemical and biological. Much of the technology and expertise involved has been obtained from the West, often by foreign agents using illicit methods. The Service is now contributing to efforts to minimise the leakage of specialist technology from the UK, and traditional counter-espionage techniques are being adapted to meet this new problem.

The Security Service, HMSO, London, July 1993

7

At 7.45 a.m. on Saturday 26 March, a woman disguised as a post office employee arrived outside an Edwardian mansion block in Kensington Court. She paused at the entrance to draw on a pair of thin transparent rubber gloves, of the sort dentists use.

Both sets of doors to the entrance hall were on the latch. She knew the caretaker left at this time each morning to walk a spaniel and a poodle belonging to two elderly women residents in Kensington Gardens. She also knew that the real postman showed up late on Saturdays, at around ten, and the roster of delivery men and women was erratic.

Unnoticed, she crossed the marble hallway to the lift beside the stairs, a slim figure who looked younger than her thirty years.

Alone inside the lift, as it climbed slowly through the floors, she removed the delivery bag from across her shoulder. It contained the tools of her trade: rolls of industrial adhesive tape, a loaded Mark 10 Smith & Wesson and a black nylon stocking.

The lift arrived at the top floor with a shudder. Just as she had been briefed, at the far end of the dim passage was an alcove and the tall, unlocked cleaner's cupboard. There was enough space for her among the brooms, brushes, cleaning liquids in plastic bottles, and a vacuum cleaner. Here, in the darkness, she would now pass the next ten minutes, until the Filipino cleaning woman arrived for work in the flat occupied by Bryan Terence Wesley CBE, a deputy director of personnel in MI5.

Anna McKeague, sister of Dee McKeague, the prisoner in the cell at Paddington Green, was about to mark her second strike at the heart of MI5: the overture to a spectacular that evening.

She had the right pedigree for the task. Born in Andersonstown, West Belfast, in those mean streets in the shadow of Black Mountain, you could say that duplicity had been in the family blood for generations. The paternal great-uncle had been a prominent IRA figure in the early years. A maternal uncle had been a Labour councillor. The father of Dee and Anna, during a lifetime's dreary work in Belfast's shipyards, had kept out of politics; his opinions, though extreme, lacked credibility, for they were expressed through an alcoholic haze, put with a verbal violence which matched the physical violence he turned against his wife and daughters.

The two sisters had been familiar with brutality, both domestic and political, all their lives. They had grown up fuelled by hate, though the genes of activism had skipped a generation. Now they were inspired by hate as much as others were by love.

Anna, the taller of the two, the more introspective and thoughtful sister, gained a place at Queen's University, Belfast against the odds. She stayed on the fringes of student demonstrations, sometimes falling victim to the fists and truncheons of the RUC. Whereas Dee spent her days as a warehouse clerk in the shipyards where her father worked and drank, Anna studied law. By night, the sisters made passing contributions to the violence, keeping proud eyes on the totals of the dead as they reached two and a half thousand men, women and children. Killing was a way of life; you couldn't live without it. Anna had been careful not to show her face and had joined the Irish National Liberation Army, the more extreme offshoot of the Republican forces. Then there came a sea change, heralded by her attempt on the life of Sir Peter Terry, the former Governor of Gibraltar.

The murder weapon, the Kalashnikov AK-47, Soviet ground force assault rifle, was traced back to her by an SAS undercover team. Her name was passed to an agent of the RUC. Instead of arresting her, the RUC man, accompanied by a woman from MI5, struck a deal in a Glasgow bar. 'Stay where you are,' they told her. 'Long term and operational. Don't approach us, we'll approach you.'

A few weeks later, under the assumed name of van der Werff, with a new passport, two bank accounts in Basel and Milan, the post-graduate student of law began a new life of murder. To the most senior officers in the INLA she remained a heroine: the killer who knew no fear. To her British controller she was a long-term investment of high value. And, when asked to do so, she killed in cold blood, methodically, with efficiency, leaving no trace. She did the business; she got paid handsomely, though she had rarely commanded the sort of fee on offer this Friday morning. The money was in Wesley's safe, on the other side of the cupboard where she was waiting in the darkness.

Moments before the cleaner's arrival, she pulled the black nylon stocking mask over her shaven head. Then she released the Smith & Wesson's safety catch.

At 7.55 a.m. she heard the lift doors and footsteps in the passage. The cupboard door opened wide; so did the cleaner's eyes and mouth.

Anna McKeague's rubber gloves squeaked. She jammed the snout of the Smith & Wesson into the Filipino's mouth, then twisted her left arm upwards behind her back.

'Give me the keys.'

Anna McKeague turned the key in both Banham locks of the white-painted steel door.

Inside, exactly as she had been told, everything was normal. From beyond the interior hallway, the living room and Wesley's bedroom, came the voice of the morning newsreader on BBC Radio 4.

She forced the Filipino to her knees. She took the gun from the mouth; then, with a knee at the back of the Filipino's neck, she pushed her forehead into the carpet and began binding her round and round with the industrial adhesive tape. She left enough space at the base of the nose for her to breathe. Once the Filipino was immobilized she walked through the flat to where Wesley was in his bath.

For a few seconds Wesley stared at the figure in dumb horror. His eyes flicked from the Royal Mail all-weather uniform, several sizes too big, to the delivery bag; the face, its features compressed, flat and hideous beneath the mask; the Smith & Wesson levelled at his head. He gave a weak smile, as if he thought she was a joker.

'Stand up,' she said. The Irish accent wiped the smile from his face.

Phlegm rose in his throat so fast he began to choke. 'What the hell do you want?'

Spit bubbled through the mask from her flattened lips. 'Stand up,' she repeated, louder than before.

Wesley gripped the edge of his bath. Bath-water slopped across

55

the floor. He struggled to stand up and keep his balance.

'Raise your hands above your head.'

He did as he was told as if clutching at an invisible bar to steady himself.

'Get out of the bath.'

He managed to get one foot on to the floor without toppling over.

'And the other foot. Keep your arms up.'

He slipped, his kneecap striking the edge of the enamel bath.

'What do you want?'

She ignored his question.

He stared at her gun; then stretched his arm towards the towel rack beneath the mirror.

'Don't touch it.'

He lowered his hands to cover himself between his legs.

'Just do as I say or I'll blow your head apart.' Her voice was extraordinarily calm. 'Walk forwards slowly into the bedroom.'

His bedside radio was blaring out the rest of the news. He tried to stop the quivering of the muscles in his arms.

'Go on,' she told him. 'Into the hall.'

'Who are you?' he demanded. 'What do you want?'

'Stop. Don't move unless I tell you.'

'Money. You want money?'

Instead of answering him, she pressed the handgun against his back. His muscles convulsed.

'You will walk into the lounge. Keep your arms above your head. Higher.' Her voice could have been an air steward's explaining emergency procedures. 'Don't touch the furniture. No hurry. You walk to your wall safe in the lounge. When I tell you to stand still, you stand still. Only do what I tell you. Understand?'

'I understand.'

'Once we reach your wall safe you will be able to touch the panic button. You won't do that. You could also touch the trigger to alert duty Special Branch, MI5 personnel security unit, and the SAS at the Duke of York's Barracks. You won't. If you even think of touching anything, unless I tell you, I will kill you. Feel the gun?'

He made no answer.

'I said: "Do you feel the gun?"'

'Yes,' he replied.

'Then don't make a mistake.'

'You're the one who's making a bloody terrible mistake. I've got nothing whatsoever to do with the Security Service.'

She made a sudden move behind him and shoved a pamphlet with a blue cover in front of his face: *Accountability of the Security Service*.

'Now slowly. Walk.'

'My wife will be back shortly.'

'I don't care about your wife.'

He caught sight of his wet and naked body in a mirror beside an art deco umbrella stand. The intruder's hideous features stared back at him over his shoulder.

'I've got cramp,' he pleaded, 'in my arm. Oh God.'

'Then lean against the wall,' she told him. 'Just the fingertips.'

'We can do a deal,' he suggested. 'I simply don't have a safe here or anywhere else.'

'You don't?' she said. 'I'll tell you what's in your safe. Two hundred thousand pounds in cash. In high denomination paper notes, in fact. Deutschmarks and Swiss Francs.'

In the drawing room he saw his Filipino cleaning woman, her face on the carpet, tied up with the industrial adhesive tape.

'You realize what the penalties are for this?' Wesley said.

'I do. Do you realize the penalties you face for thieving government funds? Face facts, Wesley. You'll get sent down for life if anyone finds out. So we're going to work together. A team. You and me together.'

He skirted gingerly round the recumbent Filipino, and the large green sofa covered in tattered Victorian quilts. His thigh banged the corner of the regency table piled high with old copies of *Wisden*.

'Stop there. At the wall. Move. To the photo. Face it. Stand still.'

He faced the framed photograph of himself. Young Wesley BA (Oxon) stood outside the Sheldonian with Mother. He was in brand new academic garb. Mother wore a hat, a straw thing with a bunch of artificial cherries in it. Young Wesley grinned from ear to ear with pride at the reflected middle-aged Wesley: naked, with the gun in his back.

'Feet to the wall. Touch the photo with your fingertips. Now edge the photograph towards you. A little sideways.'

His fingers edged the framed photograph away from the wall. Like a small neat door, the photograph opened, on two tiny hinges.

Behind it, let expertly into the plasterwork, was the small panel of numbers from 1 to 10 arranged like the fascia of a miniature calculator. Such elaborate security precautions were typical of Wesley. He left nothing in life to chance. Precaution was his business. He believed in it as he believed in Queen and Country, Law and Order and Her Majesty's award to him of Commander of the British Empire. He considered himself, like all CBEs, a man of honour; no matter the empire had been wound up sometime in his childhood. Wesley was old school suburban: a scourge of weakness. Secrets were as safe as houses in the dull mind of Bryan Wesley CBE.

'We will tap in the wife's birthday. Six figures. And if the fingers stray, even a fraction . . . Stretch your feet apart.'

The gun's metallic tip was cold and sharp against his flesh.

'Further. Go on. OK. Or, if the fingers go anywhere near the secondary . . .'

'I don't know what you mean. I'm not a gadgets man. The secondary what?'

'Listen.' She pushed the gun still harder between his legs. 'Your wife's birthday. Let's start.'

He tapped in the numbers. The safe's mechanism whirred and beeped.

'Lean forwards. Both hands inside the safe. No further. By the nearside edge. Both hands.'

'I'm sorry, I can't do this. It's too painful.'

'What d'you mean?'

'I feel faint. Why don't you just do it yourself?'

'Because you are robbing your own safe. I'm not. You're only helping me. Understand?'

'You keep on saying "understand". I want you to get out of here.'

'Shut up and look down beside you.'

The post office delivery bag lay open by his feet.

'Take out the packets of currency. Drop them gently into the bag.'

One by one, he dropped the packets of currency into the open bag. His mind was screaming: *Hit the alarm.*

But the intruder had calculated the angle of his naked body to the wall to the last degree: his fingers could reach neither the alarm buttons nor the triggers.

Fifteen seconds later the safe was empty.

'Close the door. Set the locking mechanism. Straighten the photo.'

A cry of entreaty formed in his mind and in his throat. His breaths were coming in short gasps: in and out through his dry mouth. Then he blacked out.

He must have collapsed backwards. At any rate, the weight of his body was checked before it hit the floor.

'Get up.'

Terrified, he lifted himself on to his knees and elbows.

'Ten minutes and your cleaner's sister will come to do your ironing. She'll come in. Tidy up. Make you a cup of coffee. If your wife shows up, that's thought of too. She'll find out what you've been playing at with your Filipino tarts. If they open their mouths, talk to the police . . . Well, they won't, will they? As illegal immigrants. And what happens if your wife reports it all and you get gaoled? Know what? She gets no pension. And suppose the story gets back to the Service. Jesus, I wouldn't be in your shoes.' She nudged the Filipino with the toe of her running shoe. 'You won't say a thing, will you? Should've stayed at home in Manila, shouldn't you?' Then her eyes caught the wet pool spreading beneath the naked Wesley.

'You can't even control yourself,' she said.

She took off the postman's uniform, stepping out of the baggy trousers, rolled them up and stuffed them into the bag with the packs of foreign currency.

Time to go.

Minutes later, she crossed Kensington Square into Derry Street where she passed a beggar wrapped in a blackened duvet. He was calling to her for spare change. Instead of money, she handed him the postman's bag with the clothes and the nylon stocking that had been her mask. The foreign currency, her fee for the spectacular this evening, was secure in a flat money jacket beneath her shirt.

Her brisk walk through the park, the sight of spring flowers and smells of fresh cut grass cleared her head. '*Don't let Dee weaken,*' she prayed. '*Almighty God, don't let her give in to her interrogators.*'

On a good day Dee could give them as good as she got: i.e. nothing.

8

On his way by cab to Thames House Bryan Wesley took stock.

I have kept my own secrets. And the nation's.

Until, of course, the currency he possessed illegally was taken from him. Now he realized he might be exposed as a liar and a thief at any moment. The question was when. He would have to live with the nightmare that was of his own making.

I know. I know. True. I should never have had that currency in the safe.

What he didn't know was how on earth the intruder had found out about it.

If and when his superior officers discovered what had happened, the consequences would be disastrous for him. He knew he would be given no quarter, shown no sympathy; and that finally he would, inevitably, have to face a very nasty trial and an unbearably long stretch in prison, most probably in solitary confinement. What was there left for him to do?

The only choice is to stay silent. Face it out. Deny everything. Play for time.

In the event, luck was on his side. His exposure would be a long time in coming.

Fifteen minutes later, not ten minutes as the intruder had predicted, the cleaner's sister had arrived at Wesley's flat and was, naturally, appalled by what she found. Her sister's distress upset her most. She had sobbed uncontrollably.

A humiliated Wesley had been left to clean himself up and get dressed. He didn't have to explain in any great detail that they were 'all in this together'. It was plain to see. The Filipinos begged him not to call the police. As if he would. It seemed as if they thought, reasonably, that Wesley was himself some sort of secret policeman. Which, of course, he was.

He had regained his composure surprisingly fast and made a convincing display of persuading the Filipinos they would be in no trouble. They had behaved very well. 'I'm really very grateful to you both,' he told them, giving each of them fifty pounds in cash from his wallet. 'We'll regard the matter as closed. Finished. *Finito.*'

The Filipinos had given him sympathetic smiles and set about washing the carpet and cleaning up. Wesley waited until they'd finished. And it was the Filipino women who had thanked *him* profusely as they left, not the other way round. Perhaps, having read the tabloids, they expected English gentlemen who lived alone like Wesley to be party to bizarre practices, even victims. They appreciated the value of silence. So did Wesley.

There was nothing very unusual about his being late at Thames House and he was the sort of man who always had a plausible explanation for everything he did. Including being late for work. That was part of his strength. His plausibility.

He took great comfort in his reputation. His was the safe pair of hands.

His reliability had been recognized. Was he not, after all, a Commander of the British Empire? The British still tend to trust Commanders like Bryan Wesley and all those who have been accorded similar recognition by Her Majesty the Queen.

I inspire trust. I am Personnel MI5.

He thought it to be poor taste to question such honour. Other honorands might confess to you in private that their gongs had been accepted, actually, 'Not for me' but 'for the sake of the firm.' 'For the sake of the practice.' 'For staff morale.' 'Would have even been sillier to turn it down, don't you feel?'

That had never been Wesley's view. He relished the honour he had received. And he was very proud to have been honoured for such loyal service to the nation.

Mind you: to boast would seem unchivalrous.

Honour must, as it were, be worn lightly. These were Bryan Wesley's general views. He was little different from his honoured peers who sometimes disingenuously apologized for being deserving members of the titled class: the movers and shakers; set apart in British society; the wise and the good and the great grateful for Her Majesty's expression of public confidence in their superiority. Keep your nose clean and, who could tell, a knighthood might eventually very well be offered. Sir Bryan and even Lady Wesley. Mr Bryan Wesley nurtured a secret longing for his K. The sort of thing that gets you to the office with lowly suckers competing to open doors for you. Now he realized his chances of ever getting it were in serious jeopardy. None the less, he was more than ever determined to keep up appearances.

I have a lot to live up to.

What I do with my private life is my affair.

No matter that the private life in question was beginning to give off a nasty smell.

It was clinging to him as he showed his ID to the Thames House guards. At least they seemed pleased to see him.

9

Also within the hour, the woman assistant in the sportswear department of Selfridges had her first customer of the day, who paid cash for a running suit. Made of nylon, it was water-resistant and windproof. The assistant showed her customer how to turn it inside out. 'Two outfits, you see, neat. Royal blue or royal crimson.'

Anna McKeague betrayed no flicker of her hatred for royalty, whether attached to the colour of the moment or anything else. She added a pair of black running shoes to the purchase.

Beyond artists' materials and adult games she found the ladies' toilets. Here she changed into her new outfit. She put her other clothes into the Selfridges plastic carrier. Before she left the toilet she slipped a short black wig over her shaven head. She applied make-up to her lips and around her eyes. Nothing very noticeable. Her appearance was calculated to be ordinary. Had you noticed her leaving the Ladies' you'd have thought that she was perhaps a receptionist ready with a cheery 'How can I help you?'

She took the stairs to the third floor and ladies' leathers where she bought a pair of cut-price black gloves. In ladies' outerwear she bought a grey overcoat. Then she took the lift to the ground floor where she headed for the swing door marked STAFF EXIT.

Outside, the team of men in overalls throwing plastic sacks into rubbish disposal vehicles were unwitting contributors to her progress. She swung the Selfridges bag into the jaws at the back of the nearest vehicle. Then she left unnoticed into Orchard Street in the direction of Bond Street.

She raised the hood of her running suit against the thin drizzle. Another good omen. London rain brought anonymity.

Jostling tourists barged into Tower Records. Eros was covered up, out of sight. She headed for Leicester Square, the hood around her face, breathing with the ease of the marathon runner.

She was two minutes early for her appointment with the money launderer in Gerrard Street: Vicki Leung.

The launderer ushered her into a small room with a view of the Hong Kong Bank. It was a blurred view. Layers of grease stuck to the window panes. Nicotine stained the walls a sickly yellow.

Vicki Leung's room was sparse. She had a small bank of telephones and fax machines on her desk. Beside it were two suitcases full of polystyrene of different shapes. She changed offices many times a week, always on the move. Her watery eyes stared at the packs of currency lifted from the bag marked Selfridges.

Through gold teeth she said something like 'Mewarlo an Barrel' (Milano and Basel) and 'Sliss Fwanks an Doischmwarker. OK. Name of account?'

'L. D. van der Werff.'

'Pounds sterling?'

'US dollars.'

'OK.' She jabbed a stained finger at her calculator. 'Bucks. Fifteen per cent US dollars.'

'No. Ten per cent.'

'Two currencies, fifteen per cent.'

'Ten. Or the deal's off.'

The launderers were the same throughout Europe. It was a matter of pride to up the commission. They always tried it on. The Chinese would, of course, do it for ten per cent. It was easy money for transferring money to a hidden account. This one was safe. The Chinese were the best in the business when it came to hiding big sums. Most of all the women.

'OK,' Vicki Leung said, lighting another foul-smelling Belgian cigarette. She scribbled on a form. Sums of money in a box marked 'Currency of Telegraphic Transfer'. Others headed 'Name of Beneficiary', 'Account No.', 'Name of Remitter', with an indistinct address in Harrow Weald.

'You wait for confirmation of receipt.'

'Think I won't?'

'Some people,' Vicki Leung reflected, feeding the form into the fax machine, 'some people don't believe me.'

Minutes later back came the confirmation slips from Basel and Milan.

'Take the back stairs out. Go through the restaurant. There's a takeaway for you.'

'No thanks.'

'Up to you. If you want a reason for being here. There are police everywhere. You can't always see them. Even you.'

'Maybe,' she said. 'Here, get rid of this.' She dropped the money jacket on Vicki Leung's desk.

She left by the back stairs, content that her full fee for carrying out the killings later was safe in foreign banks under the bogus name of van der Werff. She had always been careful with money. Good at deals: even better than her sister, Dee.

Off Cambridge Circus she made two telephone calls. The first was to a woman of Irish extraction, a junior negotiator in a Bloomsbury commercial property agency. They agreed confirmation of an appointment to collect keys to a vacant office suite near the British Museum.

She'd spoken to the negotiator only yesterday, who had told her she could see the office suite unaccompanied. The keys would be in a plain envelope in the Museum Street entrance hall. The negotiator was careful not to mention the address, or where precisely the keys would be. You could never be sure who was listening to your calls. The time of the visit to Museum Street had already been set for noon. No mention was made of it.

The second call was to her nameless paymaster. At the other end of the line she heard the synthesized computer voice answer.

'Fine,' she said.

'You have your fee?' said the mechanized voice, neither male nor female.

'Yes,' she replied. 'I'm ready.'

Later, another call would be the final check that her victims were in place and nothing untoward would prevent their murder.

This was the way she liked it. You kept your clients informed of progress along the line. You kept them involved at a distance until the targets had been dispatched. It was a job to be approached with the scrupulous care the doctor brings to saving life. Only in her case she was taking it. The rules for care were the same, but in reverse. She prided herself on the clinical approach.

64

The first-floor office in Museum Street was empty: unoccupied since the former tenants, partners in the Museum Mutual Benefit & Pensions Trust had gone bust in the last days of Thatcher. The envelope lay on a window-ledge beside a rotting milk carton. Inside she found two Banham keys and a used tube ticket with a pencilled number: the code to the combination lock of the defunct Museum Mutual Benefit & Pension Trust's company safe.

The safe was abandoned in the far corner of the office of the disgraced chairman of MMB & PT. Next to the safe was a lid of an old margarine carton containing rat poison. She set it aside. Fresh excreta trailed across the floor. The rats must have immunized themselves against the poison.

She turned the dials to open the safe door. Inside it, as her paymaster had promised, lay the explosive device wrapped in bubble plastic and aluminium foil.

Her watch told her 1 p.m. Time to go. Five hours until the bomb explodes.

Dead time: the last hours drag; the nervy time when, for example, street life plays you the unexpected trick.

For instance, there had been the Regent's Park cab crash in 1990 when she'd had to leg it into the park to hide her weapon. It was the day after she had gunned down that former Governor of Gibraltar in Staffordshire. In a hotel room in Kilburn she had watched the search for herself, the gunman, reported on TV. Sure enough, up came the face of Commander Harding, head of the anti-terrorist branch, whose officers now had possession of the AK-47 assault rifle, found in bushes in Regent's Park. She hated the commander's complacency and confidence. She had lain low through the long dull summer in Brighton. Why had it gone wrong? Why hadn't she killed Sir Peter Terry? Because she hadn't planned it well enough. And never rely on some oaf of a London cab driver not to crash. Commander Harding had given a public promise that he personally would nail 'the perpetrator of the outrage'. Well, he hadn't. She was playing the game both sides now.

A sullen face thrust itself in hers: 'Where's the British Museum?'

She averted her eyes. Crossed the street. Out of view behind a removal van. She pressed on, not polite or rude; only silent, a face in the crowd.

In the dead time you control your nerves, you stick to random patterns of movement in the streets and public places: stations, stores, the underground, places where people have their minds on other things or nothing.

You stay alive to police sirens, alarm bells, to any sudden alert. You stay predatory: the hunter and the hunted. You relax into the mood of people's preoccupations. By now you've stripped your mind of anxiety, any concern about being paid – she, of course, already had her fee, now safely deposited in those bank accounts under another name. It's essential for the hired killer to have the money up front, all of it. You stick to your plan like a pilot to his flight plan; you remove all clutter from your mind. But the unexpected jumps out at you.

Like the *Evening Standard* headline on the poster outside the entrance to the tube at Tottenham Court Road: POLICE FURY AT MI5 ANTI-TERRORISM ROLE. She bought a copy of the paper to read after her final purchase in the store that sold nursing uniforms. She liked to read about the enemies of terrorism. They were her enemies: she needed to know about them. There was still more pleasure to be had from the certain knowledge that she knew far more about them than they knew about her.

On the northbound tube, to Belsize Park in the Edgware train, the passengers glimpsed a nurse. Regular passengers would have seen her as one among many nurses bound for duty at Hampstead's Royal Free Hospital.

Her research had shown there to be two groups of people, readily identifiable, in the neighbourhood of England's Lane off Haverstock Hill: Japanese who leased flats in the more modern apartment blocks and uniformed nurses who occupied the nurses' hostel at the corner of England's Lane and Antrim Road. Therefore: her pale blue nylon frock, black tights, flat black shoes. She carried an overnight bag containing her counterfeit passport, ferry tickets from Stranraer, and the package wrapped in bubble plastic taken from the safe in Museum Street. She wore a light grey coat. In a brown unmarked plastic carrier bag she had the clothes bought at Selfridges to be worn when she finally crossed the sea to Ireland.

She had removed the make-up applied earlier when she changed into her nursing uniform unnoticed in the staff toilets at Foyles in the Charing Cross Road. The naturalness of her face matched the look of hospital nurse; a slip of a wide-eyed girl with the underpaid vocation the British find so very admirable.

Odd things test you in the dead time.

The second testing moment occurred when the black man turned to face her just beyond the ticket barrier at Belsize Park tube station. He asked if he could carry her bag. She walked straight past him. *You try to mug me, you black ape, and I'll knee you so you'll never pee again without screaming.* It was not, of course, violence she found objectionable: it was violence that wasn't strictly necessary.

There is a telephone box on Haverstock Hill across the busy road from the tube station entrance. From this she made the last of her calls before the bomb went off.

She heard the disembodied voice say: 'Hello.'

'Are we ready to start?'

The voice said: 'Everything's in place.'

Which meant the road to kill was clear and, later on, the getaway car, a white two-door car marked POLICE, with large letters fixed to the roof for helicopter identification, would be in place at the prearranged time in England's Lane, parked at the edge of the disaster scene. She replaced the telephone receiver.

There were no more chances to abort the bombing.

With the last of dead time running out she bought a ticket for a film at the Screen on the Hill. She closed her eyes, slouched low in her seat, breathing regularly, listening to the soundtrack, sometimes checking the passing minutes on her watch. She thought of the massive quantity of high explosive she had expertly set in place the night before. Her mind rehearsed technical matters: testing the electronics, the time to get into the white car marked POLICE, the getaway immediately after the explosion through the fire and smoke and chaos. In the dark of the cinema she practised her finger movements as they'd move later in the dark of the derelict living-room.

She thought again of Dee in prison in West London: her strong sister with nothing to look forward to except a life in jail. Well, one day soon she would get her out. That would be her triumph. The great spectacular: SISTER FREES SISTER.

They would live in Rio or in Colombia. She fancied the idea of South America.

Meanwhile, there was the murder of the two women to carry out. She was looking forward to scoring another victory. Another two deaths. It was, as father used to say, good to be alive. Two more dead Brits. It was getting as easy as counting on your fingers.

10

The last Saturday of the month: Rosslyn took the day off.

It was a Saturday for freedom in the parks. Coffee in Holland Park, two cans of beer in Kensington Gardens with a salad from Marks & Spencer, a long walk across Hyde Park with his headphones attached to his transistor radio for the news.

Still no bomb.

In these last few days of March, spring was in the air. Crocuses, narcissi and daffodils splashed the parks with pretty colours. Forsythia exploded with unusual brilliance. Where it was set against pink tree blossom, the sun shining, the yellow was dazzling. London basked in the springtime warmth. The model yacht enthusiasts had returned to Kensington pond with the wandering Arabs, the nannies with their charges in old-fashioned prams, the winos sleeping undisturbed on their backs on the grass, their zippers open to the sky.

The passivity made him restless, then anxious and finally impatient. He gave himself tea and a doughnut at the Royal Academy. In the old days, Mary would have dragged him round the latest exhibition. Now he no longer had any enthusiasm for paintings, music, novels. So he did the obvious – *Sod Gaynor, sod the day off* – and returned again to his office at Custom House in Lower Thames Street.

Which wasn't much more interesting.

Until nearly 7 p.m. when his telephone rang. It was Harding. 'Do you still have the tape of your interview with McKeague?'

No 'How are you? Good to hear you.' None of that. Harding sounded cold and distant.

'Gaynor has it in his safe,' Rosslyn replied.

'Get it to me.'

'He's gone home.'

'Don't you know the combination to his bloody safe?'

'I can find it.'

'Then do it,' Harding snapped. 'Get the tape.'

'Didn't you get my transcript?'

'MI5 have it. I want the original. Or did you copy it?'

'No. The only one's in Gaynor's safe.'

'Bring it to me here. I'm in England's Lane, NW3. Off Haverstock Hill.'

'What's happened?'

'There's been a bomb.'

The line went dead.

11

Even before he reached England's Lane Rosslyn could smell the smoke. It hung like a veil of mourning in the evening sky over the north of London.

Fire tenders roared past his car up Haverstock Hill on the wrong side of the road and a stream of police cars and ambulances overtook him, forcing oncoming traffic on to the pavements. A police patrolman stepped into the road with his gloved hand raised for Rosslyn to stop. When he lowered his car window the stench was even stronger. The air was heavy with the fumes of burned plastic and pale grey dust. Some of it gusted into his eyes. He heard a helicopter overhead.

The patrolman told him to leave his car in a space reserved for the residents of a block of mansion flats near the scene of the disaster.

Rosslyn continued on foot to the junction of Haverstock Hill and England's Lane where the streets were blocked by police cars, motorbikes and ambulances. A way was being made for more fire engines to get through. Above the din of sirens and klaxons police officers in yellow jackets shouted at the onlookers to disperse. No sooner had one group of ghouls backed away than another line replaced them. A woman yelled at some children restraining a howling dog.

A police officer raised the plastic tape at the entrance to England's Lane. He told Rosslyn where to find Commander Harding.

Fire Service vehicles and heavy equipment clogged the street. Teams of fire-fighters stood around waiting for orders. Rosslyn couldn't see Harding; indeed, he could see very little through the billowing clouds of smoke and dust. But every few seconds it cleared.

He saw the smashed windows of the houses in Chalcot Gardens which border part of England's Lane. A woman holding a child to her breast pushed past him. 'My husband's in there!' she was yelling. 'For Christ's sake. Let me through.' Two policewomen, their portable phones blaring out incomprehensible messages, managed to restrain her.

'What's his name?'

'I said he's my husband!'

'Doesn't he have a name?'

'Of course he has a fucking name.'

'Then what is it?'

A rush of smoke made the woman choke. Rosslyn covered his mouth with his coat collar. He felt an arm tug at him. A police officer pulled him away the moment before several slabs of masonry thudded into the street. The ground shook underfoot. Through the smoke a voice screamed: 'Gas!' He felt a shower of sparks rain down. He brushed them off and began to run. After a few yards a fire tender blocked his path. He turned to look back through the smoke. Several trees were on fire. Something touched his foot. He looked down and saw a dead dachshund lying on its back beside an abandoned bag of shopping.

Black smoke forced itself into his lungs from the fire in a newsagent's. One section of the England's Lane terrace had collapsed. Chairs, tables and several double beds were smouldering in the rubble. Splintered glass covered the road and pavements.

To one side of the remains of the newsagent's he saw firemen directing water jets into the blaze. Here the fires were most intense. Other figures, in yellow waterproofs, attached chains to the hulk of a burned out taxi.

He heard a familiar voice behind him: 'Rosslyn?'

Harding's face was wet; his forehead smeared with grease and dust. 'Let's talk somewhere.' He had his hand on Rosslyn's arm. 'Best not look,' he said.

But Rosslyn looked. Through a gap in the gathering of rescue service workers, firemen, policemen and nurses, he saw the corpses. Charred and roasted bits of bodies lay on wet plastic sheets. A twisted leg, the foot detached, lay in debris like a bizarre artificial limb. A transparent bag contained a pair of severed hands. Beside it lay the heads. The shock of recognition came slowly. Male or female: he found it difficult to tell. One of them seemed partially connected to a fractured shoulder bone which looked as if someone had used a hammer to smash it upwards through the skull. The flesh was peeled back, singed and tattered. He knew the faces.

'Two women,' Harding said.

One of them was about thirty years old. A few tufts of scorched fair hair stuck to the scalp.

The second woman looked older. Maybe forty. Thick blood matted her red hair. A shard of dark glass stuck out from her neck. Rosslyn noticed a gold earring in the left ear. One didn't expect a severed head to be wearing jewellery. The mouth was fixed in a dumb scream. Eyes white, open wide, one having revolved in its socket like an incorrectly inserted artificial eye. The woman's teeth were thick with blood, mucus and saliva.

'You never get used to it,' Harding said. 'No two people die in the same way. People don't think about that.'

They walked away from the horror across the carpet of splintered glass and smouldering bits of paper. The sound of glass crunched on glass was shrill. It made Rosslyn's teeth ache sharply as if he'd accidentally bitten on silver foil.

Perhaps it was too much for his mind to grasp that he had been staring into the dead faces of Monro and Watson: the women who had interrogated him on the evening of Mary's death.

There is a pub, the Washington, at the junction of England's Lane and Belsize Park Gardens, bordering where the streets join two others: Eton Avenue and Primrose Hill Road. The junction had been closed. Police officers were telling onlookers to stand well clear of the barriers of plastic tape.

Rosslyn and Harding stood in the doorway to the evacuated pub.

He handed Rosslyn a strip of sugar-free chewing gum. 'Takes the taste away. I want you to tell me about McKeague in your own words,' Harding said. 'I want your opinion.'

'Didn't Gaynor tell you?' Rosslyn asked.

'He told me what he'd heard on the tape of McKeague. He didn't tell me what you think about her. Do you think, for a start, she's telling the truth?'

'Only about being beaten up. She looks as if she's been hit by a truck. Apart from that, the rest of what she has to say sounds like pure invention. The business of an explosive device being planted on her when she was arrested. Suppose it was true? You'd have to ask yourself why MI5 would be so clumsy as to wreck the case against her.'

Harding reflected for a moment in silence.

'Do you think they'd set out to sabotage it deliberately?' Rosslyn asked.

'No. Do you?'

'Not unless they've been using her as a grass and haven't told the rest of us. That's always a possibility.'

'Think it might be?' Harding said. 'Or could the device she described be the same type that's gone off here? Whatever caused this must have been pretty well identical in strength to the item she told you about. If we get enough fragments we'll soon see if it could have been one and the same bomb, or at least identical. I thought she told you she'd been asked to do a job like this.'

'She implied that, yes,' Rosslyn said. 'But she never mentioned the exact location.'

'Not England's Lane?'

'No. Just north London. You'll have to hear it for yourself. It's in the car.'

'Later. What about the two Security Service officers as targets?'

'She just said she'd been approached by someone to do a job. Tell me – the victims, those women –'

'I'll come to them,' Harding interrupted. 'I want to know why she didn't do the job herself. Why did she turn it down?'

Rosslyn shook his head. 'Because she reckoned she was being set up. She'd have to be pretty thick to get involved in some contract to kill targets from MI5. God, it's the most obvious trap. She'd have walked straight into it. It was blatant.'

Harding was peering to where the smoke was thickest in the street. He seemed defeated.

'I know the dead women,' Rosslyn said. 'They questioned me about Mary's death. One of them was the woman who told me they intended to recruit her, as if I didn't know. Did you know them too?'

'Yes,' said Harding. 'I met Monro when she was on surveillance of UK Syrian students at the time of the Hindawi El Al operation. Watson, well, I met her at about the same time when she was Special Branch. She transferred to MI5 some time back. And I actually saw Monro only a few weeks ago at Thames House. She was an acting director.'

'Were they operational this afternoon?'

'When it went off? No. Off duty. At Monro's flat.'

'How do you know it was her flat?' Rosslyn asked.

'Because the burglar alarm's linked to the local station. It's on priority cut-out. The alarm went off at four minutes past six. So we have the exact time of detonation. So do MI5. The alarm's linked to Thames House. They've got their people here.'

'Have you told them about McKeague?' Rosslyn asked.

Harding thought about the question. He spat his chewing gum into a wrapper. Rosslyn noticed he put it into his pocket.

Harding said: 'I've told Gaynor to keep his mouth shut. I want you to do the same.'

'Isn't that a risk?'

'If so, it's my problem,' said Harding. 'I'll live with it. You too. I want to win this one. We have McKeague. Thanks to you we have McKeague. It looks to me she's making some kind of sense. The rest of it is sick. There's even been a hoax warning to the Samaritans at King's Cross. Fifteen minutes *after* the explosion. We've contacted Dublin. The IRA are swearing to Almighty God it isn't their responsibility.'

'So who the hell is responsible then?' Rosslyn asked.

The roar of a police helicopter overhead drowned Harding's answer. It was hovering perilously low. Its arc lights, two vivid beams of white, cut through the unnatural darkness.

Harding squinted up at them. He looked around to see if anyone was watching, then shouted above the din: 'Go back to McKeague and take her apart. I want to know who tried to commission her. Make her an offer. Do a deal, so she tells us who's responsible.'

The helicopter moved up a little and talking became easier.

'What do I offer her?'

'Immunity from prosecution. Say we'll re-examine the charges. Offer protection. We'll get her out of the country with a false identity. If she says she wants to stay we'll give her Special Branch twenty-four-hour protection. A safe house.'

'You would really go that far?'

'Probably not,' said Harding. 'We may not have to. But go straight in there offering anything she asks for. Say you believe her. Be her friend. Just get everything she knows. Talk all night if you have to. But don't tell her what's happened here.'

'Suppose she already knows?'

'She doesn't. I told the superintendent to keep her on in solitary. They're under orders not to talk to her.'

They left the pub doorway. Rosslyn noticed that the dismembered corpses of Monro and Watson had been removed. A police inspector approached Harding. He wanted a word with him in private.

Rosslyn watched the two men talking with difficulty above the blaring chorus of police car horns. A police dog-handler asked him to move away. The dog was straining at its leash, sniffing at his crotch, when he saw Harding rapidly making his way back to him. A man in waterproofs and bombproof clothing began to question Harding. Harding steered him angrily in the direction of a junior police officer.

'You can go home now,' Harding said. 'We can't talk to McKeague. They've taken her to hospital. She's got a blood clot on the brain. They're going to operate.'

'What's happened?' Rosslyn asked.

'Someone must have got to her already,' Harding said. 'How serious was she when you saw her?'

'Beaten up pretty badly. You know. But she made sense. Her mind was clear enough.'

'Well, it isn't now.'

'I can see her after the operation,' Rosslyn said.

The helicopter was lowering again, its rotors beating. Harding was angry and disappointed. 'God knows when that'll be.' He gave a smile of resignation, reaching out as though to say goodbye, that's it, like a gambler with his last throw lost on an outsider.

'Between ourselves, MI5 are saying you applied unnecessary violence to her.'

Rosslyn felt stunned. 'I did *what*?'

'That's what they're saying.'

'It isn't true.'

'I believe you,' Harding said.

'There's no proof I did. It's on the tape.'

'That's why I believe you,' Harding said. He patted him on the shoulder. 'I'll be in touch.'

Rosslyn walked away towards Haverstock Hill through the still growing crowd of police, rescue workers, doctors and nurses. Inside the police cordon he saw a team of forensic experts unpacking equipment from a Range Rover. Beyond the cordon, further down Haverstock Hill, the smoke was thinner. It was unusually dark. Power had not yet been restored. There were no lights in the neighbouring houses and the streetlights were dead.

He made his way through the gaping onlookers to the forecourt of the mansion block where his car was parked. Immediately he saw it he froze.

A woman with her back to him was crouching, her face obscured, next to the driver's door of his car, with a blunt instrument, a wrench or thick screwdriver, in her hands.

Rosslyn shouted at her: 'Get away from it.'

Rosslyn heard the squeal of brakes behind him. The driver yelled: 'Get out of the way.' Half turning, Rosslyn's eyes caught the dazzle of the headlights. The car swept past.

The woman had vanished. Rosslyn looked about. Then he saw her crossing Haverstock Hill through the traffic. She disappeared behind a parked bus without looking back. A looter taking advantage of chaos. One more cheap thief among thousands.

He had scared her off just in time. But when he turned his key in the door he found it unlocked.

Getting careless.

His briefcase lay on the floor in front of the passenger seat.

My luck's in. Nothing's nicked.

And it was with a sense of relief that he found his flat keys and the tape of the interview with Dee McKeague still inside his briefcase.

12

At home, alone on the Saturday night in his Pimlico flat, Rosslyn makes cheese according to Mary's method: he brings a quart of whole milk to the boil. As it starts to bubble he stirs in two and a half tablespoonfuls of lemon juice and removes the pan from the stove. He leaves the milk to curdle so the curds will separate from the whey in fifteen minutes' time. While he waits he watches the late night TV news account of events in England's Lane.

The reporter says that two women are the latest victims of the IRA. 'A Samaritans' office in King's Cross earlier received a coded warning,' the reporter continues. He goes on to say that more than twenty people were taken to the Royal Free Hospital in Hampstead. Eight of them were seriously injured. Many of them were treated on the spot by teams of motorcycle paramedics from the North London Ambulance Service.

He watches a young black man describe how he administered the kiss of life to a pregnant woman. 'There was all this screaming,' the man says. 'But I didn't listen to it. The Fire Brigade gave me bandages to cover the woman's legs.'

Another survivor, a woman with a heavy foreign accent, says: 'There was this terrible bang. I saw people lying in the street and I cradled a little girl in my arms. She had lost her foot. The street was packed with people buying Mother's Day presents.'

The reporter says that the police carried out several controlled explosions to destroy suspect shopping bags. 'The bombing bears all the hallmarks of the IRA.' He adds that security experts see the bombing as a revenge attack.

The prime minister is reported as saying: 'I was shocked to hear of the explosion in north London. The wickedness of this attack defies belief. The purpose was to kill and maim. Tragically, that is what happened. News of this latest bomb attack on men, women and children going innocently about their business on a spring Saturday will be met everywhere with sorrow and revulsion.'

The reporter ends by saying that the identities of the two dead women have not yet been released. 'The attack follows recent anti-terrorist arrests and arms cache finds in London and the north-west.' A London University professor of military history says that the war against the IRA terrorists is being lost. The anti-terrorist forces are in disarray, demoralized and wholly inadequate. The responsibility for the chaos is the prime minister's. The newsman says no politician is prepared to comment in public.

Rosslyn waits for Harding to make his customary appeal for public vigilance. He doesn't appear.

The curds have separated from the whey. He strains them through several layers of cheesecloth. The whey he's squeezed out he stores in the refrigerator. He ties up the curds in a round bag formed out of the cheesecloth. He hangs it from a hook on his kitchen shelf so it will drip throughout the night. In the morning he will flatten the cheese and it will be ready to cook as supper for one in the evening with spinach, peas and tomatoes. Mary Walker believed in the goodness of protein. Above all, the making of cheese the way she made it is a comfort to him.

He can't remember how long it's been since she made cheese for him. To find out he consults her diary. This is only the second time he's been able to face the pages, her handwriting, her voice. He opens it at random. He sees:

AUTUMN – THE FIRST CHILL OF SEPTEMBER

She's talking to herself, talking to him. They're quite alone.

R + 194
The leaves are on the turn, the grass is turning brown. There's been a dew most mornings. Today it's heavy. The London skies have been magnificent. Great streaks of white stretched overhead like the most fragile see-through silk. The sunsets are liquid – all kinds of crimson, alazarin, carmine, rose madder. R has told me about artist's colours.

There's something I can't tell R.

This – all my other love affairs have ended after six months maximum. Often less. I want to tell him about this. We're in his flat sitting at the kitchen table. Me with Calvados. R with a bottle of chilled Morgon. This diary is in my shoulder bag. I've never mentioned to R that I've kept a diary for all the other lovers. Too many. Many too many. I want R to know I've binned the record. The slate is clean.

So I begin by saying 'Aren't you curious about my past? About the others?'

77

He says he hates to think of me with someone else, some other mouth against mine.

I tell him it's all in his mind.

'No,' he says. There's real passion in his eyes.

It's on the brink of getting out of hand. So I try a different touch. 'This is my body – not yours, Alan.'

(This is the first time I've ever written a man's real name in the diary – except for THUG. And those were only THUG's initials.)

'The past doesn't matter,' I say.

He doesn't agree. He says something like 'You can only understand yourself if you value your past.'

'I can't shut it out, Alan. My past exists, I can't deny it. But I can say it doesn't matter.'

The trouble is that what I'm saying isn't quite true. I can't help seeing THUG at work. The old man, unhappy husband, says I mended his wings in bed. I turned his failure into success. I taught him how to fuck my arse.

Then Alan says 'I never want to meet the others.'

'You won't,' I tell him. 'I'll make sure you never do.'

Then R talks some more.

He says he's forced to inhabit the past – that's what he does at work. He puts people's pasts together. Then he takes them apart. He's talking about the arms and explosives dealers. He has to decide when to trust them and when not to; or when to let them think he trusts them. You have, he tells me, to think yourself into their minds, their skins, even their hearts. Above all you have to use your imagination. He thinks of himself as a cipher, like he's characterless. He has a deep need to absorb people, recreate them, then trap them. That's what makes him so good at his job. It's why his seniors seek him out for his views no matter he's miles their junior.

He says it's like the work of the art historian. Ultimately, you've got to decide whether the artefact's real or fake, a copy or a copy of a fake, and so on. Did the artist really do the picture, or all of it, or some of it? You think yourself into the artist's heart in secret and his mind to understand just what his hand really did. It's an act of cerebral detection.

'But why don't you look into yourself more?' I ask him.

'Because I don't often like what I see,' he says.

'Did any of your other women ask you that?'

Then he says he doesn't want to talk about them for fear of hurting me.

'Retrospective jealousy is ridiculous,' I tell him. 'I don't care about your other women. I've got you. Here and now. With me. And you need never

care about my previous life. In general, I associated with shits.'

(I don't mention THUG. I don't say THUG still calls me at the Yard along with half a dozen of the others. I don't tell Alan I've told them all about him. That I want to marry him, that I want your children, Alan. I want you and me to make kids.)

I won't tell him yet, or that:
1. I love him so much.
2. I want his kids so that if he ever died he'd live for ever and I'd always be reminded of him.
3. I'm secretly, deep down, pissed off with the police because there's no future in it for women.

Alan says more – he's forgotten his little bit of jealousy. (Like all jealous men he can't help dwelling on what hurts him. Unlike the other jealous lovers I love him.)

He says he and I lurch from case to case, we drown in the sea of paperwork, the grey men's committees, the boards, inquiries, working parties. We react after the event; we leave nothing permanent behind us, no books, no art, no fresh discoveries. All we do is secure convictions. That doesn't make society the more secure. We're living proof that we've put our fingers on other people's failures, broken lives and twisted minds and we shut them in prison like rotten food discarded in a bin.

Then we go to bed. He asks me to keep my eyes wide open. He looks down at me so serious. So desperate. Then he shouts like a great big broken animal. I want him to live for ever.

He can't sleep. He decides he must destroy the diary. He puts an extra blanket on his bed. Its warmth provides little comfort. A smiling Mary looks at him from the photograph in its silver frame on his bedside table and he knows he can't bring himself to destroy anything that belonged to her. He switches off the light. In the darkness the faces of the dead women are still there. Then McKeague's eyes, swollen and bloody. Then Mary's eyes.

In his dreams he hears sirens wailing and the ringing of a bell. Mary's rings: one long, two short. He wakes, smiling, sweating profusely. And, of course, Mary isn't coming tonight or any other night.

It is three-thirty on Sunday morning and there is someone at the door.

13

Rosslyn opened the door to find Harding standing in the rain. He was looking up to the street from the basement stairwell.

He followed Rosslyn into the hallway, closing the door behind him, without apologizing for having woken him at such an unearthly hour.

'Did you walk here?' Rosslyn asked.

'I parked in Ranelagh Grove. I don't want anyone to know I'm here.' He hung his soaking coat on the coat rack. 'We're too late. We've lost McKeague. Two hours ago. She never recovered from the operation.'

'Oh God, thanks very much, that's all we need,' Rosslyn said. They went into the kitchen. 'Did she talk to you before she died?'

'I talked to her,' Harding said. 'It was no bloody use. I asked her about the device. Names. She just lay there hooked up to God knows what tubes and wires and the rest of it. The nurse says "Maybe she can hear something." If she did she was cocking a deaf'un. Then this priest turns up and says, "Haven't you people had your pound of flesh, then?" Irish. Obviously Catholic. There was this hellish row before the priest administered the last rites. After she died I got the superintendent at Paddington Green out of bed. He says that MI5 have been back to see her regularly. Her condition deteriorated so fast they said they reckoned you must have roughed her up.'

'That's crap.'

'That's what I said.'

'Did she say anything to MI5?'

'Not a word, according to the superintendent. You have to give it to her. She was a tough little bastard.'

Rosslyn set a bottle of Calvados and two glasses on the table. 'How do you know MI5 didn't offer her a deal?'

'Because the custody officer was listening on the intercom. McKeague just sat there dumb. Didn't say a word. Not surprising, given the damage to her brain. But the custody officer didn't *see* what went on in the interview room. They could've done something pretty evil to her. Plenty of ways of damaging her without the doctors being any the wiser. But I don't think they'd stoop to that in

McKeague's case, do you? They must have wanted to hear what she had to say as much as us. Only she didn't say a word. Finally they carted her off to emergency surgery after MI5 left Paddington Green. What they don't know is that forensic have delivered quite a lot of stuff that's interesting. Enough of the fragments fit. The device McKeague described to you was the same sort as the one in England's Lane.'

'But it may not have been the same one she saw when she was arrested.'

'If she really did see it.' Harding sat down on the edge of the kitchen table. He poured himself a Calvados. 'Suppose it was the same one? If someone took on the job she described, the one she told you she turned down, then someone will have been paid for doing it.'

'Do you still believe she was telling me the truth?' Rosslyn asked.

'And if she was? That's the best result we've had in years.' Harding filled the second glass for Rosslyn. 'And you found her.'

'I didn't find her. She found me.' Rosslyn looked at him, puzzled, for a second. 'I'd like to know why MI5 think I was the one who beat her up.'

'So would I.'

'Because it was those prats who were responsible.'

'Probably.'

'Then I'm going to make a formal complaint.'

'Wouldn't waste your time,' Harding said. 'You wouldn't be the first to complain. Or the last. It won't get you anywhere. And I'd rather you didn't.'

'Why not?'

'Because I don't want to upset MI5 right now. Let me tell you why, Alan. They've put the blocks on me forming the usual type of investigation team. Why? Because the dead are two of their own. Whoever's on the team in an executive position is bound, eventually, to have to look at their operations. They won't welcome that. They insist numbers be restricted. We can have the usual access to forensic, but executive decisions rest with me and, now, one of MI5's officers. I've said I've no objection if I can appoint my own personal assistant. They won't wear my choice of a police officer. They must have thought: he can't get anyone else. So I went back to them with your name. I cleared it with Gaynor. He'll allow you an indefinite secondment. It's agreed, Alan. So what I want to know is what you think about it.'

'What do I think? For starters, if they're saying I might very well be responsible for McKeague's death, well, I can't see how I can be flavour of the month.'

'I thought of that,' Harding said. 'You know what I think? I believe it's an advantage they reckon they've got something on you. They'll love the idea of showing *me* in a bad light. Customs officer who stepped right out of line. Then they can argue the case for taking the investigation over altogether.'

'If they prove I used violence against McKeague.'

'If. Yes. And we know they can't. Meanwhile we've stolen a march on them. Suppose McKeague told you the truth? We know it. They don't.'

He began to pace around the kitchen. 'What do you feel, Alan? Here's a chance to settle the score for Mary. The chance to be in the front line. You once told me you wanted to face her killer. The obstacle could have been MI5's objection to you. But they've put in their man. I'm putting in mine. That's you. I don't want you to turn it down, Alan.'

'Do I have some time to think about it?'

'No. I want to know now.'

'I mean, do I have a choice?'

'You can say no, Alan. But I don't think you will.'

There was a moment's silence.

'You're right,' Rosslyn said. 'OK.'

Harding smiled and raised his glass. 'I want you to be a match for our new colleague from MI5.'

'Who is he?'

'Deputy director, personnel. Bryan Wesley, the director general's choice. Any old bureaucrat I could deal with, even one of the new women. But Wesley is operational. Liaison with MI6. He's a canny bastard. He may be all sweetness and light on the outside. Inside, he's steel. You needn't worry about him. What you have to do needn't cross his path too much.'

'What is it you want me to do?'

'Handle the witnesses. Your first one's in the morning.' He wrote something on a page of his notebook in ball-point pen. 'She's a very lucky nurse. She was only slightly injured in the blast. Minor lacerations and shock. She's in a private room at the Royal Free in Hampstead.'

'You want me to question her?'

'Yes. About eight a.m. I want her version before MI5 get to her.' He tore the page from his notebook. 'And I don't want our new friend Wesley to know about it either. I want the upper hand. The only way I'll get it right off is by cornering all the evidence.' He handed Rosslyn the page he'd torn from his notebook. 'The name of the witness is Hazel Cartaret. She's all yours.'

'Wouldn't it be better if one of your own officers questioned her? I mean, is it this bad, that MI5 don't even trust the Met?'

Harding leaned across the table, his hand flat on the wooden surface, the other positioning the Calvados bottle and his glass like two opposing chess pieces. He looked past Rosslyn to the photographs of Mary on the kitchen shelf. 'I want someone I can trust, someone who trusts himself. I want someone with an axe to grind. And then once he's ground it sharp, to use it.' He finished his glass. 'I get the feeling, when the time comes, that you won't hesitate to wield that axe. I have to tell you, from now on, you're going to find it hard to distinguish between friends and enemies. What I've learned, and it isn't much, is that the best policy is never trust anyone except yourself. Don't imagine all the paper-pushers fighting the terrorists are honourable. There's every sort of cock-sucker, self-serving, two-timing bastard behind the bars in those buildings beside the river. If the public only knew about them there'd be a tidal wave of emigration. Maybe it's as well they don't know too much about them.' He helped himself to another glass. 'Would you believe I get half a dozen resignations from my best officers every week. You know what's behind them?'

Rosslyn made no answer.

'I'll tell you,' Harding said. 'Their wives and families, and they're right. It's the wives at home who notice the changes in their men. Police work is about failure. You give the Crown Prosecution Service a cast-iron case. And then they balls it up. Or else the villain has a smart-arse laywer. Or there's a cushy jury. You never know what's going to happen when you turn the stone over. That's why I'm calling this investigation Insect. Your first job's to open up the memory of Nurse Cartaret.'

14

Hazel Elizabeth Cartaret, a large twenty-two-year-old New Zea-
lander, lay propped up by pillows in her hospital bed. She had no
objection to Rosslyn recording her statement.

'My room, or what's left of it, is next door to where the bomb
went off. Some time before six o'clock I must have turned away
from the window overlooking England's Lane. I'd been pressing a
skirt I mended last weekend. I had the radio on. Classic FM. I'd
been looking down into the street. I was walking away from the
window when the bomb went off. I had my back to it, otherwise the
glass might have blinded me. It could've been much worse. There
was this sudden enormous noise. Like *crump*. Then blue and white
flashes. I know I started screaming, because I thought, I mean, I
knew, it had to be a bomb. I thought: No one knows I'm here. So I
kept on screaming. I could smell gas. It really scared me. All the
time I was telling myself: Don't lose consciousness, Hazel. Whatever happens, don't do that. There was plaster flying about. Everything was falling on top of me. Then it went dark. I guess the
electricity must have failed. There was this wind full of dust and
flying glass. It was very hot and suffocating. I thought: Christ, I
can't see. I'm blind or something. Then there was the smoke. I
remember thinking: Why here in England's Lane? It's not as though
this is Harrods, Oxford Street, or a station, or the places they
usually bomb. Why me? What have I done? Then I thought: Jesus,
I'm a nurse. Hazel must get out there and help. So I blundered and
crawled about until I got to where I knew the door was. The door
had bust open. I managed to get out through the smoke. Then I
crawled down the stairs on my hands and knees and, somehow, I
got out into the street. And out of it.' There was a long silence.

'Tell me, Hazel,' Rosslyn asked at last, 'why did you go to the
window before it went off?'

'Because I'd heard this argument from next door. I heard two
women screaming.'

'Above the music from the radio?'

'Yes,' she said, biting her lip.

'What was the argument about?' he said quietly.

'I don't know. I thought perhaps it was some silly game. Or that I was maybe hearing things. I heard muffled shouts through the wall. Then there was a thump followed by a woman shouting something like: "It's no good. It's no good." Then: "You don't own me. You've never owned me." Then something solid hits the wall. After that I heard: "Sod you. Sod you." Then a real scream of pain. Whoever it was wasn't pretending. They were real screams. I thought: Maybe I should call the police.'

'Why didn't you?'

'Because I thought someone else already had. When I'd looked out of the window I'd seen a police car parked opposite by the bus shelter.'

'What was the car like?' Rosslyn asked.

'Just a white police patrol car with big black letters on the roof. Just big letters. I don't remember what they were.'

'Did you see a police officer inside the car?'

'No. The windows were misted over so I couldn't. Not at first. Then I realized there had to be someone inside. Because it drove off.'

'In which direction?' asked Rosslyn.

'Towards Haverstock Hill past the nurses' hostel.'

'Would you recognize the police car if you saw it again?'

'It was just a police car,' she said. 'No different from any other.'

'And all this took place just before the explosion?' Rosslyn persisted. 'You're sure you saw the police car?'

'Yes.'

'Go back to the row between the two women. Did you see or hear any more of it?'

'I heard the stereo was turned up very loud. It was k d lang's "Constant Craving". I thought these people have been drinking or something. I heard a window thrown open very hard. And more noise. This time breaking glass and this woman's voice screaming "Stop. God. Stop." I thought: I don't want to know about this. This is weird. Then I saw this woman outside. White. Thirty-something. Fair hair.'

'What was she wearing?'

'Jeans and runners. A white shirt. I think it was bloodstained. To the back of the neck. She looked a bit like a gymnast. Very supple. I thought: She'll see me being nosy. So that's when I stepped back into my room. Then the bomb went off. It was terrible, really terrible. Jesus Christ.'

'Try and remember,' Rosslyn asked. 'How long passed between the police car leaving and when you saw the woman?'

'A few seconds,' she said thoughtfully. 'It all happened, like, together. At the same time. There was all that shouting.'

'Have you any idea what could have prompted the row between them?'

'I've no idea.'

'Had you ever heard similar quarrels between them?'

'No.'

'You know who they were – the women?'

'No. But I suppose they were the ones who . . . ?'

'Died in the blast,' Rosslyn said. 'Yes, I'm sorry. They were. Their identities haven't yet been released.'

'But they were the women next door, weren't they? My neighbours. So close.'

'Did you know anything about them or talk to either of them?'

'No.' Hazel Cartaret leaned her head deeper into the pillows. 'I don't know, really. We could've said "hi", "good morning", you know, how you do to people. I don't remember more than that. It's terrible. And you don't have a clue who was responsible?'

'Not yet.'

She looked frightened. 'It's murder, isn't it?'

'Yes, I'm afraid it is. You've been very helpful,' Rosslyn said. He put his business card on the bedside locker. 'Call me any time of the day or night if you think you've remembered something.'

She seemed puzzled by the card. 'Were they involved in smuggling or something? You're a Customs officer. How come you're involved?'

'We work closely with the police,' Rosslyn said. 'Part of the job.'

That seemed to satisfy her curiosity.

'I hope you get out of here soon,' Rosslyn said.

'So do I. I'm one of the lucky ones. I feel so sorry for them, the dead women, their families, the injured. Jesus. It could've been me, couldn't it?'

'It could've been any of us,' said Rosslyn. He was standing by the door. 'You never know whose turn it'll be next.'

Hazel Cartaret gave a frightened smile. 'I'll call you, I promise, if I can help again.'

*

86

Before he left the hospital Rosslyn made a telephone call to Harding at Scotland Yard to pass on Hazel Cartaret's version of the bombing. Some people are always in meetings; Harding was one. He took an age to come to the telephone. When he spoke he sounded guarded. Rosslyn imagined there must be other people with him in the room. He listened to Rosslyn's account, interrupting only with monosyllables: 'And? . . . Then? . . . Next?'

Rosslyn said: 'The driver of the police car must have seen something. You should get hold of him.'

'I will.'

'What about the domestic row between the women?' Rosslyn asked. 'It sounds to me to have been a lovers' tiff. A fight between two lesbians. k d lang is a lesbian favourite.'

'I wouldn't know,' said Harding waspishly. 'What some women do with their personal lives doesn't worry me. There's no law against it. I can't talk now.'

He hung up, his last words echoing in Rosslyn's mind. The last time he had heard that phrase had been from Frances Monro. He remembered her assistant, Serena Watson, with the look of a gym instructress. She had blushed and Monro had changed the subject.

Waxers is the name of the bar on the ground floor of Custom House. Reproductions of the early nineteenth-century building line the walls. There's the view of HMS *Belfast* and the Thames. Here, during the lunch hour, Gaynor stood Rosslyn a glass or two of white wine. The sea captain muttered darkly about storms ahead. 'I warn you. You're going to be working with some hard cases,' he said. He seemed to be relishing his warning as the old-time sniffer of contraband, the bearded catcher of smugglers who enjoyed nothing better than showing suspects the evidence of their guilt with a 'You're in trouble.'

'You won't have room for a personal life,' he said. 'No more Mary Walkers. Have you found another woman?'

It was a nasty intrusion. Rosslyn shook his head.

'You must still be very angry,' Gaynor continued. 'Hate the bastards, don't you? I do. I hate them. I'd bring back hanging, firing squad, death by injection. All three. Let the bastards choose. Make them dig their own graves, especially the women. Believe me, the women are the worst. Remove them and the men would soon pack it in. The Irish are different. They let their women take charge. The Holy Mothers. Makes you want to throw up.'

He had never known Gaynor to show his hatred quite so nakedly. No matter he was being overheard by younger officers from drug teams, men and women in T-shirts and jeans, weary and hollow-eyed.

'Don't you agree it's a woman's war?' he asked.

Rosslyn gave a non-committal nod. Gaynor was treating him as one of his own extremist kind. The pep talk, to Rosslyn's relief, was presently interrupted by the police courier under instructions to collect the transcript of Rosslyn's interview with Hazel Cartaret, 'for personal delivery to Commander Harding'. Rosslyn gave the special courier directions to collect it from the front desk. The transcript was in a sealed envelope with Harding's name on it.

Gaynor paid the bar bill and delivered another earful: 'What you have to understand is this,' he said. 'Special Branch screw up. SO 13 screw up. MI6 are public school queers. It's MI5's day now. Harding may be ruthless, but if you think he's uncompromising, wait till MI5 start giving the orders. They belong to a different species. You may think you're riding safely with the hunt. What you don't know is that their hounds have tasted blood.'

'Thanks for the advice,' Rosslyn said, not exactly sure what Gaynor meant.

'Any time,' Gaynor said. 'You're a sceptic, like me. I like that, Alan. And a man can't survive unless he hates. Up till now I didn't think you hated enough. I've changed my mind. Like I changed it over that bitch McKeague. In the end all bitches tell the truth. It catches up with them, doesn't it?' Gaynor smiled before Rosslyn could offer an opinion. Almost as an afterthought he said: 'I was sad about your girl. You have to have been very soft on her. The thing to be said about her murder is that it's developed the mean streak in you. That's good. When you lost your cool with the CIO I began to understand you as a man.'

Meanwhile the messenger was taking the transcript of Rosslyn's interview with Hazel Cartaret across London to Scotland Yard. Its pages contained the details of the police car's presence in England's Lane on the evening of Saturday 26 March at 6 p.m. Within the hour the whereabouts of every single police car at that time would be checked and rechecked on Harding's command. But the details contained in Hazel Cartaret's version weren't enough.

Otherwise, the police officers at Stranraer in the west of Scotland might have looked more carefully at the figure in the dockside telephone kiosk.

15

'So help me God, I'll kill the murdering bastards.' It was a long time since Anna McKeague had wept. 'If it's the last thing I do in my life, I'll have the fuckers.'

She was hunched over the telephone in the smashed kiosk on the Stranraer dockside. Gusts of wind sucked open the broken door, then slammed it shut. The rain beat against her face through the broken windows. All day the storm had raged across the Irish Sea against the coast of western Scotland.

For hours she'd tried to make the connection to London. Finally she learned the truth. The tabloids had told her. There was her sister, in colour, black and white, staring up at her beneath the headlines: SUSPECT DIES. DEATH OF A BITCH.

The one person in the world she loved was dead.

She fought to control her grief and rage. 'She's worth more to the British alive than dead. They wanted a conviction. I don't believe it. They're lying.'

The computer voice on the line showed no interest in her reasoning. Without gender, it droned on evenly: 'We advise you to go to ground in the Republic until further notice. Belfast is too dangerous. You must take extreme care. Can you hear me? The line is very poor.'

She gazed across the deserted dockside to where the Stena Sealink ferry heaved against its moorings. Its departure from Stranraer to Larne was many hours overdue.

The he/she voice was saying: 'You'll take the advice.' It was part instruction, part question. Its calm contrasted with Anna McKeague's fury.

She jigged up and down in the kiosk, restless like a prize-fighter before the opening bell. She chewed on her tears. Outside the thunderstorm rolled on.

'I'm going to give you advice,' she said. 'I want proof she's dead. Of who did for her. You give me the name and you'll keep me in place. If not, the rest of your life won't be worth the living.'

'It will be sad for us to fall out,' the voice droned.

'I'll be the judge of who's sad.' She struggled to light a cigarette. 'I want the proof.'

'It's too late to do anything useful now.'

'Not for me, my friend.'

A ship's horn moaned in the distance.

'You have earned your biggest fee to date,' the voice said. 'No one is worth more than you are.'

'You don't have to tell me what I'm worth, you arsehole. I know what it would have cost to have got her out of jail.'

'It is up to you how you spend your earnings.'

'Bloody right.'

'Take some leave away from things. Then we will be back in touch.'

'Suppose I talk?'

'Do not forget we are in this together.'

'Don't *you* forget I play on both sides. We're mates, we co-operate. Suppose I blow your cover, find your real fucking name? You won't escape. I can. We have a deal. And Dee's death' – the mention of her sister's name increased the violence of her sobbing – 'it was no part of any deal.'

'We cannot continue like this.'

'Not unless you give me the proof of who killed her.'

'There's nothing you can do about it.'

'Like hell there isn't.'

'A revenge killing will point the finger of suspicion directly at you.'

There was a considerable pause. At length she said: 'I want a copy of the interrogations. Documentary evidence.'

'Will a tape be adequate?'

'Sure.'

'It may be possible to arrange for you to have a copy. Nothing else.'

'Fuck off. I want more. Twice the HE you laid on last time. You deliver it like last time. Am I precise enough?'

'What do you have in mind, operationally?'

'I want to hear how she died. The proof. I want the bastard for myself. I want to be there when he dies. That'll be Dee's memorial.'

'What is the other side of the deal?'

'You won't hear from me again.'

'That will be a shame.'

'You'll have to live with it. If you fail, then I'll kill you.'

'Let us see what can be done. We will do our best.'

She hated the disembodied voice. Hers was a human war. She understood the technologies of destruction: not the use of this voice machine, this terrible disembodied voice box speech. It added an awful new dimension. 'Do it,' Anna McKeague said viciously.

She walked into the wind, forced to step aside by a lumbering container wagon, pushing on towards the empty Stranraer streets to find her car in the driving rain.

The same evening the storm lessened enough to allow for the ferry's departure. When it drew out into the angry sea towards the livid sunset, Anna McKeague was not aboard. She was driving south to London into the dead time.

On the radio, a government minister was announcing his retirement, as he put it, 'for family reasons, to give more time to one's family and private business. I stand by my beliefs and my ideals. I support justice and freedom and free enterprise wherever it flourishes in the hearts and minds of man.'

'So do I,' said Anna McKeague, changing radio stations until she tuned into a tribute to Joan Armatrading.

16

Rosslyn was spared the pain of seeing the exact place where Mary had died outside Thames House.

He used the main entrance on Millbank when he arrived, on Harding's order, for the meeting with the director general at nine. The glass and marble foyer seemed more appropriate to the design of some post-modern luxury hotel. The ceiling of reinforced glass opened above to a view of Thames House's inner walls of Portland stone. To the right was a long rectangular observation window. Behind it he could see half a dozen guards in white shirtsleeves peering at a bank of flickering television screens showing endless corridors, lift interiors, the underground car park, rooftop clusters of aerials and satellite communication dishes and two shining metallic chimney stacks.

A guard asked him for ID and showed him to a seat in the small reception area beside the observation window. The chairs for visitors were expensively upholstered in dark red with slim backs. No expense had been spared on this most elaborate refurbishment. The guards were less interested in Rosslyn than the sign showing MI5 to be on Red Alert. Their faces looked dull. Once Harding appeared, however, their eyes lit up. His was a face they recognized. One of them got to his feet to crouch over the machine that issued ID tags. He handed a tag to Harding with a deferential smile. 'You'll be going to the eighth floor, Commander Harding, sir,' the guard said. Harding said they'd find their own way up. But when the machine produced Rosslyn's ID tag the guard dropped it on the counter top with a grudging look that said pick it up yourself. Rosslyn pinned it to his lapel. He noticed the guard had already transferred his interest to the racing pages of the *Sun*.

They were shown through one of six entrance doors, like cubicles, of steel and glass. Once they were in the lift, Harding confided: 'They can't hear us. But they can see us.' He pointed a finger at the video camera. 'I ought to tell you,' he added, 'we haven't found the police vehicle that Hazel Carteret saw. We've checked out every possible vehicle in London and the home counties.'

'There could have been a car that no one knows about,' Rosslyn said.

'A police car doesn't just vanish,' Harding said, as they came out on to Floor 8. 'I'm not getting drawn into talking about vanished bloody police vehicles.'

They passed doors marked Deputy Director General, Legal Adviser. *Cage labels from a zoo*, Rosslyn thought, *where amnesiac keepers require reminding which endangered species occupy which cages.*

'Best to take your cues from me,' Harding muttered as they walked together down the corridor.

A small man opened the unmarked doors. 'I'm the DG's temporary secretary,' he said proudly. Rosslyn looked at the man's thinning hair and Marks & Spencer's suit. 'We've been waiting for you. We're running late.' He tapped his Rolex. Rosslyn noticed the wristwatch was an imitation.

They entered a newly restored room with high ceilings. It resembled a hotel dining room. In the windows heavy steel shutters were visible behind white nylon curtains. On walls painted a light cream hung various fading reproductions of melancholy watercolours. A man was admiring each in turn, his balding head inclined in respectful admiration, until he seemed diverted by a framed photograph of the Queen propped against the wall opposite the shuttered windows. It stood forlornly next to a wilting rubber plant in a shroud of polythene.

'Commander Harding,' said the director general. 'I think you know everyone here.' She was a woman of indeterminate middle age. There were crows-feet at the corners of her eyes. The formal grey two-piece suit she wore was the sort Rosslyn's mother would have called sensible. In contrast, however, her gold necklace seemed to be a Roman replica. He remembered, with a stab of pain, that Mary had once pointed out to him similar necklaces on sale in the gift shop of the British Museum. Large fingers toyed with a pair of reading glasses and a small square cloth for cleaning the lenses. He noticed she kept her fingernails cut very short. There was no wedding ring. Instead, where it should have been, there was an indentation, the sign of separation or divorce. Rosslyn thought she had a pleasant and handsome face. An angular jaw and broad mouth. Her teeth showed signs of expensive dentistry; they were a little too white perhaps, a little too even.

'This is Alan Rosslyn,' Harding said. 'Customs & Excise.'

'I know,' said the director general. 'Do sit down.'

There were half a dozen others there. Rosslyn assumed they must be senior MI5 counter terrorism officers. He took his place at the table next to Harding and opposite a man with a florid face.

'The prime minister's delayed my meeting with him,' the director general announced. 'He wants a comprehensive report on best possible ways forward. You know: organization, management priorities, reporting systems, the chains of command. I brief the prime minister. You, gentlemen, may, as it were, brief me. Is that acceptable to you, commander?'

'Have I got this right?' Harding said. 'You are personally briefing Downing Street?'

'I already have.'

'You already have?' Harding said. 'But they don't have my report.'

'They have ours though,' said the director general. 'Let's not be detained by the old formalities, commander. Don't forget we here have lost two of our own. Monro and Watson. They were my officers. They had very important roles.'

Rosslyn detected the note of triumph in her voice.

'And my job, for what it's worth,' said Harding, 'is to investigate their deaths, no matter how important their roles were to you.'

'There is no need, commander, for us to discuss their roles. That's not why we're here. You're here as a participant in the co-ordination of the investigation into their deaths. As a police officer.'

Here, the large man with the florid face seated opposite Rosslyn raised a hand. 'Monro and Watson's roles were classified.'

Harding closed his eyes. 'I need to profile them,' he said.

'Do let's put a stop to this, commander,' said the man with the florid face. 'Monro. "A" grade. Acting director, intelligence resources and operations. Watson, however, was junior grade. Operational surveillance. London and the home counties.'

'They were friends?' Harding asked.

'Colleagues.'

'Were they known perhaps,' the director general asked quietly, 'to any of the witnesses?'

'Not by name.'

'You don't seem to understand what we're asking you,' said the director general. 'Do any of the witnesses you've questioned know they were our officers?' She was staring at Rosslyn as if he were a stupid schoolboy. 'Mr Rosslyn, we gather you've questioned at least one witness, haven't you?'

'That's correct,' Rosslyn said. 'The witness only knew the victims by sight. Not by name. They were her neighbours. Nothing more than that. Does that answer your question?'

Rosslyn's tone of insolence wasn't lost on Harding who seemed to relish it. Neither apparently did it escape the director general whose eyes narrowed.

'Very well,' she said. 'This is about damage limitation. Monro's death is a tragic loss. Not only personally. But operationally. A whole series of highly sensitive informers' networks has been jeopardized, throughout the United Kingdom, throughout the Province, and in the Republic. Her networks even extended to Europe, the Middle East and the United States. That's why the prime minister wants a daily briefing on the search for the officers' killer or killers. We need to analyse as much evidence as we can from all that your forensic officers have retrieved. Oh, and before we go any further, there's another important point to be taken on board: public relations.'

'You're not telling me there's going to be such a thing,' Harding said.

'I'm telling you there'll be absolutely no such thing,' she said. 'My officers' names will, in no circumstances whatsoever, be given to the press, TV, or news agencies. Or, for that matter, to anyone else. Not even, commander, to the commissioner. We are to follow the correct procedures. Your phrase in the first place, I think, commander.'

'And we've followed them,' Harding said.

The director general inclined her head with the same smile she'd given Rosslyn. 'I imagine you are aware that I know the identities of Monro and Watson have already been given to the commissioner.'

My God, thought Rosslyn, *she doesn't trust a soul*.

'Am I right or am I wrong?' the director general asked.

'Right,' said Harding. 'I gave their names to the commissioner because we're talking about murder and this is first and foremost a murder investigation.'

'We don't need reminding what's happened. Monro was arguably the finest operational intelligence officer of her generation. She was also a close personal friend of mine. Godmother to my son. So don't you imagine I need reminding she's been murdered. Or that I am not taking it personally. I am. We all are. So should you. Because any success SO 13 may have had in recent months is, indisputably, the result of intelligence brought here. Inside this building. Mainly from Frances Monro's networks. What you may not altogether appreciate, commander, is the extent to which the prime minister is aware of our achievements.'

Bloody prime minister, thought Rosslyn. *Doesn't know anything about my achievements, does he? About McKeague. About sod all. About Mary? She's cornering the market for herself and her lot.* 'No other officer, in the history of the Service, built up more effective networks. We think that's her most telling memorial, don't you? With the greatest respect, commander, I really do rather wonder whether you realize the appalling damage that Frances Monro's loss represents in the war against the terrorists.'

Why is she repeating herself? Does she think Harding's thick?

'All I can say is,' Harding said slowly, fighting to control his anger, 'that we are very sorry about the deaths of your two officers.'

'We're not only sorry,' the director general said quietly. 'We're angry.'

'So are we.' Rosslyn heard the tone of resignation in Harding's voice. 'We've collected every piece of relevant forensic evidence. As you know, we've questioned witnesses. We've got a good one. The nurse. Cartaret. We've kept the media sweet. What we're going to do now is to continue what we've started. Continue working. Round the clock. In the most effective way we can. We have to consider everything, however long it takes. Everything will be contained in my report. My office will send a copy through immediately it's ready.'

The director general raised her hands, spreading her fingers wide, palms down; then began to open and close her fingers. 'That won't be necessary,' she said.

'Why not?'

'I want you to tell your forensic people to deliver what they've recovered. Their evidence. The lot. To us. Here. By noon. Today. Full stop.'

Rosslyn saw a flicker of pain pass across Harding's heavy features. 'Can I have this in writing?' Harding asked.

'Very well,' she said.

Rosslyn saw Harding close his folder and lean back in his chair.

'I want it on the record that it's still less than two days since the bombing. These are the first and most essential hours of the investigation. It doesn't matter whether we're making it, or whether you're thinking of carrying it out yourselves. On your own even. But I must make it clear, in the strongest possible terms, that each and every minute is vital. We're talking minutes. When memories are fresh. When the evidence is new. What you're asking will, I have to tell you, frankly, cause delay. I can't accept delay. But if, as I suspect, you are insisting on delay, then, you must realize the risk you're taking.'

The director general looked at him. 'I hear what you say. It's been minuted.'

Harding made one last effort. 'My officers are experienced and professional. Why not just leave them to get on with their job?'

'You seem somehow to be saying I'm being obstructive.'

'I'm not,' Harding said sharply.

'I think you are.'

'I think you're saying that you are taking control of this whole investigation.'

'If that's your view, then so be it.'

Harding folded his arms. 'We can't continue sitting here like this, with two of your officers dead, and suggest a course of action, a working method for the investigation, which will play straight into the hands of the terrorists. That's what it looks like to me from where I'm sitting.'

'I'm not interested in what it looks like.'

'I am.'

'You still don't seem to appreciate what it is I want from you, commander,' she said impatiently.

'Go ahead then. Tell me.'

'I want you to do what you've always done as a police officer. Do things by the book. In an orderly fashion. Calmly. Without emotion or rancour. Without, to put it bluntly, the implicit hostility which seems to have become a rather sad feature of your approach. I want you to see your Special Branch deputy assistant commissioner. You will tell him, in your own words, that I have cleared the order already. Personally. Both verbally and in writing with the commissioner. The evidence will, I repeat, be handed over to the Security Service. In this building. By noon today. I can't, honestly, think of a way to make it plainer.'

'I'll use your exact words. And I'll submit a formal letter of complaint.'

'Now it's you who's wasting precious time.'

'That's what you think.'

'It is not what I think. It's what happens to be in Queen's Regulations for the Security Service.'

'Queen's Regs are your pigeon.'

'They're yours as well. I quote: "The death of any officer of the Security Service, serving or non-serving, may, upon the authority of the Director General, be investigated by the Security Service, or persons delegated by the Director General of the Security Service." These regulations override all others.'

Harding suddenly got to his feet. 'Director general. Now you listen to me. If anyone ever learned about this meeting they'd be appalled.' He stabbed a finger at the windows. 'There are people out there whose lives are in danger. I've been in the front line for six bloody years. I know. Unlike you, I've talked to the bereaved. The maimed. The dying. I don't need a lecture on your regulations.'

'Sit down, please, commander.'

He remained standing. 'I've a damn good mind to call the home secretary right now.'

'Go ahead. Use my phone. If you want to.'

'I don't want to lose my temper.'

'Then let me make it easy for you not to. Let me tell you: if any officer, any police officer, engaged on the investigation of the deaths of my women officers discusses any aspect of it with any-one, I mean anyone, then he or she will immediately be suspended from duty. Arrested. And charged with contravention of the Official Secrets Act and held indefinitely in custody.'

For a moment Harding looked defeated and older than before. Rosslyn felt a stab of sympathy for him.

'One more thing, director general,' Harding said, taking his folder from the table. 'Next of kin have not yet been notified.'

'I think that's one thing we can safely leave with you, Commander Harding. Monro's mother lives in a Bournemouth nursing home, the Woodside. Alzheimer's, I'm afraid.' She leafed through one of the files on her desk. 'Serena Watson has a sister coming out of a halfway house for drug addicts somewhere in west London. I have personally decided that she will not be told what's happened to her sister. Our medical officer agrees with me. She's pretty unstable and, in any case, they hardly met over the last few years. By the way, you'd better warn the witness, the nurse, Cartaret, against saying anything. Mr Wesley here is acting as liaison officer.'

Bryan Wesley, the man with the florid face who had sat opposite Rosslyn throughout the meeting, nodded in acknowledgement.

Where have they dug this one up from? Rosslyn wondered, looking at Wesley's overweight figure, the roll of flesh hanging over the waistband of his trousers. *Another armchair hero.*

'I gather the operation is called Insect, commander. Rather good, I think.'

'I'm glad you people here appreciate it,' Harding said, heading for the door. 'No doubt we'll meet again shortly.'

Outside, on the pavement facing the river, Harding said: 'Now you've seen them for yourself. When they're around it's best to keep your bum against the wall. Always remember that.'

Rosslyn said he would.

17

By noon, when they returned to Scotland Yard, Harding's desktop was covered with reports and memoranda marked SECRET. One memorandum, from the Metropolitan Police's senior explosives officer, confirmed that the England's Lane device bore the hallmarks of Belgian-German manufacture. It had originated in Dresden. There was more to come.

The force and direction of the blast, and pattern of destruction, showed that at least 190 pounds of high explosive had been planted in the derelict house next door to the one where the women died. It had been placed in a way which only an experienced professional would calculate: to achieve a concentrated demolition of lethal force. The mixture of explosives was unusual. The senior explosives officer's team had discovered traces of PE4, the British military explosive, and PETN, an explosive used both by the military and by civilian demolition companies. Additionally, there were traces of identifiable detonating cord, Cordtex, and several fragments of a German microswitch. Another forensic scientist was searching for human hair fibres and traces of blood.

'McKeague got it right,' Rosslyn said, handing Harding the interview tape. 'Everything except the extra quantity of HE.'

They scanned the other reports: lists of suspicious vehicles seen within a ten-mile radius of England's Lane during the past two weeks; calls from Neighbourhood Watch; a list of break-ins in north London; anonymous tip-offs; the complete timetable of police vehicle movements across London twelve hours either side of the bomb. 'And still no mention of the vehicle in England's Lane.'

Harding called to an assistant in his outer office. 'Send a patrol car to England's Lane in one hour. Tell them to bring a spray to mist the windows.' He tossed a folded copy of the *Independent* to Rosslyn. 'Read that in the car.'

Terrorists' recent failures in London kept secret to protect sources

Police 'thwarted many IRA bombing attempts'

BRUCE HYMAN
CRIME CORRESPONDENT

AT LEAST 10 UNPUBLICISED IRA attempts to bomb London in the past 18 months have been thwarted by counter-terrorism measures, according to a senior police source.

The claim, which is difficult to verify, was made by a highly placed source after criticisms of the police and the Security Service for failing to avert the England's Lane bomb in North London. It also comes in spite of conflict between MI5 and the police over disclosure of more details of the counter-terrorism effort.

Meanwhile, a senior Metropolitan Police source disclosed that increased patrols since the IRA bomb at Scotland Yard last year had led to an overall reduction in crime of 10 per cent. Assistant Commissioner Ian Hanson also confirmed in his annual report that a man under arrest in Northern Ireland for other terrorist offences had been interviewed over that attack.

In the wake of the England's Lane bomb, senior police officers are known to be concerned at what they see as unjustified criticism of the counter-terrorism effort, which is sapping morale. But they believe to say more could risk giving away valuable information about police informants.

The senior source said: "We have disrupted a number of attempts to bring bombs into London in the past 18 months. It runs into double figures. In addition to road blocks, we are doing a number of things in London about which we cannot be specific and which the public will not be immediately aware of. But at the moment we cannot disclose any more because some unguarded word, some snippet of information, is going to lead to the informant and someone is going to be dead as a result of it."

Another reason why information about successful anti-IRA operations and counter-terrorism measures is being held back is the reluctance of the Security Service, which took over lead responsibility for intelligence gathering last October, to release information.

The police source said: "It is taking time to harmonise matters and it is working well. But there are huge cultural differences over the release of information. We just come from completely different standpoints."

Each of the disrupted bombing attempts is understood to have been averted in the run-up to planting the device. "As a result the IRA have changed tactics and keep changing them all the time. We can make no assumptions about the sequence of bombings since they will always try to wrong-foot the authorities."

Senior police officers emphasised yesterday that a high state of alert will continue for some time since it is assumed that the IRA will attempt a repeat of the England's Lane bomb – or an equivalent – as soon as possible.

The Metropolitan Police say they devote proportionately more resources to fighting terrorism than any other force.

'The "senior source",' continued Harding, 'that's me. Wesley thinks he's so bloody clever taking the forensic evidence away from me. I've made sure our labs will have just enough time to get a thorough look at it. I can talk to the press. MI5 won't. That's one advantage we've got going for us.'

18

Rosslyn walked with Harding past the heavily boarded houses and shopfronts in England's Lane. Great webs of scaffolding surrounded the damaged houses. He slung his jacket across his shoulders, otherwise oblivious to the warmth of the sun.

'Insect will have delivered the bulk of the PE4, PETN, some considerable time beforehand,' he said to Harding. 'Under cover, in the dark, or in the rain. A hundred and ninety pounds is a heavy load. Then it must have stayed there all day. Either the device was delivered at the same time, or Insect brought it here immediately beforehand. Someone *must* have seen it brought here. My guess is, if we go along with McKeague, most likely Insect operated alone.'

Even after three days the smell of burned debris was still strong. The leaves had been blasted and burned from the trees. Many of the tree trunks were scorched and charred. At least half of them had been felled during the weekend in the interests of safety. The street seemed very quiet, at odds with the blue sky, defined shadows and dappled light.

Harding unlocked the makeshift door in the heavy wooden protective barricade to number 139. Inside the gutted steel more scaffolding had been erected.

'Imagine yourself to be Insect,' Harding was saying to Rosslyn. 'You carry the bags of HE in here.'

'And I have to bring them in off the street. A sizeable load.'

'From a vehicle. There will have been a delivery vehicle.'

Harding had copies of the statements from the shopkeepers and a dozen or so other people who had volunteered information to the investigation team. No one remembered a suspicious vehicle.

'Insect,' said Rosslyn, imagining the killer making preparations,

101

'must, therefore, have delivered the explosive by night. Must have taken thirty minutes. Someone has to have seen the delivery.' His speculation was cut short as he saw the doorway in the protective barricade filled by the figures of two women, one a uniformed woman police officer. Beside her stood Hazel Cartaret.

Harding picked his way through the debris. 'Hazel, thanks for coming. We want to reconstruct things as they could've been last Saturday.'

'Anything you want, I'll do it,' said the nurse. She smiled at Rosslyn. 'I'm much better now, see,' she said. 'Nice to see you again.'

She looked larger than he had remembered when he interviewed her in the hospital. Pink cheeks, chunky legs in black stockings, a clean pale blue uniform. Flat shoes.

'I've seen you on TV,' she said to Harding. 'You look smaller than in real life.'

Everyone laughed.

'Mind climbing up on the scaffolding with us?' Harding said. 'So we can get a view of the street.' He told the WPC to go back to the patrol car.

Up on the scaffolding, at much the same level as Hazel Cartaret's flat, they had a clear view of the street.

'Hazel, you saw the car, parked where ours is now? You didn't see the driver, or how many people were in it. The windows, we've misted the windows. So you couldn't have seen the driver. Am I correct?'

'Right.'

'There were other people in the street?'

'There's something I have to tell you. I did see a nurse. In uniform. Like mine. I'd never seen her before. I sort of know most of the girls from the hostel. I know faces that fit. Hers wasn't one of them.'

'You remember her face?'

'No. Not in detail.'

'Where was she when you saw her?'

'Near the police car.'

'What was she doing?'

'She was just standing there, beside it.'

'Try to remember, Hazel. We'd really like to know what she was doing by the car. We need to get this right.'

'I saw her put out a cigarette. I don't know any of the girls who smoke, in uniform, on the street. We just don't. She was smoking. Definitely. I know, because I've given up.'

'Was she white, black, Asian?' Rosslyn asked.

'She was white. Thin. Strong. She looked tired.'

'Then you *did* see her face.'

'I saw it, yes, but I can't remember it. She definitely put out a cigarette. Then she got in the car.'

'She *what*?' Harding said.

'She got in the car. By the driver's door. She got in the driver's side.'

'Do you think there was someone else in the car?' Harding asked.

'I don't think I saw anyone else.'

'But how soon did it drive off?' Harding asked.

'Immediately after she got in.'

Harding was standing absolutely still. 'Do you have a driver's licence, Hazel?'

'Yes.'

'So you drive. Imagine yourself getting into the passenger seat.'

Rosslyn watched Commander Harding closely. Even-voiced. Fatherly almost. His eyes bored into the nurse's with the concentration of the hypnotist, stalking the wandering memory, drawing her out. 'It's getting dark. There's rain, some wind. Now, I want you to look down into the street.'

She did as he told her. Harding spoke into his radiophone and looked at his watch. Then at the WPC.

The WPC, a Mary look-alike: *Did Harding, with some terrible perversity, choose her deliberately for her resemblance?*

'Let's watch her. I'll keep the time. Go –'

She opens the driver's door	1 second
Gets into the seat	2 seconds
Safety belt	1 second
Keys into ignition	1 second
Starts engine	1 second
Checks mirror	3 seconds
Indicators	1 second
Checks mirror again	2 seconds
Pulls out into traffic	2 seconds
	14 seconds

'Fourteen seconds,' Harding announced. 'A measurable time, variable admittedly, but measurable. I want you to close your eyes. Now try to imagine that you are this nurse, the one you saw. She goes through the same procedure. She uses the driver's door. Think.'

After fourteen seconds she opened her eyes. 'It was only as long as that,' said Hazel Cartaret.

'Sure? Are you certain she got into the driver's seat?'

'Quite sure. I saw her. The police car was waiting for her,' she said eagerly. 'And you know what? I think she wore some kind of wig. A sort of brown wig. I remember now, thinking, funny, she's so pale, like a battered face. Sort of butch. Flat nose. Now, I remember thinking, well, you know how you do. She doesn't look like a *normal* nurse.' She was talking more rapidly. 'The wig didn't fit. And the uniform was brand new.'

'What sort of age was she?'

'Around thirty.'

'Let's think about the car you saw,' Harding said. 'I want you to look at these.' He was holding some 10 x 8 index cards with police vehicle markings on them. 'And I want you to tell me if you think any of them remind you of the vehicle you saw.'

He shuffled the cards in groups of four.

'Can you do that again?' she said. 'Yes, that's it.'

The pattern was simple.
A large   V
then   P   O
then, at the bottom, a large orange circle:
            O
'And there was a red and orange strip around the doors,' she added.

'Good,' said Harding. 'Let's climb down and sit in the car.'

He handed her a copy of Rosslyn's interview with her. 'Make sure it's correct. We'll be back in a minute.'

Hazel Cartaret stayed in the car with the WPC to read the transcript.

Out on the street Harding made a call on his car radio. No police station had a record of the police vehicle with the roof markings Hazel Cartaret had seen in England's Lane at the time of the bombing.

'I don't think we're looking at a genuine police vehicle,' Harding said. 'It's a faked-up car. Like the police van outside the Yard, remember? Christmas.'

Rosslyn remembered: 'Jingle Bells'.

'We're looking at a woman, she said. White, aged around thirty, working without an accomplice. She knew who she was going to kill, and where, and when. She knew they'd be at home at six p.m. on Saturday. So we have to know what sort of people would know when they were at home. Friends, colleagues.'

'You think Wesley will give us names?'

'Who knows? We need more of a picture of the victims. I'd like you to approach Wesley for something along these lines: desk diaries, credit card expenditure, telephone accounts. He may refuse. If so, we take another route.'

The WPC came across from the car to say the witness had read and signed the statement.

'Have Wesley make the formal identification,' Harding said to Rosslyn. 'Take him to the mortuary at the Royal Free. Go there with him. Another thing, check the Hampstead sorting office. I'd like to get any mail that's arrived for Monro and Watson. Just because you die, doesn't mean letters stop coming, does it? Only a few of us know they're dead. As yet. Who knows, one of the poor bastards could've won the pools. Be warned though. The mortuary won't be nice. Not as pretty as Hazel Cartaret.'

Or the WPC, Rosslyn thought, trying to obliterate the memory of the Christmas tune, refusing to form the words in his head. A slight breeze carried the sound of bell ringers at practice. He envied them their freedom and the families they had at home.

19

Rosslyn showed Wesley through the doors of the mortuary at the Royal Free at 11.30 a.m. next day. The light fell harshly on the porcelain slabs in the middle of the windowless 70-foot-square room. The slabs sloped down towards plug holes. The air was thick with the smell of bitter chemicals.

'I didn't realize our co-operation would extend quite this far,' Wesley said.

'Someone has to identify them.'

'Why me?'

'You're from personnel.'

Wesley was understandably nervous at the prospect of viewing the remains of his dead colleagues.

'Everything's ready,' said the pathologist, dressed head to foot in white. 'Have a mint,' he offered, above the noise of running water.

Laid out on two separate porcelain slabs were the bits of Monro and Watts. The pathologist's white rubber wellingtons squeaked on the wet floor.

Wesley looked around, at the lab liaison officer's open case of tools and bottles, everywhere except into the faces of the heads perched on the slabs.

'Here is what's left, gentlemen,' the pathologist said. 'Odd how glass bits lose themselves in the skull cavities. Let's have a look at number one. Perforation of the brain pan. Must have had her mouth open, ruptured lungs.'

A black man in a green rubber gown inclined the head. The pathologist wiped the remains of the face with a small sponge.

Wesley cleared his throat. His face had turned white. 'Watson,' he announced drily. 'Watson.'

'And number two,' said the pathologist. 'Similar injuries here. Metal and stone fragments.'

'Monro,' Wesley said. 'Frances.'

'Then that's it,' said the pathologist. 'I don't often deal with bomb victims, thank the Lord.'

'Could I have another mint, please?' Wesley asked.

'Gave you my last one,' said the pathologist. 'On the whole, they're bad for the digestion.'

Wesley was hurrying from the room. His hand covered his mouth. Someone had left a National Health Service hospital disposal bag beyond the doors and Wesley reached it just in time.

By the time they were seated in the gloom of the Frognal drinking club Rosslyn noticed the colour had returned to Wesley's face. 'They know me here,' Wesley said. The solitary barman, a stooped and haggard figure, had taken his order.

'This is on the firm,' Wesley said. 'And I've got this for you.' He produced an envelope. 'Open it. Feel free to ask me questions. Since we're partners in this bloody awful business we've got to learn to love each other. Please understand, we can't provide you with the diaries and personal expenditure accounts you asked for. Such things remain classified, I'm afraid. But these will be useful to you.'

At first glance Rosslyn saw the two short paragraphs of type-script were as good as useless: bland records of bland achievements.

MONRO, Frances Melissa. Born 1953, Godalming, Surrey, UK. Unmarried. Educated: St. Mary's, Ascot; Lady Margaret Hall, Oxford. Joined Home Civil Service, 1979. Research Officer. Appointment to survey of Communist Party of Great Britain. Counter-terrorist Section B. Spain. Italy. Middle East. Northern Ireland. Staff Management Course. Assistant Deputy Director, Training. Acting Director, Intelligence Resources and Operations.

WATSON, Serena Rita. Born 1963, Stockport, Lancs. Educated: Mainwaring Comprehensive School, Stockport. Army Service, Royal Corps of Signals. NCO. Served Aldershot, Catterick, Northern Ireland. Civilian appointment to Cornell Davie Associates Ltd (Industrial Security Service). Joined Home Civil Service, 1991. London District and Home Counties Surveillance.

'That's everything you'll need,' said Wesley. 'The director general's bending all the rules for you and Harding. You must understand, that information is secret.' He passed over two small photographs. 'Monro, labelled on the back. And Watson.'

'How well did you know them?'

'Very well indeed. As you so aptly put it in the mortuary, I'm from personnel. It's my job to know about one's colleagues. I like to think I know more about individuals than they know about them-selves.'

'Do you?'

'In all humility, yes, I certainly do. You, for example. Do let me tell you how very sad indeed I was about your girlfriend. A terrible tragedy. You deserve every sympathy.'

'Thank you. Do you have a family?'

'Two boys at university. Manchester. Felix, a budding anthro-pologist. It runs in the blood, I think. Jonathan, the younger, is doing drama. Takes after his mother. A separate soul. Prefers his own company. Like his mother. We are separated, you understand.

Still, the best of friends. Pitched our tents apart. Divorce is such a messy business.'

'Mrs Wesley, does she have a job?' Rosslyn asked.

'She does indeed. In the firm. And very content she is too. The lovely cottage in Amersham. Dogs. Cats. The garden. A bit of a zoo. And you? Perhaps not, so soon after Mary's death. A woman friend, I mean, anyone to keep you company?'

Rosslyn shook his head. The barman brought drinks in chipped glasses. A wasp settled on the table.

'Perhaps you'd rather not talk about it,' said Wesley.

'Not now,' Rosslyn said. 'How well did you know Frances Monro?'

'As well as anyone, really. Matter of fact, I interviewed her way back, when she applied to be an instructor on staff management. She interviewed very well. A woman of wide interests. Very supportive of her juniors. Davina – my wife – knew her well and liked her. A potential director general. High-flyer. Someone you looked up to. Shall we say, in the top rank.'

'With access to all departments?'

'More than most officers. Bear in mind we operate a strictly need-to-know policy. Only senior, the very senior ranking officers, have general access across the board.'

'You said she was in the top rank.'

'Why do you ask?'

'To get an idea of how significant her work was. What it would mean, for example, to your set-up, to lose her; how far the IRA would have considered her a major target.'

'I follow. Leaving aside the director generalship question, I can tell you she was very important. Without going into specifics. She was, naturally, a bigger player than her friend, Watson.' He turned his attentions to the wasp. His effort to squash it beneath the plastic ashtray failed. 'Tell me, what will you do with the info I've produced for you?'

'Consider it with care, Mr Wesley. We need your help.'

The photos of the two women lay next to the crawling wasp. 'I think, Rosslyn, you do need it. You must be feeling a little out of your depth. There are dimensions to the Service officer's life that can't be touched on. Monro was a fine officer with a complex intelligence portfolio. For example, I can tell you she carried a hell of a workload. Lockerbie, for one. On the fringes of the Saddam arms deals, another. She was so very good on the Iraqis. Your sort of territory – arms, explosives. Shall we say, suitcase opening? Cans of worms, jobs. Insect elimination, as your friend Harding would tell us. She is supposed to have ditched Cresson for the frogs. So the bloody French are for ever in our debt. Covered up the Clinton mess in Oxford. The Americans didn't love us for that. Don't imagine the Yanks backed off a trade war because they wanted to. We whipped them till they begged us to stop. We've got the White House where we want it. Frances Monro had all that to her credit, and more.'

'What about Northern Ireland?'

'Haven't I given you enough? We're talking serious operations. Baghdad. Paris. Washington.'

'Isn't that MI6 territory?'

'Naturally. But the world's a smaller place than I dare say the world of Customs may lead you to imagine.'

'Her CV, this biography, it says Northern Ireland.'

'She was operational there too, at arms' length.' He gave Rosslyn the bully's smile: hit me if you dare, his eyes were saying, the edges of his front teeth sucking his bottom lip. 'Absolutely nothing we can connect with England's Lane.'

'You're certain?'

'I know it.'

'And what do you know about Frances Monro socially? Did you and your wife meet her on any sort of regular basis?'

'Not in any meaningful way.'

'But you said your wife, Davina . . . ?'

'Davina. That's the name of my *estranged* wife, if we're to be logical.'

'You said she worked, where was it, in Amersham?'

'Correction. She *works* in Beaconsfield. She *lives* in Amersham.'

'Yes,' Rosslyn said. 'I should've made a note. But I suppose it isn't material.'

'Not in the slightest.'

It is material, Rosslyn thought: *if she, Davina, knew and liked her, well, that's what he said*. A second wasp had joined the first. 'I thought, perhaps, Mrs Wesley could give me a more up-to-date picture of Monro, more detailed anyhow, than the one we've got here.'

'I can read your mind, Rosslyn. You're perfectly right. And why not? Have a word with Davina. Bear in mind, Beaconsfield's a fancy set-up. State of the art technology, labs, research. Davina, you'll soon see, is a highly gifted scientist.'

'I'm not asking you what she does,' Rosslyn interrupted.

'And I'm not telling you. If you'd let me finish.'

'So Monro *was* a candidate for the director general's job?' Rosslyn said.

'I didn't say that.'

'Well, either she was, or she wasn't, a candidate for the job.'

'You're going round in circles, Rosslyn. She was not a candidate. You forget, I am personnel.' Now a smirk. A brief sneer. The smug face. The public school bully. 'Let's suppose she was. What are you saying? The IRA targeted the candidate for the best job in security in the free world?'

'We're all targets, Mr Wesley.'

'I can assure you I am not. I'm sorry if you are.'

'You're forgetting. I lost someone very close to me. She was a target.'

Wesley gave him a patronizing smile. 'My rather trivial point is that, quite frankly, officers like Davina and Monro are separated by a world of difference. Rather, they were. Davina is Scots aristocratic. Née Macleod. The family. The clan. Monro, *pace* the Scots lowland name, is, rather *was*, Surrey. Minor Catholic. Minor bridge club. A scholarship entrant to her girls' school. Some minor scholar at Lady Margaret Hall. But lower middle class. The sort of woman who offers you a serviette, calls a lavatory a toilet. Get my drift? With more than two thousand staff we are a broad constituency of the British class system, divided sometimes by our social backgrounds, but united by trust, the sense of family, the common cause. That's what makes it possible for us to recruit people from such divergent backgrounds. I like to think we pioneered the notion of equal employment opportunities. We need every sort. Black. White. Gentile. Jew. The bent, the queer. United in trust. Nowadays everyone's a little more open about *everything*.' He crushed both wasps dead beneath the ashtray. He touched his closed lips with a finger. 'Don't answer me here and now. Too important an offer for you to accept in a hurry. Have you thought of joining us?'

Rosslyn leaned back in his chair. A spring creaked. 'Is this an offer from you? I mean, is this *your* personal initiative?'

'Perhaps, a feeler. You could get an appointment at senior grade. Along the same lines as the one we offered to Mary Walker. Frances Monro thought Mary was one of the finest potential recruits she'd seen in years. Your cloth is cut the same way.'

Rosslyn felt numb. The blood beat in his head, through the veins in the back of his clenched hands.

'She was an extraordinary young woman,' Wesley rattled on. 'I can see exactly why you liked her. Do think about what I've said. Here.' He handed over a visiting card: Bryan T. Wesley CBE, Kensington Court, London W8 5BH. 'Call me there.'

He scribbled a telephone number below the address. 'We can share a bit of supper. Not here. This place is a touch grim. Not what it was. Would you prefer to dine with me at the Garrick? Do you have a London club?'

'Custom House Fitness Centre.'

'I'm a Garrick man,' Wesley said and paid the bill. 'The only way to destroy the IRA is for decent people to carry on as normal in the face of murder and destruction. The old invocations remain the best. Whatsoever things are pure, just and of good report.' He tapped his chest below his heart. 'It's all in here. Tell me, Rosslyn, what do you feel your answer might be to us, subject, as it were, to survey and contract?'

'Probably no.'

'Think about it carefully. For Mary's sake. You've got a lot on your mind. I dare say a visit to Davina will be a welcome break. I'll tell her to expect you.'

The Hampstead sorting office is at the end of Shepherd's Walk, a narrow street off the main thoroughfare. Rosslyn signed for the dead women's undelivered mail. Most of it consisted of circulars from local estate agents addressed to Ms S. Watson.

She had been looking for a flat to buy, a leasehold, with one bedroom, something in the region of £90,000.

Ms F. Monro had failed to pay her accounts at Marks & Spencer, Selfridges and Peter Jones. She owed a total of £457.62. She was invited to a private view by the Trustees and Director of the National Portrait Gallery. She was being reminded by the *Spectator* that her subscription had recently expired.

A post office worker came down the short flight of steps from the entrance to the sorting office whistling a hymn tune. He looked at his watch and without a glance passed Rosslyn who was leaning against the wall halfway down the street, opening another letter to Ms Monro, a circular, a printed letter of intent from Glenda Jackson MP. Another envelope yielded some travel brochures from Hogg Robinson's branch in Gower Street. The next envelope bore a blurred postmark. It was marked PERSONAL AND PRIVATE, and addressed simply to Frances Monro.

Slowly he became aware he was being watched by the post office worker, the whistler of hymns, who had paused at the end of Shepherd's Walk to look back.

He read the letter quickly.

Dearest Fran,
I've finally decided to put pen to paper and let you know how very sad I was to hear you didn't get the DGship. No one deserves it more than you do. At least you must take comfort from that general knowledge. Your many supporters in Box will be as disappointed, as *disillusioned* as I am. But the future will be bright for you in other ways, I'm sure. Could you let me have Ingenue back when you have a moment?
Commiserations,
Always,
Davina

He attached the rubber band to the bundle of letters and headed down Shepherd's Walk towards the High Street, his mind filled with more disturbing thoughts, about the dead women, and the letter from 'Davina', with no date, the postmark blurred, no address. Surely this was from Wesley's wife.

20

'Wesley can look after himself,' said Harding, in his office at Scotland Yard. 'He's what he says he is, Alan, an observer, and that's how he stays. If he wants to muddy the waters with half-arsed attempts to recruit you into MI5, that's his business. He's only trying to get you on his side. What he forgets is that we're already in this with him. We don't need him to do our thinking for us. It's a matter of trust, all that crap. The hopeless inadequacy of the CVs. I could have told you everything he gave us. Of *course* Monro was a major target. But I have to tell you that Wesley isn't going to give us *relevant* details of her operational work.'

'He mentioned Lockerbie, the Iraqis, the French, even the Americans,' Rosslyn said. 'Sounded to me she was working with MI6 as well.'

'He's steering you clear of what McKeague gave you, what she *might* have given you, to confuse you by talking about Mary. Bloody MI5 *personalize* everything. It's a ham-fisted psychology they use and it doesn't work.' Harding was looking at him very seriously. 'You've got to see Wesley's wife about that letter. Go to Beaconsfield. Ask her for the picture of Monro's life. We take a leaf from Wesley's book and make it personal. They can try to deny us further access to the forensic, but they can't stop us looking at their dirty laundry. MI5 is a hot house of little rivalries, petty affections, in-fighting and such like. It spreads outwards like ripples on a pond.'

Rosslyn looked out of the window. Black clouds hung over south London. Pigeons twitched on the window-ledges. 'I'll go and see her this afternoon.'

'Before you do, there are two more things I want to tell you. What do you want first, the good news or the bad?'

'The bad.'

'Our friends in MI5 have logged a formal complaint about the treatment received by McKeague at Paddington Green. Their medical officer claims she died as a result of injuries sustained in her interrogation. If they can prove it, this investigation passes over to MI5. They're claiming it was you. They say they have concrete evidence.'

'Like what?'

'The tape of your interview with the prisoner. It's down on tape.'

'But they never got it. They got a transcript. The tape was in Gaynor's safe. Listen to it, that's all you have to do. Jesus, there was a table between us, the observation slit was open, anyone could've heard me hit her or seen me touch her. I did neither.'

'I'm afraid the evidence from MI5 points to you.'

Rosslyn shrugged. 'I don't believe this. Why would I lay a hand on her? I didn't have a chance, even suppose I'd wanted to. Which I didn't. It's not my style and you know it.'

'Yes, I know it,' Harding said. 'But you had a motive. You wanted the name of the person behind Mary's murder.'

'And more besides.'

'You said it, Rosslyn. I didn't. And there's the issue of the tape recording.'

'You've got it. Don't tell me it's been nicked here, in bloody Scotland Yard.'

Harding shook his head. 'Here.' He slid a tape across his desktop. 'That's it. The one you gave me. It's completely blank.'

Now Rosslyn saw it: England's Lane after the bomb. The door to his car forced open. His briefcase on the floor in front of the passenger seat. The woman disappearing through the traffic on Haverstock Hill. He told Harding what had happened.

'She will have taken your tape and substituted a blank one for it. Now, we have this.' He started the tape recorder on his desk.

It was a sickening piece of work. The record of a woman being beaten to near death. Her screams. Her pleas. The thud of fists in her face. Distorted. Rosslyn's questions cut in between McKeague's pleas. His own reasonableness had been translated into the arcane logic of the sadist. It nauseated him.

'They want you off the job, Rosslyn. Your immediate removal from duty, suspension, disciplinary action. The lot. I've discussed it with the commissioner.'

'What did he say?'

'He's leaving the decision to me. I've submitted a report to the director of public prosecutions. That's worse,' said Harding indifferently. 'Much worse. Sooner or later everyone stoops to the same level as the IRA. Harding's Law. Scum always sinks below the surface.'

'You're telling me you believe this?'

'No. I don't. But we won't tell MI5 that. We say you'll be reprimanded pending the view of the DPP. Don't worry yourself about it. She's a personal friend of mine. One of the few women in high places I like. She'll take her time looking at the case. Even MI5 can't mess her about.' He hesitated. 'What's bad news is that the smell of cover-up, the covering of the arses, is getting stronger.' Again he paused to study Rosslyn. 'The good news,' he continued, 'is that I'm in remission. Sooner or later I was going to tell you. You need to know. I have cancer.'

'You?'

'Yes.'

Rosslyn took a deep breath. 'When?'

'There's no more to say. I could have two years, even five.' He gave a bleak laugh. 'I can think of quite a few people who'd be pleased to know. We won't allow them the pleasure.' His voice assumed an air of resignation. 'Success is the best revenge. We'll go on as we are. What happens after doesn't matter.' He was smiling to himself, as if lost in some private story.

There was a long silence. Rosslyn managed a brief smile. He realized Harding had begun to mean far more to him than he'd have believed possible.

'Now you'd better get to Davina Wesley.' He handed over a typewritten address in Tavistock Crescent. 'This is where you stay from now on. Out of sight.'

'I'm sorry about –' Rosslyn said.

'The tape?' Harding interrupted.

'No,' said Rosslyn. 'About you.'

'It happens,' Harding said. Suddenly he turned his back so Rosslyn couldn't see his face.

21

MI5's Scientific Technical and Research Unit (STRU), three miles beyond the outskirts of Beaconsfield, was in the Red Alert state when Rosslyn stopped his car at the barrier. At the end of a short road stood a pair of high solid-steel gates. These were set into a continuous brick wall like a jail with barbed and electrified wire. The video surveillance cameras looked to have been installed more recently than the wire. Two Alsatians and their handlers were patrolling the perimeter of the sand strip around the wall. Rosslyn glanced at the notice in front of the guardhouse.

WARNING
MINISTRY OF DEFENCE: STR UNIT
(Beaconsfield)
THIS IS A PROHIBITED PLACE WITHIN THE MEANING OF THE OFFICIAL SECRETS ACT.
UNAUTHORIZED PERSONS ENTERING MAY BE ARRESTED AND PROSECUTED.

The duty guard, a uniformed Indian in a turban, told Rosslyn he was expected by the chief administration officer. 'You can park your car next to Mrs Wesley's space,' he said.

Rosslyn put his briefcase on the X-ray machine.

'No cameras or tape recorders?' the guard asked.

A second guard was examining the underneath of his car with a wide mirror on a pole.

Once Rosslyn had satisfied them he was risk-free, he was shown through the steel gates operated from inside the guardhouse.

'Mrs Wesley will see you in forensic,' the Indian told him.

They passed a few men and women wearing white overalls in the compound. At the far end of it the Indian used plastic cards to open a black steel door. None of the doors was labelled. Rosslyn assumed the different colours of the doors were codes for the work carried on behind them. Black seemed appropriate to forensic.

Inside, and out of the daylight, they were in a narrow corridor leading to a lift. The guard stood aside to let Rosslyn in. Its light was very dim. 'Take the lift down to the fourth floor. Mrs Wesley will meet you there.'

The lift went slowly down. Floor 4 seemed to be in the bowels of the earth. Rosslyn was reminded of a mineshaft. His eyes grew accustomed to the feeble light.

So when the doors opened he was dazzled and it was at first hard to see the woman standing in the passage.

'I'm Mrs Wesley,' she said. 'Davina.'

'Alan Rosslyn.'

She was a striking and attractive woman who must have been a beauty in her twenties, with thick black hair and perfect teeth. She wore a pale green cashmere cardigan over a summer dress and gold chains around her neck and wrists.

She gave him a smile of motherly enthusiasm. 'You're Bryan's young friend. I worry about him on his own. How is he?'

'Seems fine to me,' Rosslyn said, uncertainly.

'We all have our hands full with this latest bomb.' She opened a door to a long and brightly lit laboratory. Rows of men in white coats were poring over piles of fragments in silence broken only by the hum of the air-conditioning. They paid no attention to Mrs Wesley and her visitor. She led Rosslyn to a glass cubicle at the end of the laboratory.

'We won't be interrupted here,' she said. Set in the wall was a row of small video screens showing the forensic technicians working at the lab benches beneath the glare of lights and a variety of corridors and passageways. There were also two screens which showed computer rooms – one screen was marked 'Live Index', the other 'Research Index'.

But the bottom row of screens was the one that chiefly caught Rosslyn's eye. The pictures seemed incongruous. He saw fish swimming in one tank; some newts in another; and, in a third, some frogs.

'You keep pets down here too?'

'Yes,' she said. 'Not, though, for our amusement or, indeed, theirs. Pets and their products three doors down.'

'You breed them?'

'Uh-huh, we do.'

Rosslyn watched the screens. 'I've only ever seen these in pictures. They're Japanese, *fugu*.'

'You know about puffer fish?'

'Yes, I do. Last time I saw one was in a bag I confiscated from a Japanese automotive designer at Heathrow one New Year's Eve. The bloke had it wearing this small top hat and lipstick. Do you believe that? That's how they decorate the *fugu* hanging outside their restaurants. It wasn't so funny. Christ, there was enough tetrodotoxin in its liver to poison most of London. The Jap says: "I would like to eat *fugu*; but life's too sweet." I said: "You aren't even going to touch the thing." TTX is the most powerful poison known. What are you doing with *fugu*? And salamanders – it's in their skin; and in those nasty Costa Rican frogs. Have you ever seen the effects of TTX?'

'Only in rats. How do you know about tetrodotoxin?'

'Because I studied those fish as part of my university degree. And newts and frogs and toads. As in *Macbeth*. They're evil. So what are you doing with them here?'

'It's part of a research project for our counter proliferation people. We're sealing up the leakage of specialist technologies. And generally we're looking at the illicit processing of toxic substances. It's horribly easy to manufacture synthetic tetrodotoxin.' She gave him a challenging stare. 'We're not here to discuss the gonads of the *fugu*, Rosslyn-san, are we?'

'We're not,' Rosslyn said. 'Tell me about the constituents of the bomb.'

'Commander Harding will be pleased to hear the bomb ultimately falls into two parts: the primary device of Belgian-German manufacture. In addition to what the Met's senior explosives officer found, we've discovered signs of French plastique. No tracer elements, of course. You'll be familiar, in your work, with the composition of the English PE4, plastic explosive 4. That was the basis of the secondary device that provided most of the explosive force. Our view is that the overall composition marked the technology of the IRA.'

'How can you be sure?' asked Rosslyn.

'Because we have assembled exactly similar devices on a *pro rata* basis, proportionately as it were, to test the direction of blast. Once we know that, we can piece together the fragments to construct the evidence. One can eventually reconstruct the movements of the bombers up to the moment of detonation. In the case of England's Lane you're probably looking at two or more people involved in the delivery of the explosives.'

'Unless the delivery was made by someone of exceptional strength,' Rosslyn suggested.

'And then they would've taken some considerable time to put the explosives in place. But you must understand, in that confined space, the force was massive and the heat-core of the fire highly destructive. In our view, there's no chance of finding evidence to trace the identity of the bombers. The evidence has been incinerated.'

'Is that the view of your chief scientific officer?'

'Yes. You're welcome to a copy of his report. We've already sent one to Commander Harding.'

'Do you think there's any chance the bomber could have been caught in the blast?'

'None whatsoever. We'd have discovered human traces. But I think I can read your thought. If the bomber were to strike again we might be on easier ground the second time around.'

'Is anyone here suggesting another bomb?'

'None of us is in a position to speculate.'

'You're telling me, Mrs Wesley, we're at a dead end?'

'I wouldn't be that pessimistic. But from the point of view of forensic investigation, I wouldn't hold out much hope it will yield an identity. None, that is to say, that will give you a swift conviction. That's the problem with murder by bombing. The weapon destroys itself by definition. It isn't the same as a knife or a gun. The bomb eliminates the traces. I'm sorry I can't be more helpful. We don't have luck on our side, do we, Mr Rosslyn?'

He saw, on the video screens, several of the men leaving the benches. And the *fugu*: slow moving, listless in their tanks.

'There are more personal things I'd like to ask you,' Rosslyn said. 'About the two victims. If you don't object.'

'Of course I don't. Why don't you find your car and follow me home to Amersham? We can relax over a bottle of white wine, or something stronger if you prefer.'

'I'd like that,' he said. 'We're not expecting any sensational results from the forensic side.'

'That's a wise policy,' she said. 'One can only get so far with science. It's the hand that squeezes the trigger and the mind behind it that matter finally. You and I think alike. I'm pleased you like our aquariums.'

He followed her out of the glass cubicle.

She said: 'I'm looking forward to some fresh air. Spring is almost summer. Isn't it extraordinary how early summer comes nowadays? There was all that talk about the greenhouse effect. My children used to sing God has left His hosepipe on. To the tune of "The Sun Has Got His Hat On" or some such song. I suppose they missed the point. Or was that before the greenhouse effect? Now no one seems to worry. Is it still a fine day up above?'

'Very pleasant.'

She sighed. 'Summer. We can sit outside in my garden.'

Going up in the lift, Rosslyn's ears ached. He felt her dark eyes on him. The dim light glinted in them. The Wesleys made an odd couple. Hardly surprising they had grown apart. Perhaps they proved the cliché that opposites attract. In the Wesleys' case it was hard to see the proof.

On the way out, they were subjected to the search procedures. No exception was made, even for Mrs Wesley. If anything, he noticed, the guards were more thorough with her than they were with him. Perhaps it was because of her senior rank. She was officer class; they were other ranks. They seemed rather frightened of her.

'Thank you,' she said automatically. 'Good evening and see you tomorrow.'

She smiled at them, rather sweetly; and turned to Rosslyn who was holding open the door to her car. 'With one bound she was free,' she said, almost playfully, like a schoolgirl. 'Bryan told me I would like you. He's not always right about my taste in men. But he's right about you. Follow me home to Amersham.'

He was warming to her. The *fugu* fish were in safe hands. God knows what she'd ever seen in Bryan Wesley.

Her garden was an early springtime British wilderness. A tangle of old climbing roses, ivy, forsythia dropping blossom; the lawn more of weeds than grass, soggy with moss. Beyond the lime trees blue smoke drifted in a vertical line to the sky.

Rosslyn wiped green mould from the garden bench.

'I expect you'd really rather hear about Frances,' she said, setting down a tray with a bottle of Meursault and wine glasses on the rocky wooden table, oblivious of the green slime patches and the snail stuck perilously to the table's rim. She handed the bottle to Rosslyn for him to open and she wrestled to split a plastic bag of Greek biscuits, *paximati*.

Suddenly, the verandah filled with yapping mongrels. 'Don't feed them,' she said, 'or they'll never leave you alone.' Her half-smile seemed fixed. He reckoned she was a lonely woman, unhappy with middle age.

'Frances was a dear friend,' she said. 'I'm so touched you rescued my letter to her. I terribly regret she never read it. You never know when the worst will happen. One shouldn't think of oneself, though. I can't imagine a worse death. One only hopes she knew nothing about it. What strikes me as so extraordinary is that Serena was there too. Such awful bad luck. Of all the moments to pay a visit. It could have been me, even you, Mr Rosslyn.'

'I didn't know them.'

'Oh, I thought you did.'

'You're thinking of Commander Harding. He once worked with Frances.'

'So he and Bryan will have told you something of her life?'

'Only what's permitted. Your husband, your estranged husband, he seems so open but he's not exactly forthcoming.'

'That's MI5 for you. Comes with the territory, I think.'

The dogs were joined, at a wary distance, by cats. A fat grey squirrel watched from its tree perch. The audience of animals fell silent.

'My work's something of a restricted area, you understand. I can help, I expect, with matters of a more personal kind.'

'I'd appreciate that,' he said. 'Your letter to Frances. You posted it from near here?'

'In the post box down the road. On my evening stroll. Walking in the open air is a precious relief from days beneath the ground. By the way, we wanted you to see the forensic team, so you can be sure you'll get the very best results. Between you and me, we're streets ahead of the police equivalent. But my letter – you'll have gathered I was upset Frances failed to get the appointment she deserved. No disrespect to the DG herself. Just that Frances gave her whole life to the Service. I suppose you can say she's now given it. A sort of ghastly sacrifice. It's classified information about Frances failing to get the director generalship, by the way. Or perhaps it isn't, when you bear in mind the papers have even so stupidly revealed the DG's shopping habits and her home address. How the IRA must be laughing. Forcing her to move house. Had Frances been appointed, matters would've been very different, believe you me. Personally, I don't believe in a security service which is insecure.'

'You dislike the new look MI5?'

'I can't say I particularly like the new look. Frances certainly didn't.'

'She had enemies in MI5?'

'A woman with an original mind in any branch of the Security Service makes enemies, Mr Rosslyn.'

'Any in particular?'

'I mean enemies in the institutional sense. Generally, she was widely liked. And very close to the director general.'

'Godmother to her son, wasn't she?' Rosslyn said.

She looked surprised. 'Bryan told you that?'

'No, the director general did.'

'Well, well, I didn't know you're on such close terms with her.'

'Only professionally, Mrs Wesley. Co-operation is flavour of the month. That's why I'm working closely with your husband.'

'My estranged husband is investigating the murder of Frances and Serena? I must say I wouldn't have thought Bryan qualified to contribute to a murder investigation. There we are. He can tell you that Frances was very good to me during the break-up of our marriage. The listening ear. A woman's shoulder to cry on. We were the greatest friends. We dined out locally. Usually the Bell at Aston Clinton. Went to concerts. My preference is for the Proms. Not k d lang. Though I gave her the compact disc. I never did get it back.'

'The one you asked her to return?'

'Yes. *Ingenue*. Not that it was ever my cup of tea. On the contrary. It was my son Felix who wrote to me from Manchester to ask if I might take it to him. I was there for the week before Frances and Serena died, for my other boy, Jonathan. To see his student theatre production. Jonathan's the actor in the family. That was when I heard the awful news. But I don't think we should discuss unimportant family matters, do you?'

'Your sons knew Frances?'

'Only as a friend.'

'They got on well with her?'

'I think so, really.' She seemed evasive.

'Do you think your sons would talk to me about her?'

His question seemed to worry her. 'I'd rather keep the family out of it,' she said. 'I've always encouraged the boys to lead their own lives. Our world imposes enough strains on family life as it is.'

'You'd rather I didn't talk to them?'

The same look of anxiety. 'It's up to you. I'd prefer you didn't. And, frankly, I don't think they could be of any help. They definitely are in no position to tell you who killed Frances and Serena. They're only students.' She smiled. 'Who do you think was responsible?'

'The IRA,' Rosslyn said. 'I share your view. But they haven't claimed responsibility for it.'

'Of course not. The identities of the dead can't be revealed in the press.'

'The IRA could reveal them,' Rosslyn suggested.

'And MI5 would make no comment.'

'And be forced to parade Frances and Serena alive and well?'

'That's a rather absurd line of thought,' she said. 'We don't confirm or deny what our officers do. All records of service are secret. That doesn't alter one's belief that the IRA was responsible. There can be no possible motive other than political. Unless it was of a personal nature. Domestic. Most murder is domestic in origin, so I'm told.'

'But the murder weapon's usually a knife or some kitchen implement. Not a few hundred pounds of high explosive. We're talking of carefully calculated killing.'

'I agree,' she said. 'You prove my point. IRA. Their crimes seem so very easy to commit. The domestic angle is a non-starter. We aren't dealing with relatives, family friends and so on.'

'Did you ever meet any relatives of Frances or Serena? The mother, or Serena's sister?'

'No. I didn't realize Serena had a sister. Frances' mother has Alzheimer's. She's in a home on the south coast. But she did sometimes speak of a friend, an officer in the RAF. A married man. The wife discovered her husband's adultery and put a stop to things.'

Wait a moment. This doesn't fit.

She seemed to read his thoughts. 'It was several years ago, I think,' she added quickly.

I must have touched a raw nerve.

She was anxious to change the subject. 'I think Frances was glad to be rid of him. Nothing was going to come of it. He was a heavy drinker.'

'Do you know his name?'

'No. But Bryan could give it to you.'

'How did he know about the boyfriend?'

'Because the wife wrote a letter of complaint to Thames House. The legal department handled it with considerable skill. By the way, if you're thinking of contacting him, don't bother.'

'Why not?'

'He was killed in a motorway accident on the M25 two years ago. His wife emigrated to Canada soon after. Frances took it badly.'

'And the matter was closed?'

'The legal department closed the file.'

'Do you have any letters from Frances, or photos, personal things, anything which would mention the affair?'

'I'm afraid not. All I have is a photo of her. Taken here in the garden with the cats and dogs a few years ago. I'll show it to you.'

She led him into the house, to where the photograph of Frances Monro, smiling rather self-consciously, was hanging in the hall beside a small mirror in a gilt frame.

He watched Davina Wesley's dark eyes reflected in the mirror with a far-away look. 'Such a waste,' she said. Then she sighed. 'Unbearable, isn't it? Almost too terrible to imagine.'

'You have my sympathy,' he said.

She took a deep breath: 'You have mine too. This investigation must be very painful. I think the strain on Commander Harding must be dreadful. Do you get on well with him?'

'Yes. I do.'

'He looks a remarkable man. Judging from the TV. I'm so sorry he's unwell. You do know he's not well, I suppose?'

Rosslyn gave her a noncommittal nod.

'Between ourselves,' she said, 'I imagine it must be serious. We were approached, formally, in the general run of things about security at St Paul's. When he first went into hospital, and I gather the doctors thought he wouldn't pull through, the question was advanced: would it be advisable to hold a memorial service for him at St Paul's? I thought it rather premature. We had to produce plans, and so forth, of which we didn't have any, naturally. Then suddenly it was all postponed. Now he's fought back. That's good news. But to plan a service when he was still active . . . I suppose the Met likes to organize things well in advance. He's somewhat of a public figure. Rather attractive in his lugubrious way, don't you think?'

'I'm never sure what women find attractive in men,' Rosslyn said, wanting to be gone. His observation made her laugh. Her laughter started the dogs barking in the garden. A cat bolted through the hall. Another, a fat ginger, leaped on to a shelf next to a vase of dying roses. The creatures in her menagerie were nervous.

'If I can help you, please don't hesitate to get in touch, Mr Rosslyn.' She shook his hand, holding it firmly, a fraction too long to be formal. 'I've enjoyed your visit,' she said.

He walked quickly to his car.

In his rear-view mirror he caught sight of her watching him from her front door. He found something both attractive and slightly worrying about her. And he wasn't quite sure what it was.

The surveillance officers had been waiting for his return to the flat in Pimlico. A senior man explained the mechanics of the trip alarms, the bugs and hidden video cameras. If Rosslyn needed to return there for any reason he should warn the watchers. A team of three had occupied a top-floor flat across the street. Otherwise, he should carry on as normal; use his car, let the newspapers keep on coming. They'd thought of everything. There was even a black WPC who would show up daily disguised as his cleaner to answer callers. 'Mr Rosslyn will be back later,' she had been told to tell the curious. The senior man was sure his boys would catch Insect red-handed if she showed her face in Pimlico.

Rosslyn packed for an indefinite stay at the safe house in Tavistock Crescent. He made room in his case for Mary's photograph, her kimono and her diary.

At Hyde Park Corner the traffic was at a standstill. His car radio explained why: motorists were being advised to avoid the West End because a fire bomb had exploded in Chinatown. Two storeys of a house in Gerrard Street had been gutted by fire and a woman had jumped to her death from an upstairs window. The police said she was a Chinese dealer in foreign currency. Her name was Vicki Leung, aged forty.

They were asking for anyone who had been in the vicinity of Gerrard Street earlier that afternoon, between 4 and 5 p.m., to telephone New Scotland Yard on 071–230–1212.

A police source said the murder was believed to be connected with the IRA.

22

Anna McKeague saw the news of Vicki Leung's death on *Channel 4 News* at seven in a Covent Garden pub. The photograph of her money launderer on the TV screen scared her.

For a third time that evening she returned to the call box to establish contact with her paymaster.

A recorded voice said the number wasn't answering. She should 'please try again later'.

She hoped Chinese Vicki Leung was well and truly dead. Slam. The telephone receiver holder shook. She was in the grip of anger. 'They' must have traced the money; it had been planted on her. Vicki Leung had grassed on her. Step by step she was being out-manoeuvred.

Drinkers spilled out from the pubs to the street. A fat policeman spoke into his portable phone. London smelled of rotting garbage.

Answer me. This time the familiar disembodied voice picked up.

She'd make out the death of Vicki Leung meant nothing to her. She wanted very much to mention it; good sense told her not to: there was more pressing news to hear.

'Your material will be in place at five tomorrow morning. There is a problem. The proof of identification you require is available on condition.'

'No conditions,' she said.

'You cannot take possession of it.'

'You agreed I could hear it.'

'You will. We have made secure arrangements for you to hear it. And there will be a fee.'

She stayed silent.

The tables were being turned against her. She said: 'I don't deal with blackmailers.'

'Neither do we. Our runner requires a fee of five thousand pounds in cash. He will not allow you to listen to the tape unless you pay it to him.'

'You provide his fee.'

'We are not in a position to pay him.'

It was unbelievable. Her paymasters were unable to come up with five thousand pounds in cash.

'I am asking you to pay his fee.'

'You are asking us for information. It is not us who are asking you. The provision of HE material presents no difficulty. But the tape involves human factors. Your objection to making payment for it is illogical.'

'It's too dangerous. The money can be traced. It's too late to organize a dead delivery drop. You're talking of human factors and I don't want a human contact. You established this communications procedure, not me. You can't guarantee your people won't identify me if I show my face to them.'

126

'You need not be concerned. We can reveal your identity to the delivery man. He's disabled, in no position to identify you even if he wanted to. He knows nothing of your existence. He is on a retainer from another department of the Home Office. A senior registry clerk to the Security Service Commissioner. We will give you access to the SSC Annexe in Queen Anne's Gate. You have a pre-arranged appointment with a Mr Levy.'

She was in no doubt the trap was being set for her. Her silence must have conveyed her suspicion down the line for the voice continued without hesitation: 'The question of you being compromised at Queen Anne's Gate does not arise. Levy is our conduit within the commissioner's office. He cannot see your face because he is blind. If you wish, you can reach him on extension 2828. The Home Office number is 071–273–3000. He is expecting a Mrs Margiesson to call. The provision of five thousand pounds in cash, one hundred fifty-pound notes, will prove your authenticity. You must see it from his standpoint. He requires to be confident no harm will come to him. It goes without saying you should not be carrying a weapon. The risk is not yours, my friend. It falls on us.'

Anna McKeague lit a cigarette. She'd force a compromise. 'I'll go along with this. If I pay, the business is completed on my terms. This Levy. We'll meet on neutral ground. He'll get his fee. He'll come to no harm. You tell him to be on the southbound platform, number two, of the Northern Line at Camden Town one hour from now. There's a wooden storage case for fire equipment underneath a broken clock. Tell him to wait by it for thirty minutes. If I don't show up, the deal's off. If he doesn't show up, God help you. If he shows up with anyone else, God help them. I'll be armed and I'll kill your Levy and anyone else who gets out of line.'

'We will have to confirm the new arrangement with Levy.'

'You fucking tell him to be there.'

'Very well. You will not be able to reach us again on this number. Arrangements have been made for its disconnection.'

'Next time remember to pay the bill. Don't expect me to pay it for you. Levy's one thing. Your fucking phone bill is something else.'

The line was already dead.

Anna McKeague came out into the crowds in Covent Garden to find a cab for a quick drive to Camden Town.

*

127

From where she stood, in the entrance to the Penguin bookshop, she saw the blind man pay off his cab at 8.05, ten minutes before the time agreed. She reckoned Levy would present few problems if things turned nasty. His name suggested he was Jewish so she was surprised to see Levy was a black man. She put his height at 5 feet 4 inches; his weight at around 170 pounds. He arrived accompanied by a guide dog, a golden Labrador.

She crossed the road to the station entrance filled with winos quarrelling over a discarded pizza. Levy was in the queue for tickets. She turned her back on him to buy two cartons of cigarettes in 200s from a kiosk. The proprietor put them in a plastic bag for her. Once more she scanned the station entrance hall. There was no one there she couldn't handle in an emergency. The woman ticket collector was being harassed by a mad person who might once have been mistaken for Andy Warhol. Experience told her MI5 special duty men denied themselves disguises as imaginative as dead icons from the pop world. She decided Levy was a cleaner kind of delivery man. Once he was through the ticket barrier she bought a ticket from a machine and then followed the way he'd taken underground, drawing on a pair of gloves.

And there he stood, as he'd been told, beneath the clock by the fire equipment unit.

His eyes were completely white.

'Mr Levy?'

'Mrs Margiesson.'

The Labrador eyed the new arrival. A southbound train disgorged its passengers.

She kept her eyes on the video surveillance cameras and put her arm round Mr Levy's shoulder. London Transport would have seen a smiling face giving the blind man sympathy. Except, as she knew, the system had been out of commission since Christmas. It had proved its worth when she'd met the bombers before the failure outside Thames House.

For a civil servant, Levy had expensive tastes. His accent matched his Savile Row suit. 'Perhaps we can settle the question of my fee,' he said quietly.

She let him touch the carrier bag. 'As agreed, packed in cigarette cartons.'

He held the bag in front of the Labrador. It sniffed the bag suspiciously.

'I wouldn't open it here,' she said.

He set a small tape machine on the top of the fire equipment unit. She was careful to keep hold of the carrier bag. 'If you'd listen,' he told her, holding up the ear piece at the end of a wire in the tape machine.

The disembodied voice said: *'Paddington Green police station. Friday the twenty-fifth of March.'*

It went on: *'You have to understand, I'm a Customs & Excise officer. We don't do deals, McKeague. You're looking at forty years at least. You'll be an old woman by the time you get out.'*

'You're a hard man, Mr Rosslyn.'

Recognition of her sister's voice was instant. She fast-forwarded the tape, stopping and starting at random.

'I want to talk about MI5 . . . planted a serious HE device on me.'

That was good. Dee had been leading this bastard interrogator on.

On and on: *'Who was this person then? Who asked you?'*

'No comment.'

Her sister began to scream.

'Then who was this person working for?'

There was a confused sound, a thud, a crash of knuckles on bone, followed by a whimper.

'Then Mr Rosslyn, for God's sake, you tell me what else you want.'

She was begging, wheezing.

'Listen, McKeague. I've never needed you.'

Anna McKeague continued listening to her sister's screams of pain: she heard her panting, her gasps, her choking. She was hearing her sister die while this interrogator kicked and punched her. She imagined Dee being strangled then struck repeatedly with some smooth metallic object wrapped in cloth. The man's voice grew louder, more insistent. Then, for several seconds, there was only moaning.

It was interrupted by the sound of an approaching train. The rails strained, vibrated. Stale air was being pushed out of the tunnel's mouth.

She grabbed the tape from the machine, at the same time shoving the carrier bag into Levy's arms. His vacant smile evaporated.

She leaped at him, her hands around his neck, shoving him to the edge of the platform.

The train's lights appeared in the mouth of the tunnel.

She held Levy tight in her arms, bending him sideways and further backwards. The carrier bag fell on to the platform and then, knocked by Levy's flaying feet, spilled its contents, the cigarette cartons, over the platform edge.

The tape was still in her hand. But she hadn't reckoned with the Labrador. It jumped at her, tearing at her coatsleeve.

She rocked sideways and pushed Levy backwards and downwards to the tracks. The tape cassette was jerked out of Anna McKeague's hands. The dog leaped after its master on to the tracks. The full force of the train crushed Levy's head and chest.

Long before the train had come to a halt, Anna McKeague ran through the passages to another platform.

Northbound on the Northern Line, the only other passengers in the carriage were three Japanese men with identical black briefcases studying a catalogue from Harrods. She removed her gloves. Apart from the Japanese, she was travelling alone. She had wanted to know everything about Rosslyn. Now she had something to go on. The proof of his guilt. She knew his name. But she needed to put a face to the name.

The doors opened at Chalk Farm. She breathed the cool stale air. A voice over a loudspeaker was announcing delays in the other direction. She turned her head away from the Japanese who were staring at her in confusion. A few minutes later she emerged into the fresher air, on the streets, into the dead time she began to share with Rosslyn.

SPRING SUMMER

The perfect murder, i.e. a premeditated killing where the murderer makes such arrangements as to make all aspects of the death look like an accident, is only possible in theory. Someone may object that many murders have been judged to be suicides or accidents, and murderers have gone free. However, such crimes cannot be considered perfect crimes; they are simply failures in bringing out evidence of deliberate killing.

Arne Svensson and Otto Wendel, *Techniques of Crime Scene Investigation*, American Elsevier Publishing Inc., NYC, 1965

Some agents, who can include members of the public as well as members of target organizations, regularly run considerable risks in their work for the Service. Substantial resources are devoted to providing support, both for the agent and the Security Service case officer, particularly to maintain the security of the operation. Close attention is also paid to the welfare of the Service's agents, both during and after their agent career.

The Security Service, HMSO, London, July 1993

23

'There are 58 million men, women and children in the United Kingdom,' Rosslyn wrote to Mary's mother some weeks later.

One of them is Mary's killer. I am going to bring her to justice. I say 'her' because I can tell you we think the killer is a woman. This halves the population for us. If you reckon there are around seven million women in the UK who are over 65, then you can reduce the number of suspects still further. We also believe she's white and that reduces the number too. And if we are thinking of Northern Ireland female residents, we're talking of some 300,000. We can gain some succour from these statistics.

I can also tell you that the Security Services, Police and we in Customs have combined forces for the hunt. Our target can run and hide, but not for ever. Everything possible is being done to avenge Mary's death. Like me, I know that's what you want.

I'd like to hear from you. There are many questions I want to ask you about Mary. If you are prepared to answer them, please send me a line c/o HM Customs & Excise, New Kings Beam House, 22 Upper Ground, London SE1 9PJ.

The idea of writing to Mary's mother along these lines came to him during the days of waiting in the safe house in Tavistock Crescent provided by the protection unit of the Special Branch. He felt he should thank her for the gift of Mary's diary: the bequest he both loved and hated. Moreover, another idea had formed in his mind: that Mary might have embroidered the truth. Her mother might be able to confirm it for him in so far as one painful diary entry involved her and its content persuaded him to make an exploratory overture to her. She was, as it were, the only available witness to Mary's secret life who might substantiate its truth or falsehood; and the entry decided him to open a line of communication to the mother in the north of England.

Mary had written:

Spring is turning into summer and I've discovered I'm pregnant.
By R or THUG I don't know. I'm supposed to know, but I don't.
I have tulips from Amsterdam in my office.

*Two dozen white tulips from THUG. Three dozen red ones from R. Red
and white = pain and grief.*

*So, I tell them both, I'm using up some leave for a few weeks. I need to get
away alone. Please understand. Going to the Western Isles. Away from the
phone, away from duty. I'll be back.*

*Now I've come back to Mother who offers help. I wish I knew the child
was R's. Are there tests which give you the answer in advance? If so, I
don't want to know. Easier, I think, to face abortion if I don't.*

R's not ready to be a father. He might tell me he is. But he isn't.

*He looked so sad when he saw me off. He ran, like a kid, along the
platform beside the train. His last words ring in my head: 'I don't want to
live without you.'*

*Have a good time, I tell him. Enjoy yourself. It's good to be on your own.
You know I love you.*

*He looked so downcast. He's so bad at goodbyes. Unlike me. I've got good
at goodbyes down the years. I breathe more easily. I love journeys. Best of
journeys are by train.*

Soon it's all over.

Goodbye Baby.

R is waiting for me in London. Life goes on.

Thank God he will never know.

'Things go dead,' Harding said one morning in the Tavistock Crescent flat. 'You have to steel yourself against the waiting.' He stood
at the window. 'Do you mind it?' he asked, fingering the security
grille.

'Don't you?' Rosslyn asked.

'It's part of the game. You get used to it. You wait for them to
come out from cover, the head over the parapet. The one mistake.'

'If she's given up?'

'She hasn't,' Harding said. 'I know it. I know her mind. She's like
an addict. The alcoholic who dries out, then drinks a hundred pints
of coffee a day. It's in the mind. You can't cure addiction. The killer
is the same. She gets a high like an undertaker handling stiffs. It's a
power trip. Or the ladies' man who keeps his score. Killers aren't
much different from the rest of us. Anyone who thinks they are is
very much mistaken. And we're addicted too, Alan, to beating her
at her own game. The evil bitch.'

*

Another day they spent a few hours discussing the Wesleys.

Bryan Wesley had grown increasingly uncommunicative. He was avoiding their calls. 'I will let you know when I have a relevant item to report,' he would say. 'There will be a strategic meeting at Thames House in due course. We are on the case. Patience is what counts.' The platitudes were infuriating.

Then there was Davina Wesley who, it seemed, knew the victims, or at least Monro, better than most with the possible exception of the director general. The latter had turned down a request for further meetings 'until we have the clearer picture'. Had she now silenced Davina Wesley?

'Best to let her brood,' Harding said, 'until the director general calls her big session.'

'I ought to question the Wesley sons,' Rosslyn said, 'the students up in Manchester. They must have known Monro. Look, their mother keeps her photograph in pride of place at home. She was a family friend. The mother must have talked to her sons about her. I should see them.'

'Later,' Harding said. 'We won't create unnecessary hostility. Bad enough having the tape of your McKeague interrogation being held over our heads. I want to see how they use it against us.'

'I'm seriously pissed off with waiting,' Rosslyn said. 'Ironic, isn't it? I'm a virtual prisoner here. And the killer's out there. God knows where. Am I the hunter, or the hunted?'

'Both.'

'Then let's move it on.'

'Patience,' Harding said. 'A steady hand on the tiller.'

'Christ, you sound like Wesley,' Rosslyn said.

He received no reply from Mary's mother. Perhaps his letter hadn't reached her; perhaps she had replied and her letter had been intercepted. He would have dwelt upon her silence more had it not been for the incident in the rush hour at the Angel, Islington.

It began with a call from Gaynor.

'Alan, we've got a grass who's asked for you by name,' he said. 'She won't say how she got it. She's called from a phone box in Hammersmith.'

'Who is she?'

'She won't give a name.'

'You know why I can't see her,' Rosslyn said.

'Then ask Harding to clear it, Alan. She's offering us names of a Cypriot who's bringing in a load of Franchi Spas 12 semi-automatic shotguns.'

'Can't you send someone else?'

'She will only speak to you,' Gaynor said.

'I'll ask Harding.'

But when Rosslyn put it to the commander, Harding said firmly that he did 'not like the sound of it'.

Rosslyn thought differently. 'We can't be looking at Insect. If it's her she'll know any meet will be swarming with armed plain clothes officers.'

So a deal was struck. Rosslyn would see the woman grass in the ticket hall at the Angel underground station. Gaynor acted as go-between. The grass asked that Rosslyn identify himself by carrying a copy of *Yellow Pages*. She would be wearing jeans and a Bob Marley T-shirt.

The meeting was set for 9.15 a.m.

Rosslyn was there ostensibly alone. The armed plain clothes officers seconded from the SO 19 Firearms Unit next to Old Street magistrates court took up positions in the station, their guns and stun grenades concealed and at the ready.

Harding had insisted his man have full protection and Rosslyn waited, the copy of *Yellow Pages* under his arm, searching the faces of the morning travellers for the woman in the Bob Marley T-shirt. She never appeared. At 10 a.m. the operation was called off.

Back at Tavistock Crescent Rosslyn told Harding it had been a waste of time.

'Perhaps she did show up,' Harding speculated.

'And smelled the guns?'

'Probably. Then she must have legged it.'

The summons from Thames House came a few days later.

'They've connected the death of the Chinese with Levy's,' Harding said in Rosslyn's car on the way to Millbank in the pouring rain.

'What connection?' Rosslyn asked.

'They aren't elaborating.'

'Christ, I really wonder whose side they think they're on.'

'We won't blow our fuse, Alan. There are new players at the table now.'

'Who?'

'The Home Office,' Harding said grimly. 'As well as MI6. I have the feeling things are shifting beneath our feet.'

This was Harding, master of the unspecific, who seemed to Rosslyn to be lost in his thoughts. He could have been talking to himself. Earlier he'd told Rosslyn to prepare himself to move out of the flat in Tavistock Crescent. To pack his bag, no more than that.

When they neared the Embankment, Harding said: 'The director general was too cheerful on the phone with me.' He gave a passable imitation of her voice: '"I want you and Mr Rosslyn to accept my hospitality."'

'What hospitality?'

'Let's see,' said Harding. His patience was showing signs of exhaustion. 'I've never liked not being in control,' he added. 'I get this queasy feeling inside my gut each time I see Thames House.'

'So do I,' Rosslyn said.

'It's so destructive,' Harding said, 'for us to be at each other's throats.'

'That's what I was saying.'

'And I think you're right.'

They drove out of the rain into the Thames House car park on Thorney Street. Had they not been so preoccupied they might have noticed the minicab that had been following them.

The minicab, with Anna McKeague in the back seat, was parked unobtrusively on John Islip Street. *Feeding time*, she thought. *The animals are entering the cage. Put it another way – they're dead meat in the dead time. This is when I keep my head. Tonight the bastard duty man will be where I want him.*

24

'The leading strategists of our war against terrorism have been wiped out,' Wesley says to Rosslyn at the far end of the Thames House conference room. He speaks as if it was confidential, though of course the whole world already knows the Chinook helicopter crash on the Mull of Kintyre claimed twenty-nine lives. The victims were from the army, the Royal Air Force, the Royal Ulster Constabulary and MI5. 'I knew John for twenty years,' Wesley goes on. 'A great deputy director general. It's a terrible loss. Six friends too – that's a tragedy. Catastrophic.'

'*Was* it an accident?' Rosslyn asks.

Wesley shrugs. 'We'll be told sooner or later.'

'Later, I'd say,' says Rosslyn. 'There isn't just one inquiry into the crash. There are three.'

'Safety in numbers,' Wesley offers.

'I think the opposite,' Rosslyn says. 'It's astonishing that the principal officers, strategists, were allowed to travel in the same aircraft.'

'It was an act of God.'

'That's what the IRA will be thinking.'

Wesley pours himself coffee from the refreshments trolley.

Everyone is waiting for the director general to start the meeting. Rosslyn looks away from Wesley to the wall clock which says 9.15 p.m. The director general is fifteen minutes late.

'If Sinn Fein is honestly thinking of getting into bed with us for talks about the constitutional future,' Wesley is saying, 'then dear God, one does have a right to expect the violence to end. Don't you think so?'

Rosslyn glances past the others in the room to where Harding stands alone reading a newspaper and looks to be keeping a deliberate distance from the others.

'And I'm bound to say the United States attitude to Northern Ireland is a bit bloody rich,' Wesley goes on. 'Suppose an American Airways Jumbo gets hit at Heathrow and a whole lot of Americans are killed? That might bring the Americans to their senses about the IRA. They may ask for "demilitarization", "clarification" and "persuasion of the Unionists". Attrition is what they want, my friend. Attrition pure and simple. That was the point of the mortar attack on the Gulf War cabinet at Number Ten, Bishopsgate, Heathrow. I ask you, what's next – British withdrawal, peace, surrender? Take your pick. What worries me is the

Protestant backlash. It'll always be there, whatever agreement is reached in talks.'

'Why doesn't the president unequivocally support us?' Rosslyn says.

'Search me,' says Wesley. 'I don't like Americans. It's almost a racial thing. I love to tell them to their faces that I don't like them. God, you should see the pain. The bafflement. The way they cringe over Vietnam. Everyone's a protester against Vietnam. So easy to protest about last year's wars. So very easy. No. They love bombs. They love to bomb innocent people, don't they? They talk of freedom. Whose freedom? I'll tell you. Their freedom to do what *they* want. And always, *always* they so desperately want to be loved and liked and admired. Popularity is everything to Americans. I dare say their frightful universities offer degrees in it. Wouldn't surprise me. Popularity. For what? For why? Special relationship, my arse. Cousins. *Bullshit*. The IRA is being rewarded for what they shouldn't be doing anyway, i.e. killing people.'

What's he after? Trying to make out I'm some sort of peace-kissing anarchist. Trying to get me to give an irresponsible view?

'That'd bring the president to his senses.' Wesley grins. 'Blood on the streets of Washington.'

'Isn't there enough already?' Rosslyn says.

'Take your point, take your point,' says Wesley, laughing as if Rosslyn had intended a good debating joke.

'Perhaps,' Rosslyn says, 'the White House realizes the peace process is a shambles. Don't you think so?'

'I do, yes,' says Wesley. 'Oh, yes, I'm afraid I do. I wish I could say I'm a peace man. But, well, between ourselves –'

'You're not?'

'We won't spread it about,' Wesley whispers, walking away with a smile. As he passes Rosslyn catches the mixed smells of stale alcohol and nervy acidity on Wesley's breath.

Left alone, at the edge of the gathering, the outsider, Rosslyn catches fragments of the conversation of a man who seems to be from the Home Office and clocks his name: Julian Lucas, a squat figure who sports a Garrick Club tie. The colours of the imitation silk clash with the redness of Lucas' sore nostrils. *Has he got a drug problem? Cocaine? Lucas, he's kind of hyper.* Then he sees Lucas pop an antihistamine tablet. He's talking to a woman called Verity Cavallero.

She's needling him. It strikes Rosslyn that everyone is on edge: poised to get at everyone else's throats. He sees other faces he doesn't know and presumes they could even be observers from the new committee co-ordinating intelligence gathering and active operations in the Province.

The IRA have been tossed a lucky gift. If they could sense the mood they'd be even more pleased with themselves.

An unseasonally high pollen count must be making Lucas' life a living hell. He sniffs, wipes his dripping nose. More likely it's the stale dry air being pumped from the Thames House new and powerful air-conditioning system that's causing Lucas so much grief. Or is it Verity Cavallero? She's beaky, with fine platinum blonde hair cut in a pudding-bowl shape which gives her a kind of schoolgirl look. *Roedean, Benenden, I should think.*

Her fringe is low and straight above sharp blue eyes. Her eyebrows are dark and heavy. *Of course, the platinum is fake, another deception.* 'The word I have,' she's saying to Lucas, 'is that the present cost of refurbishment around here is running much higher than the estimated £240 million. Am I right, or am I wrong?'

A look of defeat and animosity spreads across Lucas' face. He tightens the knot of his Garrick Club tie, stretches his jaw, juts it.

Cavallero won't let go. 'Is it true the staff restaurant carpet costs more than £70 a square metre? That's what *we* hear. And exactly what did you pay for the whole property, Julian? A hundred million? Don't look so wounded. Do tell.'

'Classified,' says Lucas, reaching desperately for his handkerchief.

'Well, did you, or didn't you?'

'Lay off me, Verity. You're Six. Finance resource management and audit branch. For God's sake. If anyone knows what's been spent on bloody anything in this country by anyone, at any time, you know. You've got the Treasury, the City, the banks in your playpen. Why ask me? And you know it has approval.'

There's someone at Rosslyn's side. It's Harding. So Rosslyn doesn't catch the end of the bitching between Cavallero from SIS and Lucas from the Home Office.

'Why doesn't the woman show up?' Harding says.

'The Chinook crash,' Rosslyn suggests.

'At this rate we'll be here for ever. Here.' Harding's holding out his folded copy of tonight's *Evening Standard*. 'Read that. It's enough to make you puke.'

BOMB CAN'T
BREAK MI5

A Bomb Threat to MI5 showed that secretive old habits die hard. The new openness proclaimed by the Home Secretary and MI5's Director General has apparently not filtered down to at least one agent. The agent rang Scotland Yard to say that someone had made a call threatening to blow up the secret service headquarters, according to the Police Federation's *Journal*.

"Fine," said the Yard. "We will send someone along. Where are you?" "Can't tell you that," said the agent at the other end. "It's classified."

After much "cajoling and not a little swearing", the information was reluctantly given. For future reference, the Box 500 address is on the Embankment, very close to Lambeth Bridge.

The director general has come into the conference room while Rosslyn's been reading. Rosslyn and Harding find their places at the table. The director general settles herself into her chair at the head.

She begins: 'If the gentlemen would like to remove their jackets, don't hesitate.'

All do so except Rosslyn and Harding. It's an invitation Rosslyn has often given himself. It's one of those small psychological tricks intended to relax the suspect. To put your victim at ease. Once the jacket's off a protective shell is removed. Rosslyn recognizes, in this small move, in the director general's casual offer, the mark of the professional like himself. He notices Lucas, now seated next to him, is down to his Jermyn Street shirtsleeves and bright red braces. The odour Lucas gives off is reminiscent of a chemist's shop, the mixture of disinfectant, cheap soap and air freshener masking the odour of infected customers.

'The agenda has been circulated,' the director general says.

Rosslyn and Harding glance at each other briefly. No agenda has been sent to them. There isn't even a spare one for them on the table.

The director general is leafing through her papers fast. Rosslyn notices she turns her copy of *Country Life* face down.

Surely, she must have brought it to the meeting by mistake.

'No minutes of the last meeting for approval,' she announces. 'No matters arising. If those around the table would introduce themselves, then we can begin.' She makes no apology for being late. Offers no explanation. By way of introduction to oil the troubled mood there's even a hint of the blustering niceties favoured by hefty Wesley.

'Round the table,' she says. She turns to:

'Bryan Wesley. I think I know everyone.' And everyone seems to know him too.

Then: 'MI5 legal adviser.'

And: 'MI5 deputy director of operations.'

Harding is scribbling on an MI5 notepad bearing MI5's motto beneath its crest which is as vulgar as a brewer's trademark. The motto says REGNUM DEFENDE.

And: 'MI5 staff counsellor.'

Then: 'Director of intelligence resources and operations.'

And: 'Acting, counter-terrorism, Irish and other domestic.'

And: 'Counter-espionage and counter-proliferation.'

And: 'Counter-subversion.'

Then Verity Cavallero, MI6; Julian Lucas, Home Office; Commander Harding; Mr Rosslyn.

Harding slips the note he's been doodling to Rosslyn beneath the table. Rosslyn reads: 'See your friend tonight. Put the screws on her. Take the underground. I need your car. *Regnum Defende* means watch your arse. Remember. I play HARDING as in HARD. HARD INDIGNANT. You play sweet and light. Nod if you read me. Get rid of this note.'

Rosslyn has a blank look on his face, then glances up, nodding, caught for a second by the director general who gives him a pointed stare of irritation. When he looks back to Harding he sees the heavy features have the look of a schoolboy's sweet innocence. *Wasn't me, teacher. What ME, ref?*

'If we can focus our attention on Insect,' says the director general pointedly. Presumably, Rosslyn reckons, this is for his benefit as well as Harding's. 'There are several immediate and urgent secret aspects in the situation which I have asked my officers to address in turn for the meeting's benefit. Perhaps you'll start, legal adviser.'

'I find no cogent reason,' MI5's legal adviser says, 'for any aspect of the operation, Insect, at present underway, category red, to be in conflict.' He speaks in a monotone with the voice of some recorded Telecom announcement. 'I refer, of course, to conflict which, I am advised, after consultation with the attorney-general, might affect, or be of interest to, the European Convention of Human Rights.' He drawls on. About 'chapter', 'verse', and 'precedent'.

Rosslyn glances at Harding's doodle: 'The Europeans couldn't give a SHIT.'

Then it's the turn of the first of the directors. As he speaks, he inclines his head towards the director general, threading and unthreading his long fingers like an effeminate nervous courtier. 'Responsibility,' he says, 'remains where it was defined by you in your memoranda based upon your first and basic policy decision. No aspects of apportionment and devolution as might affect operational thrust may be said to have changed.'

Rosslyn doesn't have to glance at Harding to know he's struggling to prevent a yawn. But Harding's effort catches the eye of the director general.

'Do intervene, Commander Harding, if anything we say seems unacceptable.'

'There's nothing I've heard so far I can't live with,' Harding says bluntly.

'Then if I may review the present position,' says the director general. 'Please do, anyone, stop me if you wish to comment. First. The prime minister is being kept informed, fully, by the home secretary who is in turn kept informed of progress by me. And Mr Lucas serves as conduit in that respect.'

Lucas sniffs.

'Our analysis,' the director general continues, 'is that we are looking for one target. This is a different location spread from Bishopsgate or Heathrow. I won't comment on that now. I have been speaking to the prime minister. A single terrorist agent. An agent, our profiles suggest, who views any serving officer of the security services as a potential target, just as Frances Monro and

Serena Watson were singled out for murder. There is, as I'm sure Miss Cavallero will confirm, from the point of view of Six, no reasonable justification for assuming that the agent is a *bona fide* member of an overseas terrorist organization.' She pauses a moment to look down the table to Cavallero. 'Would you comment, Verity?'

Lucas blows his nose.

'You've put it succinctly,' Cavallero says. 'Our traces in the Middle East, our cousins in Washington, new and open Moscow conduits via Bonn, Paris and Geneva, find no evidence of any link with, for example, Hizbollah or any surrogate cells. Obviously, as you'd expect, we continue to review key and active sources, as well as some non-active, within the Provisional IRA, the Irish National Liberation Army, and the Irish People's Liberation Organization. Not one of these do we consider to have direct responsibility for the murders of either Frances Monro or Serena Watson on the twenty-sixth of March in north London. Nor indeed do we judge such organizations or their surrogates or offshoots to have been responsible for the murder of Woman Police Officer Mary Walker last year.'

Mary Walker. Rosslyn tenses at the mention of her name. He hears her voice ringing in his head. He blinks. *Mary*. A phantom. Her sweetness. The longing returns like a spasm. It's physical. *Mary*. And the reality? Of course. *Mary isn't here*. And the emptiness returns. He closes his eyes. Opens them.

Mary Walker. Last year. A hundred years ago.

'Clearly, it is advisable for us, as indeed it is no doubt for you, to review the *inter-connectedness* of the killings. Especially, of course, in respect of the forensic evidence and the statements of witnesses. Such matters, as they exist, have been intensively scrutinized. I must also add this. We have, additionally, considered the possibility of involvement of other organizations in the Province. Such as the Ulster Volunteer Force and the Ulster Defence Association. My colleagues in the relevant departments find no links with those organizations. I realize that your task would be made easier if I were able to report connectedness to at least one formal, even informal, organization. But it would be dangerous to do so whilst there really is no existing connection that we can trace. Indeed, there isn't even a remote hint of one. At present, I can't even say that one will, even may be found, either in the long- or the short-term future. Beyond that I think I have nothing further to add.' Her tone is the headgirl's.

'Thank you,' says the director general.

She turns to Bryan Wesley who clears his throat, coughs and reaches for his wine glass. His swallow is audible. A long hiss between his teeth.

'We have made very considerable advances,' Wesley says. 'I do hope, director general, that the minutes will record the gratitude of the Service to the highly professional work done to date by Commander Harding and, from Customs & Excise, Mr Rosslyn. They have, as all of us round the table would expect, brought an expertise to the prosecution of this operation, Insect, which we have traditionally come to expect from the respective services.'

Harding is staring, expressionless, at his latest doodle on the MI5 crest. The ugly winged animal with the fish tail is by now seated on a lavatory. Rosslyn glances sideways at the doodle. The meeting is pissing in the wind like the beast in Harding's revision of the vulgar crest.

'My progress report is paper A.1,' Wesley says.

There's a rustling of papers around the table.

'Talk us through it,' says the director general.

'Indeed,' says Wesley. 'The untoward motive for the killings: an option, but vague. The individual with a political motive – again, vague. The staff counsellor's file.' He raises his eyes to the staff counsellor, who blinks. 'Here we can be precise: we have no mention of Monro, Watson, their colleagues, friends or families having sought an interview with the staff counsellor concerning any aspect of personal or professional anxiety, conflict, distress, psychiatric problems or financial difficulties. Commander Harding's and Mr Rosslyn's evidence: this is more detailed. There is the forensic evidence. It is confirmed also by STRU, Beaconsfield. The nature of the explosive device, locations, timings and so forth. All such matters are confirmed by the statement of the witness, Nurse Cartaret. She offers no material evidence of consequence. Other, of course, than to confirm the inexplicable presence of a police vehicle near the scene prior to the detonation of the bomb. No such car has been traced. Other details are set before you. But, as I'm sure both Commander Harding and Mr Rosslyn will confirm, they do not add up, when seen as a whole, to a picture which takes us very much further forward. If there are questions, I know the commander and Mr Rosslyn will be happy to answer them.'

There was none.

'This then is the picture we have before us,' the director general declares. 'The same one I have presented to the prime minister who remains adamant there will be no statement to the press. On the one hand, it generally fails to identify known enemies. On the other, well, the objective observer will say some progress may have been achieved. I am bound to say – and this is very strictly off the record, commander – that the ball is bouncing into the court that you share with your doubles partner here, Mr Rosslyn. And we rather wonder if you have, at any rate *so far*, seen the opposition preparing to serve, if you will permit the tennis metaphor. It's you to return serve.'

The knives are coming out.

'I don't, with respect, see it as a game,' says Harding; i.e. *Balls.* Rosslyn doodles a pair on the *Regnum Defende* pad in front of him.

'As you wish,' says the director general.

Harding snaps: 'Perhaps our evidence has been delivered to the wrong address?'

'I think you'll find that I'm very well aware that our address is, by now, common knowledge, as your Police Federation has confirmed in tonight's *Evening Standard.*'

'And you may live to regret you made it possible.'

'I rather prefer, unlike you, the notion of openness about the Service. No matter what the media are saying about us. We don't answer to the press, commander. Bear in mind my personal commitment to openness, as well as the prime minister's, and the home secretary's. We report to the same masters.'

'I'm a police officer. So do I.'

'Then try not to keep on telling us, commander, what we already know. Rest assured you won't be asked the time of day in Thames House. One can hear the chiming of Big Ben from here and it's saying that time isn't on our side.'

'Then, one day,' said Harding, 'when you come to Scotland Yard, you'll hear the chimes from there too. As well as sirens. Alarm bells. And the muttering of officers who don't need armed protection and some palace preserved and refurbished by lunatics in English Heritage for the benefit of readers of *Country Life.*'

'Commander,' the director general whispers. 'Some of us do have homes to go to tonight.'

146

Christ. Country Life. *He's sailing a bit close to the wind with that one.*

It is Harding's turn again. But he has turned pale. His hands are shaking. 'I'm sorry.'

'A problem?' says the director general.

'I don't feel too good. If you don't mind . . .' He turns to Rosslyn. 'Mr Rosslyn will answer your further queries.'

Suddenly he leaves the table to head for the door.

God. He's doing a runner. Rosslyn is confused. *Is he expecting me to leave with him?*

He follows Harding to the door.

'You stay,' Harding tells him. He looks exhausted.

'Are you sure you're OK?' Rosslyn says with his back to the meeting. He hands over his car keys.

Everyone else is affecting to ignore the mood of war. Several voices are raised at once in a joint effort to stifle anger and embarrassment.

At the door: 'I'll be fine,' Harding says. 'If you want to know, I'm supposed to be at a lodge meeting at the Café Royal. Don't forget my order. Get her on our side. *Regnum Defende.*'

'Same to you.'

The SIS woman, Cavallero, sets out her stall, a new tack: 'We have a specific interest in the financial side of things,' she says. 'Some high denomination notes in rather sizeable quantities are showing up in Hong Kong. Our friends there have traced them back to the Mint Annexe. Purely for the record I'm asked by our finance director to say they weren't notes produced for Tripoli, more to the point, the numbers show they were issued to you. Apparently, to personnel.'

'We've discussed this before,' the director general says impatiently. 'Bryan?'

'It's not strictly the business of this meeting,' Wesley says, 'but yes, the notes did indeed pass through us some months ago to an agent we have run successfully for some considerable time. Before I took over my responsibilities in personnel at the present level, I saw to the payments.' He smiles at Cavallero. 'I take full responsibility.'

She says: 'I think Mr Rosslyn of Customs & Excise might like to set his sniffer dogs amongst our little Chinese chums.' She turns to Rosslyn.

All eyes are on him.

'We haven't looked into a Chinese connection,' he says.

'Not something we've needed to raise either,' Wesley interjects with an air of approval.

'What I do advise you to consider,' Cavallero says, 'are the stakes you are playing for. If we're talking of some Far Eastern manoeuvre then, it seems to me, you should be concerned for your personal security. One of the newer money launderers was murdered. I'm very slightly surprised our Home Office representative has never raised it.' She looks at Lucas.

'She fell to her death,' Lucas says. 'Nothing proven.'

'Other than her workplace was fire bombed,' counters Cavallero. 'Or was she one of yours, Bryan?'

'No. She wasn't one of ours,' Wesley says wearily.

'I didn't say she was, Bryan.' Cavallero offers a sympathetic smile. 'Neither was she one of ours. But don't you think it might be worth looking into?' She leans back in her chair. Threads her fingers behind her neck. 'And we're still waiting to hear why Levy died. Clerks in the Security Service Commission usually live out their allotted span.'

'We're keeping an open mind on that one,' Lucas says. 'Foul play still hasn't been ruled out.'

'Hasn't been ruled in either, has it?' asks Cavallero, who begins to write on a notepad in her open wallet on her knee. 'It operates both ways, the open mind. It lets things in. It lets things out.'

Rosslyn notices she is shielding the notepad from view.

'The structure of the investigation is ideal,' Lucas says. 'It reflects interservice co-operation at the level the prime minister has asked for.'

'Mr Rosslyn. In the absence of Commander Harding,' the director general says. She seems to be tightening her rein on the proceedings. 'Mr Rosslyn, if I may speak for the Security Service' – she looks sharply at Wesley who is breathing heavily – 'we take it Scotland Yard is actively considering the implications of the death of the Chinese. But we don't feel it needs alter the core investigation. Similarly, the death of Levy, the Security Service Commission clerk. The argument I would have put to Commander Harding before he left is this: it is more than ever a matter of sharpening the focus on what happened in north London. My reason for arguing this is simple. There is no precedent. No clear link with previous terrorist incidents. Therefore, we insist greater attention is paid to the evidence.'

'That's what we're doing,' Rosslyn says.

'And without reliance on untoward pressure being applied to suspects under interrogation.'

Jesus Christ. I see what's happening. She wants me by the balls. The bogus recording of his treatment of Dee McKeague. *The director general has to be the person who's sought my removal from the investigation. I'm staring her in the bloody face. Suspension. Disciplinary action.*

'We have no suspects, director general,' he says.

'As we are sadly aware. All you seem to have achieved so far is your prospective reprimand pending the view of the director of public prosecutions. I suppose Commander Harding contrived this particular degree of leniency? Pending the view of the DPP.'

He assumes she doesn't know what Harding's achieved on his behalf. He wants to make his protest here and now.

Let her have it. The tape has been a deliberate and skilled attempt to discredit ME. The temptation to strip off his mask of indifference seems irresistible.

He decides to make no comment.

'I think you catch my drift,' the director general says. 'If not, so be it. If so, I can tell you that the sorry history of the suspect McKeague's bungled interrogation, the violence that prompted her death, will in the course of time be a matter for inquiry.'

'I'd welcome it,' Rosslyn says. 'If she hadn't died we might have got a crucial lead. I have to say the violence she suffered had nothing to do with me. I appreciate it's past history, but I don't like the implication that I behaved towards her in any way that was out of order. The recording of my last interview with her was seriously altered.'

The director general leans lower across the table. She gives something like a shrug. 'We don't believe it, Mr Rosslyn. Why would anyone *want* to tamper with the tape? Surely, it would have been the other way around? You, or your colleagues, would have sought to edit out the record of wholly unacceptable violence administered to the detainee. And there are two versions, are there not? One which has you behaving correctly. The other which tells a very different story.'

She looks around the table. The prosecuting counsel with the look of mild outrage. The wry smile which says the defendant is in it up to his neck: I know it, you know it, he knows it. How do you find him? Guilty.

Rosslyn feels sick inside. He could say the reason for the doctoring of the tape is that MI5 needs to discredit him.

It's getting too close for comfort. Regnum Defende.

'You see,' the director general says, 'I want the record of this meeting to reflect our view of your care and conduct of the McKeague case. The essence of an effective security service can be seen not only in how it sees the enemy, but in how it sees itself. I think you'll find my colleagues in SIS agree with me.' She turns to Verity Cavallero for confirmation.

The heat's off for the time being.

'In principle,' says Cavallero, 'I'd agree entirely. Obviously, the matter of Mr Rosslyn's handling of a prime IRA suspect should be a matter for possible adjudication at a later date. Meanwhile, if the view of the meeting, assembled in the spirit of agreed interservice liaison, is that the investigation be allowed to continue supervised at operational level by Commander Harding, Mr Wesley and Mr Rosslyn, then I have no objections. We, across the river, may have reservations. But we have no intention of getting involved. One can offer advice. But no more than that.'

'Thank you,' the director general says, finally. 'Any other business?'

Wesley has an item. 'I'd like approval to talk further to Mint Annexe about the record of forged currency to agents. It might yield some new pointer to associates of agents formerly handled by Frances. I'll be happy to take control of that aspect.'

'Agreed,' says the director general.

The meeting is at a close. Its participants drift into two groups. The director general is surrounded by her people with Lucas hanging on her every word.

Cavallero tells nobody in particular that she has to leave. 'Late for a dinner date,' she says. Then, to Rosslyn: 'Can I give you a lift anywhere? I'm heading for St John's Wood.'

'If you could drop me off near Baker Street,' Rosslyn says.

Outside, on Millbank, it's raining. The usual English summer. Rosslyn sees a familiar face: the motorbike courier who had shown up in the ground-floor bar, Waxers, at Customs House to collect the transcript of his interview with Hazel Cartaret.

'A delivery from Commander Harding,' he now tells Rosslyn. 'He asks that you open it in privacy. Sign here and print your name.'

The package is nondescript, carefully wrapped. A written note on the brown paper says: *'Regnum Defende.'*

'And this is your bag. Personal belongings. Commander Harding said be sure to see you got them for your trip.'

'Thanks,' Rosslyn says.

'Any time.'

He gets into Verity Cavallero's black VW.

Everything, from Wesley's confidential remarks about the Chinook crash at 9.15 p.m. in the conference room, up to now, as Rosslyn shields himself against the driving summer rain – every detail, word and gesture, has been faithfully recorded inside Thames House by the surveillance cameras with zoom, night enhancement vision, and the twenty-four-hour recording facilities. Total recall has been achieved.

Rosslyn knows MI5 hasn't missed a trick. Not even the futility of its own deliberations. *That woman. She'll even video her own death when it comes. The ultimate snuff movie. Like the ones I nick from the homebound pervs from Amsterdam. 'Strictly for my personal use,' they always say. Well, they would be, wouldn't they?*

25

'Off the record,' Verity Cavallero was saying, as she steered a careful path through the traffic in the rain, 'my interest is in the passage of bogus currency from the Mint Annexe. MI5 has indented for ten times the normal amount during the past three years. Over three hundred thousand pounds, usually in Deutsch-marks and Swiss Francs. The standard maximum payment to a single agent or informer is set at five thousand in a year. Are we to believe MI5 is suddenly operating two hundred and fifty new agents in the UK and Northern Ireland? I think not. We're looking at sums of money which haven't found their way into the coffers of the IRA, Provisionals, INLA or IPLO. Write out the Irish. And write out Abu Nidhal, terrorist groups in India. I believe the money's gone quite elsewhere.'

'Like where?' asked Rosslyn.

'Who knows?'

'It can't be too tough for you to get access to the Thames House finance department.'

'I've already been there,' Cavallero said. 'They're not fools. They use the crab system. One claw passes the cash to another claw. Their finance section doesn't control bogus foreign currencies.'

'Who does then?'

'Take your pick. Any one of the five operations departments, even admin, personnel or support services. I'd advise you to take a look at that Chinese and her clients. Also Levy. He has a boyfriend. Here.'

She handed Rosslyn the note she'd made surreptitiously at the Thames House meeting. 'His name's Patrick Coker. That's the address of the cottage they have in the Cotswolds. MI5 may reckon there's no connection between Levy, the Chinese and Coker, in that order or any other. No reason necessarily why they should. But we've long held doubts about Levy. He's kept Coker in considerable luxury beyond his means for years.'

'What sort of man is he?'

'Coker? Thirty-five years old. Six years in a tank regiment in Germany. Habitué of gay clubs in Dusseldorf. Left the army as a trooper for drug abuse. An ignominious departure. Becomes a minicab driver and gets picked up by Levy, and Bob, or rather Levy's, his uncle. We've got Coker on our record because of a relationship way back with an East German agent. Enough said.'

'Why aren't you going after him now?'

'For the same reasons the initial block was put on Harding. Rivalry. Jealousy. Call it what you will. But if I were you, I'd get to him as soon as you can. And, for what it's worth, I take your side over that taped interview of yours with the Irish woman. You've been set up by someone and no one cares to admit responsibility. You don't seriously believe all this cod about openness, do you? Look, it's the old double-door trick. One door's opened and everyone says, "Now children, you can all see in." And what do you see? Another door, locked and bolted, with no windows. Politics is now the art of the impossible. It's dying. The new Them and Us is government *versus* people. Once the bastards get elected they obfuscate.'

'It's easy to be pessimistic.'

'I know. That way you see the truth more clearly,' she said. 'Where do you want me to drop you?'

'Here will do.'

They were near Madame Tussaud's. 'The most popular institution in the United Kingdom,' said Cavallero. 'A waxworks. Like GB plc. One bomb and the whole lot melts.'

Rosslyn took his case from the back seat. 'Thanks for the ride.' He was out on the street and Cavallero had more to say: 'Your friend Harding must have been a bit thick to pass you a note inside Thames House. It'll all have been recorded by the video cameras. Hope he didn't tell you anything of consequence. By the way, watch Wesley. He's a double first, XXL shit. You should ask his wife about him.'

Rosslyn gave her a vague smile. 'His ex-wife.'

'You know her?'

'Not really.'

'You know what her problem is?'

'No.'

'She's disturbed. Has to be to have married a shit like Bryan. Seriously disturbed.'

Out on the street Rosslyn was getting soaked. 'You know them well?'

'Not Wesley in the biblical sense. He prefers Filipinos, the meek and the mild. He's like all card-carrying bullies. And he's got a string of them. Cleaning women. Illegal immigrants. You should speak to them too. You might learn something else.' She was laughing at him. 'The wife's a health hazard.'

'You really hate MI5, don't you?' Rosslyn said.

'Don't you?' said the smiling Cavallero, reaching over to close the car door. 'Remember once you've started working with them they get under the skin. Like sea urchins. The spines soon get infected.' The car door was still open. 'Surely they've tried to recruit you?'

'Wesley gave it a feeble shot.'

153

'Well, my friend, you're as good as in anyway. You should be rather more watchful. Of them. Of Harding. One never knows where the knife will stab you. The trick is to see it coming. Get your eyes accustomed to the darkness, Mr Rosslyn. You'd better go. You're getting wet. Call me sometime when you're free. It's been nice talking to you.'

'You too. Thanks for the lift.'

He watched her car disappear in the traffic. Then he headed for the station at Baker Street through the rain.

26

A handgun, rounds and a lightweight shoulder holster. The Mark 10 Smith & Wesson. Standard issue for personal protection. These were the contents of the package Rosslyn unwrapped in the privacy of the lavatory on the train en route for Amersham.

He searched the wrapping paper and bubble plastic for an accompanying note from Harding, without success. The gun carried its own message. Keep me near. Use me when needs be. I am your best friend, more trustworthy, with a better bite than an Englishman's best friend, without a mind of my own. Such things had been drummed into the minds of the trainees at Lippitts Hill way back when. The loading of the gun excited him. He fastened the holster around his shoulders. It was a perfect fit. Harding had got the measurements exactly right. Once he had put his jacket back on he sought out tell-tale signs of a bulge. Satisfied none showed, he shoved the packaging beneath the pile of discarded food cartons and newspapers below the leaking basin. An empty beer can rolled this way and that across the slippery floor to the crazy swaying of the train.

Back in his seat, in the deserted carriage, the seats' fabric slashed by vandals' knives, the windows sprayed with graffiti, he checked his bag. Always the Customs man, the basement man, the maker of lists. He rummaged through his things in the bag for a false bottom. Couldn't help it. Always would. Curiosity, the manual said, is the best natural asset of the Customs man. Search and search again.

First use your eyes. Look. Feel. Search. Let the guilty come to you. Let the enemy come to you. His first instructor, 'M.A.J.' the Martial Arts of Japan freak – 'Madge' they'd called him – always held that the most brilliant of smugglers will eventually show himself to you. Relax, let him think you're the underpaid fool. Let him dig his own grave.

Madge, the self-taught philosopher, used to say we can do worse than learn from the Japanese, another island people: stay composed, feign embarrassment, show respect, be passive, always passive. You know you're in the right. So, with the gun, secure and warm, hidden inside his jacket beneath his armpit, Rosslyn was in a more buoyant mood. Of course there was no false bottom in his bag. He went through his things. The solitary traveller heading through the dismal northern outer suburbs in the rain.

He listed: change of underwear, shirt, socks; Mary's photograph, her kimono; toothbrush, toothpaste; Mary's diary and his letters to her, which brought her back close to him, the diary entries, day by day, staring at him like snaps of her taken by someone else. Or were these descriptions more like some camera she'd set herself so she could face it alone and take her own portraits? Mary the secret self-portraitist was inviting him to examine her work again and the diary assaulted him with its dreadful honesty.

SUDDENLY LAST SUMMER
R + 99

My mind is too full of secrets for my own good. I long to start all over again, to wipe the slate completely clean, to regain some innocence. There ought to be a pill you can swallow to obliterate memories once and for all. Perhaps there is one the shrink never told me about.

She was the shrink I went to when finally the THUG affair went too far. I said to her there was nothing I wouldn't do to please THUG. She asked me for his real name but I wouldn't give it to her. You don't feel able to trust me? she said. Yes, I said, I trust you. But I don't trust him now.

Why not? she asked.

Why not? I'll tell you. Because he'd kill me if I tell you his name.

Tell me about it.

About why he'll kill me? Because he'd lose control of himself. He likes pain. More and more pain. He's addicted to pain.

And how do you feel, Mary, about that?

For Christ's sake. How do I feel about pain? The shrink has to be thick-thick-thick.

It hurts, I said.

Of course, she said. We all experience pain differently.

How she knows that I'm not sure. But I dare say it's a fair bet.

Tell me about it, she says. You and him. It.

It began, I tell her, when he'd booked a room at the Kensington Hilton. At the end of a corridor. One of those rooms which you sort of think is soundproofed but you can hear the traffic outside. I'm late. He smiles. Puts the Do Not Disturb notice on the door handle. Double locks the door. He says I'm a bad girl. Daddy says you're very bad. Daddy has brought a friend to punish you. I'm pretty insulting about 'Daddy's Friend'.

Where is he? I ask.

You're not allowed to see him, he says, and dims the lights. Trust me?

Yes.

Good. He produces a large black cotton handkerchief and blindfolds me. I can't see a thing. I feel his hands undressing me. Done this a thousand times before.

Once I'm naked I hear him open the minibar. The clink of glasses. The snap of metal when he opens a miniature. It's Cointreau. Very cold. He parts my lips and pours some down my throat. Then he sets the glass down. I hear it clink. He pulls me down across his knees.

Do you want me to do this?

If it pleases you.

Will you cry?

No.

I want you to say sorry.

Sorry.

That's good.

Then he slaps me. Hard. Then harder. Till the cheeks of my arse are stinging.

Hot now?

It hurts.

Then he fondles me between my legs and I feel something freezing cold slip up my arse.

Relax.

I do as I'm told. What is this – up me?

Like it?

Yes.

It's a candle.

Then he turns me over on the bed and slips himself inside me while I feel the pillows in the small of my back, my legs spread apart, and the freezing candle still up my rear.

I realize he's planned this thing long before. He's been waiting for me here, sadist that he is. He removes the blindfold, and the candle, and his prick. I ask him why he hasn't come inside me.

Because it's your turn, sweetheart.

Now I see there's a very thin bamboo cane on the bed and there's a look of fear in his eyes and this strange sort of smile on his face.

He blathers on to me about how foul and depraved he is. He feels 'so guilty and ashamed. I deserve whatever you know you must do to me.'

2 and 2 makes 4, I say.

6, he says. 6. I don't want to see you do it.

I take the hint. Blindfold him. Force him to spreadeagle himself across the bed. Pull off his clothes down to his pants, then pull them down too.

I deserve to be marked, he says.

You will be, I tell him.

Please, he says. Though I don't know if he means, I mean really means, 'Please do' or 'Please don't'.

Please.

Then I thrash him. If it pleases him I'll show him. And the last three times are terribly hard. The bamboo splits and the last stroke draws blood.

I see he's started to weep.

Love me, he says, love me Mary.

So I turn him over and slip him inside me. It's all out of him in a minute. As fast as that. We're both soaking wet and the sheets are bloody.

Now, if I read this over again, what I told the shrink about the Kensington Hilton incident, I find it's the sort of story I'd totally condemn if it were someone else's, if say, I'd read it cold.

The trouble is, I told the shrink, I enjoyed doing it to him. His pleasure. His feebleness. His pathetic passivity. It was as if the only moments he'd savoured concentrated attention at the hands of someone in a hotel room or, God knows, at the hands of his mother or teacher or someone.

It had gone too far. I realized that as soon as we lay together on the sticky sheets. Me and my old man who I've just thrashed and fucked.

We bathed together, dressed, left the hotel for a restaurant where, he said, there'd be candles on the table.

THUG is the only man I've known to reserve a table at a restaurant on the basis they have candle-holders.

We had dinner to the light of the candles we'd used at the hotel only an hour and a half before. 'If you ever tell a soul,' he said, 'I'll kill you.'

'How many women have done that to you?' I asked him. 'And the other way around.'

He smiled at me in silence.

The shrink said, 'He never told you?'

'No.'

'What do you feel about that?'

'I hate it.'

'You hate it?'

'Hate it! Yes. Wouldn't you?'

'It's a perfectly normal reaction.'

'And I hate him too,' I said. Here I began to cry.

She knew. I knew. I was in love with him. Always was. Always will be. He must have known, all along, I liked him to punish me, I liked to punish him. The pain brought us so very close. That's the point about pain. There are no barriers between you and it. It's inside you and it's the sweetest pleasure I've ever known.

The trouble is I hate myself.

And yet. I know, if R knew that any other man loved me and I loved him, he would kill him. Definitely.

Now I must turn the mask around.

I'd like to thank my shrink who cured me of SM, THUG who'll always watch over me through the shadows, and R who's so sweet, who cares for me, whose kids I want. That's the good news and there's too little of it about.

I still can't look at a candle without laughing, without thinking, without wanting to tell men everywhere – you want a woman to be yours? Then invest in candles and a fridge freezer.

How I miss the old days.

How I love THUG for being a bent jealous lover.

How I love R for being a straight jealous lover.

Some women have all the luck. Let's hope it doesn't run out. Anyhow, not yet.

He was cold; then hot: awash with a sudden fever. Shaking in his hands, the diary he had cherished smelled corrupt. He hated it. Sweating, he rested his head against the cold glass of the carriage window, almost suffocating. The initial stab of fear turned to resentment, against Mary, against her loathsome perverted lover, against himself. The innocence of his love for Mary, the sweet memory of her, kept alive by not reading to the end of her secret life, had evaporated. Blood beating in his ears blocked out the rhythm of the train.

27

The taxi rank at Amersham station was empty. He dialled several numbers for a taxi to take him to Davina Wesley's place. Each time women's voices said his call was in a line. 'Please hold.' And each time he was left listening to the same electronic version of Vivaldi's *Four Seasons*, a snatch from summer in the rain. He decided to walk. Thumb a lift. Someone would surely stop to pick him up. No one did.

Soaked through, he trudged through the streets. The rain penetrated his jacket and shirt. Whoever had designed the gun holster had failed to allow for it getting wet. The straps rubbed his skin painfully. He tried to analyse his feelings to himself about Mary, the diary, her role in his deception. He failed to come up with a word for what he felt. He tried hatred, regret, sadness. Sickness and anxiety were nearer the mark. And disbelief, a corrosive disbelief. It made him breathless, his mouth dry. His eyes seemed to burn. He was a victim: not of his past, but of someone else's, Mary's. What the man had done with her in that West London hotel bedroom sickened him. He imagined – perhaps it had been the reference to the Hilton – that the man was an American. The idea of him bathing with Mary after lovemaking, wallowing in the suds with her, somehow confirmed his view. THUG – the name, why, it was American. THE UGLY.

A Volvo towing a swaying caravan passed by in a spray of water. He saw children's faces grinning at him. A girl, about ten years old, stuck her tongue out and waved two fingers in obscene reply to his thumb jerks.

He asked himself why this investigation had taken such a

numbing turn into an emotional abyss. Perhaps he was really to blame for it. The failure to understand her, her past and her spirit was, by any standard, a desperate failure. Desperation was what he reckoned he was feeling. Here am I, he thought, tired and drenched, heading into the darkening countryside, alone, with a gun, to do something, God knows what or how, about some disturbed ex-wife of a shit in MI5 who's supposed to be my colleague. And two of his own have been blown to bits by God knows who or why. Beat that if you can.

'I can't,' he said out loud.

By the time he reached Davina Wesley's house he knew that he presented a pathetic sight. Drenched, half-human, the lean creature from the slime that had haunted him in childhood dreams. Judging from her look of astonishment when she saw him, Davina Wesley shared this view. He was aware of a moment's silence after she opened the door to him. Somehow she seemed to have been expecting him.

'You'd better come in,' she said. 'Has your car broken down?'

'I came by train. There were no taxis at the station.'

He stood in her hallway shivering.

'I could've met you at the station,' she said. 'All you had to do was telephone in advance.'

He wasn't about to tell her there was the chance her telephone might be bugged. The listeners would have been alerted to his visit. She probably realized as much herself. Perhaps she took it as a sign that he wished to keep his visit confidential.

'Did someone tell you I'd be here?'

'I gambled on finding you at home.'

'Your lucky night.' She told him to stay where he stood, soaking wet, watched by her dogs and cats, while she went upstairs to find some dry clothes. When she reappeared she was carrying a long blue silk dressing gown. 'Have a hot bath. The bathroom's first on the left, opposite my bedroom. You can leave your bag in the mending room. I'll dry your clothes.'

'I don't want to put you to any trouble, Mrs Wesley.'

'One doesn't offer to help unless one wants to. And I'd much prefer you to call me Davina, Alan. Stay for dinner. Then you can tell me why you've appeared like the monster from the deep. Come down and join me when you're ready. I suppose you've got something important to tell me.'

She smiled. Then she disappeared into her kitchen. 'Make yourself at home.'

Wearing the dressing gown, he went upstairs. He left his bag in her mending room, a tiny passage full of laundry baskets, a wardrobe and a sewing machine.

The doors to the other rooms on the top floor were open. One of them was a study, its walls covered with floor to ceiling shelving packed with books, files and what looked like scientific journals. A sea of paper covered the floor: typescripts, faxes, Xeroxes and catalogues from international chemical and computer manufacturers. Just inside the door were two dog baskets padded with old blankets and a cat litter tray which explained the smell. The room next to the study was her bedroom. More books lined the walls.

In all the rooms the heavy curtains were closed. He noticed the powerful smell of her perfume, stronger than the cats' smells. It followed him everywhere, and when he hung the blue silk dressing gown on the hook of the bathroom door he realized the dressing gown was the perfume's source. She must have drenched it recently from the bottle of Chanel's Coco on the table by the bathroom door. It was the sort of gesture Mary had made, the laying of the animal scent; a hint, to be interpreted as he wished.

Like the general invitation to make himself at home: wallow in her bath, use her soap, her white and rough bath towels, wear her dressing gown, sit opposite her at her kitchen table.

'Poached chicken with almond sauce,' she said. 'My version of a Middle Eastern dish, Circassian chicken. Tell me you've made a breakthrough in your investigation.'

He summarized the meeting at Thames House.

'So you think it's the work of a solitary psychopath?' she asked.

'That's what it looks like. But someone working alone has to have back-up. The finance. Ways and means to get explosives. Someone to assist the disappearance to a safe haven. There's no precedent for a single killer carrying out this sort of bombing. There has to be a group behind her, even if only at one remove. There must be some controlling agency.'

'You say "her". Are you sure the killer is a woman?'

He rehearsed the evidence of the witness, Nurse Cartaret.

'Who knows you've come out here to see me?' she said.

161

'Commander Harding. We don't have any secrets from each other.'

'Does Bryan know?'

'No, and I'd be grateful if you wouldn't mention it to him.'

'No reason for me to mention anything to Bryan. Don't look so worried. He isn't about to call here. Not like you. He never turns up anywhere unannounced. Not his style. Bryan doesn't approve of surprise visits. He's a creature of strict routine.'

'Was Frances? Was she a creature of routine too?'

'Pretty much so. She lived a very tidy life.'

'Can you tell me,' Rosslyn asked, 'anything else about her work – career, or home life, which might suggest she could've been a prime target?'

She considered his question carefully. 'No. Believe me. And I owe her a great debt. I've told you already. She was a great support to me when I broke up with Bryan.'

'Did you talk to her about him?'

'Naturally.' She laughed nervously. 'He was the source of my misery. We talked about him in great detail.'

'Frances didn't like him?'

'She didn't approve of him.'

'Professionally or personally?'

'Both. Yes. He's actually something of a bully.'

'Verbal or physical?'

'Both. He hit me more than once.' She looked aside. 'He hit me hard enough for it to hurt. I do have to say it was intolerable. It was when he punched me in front of the children I finally decided everything was completely finished. I deeply dislike violence. I think it's the one reason, philosophically as it were, I can finally justify my work. I want to see an end to the violence. Bryan, however, believes in the efficacy of violent confrontation. His cheeks are not for turning. He admires "the iron and steel of the warring soul". His phrase that. "When push comes to shove," as he says, "we should string up the terrorists by their balls." He practises what he preaches. And what he practises is sometimes frightening. Professionally, he's the master of dirty tricks.'

'Professionally?' Rosslyn asked. 'Is that why SIS disapprove of him? His handling of bogus currency produced by the Mint Annexe?'

Her face showed consternation. 'How do you know about that? Did he tell you?'

'No.'

'Who did?'

He avoided giving her a direct answer. 'Customs search out and seize counterfeit currency in many different centres.'

'I know that,' she said quickly, 'but how do you know Bryan's acted as paymaster to terrorist agents?'

'I don't have chapter and verse,' he replied. Which he didn't. Unless you counted Cavallero's little story. Given her SIS pedigree she was possibly flying a kite. 'You're frowning,' he said. 'It's only a rumour we've latched on to. That some counterfeit money Bryan handled has shown up in Hong Kong. The word is that SIS are pretty sick about it.'

'And is Bryan?' she asked.

'Sick about it? Probably. We've got our hands full with other things. You could always ask him about it yourself.'

'We don't speak to each other,' she said.

'Never? Not even about operational matters? What happens when your work overlaps?'

'It seldom does, fortunately. I'm not going to start helping him out.'

'You think he's in trouble?'

'Bryan? No. He protects himself from trouble by dropping others in it. That's why he loves personnel. When it comes to putting others down there's no one in the world who does it better than he does. He's raised the wrecking of others to the status of an art form. Friends, enemies, lovers, his wife. Cross him at your peril. He doesn't take prisoners. Take his family, me, his mother who left him a small fortune. He couldn't wait for her to die before he got his paws on her money. He has the confidence of old money without the style. He's utterly selfish. If he ever gives a present he leaves the price tag on it, probably a bogus one he switched in the store where he bought it.'

'He still gets under your skin?'

She shook her head. 'I make it a personal rule never to talk about him.' This, Rosslyn could easily see, was a rule she broke with ease. 'I'm indifferent to him. Deeply, irrevocably indifferent. Indifference is the best of weapons against the lover who's hurt one terribly.'

He thought of Mary and wondered if she'd intended him, one day, to read the history of her sexual adventures. Was that her weapon? Perhaps a fairer view might be that she had been inept.

'You see, Bryan has always been careful how he hurts people. I could talk to you all night about it.'

'If you want to,' he said.

'Not really. It's in the past. There's no profit to be had in retrospective hurt. There's something so very vulgar about self-pity, don't you feel?'

'I wouldn't know,' Rosslyn said. 'Most of us find a reason, sooner or later, to pity ourselves. Perhaps it's best to keep it to oneself.'

'Is that why you don't talk about your girlfriend?'

'It's in the past too. She isn't what she seemed to me when she was alive.'

'Then perhaps it's best you shouldn't talk about her.'

'Except I don't have a choice. I want to know who killed her.'

'The punishment,' she said, 'you want the punishment to fit the crime?'

'Why not? You have to see my point of view. All I want is to know who killed Mary and why.'

'And Frances and Serena?' she said.

'My job as well.'

'Mine too,' she said. 'We share the common goal. You should follow my method.'

'Which is?'

She said she was a scientist. As such she constructed models. Her first was straightforward: 'Frances ran countless agents, often under the pressure of extreme danger, sometimes through a second party, even a third. For example, she had a target, a Libyan diplomat who was infatuated with a public relations bimbo representing the British Tourist Board. She was married. The Libyan had got her pregnant. He was married too. Frances had the couple put under surveillance. The girl sought an abortion. The girl's father was a High Court judge whose brother was a junior minister in the Treasury. It was a "family tree operation". Dead easy. Dead wood burns brightest. All sides would be damaged by the girl's mistake. But she told the Libyan she wanted the baby. The visit to the abortionist was some willing gesture to the sweating Libyan. Frances paid off the abortionist to say the pregnancy was too far gone which, of course, it wasn't.

'The Libyan received letters of warning, anonymous of course, containing death threats. Unless he was prepared to meet a "friend who'll help". Who turned out to be, you've got it, Frances. The Libyan was beside himself. He talked, he'd talk about anything, and he did so to the tune of revealing times and places and methods of arms and drug importations from Algiers to Portsmouth, even Bogotá to Southampton. It was a classic. Eventually, the Libyan turned sour. The girl was bought off too. She had the abortion but, a few months later, turned up in Paris with "the baby", "to show the child", a substitute of course, to the Libyan's wife. A week later the body of the Libyan was found on the pavement outside the entrance to a hotel in rue de l'Université. Skull smashed in. Victim of a fall, a push, a topple, call it what you will. End of story. A perfect model of sound and circular construction, with a tidy end except for one thing, a flaw. Can you spot it?'

'What is it?'

'Her refusal to delegate led Frances to handle the Libyan herself. She made an enemy of him. He grew desperate. He talked to someone on his own side. Sooner or later, it always happens, especially with the Arabs. They confide in someone, if only to tell part of the story. Like a soldier's friend. Few people can take the pressure entirely alone. The hard core of professionalism doesn't always extend to the personal life. So, the Arab has a friend now. And this friend becomes the enemy of Frances. There's a very nasty incident one night outside Dover where two cars deliberately ran Frances' car off the motorway. She suffered minor injuries. She was fortunate. One of the cars had been bought with cash in Maidstone the day before. The Kent police traced it to a chauffeur who'd worked for the Libyans way back. By the time they'd got his name he'd already fled the country. The identity of the second car was never established. But the whole incident proved that Frances was on a blacklist. She only had herself to blame. She hadn't delegated; she hadn't isolated herself. You could say she was her own victim. She had believed too much in her ability to do things herself. It wouldn't surprise me one bit if a similar pattern repeated itself and led to someone taking revenge down the line. Someone from way back in her career.'

Her exposition was credible if you believed an officer like

Frances Monro hadn't learned from experience. The old habits of the intelligence officer die hard. Presumably, Monro believed in her own indestructibility; in the protection of anonymity the Service offered her. One more stab at handling an operation herself, as the lone star rider in the murky territory of deceit and violence. Perhaps her reach had exceeded her grasp.

Rosslyn explained why her model seemed to him unworkable: 'I'm taking it as read that the director general will have had people sift her past.'

'That's a fair assumption. She kept a great deal to herself though.'

'But she would have kept very detailed records of her cases, her agents, her cut-offs, the whole paraphernalia of her working life. A woman like her must have wanted her in-house records to withstand scrutiny. She must have wanted her candidature for the top job to look entirely plausible.'

'It was.'

'So she wouldn't dare to have pursued it had there been skeletons in the cupboard, spectres of revenge, anything like that?'

'I think you're right. Yes.'

'Then what's your other model, that she was some kind of double agent, traitor, or something?'

She seemed to smile. 'It's reasonable for you to imagine that,' she said. 'But it really could not have been applied to Frances.'

'Or Serena Watson?'

'No.'

'You see, I've got to search. It's hard, I know. But you have to search too, Davina. Tell me her mistakes. Her defeats. Her flaws. Search your mind. You have the advantage. You knew her.'

'Right,' she said. 'You have to realize that there was nothing in her make up to persuade anyone to kill her. I've told you about her major flaw. She wouldn't delegate. Thames House will already have reviewed her previous cases. My first model, I admit, doesn't apply. The second's a red herring. You're left with the forensic report. We both know it's yielded nothing you can latch on to. It puts you and Commander Harding in an unenviable position. The spade work, the digging in the Thames House files can't in any circumstances be carried out by you, or Harding, or any of his officers. By the way, there are areas even Bryan isn't allowed to look into. The one person, the only person who can see everything

166

is the director general.' She shrugged. 'You could ask her for a confidential meeting. Lay your cards on the table. Offer to give her a second opinion on what she's pieced together so far. But if I were you I wouldn't bother.'

'Why not?'

'Because she won't agree to open the files to you. Or Commander Harding, or even dear old Bryan. Thames House does its own dirty washing. You can't expect departments to down tools, call in officers from all over the country from active operations. No. The show goes on. Grinding on remorselessly. You can't stop the play because someone in the audience wants an interval to make sense of the plot. It's never happened in the past. And, believe me, it won't happen now. All you can do is wait.'

'For what?'

'For the other side to make a move. Don't look so bleak, Alan. One has to search oneself, one's own past, for the jealous lover or the professional adversary bearing grudges. Someone driven to the limit. You construct a model for me. Imagine the events before Frances and Serena's deaths. Your own life before Mary's death. You tell me. Begin at the beginning.'

Once more he told the story of the operation which led to Dee McKeague's arrest. He described the heart of the interview with her. How Dee McKeague was convinced Monro and Watson would be murdered. How she had been offered the commission. That she could name Mary's killer who had been a key player in the attempt to bomb Thames House before Christmas. He retold the events with conviction, and in great detail: he rehearsed the story of his interrogation of her and the lengths, he believed, someone had gone to remake the tape, evidence that would have led to his immediate suspension had not Harding intervened on his behalf. 'I'm convinced it was someone within MI5.'

'Unless it was an IRA sympathizer, or someone prepared to take their money for doing it. It will have been a hefty fee and there will always be police officers who have their price.'

Rosslyn shook his head: 'Harding knows them at Paddington Green. Makes it his business to have ears in all the high security departments.'

'Then you're back to the director general,' she said. 'And, of course, she will have been through every contact of McKeague's.

Her associates. Her family, her friends, all the way back to when she was a little innocent Catholic girl. There are millions like her, and thousands who sympathize with the IRA. Hundreds who, at any one time, may be more or less active in the towns and cities. The proof of guilt is in the thousands of tons of wreckage cleared from the streets. Finding it is a hopeless task.'

'None the less,' Rosslyn said, pushing his chair back from the table, 'there are still more facts to be found. And statements to be taken. Remember, I'm a duty man. They've all got something to declare.'

After dinner, while she put the dogs and cats out in the garden, Rosslyn cleared the table. The rain had stopped. He heard her talking to the dogs; she was calling each by name, wishing them goodnight. For a time he watched her standing very still with her face turned up as if she were contemplating the moon. Briefly, alone in the silence, he thought again of Mary. He was aware of a new sensation: calmness, the illusion of temporarily being removed from the strains of the investigation. And the anger he'd felt that short time previously, as he'd read Mary's entry in her diary, subsided. It was something to do with Davina Wesley's composure and the feeling that he could trust her. In their different ways, they both seemed to be victims.

She locked and bolted the door to the garden. 'To state the obvious, Alan,' she said, 'you're going to have to stay the rest of the night here.'

It was by now almost three in the morning.

'There's an early train in an hour or two,' Rosslyn said. 'If you don't mind I'll stay down here and read.' There was a day-bed beside the kitchen fireplace. 'I can sleep on that.'

'No,' she said. 'Come and sleep upstairs.' She turned out the kitchen lights and took his hand. 'There's much more I can tell you, Alan, about what happened to Frances and Serena. And why Mary died. Who killed all three of them. I'd feel easier telling you if I was completely close to you.'

There was a single bedside light in her bedroom. 'It'd be nice if we slept close together,' she said. 'Just for a few hours. Longer if you want. I could take the morning off.'

She went into the bathroom. Through the door she called out:

'You could do the same, couldn't you?'

'Not tomorrow,' he answered.

'Well then, undress and get into my bed.'

He lay waiting between the sheets. And then heard her say: 'Turn out the light.'

28

Even a half-wit could tell the surveillance officers had taken up residence around Rosslyn's flat in Pimlico. Anna McKeague had seen them weeks ago from the safety of a cab, their faces in the windows of the top floor opposite the basement flat. And from the wine bar on the street corner she had also seen him talking with a senior officer. A superior plod. Rosslyn had been standing by his car with his bag. She had called a minicab and followed his car to the block of flats in Tavistock Crescent. Waited there, unseen. The cat by the mousehole.

Now, when Rosslyn emerged with Harding she followed him to Millbank. She had seen enough to know they had gone inside Thames House.

Her minicab driver said that it was time for him to go off duty. 'Who are we waiting for?' he asked sourly.

'I'm waiting for a friend.' She offered to double the price of the fare.

'I'll need a score at least,' the driver muttered.

Two hours later they caught sight of Rosslyn's car leaving Thames House. By now it was raining heavily. They tailed the car to the West End and lost sight of it as it entered a National Car Park.

She paid the cab driver with two ten-pound notes and then sheltered in a doorway in view of the car park's main exit. There was no sign of Rosslyn, though. Perhaps he'd left by some other exit. A few minutes passed. Then she decided to enter the car park and look for the car.

She eventually found it on the top floor. She was alone. Approaching the car she walked, close to the darkest wall, towards the single video security camera. Stretching to her full height, she smeared the lens with a trace of Vaseline; enough to obliterate the record of her presence, and to suggest to the attendant in his booth below that the camera must be temporarily on the blink.

Now she dealt with Rosslyn's car.

She lay on her back underneath it and attached a small pack of high explosive to its chassis. She checked the wiring, felt for the timer, and set it. Then she smeared it too with Vaseline, and covered that with a layer of grease and dirt.

Now the device was properly camouflaged, ready to explode minutes after the car moved out of the parking space. Its movement would activate the timer. It was as simple as setting a firework. Only this one was lethal. Another perfect job.

A rush of excitement followed. On her feet again, she was light and heady. The car would disintegrate. Glass and steel would carve up Rosslyn's flesh. Tear him apart. His remains to be taken away in plastic bags. The slow and time-consuming work by the forensic team to reconstruct her handiwork would begin. She longed to see Rosslyn die. But she knew it wasn't safe to hang around any longer. So she left by the stairs.

Outside once more, in the rain, on the way to the station and the early train that would take her out of London to Amersham, she told herself to relax.

The journey was the prelude to bigger things.

It's down to me, she told herself. She wanted the pigs to suffer the agonies of the most unpleasant death imaginable.

Once I've got the means, my weapons, it's going to happen.

And I'm going to use their brains, she told herself: *their own researches to wipe them out.*

You're going to open up your storehouse for me, Mrs Wesley. You're the one who'll show me your secrets.

29

At first, when Rosslyn woke, his body ached and he pressed himself deeper into the softness of her bed to ease the stiffness in his shoulders.

Her bedside clock showed five-thirty.

He heard the dawn chorus from her garden and beyond. The telephone ringing. Her barking dogs. Her voice, on the telephone, downstairs. The whistling kettle.

He remembered that she had said: 'There's much more I can tell you, Alan, about what happened to Frances and Serena. And why Mary died. Who killed all three of them.' And what had seemed to be an odd prerequisite for the revelations: 'I'd feel easier telling you if I was completely close to you.'

It seemed as if she needed to complete a reconnaissance. As Gaynor had once put it to him, in the phraseology he claimed to have learned in the military: 'Time spent in reconnaissance is time seldom wasted.' He reckoned her recce had removed whatever misgivings she might have entertained about him.

She came back to the bedroom with a breakfast tray.

'Did the dogs wake you?' she asked.

'No. I heard the telephone ringing,' he said. He was curious to know who might have called her so early in the morning.

'No prizes for guessing that it was Bryan,' she said.

'What did he want?'

'To know whether, by any chance, I knew where you were.'

Rosslyn peered at her uncomfortably for a moment. 'Did you tell him?'

She hesitated, then gave a laugh. 'What do you suppose I told him? "Yes. Actually Bryan, he's in my bed. We're lovers. There's something rather flattering about a younger man who's such a good lover. Unlike you."' She gave him a long look of disappointment. 'I hope it's more than that, Alan.'

'More than what?'

'You didn't sleep with me only because you think I might be of use to you.'

It's the other way round, he thought, but he wasn't going to tell her that. After all, she had taken the initiative.

He was about to reassure her when she said: 'Look, I've got some bad news for you. Commander Harding's in hospital. A bomb exploded last night.'

Rosslyn felt cold. 'Is he dead?'

'No,' she said. 'He's not. But they say he's been seriously

171

injured. He's conscious. "A very close shave," Bryan said. "A very close shave." Bryan loves to be the bearer of bad tidings. And your friend Harding has had enough of his senses left to have asked to see you immediately.'

'Jesus Christ. I don't understand why it was Bryan who called.'

'Because he's been told to telephone all the people you might be seeing, and those you've questioned already. I don't know who the others are, Alan. But I'm number one on the list, aren't I?'

'Do they know who's responsible?' he asked.

'I don't know, didn't ask. Drink your coffee before it gets cold. Don't worry, your clothes are dry. By the way, do you sleep with *all* your witnesses?'

'You're not being fair, Davina.'

'I am. To myself. I don't need to get hurt. There's something I want you to do for me. I want you to write to me.' She pressed a finger against his mouth. 'Something. Don't tell me now. Something nice.'

He smiled in agreement.

'Good,' she said. 'I'll be waiting for you here. Whenever.'

'When it's all over,' he said, 'we'll go away. Up north. To the Lakes, perhaps. Visit your sons. Jonathan, isn't it, the boy at Manchester, and . . . ?'

'Felix. Yes. But I think we ought to get to know each other better before that. Meanwhile, you must get back to London.' She hesitated. There was a look of fear in her eyes. 'Alan, it was your car they blew up last night.'

It hadn't occurred to him that the bombed car was his. Suddenly he remembered.

'Did Bryan say it was *definitely* my car?'

'Yes, he did. That's one reason why Harding wants you off the streets. So do I. You could have been blown to smithereens. You're now very plainly a prime target. I don't want anything to happen to you, Alan.'

'It won't,' he said. 'But please, if you do have something else to tell me, something you're holding back, tell it to me now.'

'I've thought a lot about it.'

Again she hesitated.

'Anything and everything,' she continued. 'Frances' past. It'd be a pity if her death finally turns out to have been meaningless.

Remember, I told you about the officer in the RAF. The wife who complained about Frances. Her obsessive jealousy.'

This again.

'She came into a lot of money when her husband died. Life insurance. A house in Lincolnshire. A flat in St John's Wood. She sold up, though, and left for Canada. She would have had the means to dispose of Frances.'

'What? By offering the job to the IRA? I doubt it.'

'Well, the husband had been in Defence Intelligence. He'd have known the ropes. His wife wasn't stupid. Service wives talk among themselves more than ours do. Or the wives of SIS officers. The tradition of security doesn't run so deep in the armed services.'

'Why haven't you mentioned this to anyone else? Bryan, for example?'

She gazed out of the window. The sun was rising above the trees. 'It's going to be a lovely day,' she said. Then she turned back to him. 'I don't know why I haven't spoken about it to anyone else. Perhaps because I wasn't asked. Anyway, it's purely supposition. I admit, it doesn't explain why Mary died. Or Serena Watson who just happened to be terribly unfortunate. Being in the wrong place at the wrong time.' She buried her face in her hands. 'I'm so sick of it,' she said.

'But I'm glad you told me,' he said gently. 'Every little helps.'

'I haven't disappointed you?' She kissed him on the mouth. 'I rather feel I've let you down.'

'You haven't,' he said.

He went downstairs. His clothes were dry. He dressed in silence hurriedly, watched by the sullen dogs.

They drove the short distance to the station. She kissed him good-bye gently and once again reminded him to write to her. He said that he would.

There was a short queue in front of the ticket counter. Men and women in suits carrying rolled umbrellas, some with portable tele-phones and bulging briefcases. One with a masonic case like Gaynor's.

As he made his way to the platform for the London train, Rosslyn glanced back to the station forecourt. Davina Wesley had gone. Where her car had been parked before he saw the figure of a woman getting into a cab. She had short hair, and a rather athletic build. Dressed like a nurse, she looked like a woman he'd once seen before, rather intense and slightly scruffy. Probably an off-duty nurse, a policewoman, a schoolteacher even, he thought. There was something familiar about her. A look of Mary? Duty men are trained to remember people's identities and he was worried he couldn't place her. She was carrying a red plastic collecting box, the kind women rattle at you in the hope of spare change for some charity or other. No. He couldn't place her. The cab drove off.

At least there was a free seat on the London train.

30

In the privacy of the lavatory, he loaded the handgun and set the safety catch. The bulge of the gun and holster seemed to him to be conspicuous beneath his jacket.

When he returned to his seat, carrying his bag, he sat hunched up, his arms folded, content to hear the tinny sss-sss-sss-sss-dum-dum from the Walkman of the man in the next seat. The noise was irritating the other passengers near by and satisfactorily diverted suspicious glances. Like going through the Nothing to Declare section. Always a good idea to stay close to an unwashed student.

Rosslyn felt inside his bag, his fingers checking the contents. He found something in the bag he hadn't packed himself.

'Did you pack this bag yourself, sir?'

Yes.

'Has anyone asked you to carry aboard some other item for them?'

No.

He wasn't to know Davina Wesley had slipped something into his bag when he wasn't looking. It was a stamped addressed envelope with Davina Wesley scrawled boldly across it. Her address. And there was a Biro inside the envelope.

He began writing: 'Davina, Thank you for last night.'

He wondered what to add. She had wanted him to write something 'nice'. Like what? Not as crass as 'Thank you for the sex.'

He lifted the paper to his face. It smelled of her perfume.

The woman opposite looked up from the *Telegraph* crossword on her lap.

She gave him a smile, but Rosslyn looked aside and wrote: 'If there's something you need to tell me, call, or write, or fax my office. I'll keep you posted on progress. Let me know where and when it'll be easiest to phone you. Thanks again. Yours, A.R.'

He posted the letter outside Baker Street Station. Then he called Wesley with a view to visiting Harding straightaway.

Waiting for Wesley to come on the line he suddenly felt uneasy. Had he not now embarked on a deception no different from Mary's betrayals? He wanted to get back to the job, not just because it had to be faced, but because it offered an escape route from his anger about Mary; the fact that there was, so to speak, unfinished business between them. He was investigating her death as well as Monro and Watson's, undercover, and in secret, while someone out there wanted to see him dead. Why else had *his* car been blown up? The cold returned. He had the frightening sensation that he was investigating himself. It felt as if he were the quarry now. And it seemed to him that someone else, the Insect, was in a similar frame of mind. Insect knew him. But he didn't know Insect.

Wesley was speaking to him. The same plummy voice, breathless, a little too intimate, was reciting the details of Harding's whereabouts. 'Nearly pulled the plug on him,' Wesley said. 'Where, actually, are you?'

'Regent's Park,' Rosslyn lied.

'And last night. When we needed you?'

'Man about a dog.'

'I think in future, Rosslyn, you should let me know your movements in advance,' Wesley said. 'Go and see Harding now. I'll tell the protection unit you'll be there in thirty minutes.'

Rosslyn could tell Wesley had something more to say. It wasn't long in coming.

'By the way, Rosslyn, I'm in charge, now that Harding's *hors de combat*. We're turning over a new leaf. Log your movements, please. And do not, repeat do not, discuss the operation with anyone without my personal authorization. No comment to the press on who you see, and so forth, if it's crossed your mind.'

'It hasn't.'

'Just as well,' said Wesley. 'Hurry through with Harding and then join me at Thames House. I want to talk to you. My office. Twelve-thirty. What I have to tell you, Rosslyn, is personal and unpleasant.'

'To do with *what*?'

Without another word Wesley hung up.

31

Last night's rain had brought a sheen of rich green to Davina Wesley's garden.

She sat with her morning coffee at the garden table listening to the hum of a tractor in the distance. Wood pigeons beat a way through the beech trees. She watched them fly upwards, then drop, swerving away in an arc. Her dogs watched the pigeons glumly. The cats eyed them with predatory intent.

She stared at the tangled creepers, the ferns and rambling roses. Summer had come early. The thought disturbed her as if a trusted clock had suddenly gained an hour. Wild flowers had already found a sanctuary here. Butterfly orchids were flowering, the colour of ivory. There were water avens in the wetness of the shadier corners of her garden with drooping heads of orange-pink. A good day, she thought, to be absent from the dry chill of her underground world at Beaconsfield.

One of her cats lay on a dry flagstone edged with moss. It reminded her of Alan. Wiry, solitary and also, she felt, probably gullible, a little brave. She had always thought cats brave, which was why she'd called this one, her favourite, Meg, after Keats's Meg Merrilies:

Brave as Margaret Queen
And tall as Amazon.

She saw Meg's ears twitch, the hairs on her neck bristling. Meg raised herself, slowly arched her back. The dull sound of the doorbell inside the house had alerted them both.

Davina got up from her garden seat. One of the dogs began to bark. 'Stay,' she called. 'Stay. *Sit.*' And she went indoors.

176

Her eyes, accustomed to the sunlight, strained in the dimness of the kitchen and hall. She felt dizzy; perhaps, she thought, from too little sleep last night.

'Who is it?' she called through the door.

'Save the Children,' a woman's voice replied.

'Fine. OK, wait a moment.' She found a five-pound note in her handbag. This was a collector from HRH the Princess Royal's charity and she vaguely approved of the Princess Royal. 'I'm afraid the flap over the letter box is jammed,' she called. 'Here.'

She pushed the fiver through the narrow slit.

'Are you Mrs Wesley?' the woman asked. 'We have you on our list.'

'Why do you ask?'

'I wonder if I could come in for a moment? I'd like to explain the advantages of taking out a covenant.'

'I'm afraid it's not convenient at the moment.'

'I'm sorry. You have visitors?'

'No. But it really isn't convenient.'

The woman sounded disappointed. 'If I could just show you a brochure. It won't fit beneath the door. Just for a minute?'

'Very well then.'

She opened the front door.

It was the harshness in the eyes which struck her first. They were unblinking. Not the eyes one would expect of a charity worker. A fraction of a second later she saw the gun in the woman's hand. The accent changed from flat home counties to Irish. 'Move back. Slowly. You're going to do what I tell you,' the Irish woman said. 'Or I'll blast your tits off.'

32

Rosslyn saw new faces at the King Edward VII Hospital for Officers. Only yesterday, it seemed, he too had been kept here under armed guard like Harding. The shock and injuries had aged him. Rosslyn hid his pity for Harding's frail appearance.

They talked for half an hour. Harding explained how the latest bomb had nearly killed him.

'I was shining my pocket torch at your car. Underneath it, all around the bodywork. Nothing. Then I'm about to get in when I see these smears in the dust, more grime really, as if something has recently been dragged out from underneath. So it seems likely someone has taken a look and got out in a hurry.'

'So what triggered it?' Rosslyn asked.

'I'll come to that. So I go downstairs to see the duty attendant, some Asian, who says, "I've seen everyone who came in, everyone who came out." I check his till, his receipts, the works. Then his surveillance system. And bingo, the camera on the top floor is blurred. Totally out of focus. I notice he's got his own TV showing some late night shit. I tell him, "Close the doors." He says, "But what about the customers?" So I tell him, "I suspect there's the possibility of an unexploded bomb on the top floor underneath my car." I tell him, "Stay with me." And I call the Yard. Then, and I still can't credit this, or what gets into his brain – his takeaway tandoori, the lager, or the news of a suspect bomb. But he belts out of the cubicle saying, "I'm going to throw up."

'He's outside like a shot, running for his life, up the fire stairs. If he feels like throwing up he's doing a good job of swallowing it down. I slip on the stairs and twist my ankle. Then I go on and find him with his head in the boot of the car next to mine – *your* car. Here I pull my gun. He's holding a carrier bag. "This is only cash," he says, shaking. "My winnings from William Hill." I say, "Put it down. Gently. Slowly. By your feet. Do it. DON'T HAND IT TO ME," I shout. "Do as you're told or I'll blow your legs off." He's shaking like a limp dick in a microwave. Then there are the sirens. The boys are here. Our friend freezes. Then he throws up the tandoori and lager all over the shop. Even pukes into the carrier bag. I make to grab him. But he passes clean out, slams against your car, jolts it. If there's a bomb, well, how long have we got, him and me, to get the hell out?

'So I drag him and his stinking bag across the floor. He starts to come round. Now he's crawling. I get my arms under his armpits and lift him up. We're almost through the swing door, the fire door to the stairs, when the bugger goes off. If it hadn't been for the fire door, the direction of the blast downwards, well, we wouldn't be here now. Not you. Not me.'

'Christ, I'm sorry,' Rosslyn said.

'It's not the end of the world. I'm alive. Even the Asian's alive. Stunned and bruised, and alive. Turns out it was kosher – he'd won a tidy sum. But my legs are smashed. It'll be a time before I'm back. I could kick myself for not having noticed the duff video surveillance unit. It'd been Vaselined. Even if the Asian hadn't been half-pissed he wouldn't have seen a thing. Sometimes I wish some Asians wouldn't hit the booze so much.'

'Has anyone claimed responsibility?' Rosslyn asked.

'No,' Harding replied. 'But this *has* to be Insect. The pity is that the fucking car park hasn't got a recording system. We could be watching her on video here and now. There have been so many near misses. I'm telling you – we're going to get her. Not MI5. They won't. We will.'

The injured Harding was even more determined than before. Not surprising, Rosslyn thought, his legs were badly damaged and, moreover, he was as good as off the case. 'Is it true Wesley's taking over? That's what he's told me.'

'Yes. It's true. It won't matter in the long run.' He shifted his body on the bed. 'Sometimes it's good to have an arsehole in charge. He's a loudmouth and a shit.' He shook his head, then winced. 'My legs. Oh Jesus.'

'Don't they give you painkillers?'

'I don't believe in them. I want to think straight when you tell me what happened last night. By the way, Wesley doesn't know, if it matters, that we're opening up his so-called wife. I had him telephone all the people you've seen. Including Mrs Wesley. He didn't catch on. Tell me what she gave you.'

The nurse brought coffee. Rosslyn used the break to order his thoughts, to separate the professional from the personal.

The nurse left and he began: 'It's true she was very close to Frances Monro. The break-up of the marriage brought the two of them even closer. Monro was the sympathetic ear. And she told me quite a lot about Monro's operations, maybe more than she intended.'

'Like what?' Harding asked.

Rosslyn told him the story of the Libyan, the first scenario, the theory that Monro had been the victim of her refusal to delegate, that someone had taken revenge, as Davina said, 'down the line'. Someone from way back. Then there was the second scenario or model: that she could've been a double agent.

'Did she suggest that idea?'

'No. I did. But she threw it out. She didn't point to a single fault. She managed to turn what looked like bad points into good ones in Monro's favour. So we talked on. I told her about Dee McKeague. She dismissed the story really. And about the tape of my interview. She suggested it might be a bent copper.'

'I don't think so,' Harding said. 'I know Paddington Green inside out. I know it wasn't one of theirs.'

'I said, maybe MI5.'

'Them, more likely. But I don't see how that would persuade anyone to have a tilt at you or me. Even they aren't going to stoop that low.'

'Finally,' Rosslyn told him, 'we get another version. This one's to do with some extra-marital affair Monro had with an air force officer who's dead and whose jealous wife complained to MI5, as if they'd be interested in who she was in bed with. And Davina Wesley says the wife came into a fortune when the RAF man died. So she has the means to dispose of Frances. Well, I don't think much of that line.'

'Neither do I,' Harding said. His eyes were watery and drifting. 'Listen, Alan, level with me, how personal did she get with you?'

'Nothing.'

'What does "nothing" mean? You stayed the night there, didn't you? She's an attractive woman, isn't she?'

'I know what you mean. And to save you asking something out of order, the answer's nothing.'

Harding hadn't finished. 'But do you think there could've been? What I mean is, do you think she's interested in men? Or is she queer, lesbian or whatever?' He raised a hand. 'Spare me any details, if there are details. I mean, I'm not interested in whether you had a cuddle with her, or more besides. My question is this: is she lesbian?'

'Christ, she's got a husband and two kids.'

'Makes no difference. People change. Answer me. Yes or no.'

'If I'm any judge of these things, she likes men.'

'How much does she like men?'

'Quite a lot.'

'You're sure?'

'Totally.' Rosslyn gave a short laugh. He couldn't help it.

'What's so funny, Alan?'

'Only this is the second supposition about Davina Wesley I've heard in twenty-four hours that sounds, well, really odd. First, the woman from SIS, Cavallero, tells me Davina Wesley's disturbed, "a health hazard" was how she put it all la-di-posh. She's got it in for MI5. Hates the lot of them.'

'What you don't know, Alan, is that Cavallero's given me a break. Not on Davina Wesley directly, maybe on Monro, certainly on Serena Watson who SIS looked at when she was in the army. Watson was a dyke. She got into trouble for it in Aldershot. As Cavallero puts it, "SIS stuck the finger in her." But this is the thing: MI5 had no problem in recruiting her. So why? She was between the sheets with Monro. This is why I'm interested in Davina Wesley. Remember the letter you retrieved. Keep it in mind. Now, let's leave it aside a while. Tell me what Cavallero said to you.'

Rosslyn went through the payments Wesley was supposed to have made. The advice she'd given him to see Levy's boyfriend, Coker, the disgraced soldier who'd been running with the hare and the hounds in Germany. SIS, it seemed, had used him. But given Coker's East German boyfriend it seemed more than probable that the East Germans had used him too. 'She told me to visit him, and I think I will.'

Harding peered myopically at the untouched coffee cup on his bedside table. 'Coffee's cold,' he said. 'Ask the nurse for more.'

The nurse came in and rearranged the pillows behind Harding's head and shoulders. Another nurse brought fresh coffee. Once she'd left Rosslyn said: 'Have you any objection to my using Dickie Gaynor? Just this once. He's hard and there are people I'd like him to see.'

Harding sipped his coffee. 'Like who?'

'Like Wesley's Filipino cleaners. His family: the sons. Cavallero. Whether the money's been used for something it shouldn't have been. I want the details. I'll see Wesley's sons myself maybe; I want to know if their mother is telling me the whole truth. And I just want to be sure of Wesley. He's pissing on me and then he tells me it's raining.'

'So you want to piss on him?'

'Don't you? He's in charge now. They've stitched us up. Perhaps they bombed you last night to get you off the case. Nothing surprises me.'

Harding laughed bleakly. 'And I don't think it was me they wanted to kill last night. It was you. But Wesley's not the one we're fighting, Alan, unless you've gone soft on his wife. That makes things, shall we say, a bit trickier.'

'It doesn't enter into it.'

That met with Harding's usual gesture of protest. The hands raised, palms outstretched, pushing the air: 'Of course it doesn't, Alan, of course it doesn't. She's fanciable. I could fancy her.' His smile returned. 'We could do worse than Dickie Gaynor. We can trust him. I've good reason to trust him.'

'He's a member of your bloody masonic lodge.'

'And that helps. He doesn't deserve to be dropped in the shit by us. Remember, he's your boss. He doesn't owe you any favours. There again, he owes me one or two, two drunk-driving offences dropped. We all owe someone something, don't we? White and black, debtors and creditors, that's how it works, Alan. Know what you owe me? To win this thing. Soldier on. Lift the phone. Call Gaynor. Make sure none of Wesley's people follow you when you see him. They'll be on to you, you watch and see.'

The clock on the radio said 11.05.

'Wesley wants to see me at twelve-thirty.'

'Sod him. See Gaynor. Call him. I know what Wesley wants. He wants you barracked in accommodation at Thames House. He told me. He wants you off the streets. I advise you not to go to Thames House. Find some other bunk.'

He thought: *Davina's place? A hotel room in Bayswater?*

He was waiting for Gaynor to answer his telephone. He wasn't at his office. No one seemed to know his whereabouts. There was no reply from his home. Where was he – ballroom dancing in his lunch hour?

'He's in the city, somewhere,' Harding said. 'I know. I saw him at the lodge meeting last night. Oh Christ, I remember, he's in Docklands today. Is that what he said?'

'I don't know,' said Rosslyn. 'I'm not on the square, am I?'

'Not yet.'

Harding was on the telephone now. 'Give me Richard Gaynor's car phone number.' He memorized it, dialled.

When Gaynor answered Harding spoke quietly: 'Drop it. Yes. Now. Meet a friend of yours in the staff quarters at the Angel in

Rotherhithe. Mention my name . . . No other names. I want you to do everything he tells you. Forty minutes. Two of my officers will be in the background.'

The effort of replacing the receiver drained the remaining colour from Harding's face. 'I have to admit my bloody legs hurt. I only hope they don't have to take them off. I'd rather pack it in before they do that to me. And you?' He closed his eyes, drew a breath between his teeth, a long hiss. 'Going to Amersham, then. Tonight, are we? Oh no, don't tell me if you don't want. Best see Coker, then the Wesley sons, then the mother. She hasn't levelled with you Alan, believe me. And if you fail to get them talking . . . I'm telling you, Insect's slipping away from us. I have this nasty feeling inside. She's winning.'

Rosslyn had never seen him look so grim.

33

The early afternoon news bulletins carried details of the car bomb in London's Soho. A car park attendant, an Asian, had apparently suffered minor injuries and was at present detained in University College Hospital. An unnamed civil servant (no mention was made of Harding) had sustained more serious injuries, to his legs. The reason announced for holding back the civil servant's name was that his family was holidaying somewhere in southern Spain. Thus they were unaware of the tragedy which, said a spokesperson, 'could have been very much worse had not the victims been so vigilant'. As it was, the damage was put at 'several million pounds', a piece of exaggerated guesswork.

Once again, for the thousandth time so it seemed, the public was asked 'to remain alert to suspicious packages'. And once again the warning to the public fell on deaf ears. But the London Transport staff, the men and women in the front line, heard the latest warning and most heeded it; especially those who'd turned up for work at those stations listed as A-grade targets. Most of these are the stations connected by tunnels to the main rail termini, particularly Waterloo, Victoria and Kings Cross, where staff remember what it's like to be trapped in the horror of an underground inferno. And not far from Kings Cross are two other A-grade targets, Warren Street and Euston Square underground stations, used every day by the staff bound for 140 Gower Street, an outpost of MI5, still occupied by those staff not yet allocated office space in Thames House.

At Warren Street, more precisely just outside the entrance, by the news stand, lay a pile of uncollected plastic garbage bags. And the station supervisor was alerted to something wedged between two of the bags on the top of the pile. It was a carrier bag, tied at the top with insulating tape. The newspaper seller told the station supervisor he 'didn't like the look of it'.

The forensic officers at New Scotland Yard opened the carrier bag. It had, of course, already been X-rayed and declared safe. But the contents intrigued the examiner. The senior officer decided Harding should be informed about the contents of the bag. The problem he faced was: where was he?

Harding's office said the commander 'was on temporary leave'. Where, they weren't saying. The senior officer was not prepared to let things rest. He decided to make a more personal approach. Wasn't it common knowledge that the commander was a freemason? This senior officer, a Catholic, held no truck with the Brothers and their anti-papist, misogynistic secret plots, but he had to accept they could have their uses. He would activate the chain of communications. He spoke to a Brother, a member of Harding's lodge. He had, he said, a piece of intelligence under wraps which, it seemed to him, should find its way to Harding as soon as possible. He wouldn't say where it was, over the telephone. The Brother he'd contacted faced similar difficulties in tracing Harding's whereabouts. No one at the Yard knew where the commander was. It was all very odd.

So he telephoned Richard Gaynor, at present, like Rosslyn, on his way in an unmarked car to Rotherhithe. And it was Gaynor who spoke by car telephone to Harding. 'Your forensic people have something for you.'

Harding didn't hesitate to tell the forensic officer to send the bag and its contents to Rotherhithe.

These, then, were the circumstances in which the architects' plans for the renovation and restoration of Thames House ended up, early that afternoon, in the top-floor room at the Angel in Rotherhithe, an unexpected item on the agenda for discussion between Rosslyn and Gaynor.

Attached to the bag was a typed note, in an envelope on which was written, by hand, 'Personal and Strictly Confidential. For the Attention only of Messrs Rosslyn and Gaynor, HM Customs & Excise.'

10.30 15 June

Sir,
The contents of this package were discovered at approximately 07.45 hours this morning outside Warren Street underground station by a news vendor who had alerted the station supervisor to the presence of a suspicious package.

After standard precautionary measures had been taken, the package was brought to me for further inspection and analysis. My preliminary findings indicate the following:

1. The main contents of the bag comprise summaries of an architect/ structural engineer's report on major building works, mainly complete, at Thames House, Millbank, London SW1. You will notice the summaries are headed with TOP SECRET classification.

2. It may be of relevance that certain sections have been recently photocopied. These are the sections describing technical specifications for fibre optic communications ducts, air-conditioning and ventilation systems, sewerage facilities and water supply systems. There is also a reprint from *The Architectural Review*, Vol LXX, November 1931, pp 165-167.

3. No trace of fingerprints have been found on these documents which suggests they are in a pristine state, possibly stored with other documents of a similar type of paper and printwork.
However, there are traces of handling by a person/persons wearing rubber gloves.

4. More significantly, various human hair fibres, as well as artificial hair fibres from a brown wig, have been retrieved from within the pages of the documents. In addition there is a residue of Vaseline or unguent. And, unusually, though not exceptionally, on the inside of the plastic carrier bag are traces of menstrual blood, suggesting that whomsoever most recently handled the bag is
   (a) obviously female
   (b) the blood is type Rhesus negative
   (c) the blood is of sufficient quantity to allow for a DNA categorisation and samples are at the path. lab. accordingly.

5. Additionally, whomsoever tied the carrier bag, fastened it by using her/his teeth and there are imprints in the plastic, again not of a specially distinctive type, but of an identifiable pattern.

6. Again most significantly, on the insulating tape used to fasten and secure the neck of the bag, there are traces of SEMTEX high explosive.

7. Identical traces of the same blood type, Rhesus negative, SEMTEX, insulating tape, and human and artificial brown hair fibres were recovered from the site of the bomb blast in the early hours of this morning at the location north of Shaftesbury Avenue in which two persons were injured.

8. Likewise, though there were no traces of Rhesus negative blood, at the site of the bomb blast at England's Lane, NW3 of 26 March last, there were, nevertheless, traces found of both identical human and artificial hair fibres.

9. Similarly, though there were no traces of Rhesus negative blood, at the site of the death of a Mr Levy at Camden Town underground (see: LEVY Report, Page 7, para 1(e)) there were identical traces of human and brown artificial hair fibre found both on Mr Levy's body and clothing and on the platform.

You will appreciate this is a somewhat curtailed and, given the constraints of time, not necessarily formal or conclusive analysis. Nevertheless, it will be wise to consider the initial assessment of the findings. These point to the likely, not proven, presence of the same individual, a female, possibly aged 30 or about, white, of the rarer blood classification who, certainly at the incident in the early hours of today, had or was handling and was in possession of SEMTEX.

You will appreciate that a vast quantity of human and artificial hair fibre can be dispersed at a crime scene, and it has only been the recently concluded tabulation and analysis of what has been collated that enables me to affirm my analysis.

If I can be of further assistance please do not hesitate to get in touch with me, personally, at my office.

Rosslyn and Gaynor read the memorandum in silence. From the upstairs windows of the staff rooms there were magnificent views of Tower Bridge and the dome of St Paul's Cathedral. The tide, on the turn, was pulling slightly downstream to Greenwich Reach. Opposite, on the north bank, was the old site of public executions. It was from here, in the Angel, that Judge Jeffries would enjoy a drink watching the death throes of those he'd found guilty of far lesser crimes than Insect's.

Then they read through the dossier prepared by the architects and engineers for the reconstruction of Thames House. It was numbered 87.

'This,' said Gaynor, when he'd finished reading the dossier, 'is in the hands of the bomber? It gives me a very nasty feeling. She knows *this*. Jesus, it's so easy. How long do we have before she does it again? What the hell is stopping her blowing anything up, including Thames House?'

'She's tried before,' Rosslyn said.

Gaynor must have thought of Mary. Must have read Rosslyn's mind, who added, 'I was there.'

'I'm sorry,' Gaynor said.

'No. It's OK. In a way, you know, I'm glad I was. But that time, perhaps, she hadn't done the research. Now, she has.' He tapped the dossier with the tips of his fingers. 'At last we have something physical, we have, sort of, the benefits of her research. It's a big moment, isn't it?'

'You tell me,' said Gaynor. 'This isn't why I'm here, is it? To read some clumsy architect's plans. Don't those berks have safes or anything? And look at this. The *Architectural* bloody *Review*. It's all in print. The site. The basement. The steel frame. Ground plans. The whole bloody edifice.'

'It's from 1931,' Rosslyn said.

'So what? They've restored the building, haven't they? I pass the bugger every week within spitting distance. Even a child could see how vulnerable it is.'

The manager appeared with a tray of drinks. Rosslyn stood up and went to the windows. He should have felt wearier than he did. He was trying to imagine where Insect could be. Where, if he was in her place, where would he be now? Not far from Warren Street? He couldn't tell. They knew when the bag had been found – not when it had been dumped by the station entrance. Was she, like him, down by the river? Nearer Thames House?

Back again at the table he scrutinized the specifications:

The weight of the structural steel employed was 11,208 tons; 137,000 cubic feet of Portland stone and 9,000 cubic feet of granite have been used for the elevations. The illustrations on these pages are: plans of the fourth floor; a drawing of 'A' staircase hall on the seventh floor; Thames House and Imperial Chemical House from the embankment in front of St. Thomas' Hospital; drawings of entrance vestibules, entrance doorways; a working drawing of the east elevation of the south block. Thames House and Imperial Chemical House were both designed by the same architect, and form one architectural composition.

'Suppose you and I were going to bomb Thames House – imagine. How do we really bomb it, what are the models?' Rosslyn asked.

'The *what*?' Gaynor said. He wiped some beer from his beard.

'Models, scenarios. Our plan. On land, what do we do? We get inside with HE. Or we just do what they tried before. We leave a van packed with HE outside and set a timer. Say we do? What happens? There's a big local blast. But it comes up against a stone and granite skin, then a steel frame. The blast will be localized. Sure, it'll knock out windows and so on. But it won't do that much damage. It'll just show how bloody strong the building is. Suppose we bomb from the air?'

The watery sunlight made patterns on the table, and the open dossier, and the photocopy of the magazine article. And here was the plastic carrier bag like an object taunting them. *She had touched it*. Like a silent challenge. Once more, Rosslyn went to the window. This time he opened it. He could smell the Thames: mud, sweet, slightly rotten, like stale water from a flower vase. A barge's steel cable twanged.

'There's radar and satellite warning systems,' Gaynor said. 'So the air's out.'

'Right.'

'The air is out, exactly. So, I reckon, is high explosive. And we're not going to fantasize about limited nuclear attack. We're looking at a localized attack.'

'Using what?' Rosslyn persisted.

'I don't know.'

'Poison in the water?'

'She couldn't get up there.' Gaynor turned to the plans of the roof spaces. 'You just can't get in there.'

'So how do *we* get in? The whole place is self-contained. Looks like a thermos flask. A cell within a protective cell. A kind of Russian doll thing.'

Rosslyn thumbed through the pages of the dossier. 'She's Xeroxed these.' He turned the dossier round. 'Fibre optic ducts. Air-conditioning. Ventilation systems. Sewerage and water. And there's no space there to get in.' His finger pointed out massive walls of reinforced concrete.

'It's all self-contained,' Gaynor said.

'Come on,' Rosslyn urged him. 'You're the smuggler. How do you bust in?'

Gaynor shook his head. 'I don't. I really don't.'

'Correct.'

The portable telephone began to ring next to Gaynor's chair. 'Here,' he handed it to Rosslyn.

It was Harding: 'What have you got?'

Rosslyn read out the memorandum. 'We know finally we're looking for a white female, in her thirties or so. Maybe she wears wigs or something. Most probably she has stolen plans from some architect's office for the restoration of Thames House. But, I wonder, has she junked the idea of bombing it? It's impossible to do it. She's photocopied the pages showing the best clandestine routes into the building. But there's a bloody great protective concrete wall. Better still, we have her blood group, hair samples, teeth marks, and SEMTEX traces. She was almost certainly the one who did the car in, and you, this morning. And she was there when Levy died in Camden Town. She's having her period, if you're interested. And all of it shows up in England's Lane.'

Rosslyn felt the silence at the other end of the line. He looked out of the window towards Tower Bridge. He saw Gaynor likewise staring upriver.

'Either she plans to hit Thames House,' Harding was saying, 'or she plans to hit us, or the usual round of outspoken Tories, or the odd general. Whoever. But one terrorist can't bring off a Thames House attack. I still can't believe this woman is working alone, I really can't. And I don't think Wesley can be thinking so.'

'When do I report in to him?'

'You keep in touch with me, Alan. Wesley doesn't owe us any favours. And we don't owe him any. I think, I believe, somewhere and somehow, he's up to his neck in shit. Personally, I want to see him drown in it. And, you know, I still believe you've got to crack that wife of his. I'm convinced she's hiding something –'

'Why do *you* think she's so suss?'

'She's MI5. She knows what sort of man Wesley is, as wife, ex-wife, whatever. It feels like there's some residue of protectiveness somewhere. If Insect's about to blow up Thames House, let's not be there when she does it.'

'Do we warn them?'

'There's no use warning them about what cannot happen. Listen, I was in on the discussions about the restoration of their head-quarters. There's no one who could destroy it. Believe me. No one. If, by the way, it were to happen I'd be one of the people held to blame. I know what I'm talking about. Just get in there among the scum with Gaynor. You've got the list. Tick them off. If either of you have to use violence – use it.'

'Is that permission?'

'It's common sense, Alan,' said Harding.

'I'll bear that in mind,' Rosslyn said, and turned back to Gaynor.

'Don't forget it,' said Harding and rang off.

'I think he's wrong,' Rosslyn said to Gaynor. 'I think Insect is finding a way of bringing off the biggest spectacular of all time. Something the whole fucking world will see.'

'He doesn't think so?' Gaynor suggested.

'No,' Rosslyn said. 'He wants us to carry on. You. And me. Searching bags. Grilling suspects. "This way, sir or madam." Strip search. And we'll get the usual protests: "D'you know who you're speaking to? Lord Prick, Lady Prat." And "This won't look good in the papers, will it?" So, we divide them up. A gay in the Cotswolds. Two students, the Wesley sons, in Manchester. Ms Cavallero, she of Six. Wesley's Filipino cleaners for what they're worth, and Davina Wesley. You don't mind taking orders from a junior?'

Gaynor smiled. 'Listen, Alan. I don't know whether you realize this. But Tom Harding's dying. He may never come out of hospital. You know what's wrong with him?'

'Yes, I know.'

'I'm not a doctor – I mean, I don't know if they can operate on him or whether they can't. But it's much worse than people know. So you see, I want to give him this one last win. He's totally alone. His wife quit, I don't remember when. He's given his whole life to fighting the IRA. His last reward will be to win this one. Find this woman, whoever, wherever she may be. And I know that's what you want, for Mary's sake. There's no going back. Harding's always believed, as anyone who's reasonable might believe, that we're never going to win if we're deep in bed with MI5. They couldn't even search a lady's handbag. I mean, they haven't seen heroin-filled condoms pulled out of women's parts or blokes' arseholes covered in slime and shit. Well, I have. I know what it takes. They haven't seen the stuffers and swallowers. And it doesn't take a whole bunch of little women graduates, Ms turned-up-noses, fresh-cheeked sweeties to smell the stink of terrorists' breath. Frankly, we're not throwing this away. Fuck Wesley and MI5. No one's going to stop us moving. It's too late. Tom Harding knows you're bloody good. Best of all, you've got a reason to do the job like no one else. It's personal.'

'Yes, it is. You'll take my orders?'

'I'll take your orders, Alan. I'll see whoever you tell me, give you a written report down to the last whisper.'

'I want you to open them up,' Rosslyn said. 'Cavallero. The currency transfers. The whole story. The Filipino maids Wesley uses. You stick to London. I'll see the Wesleys' sons in Manchester and the man Coker in the Cotswolds.'

'And the wife?'

'Her too,' Rosslyn said.

'OK. Fill me in. And let's work to fixed liaison times.'

'I'll call you on your car phone,' Rosslyn told him.

'You?'

'I'll need a car from the pool. And fifteen hundred pounds in cash.'

'We'll call one over here. But the cash – what for?'

'Because I'm going to pay the bastards to talk.'

'If you say so,' Gaynor said. 'When do you need the reports?'

'This time tomorrow.'

It took almost an hour for Rosslyn to brief Gaynor fully. On the way out of the Angel the manager said he was sorry they hadn't stayed 'for lunch on the house'. He shook hands carefully with Gaynor. Rosslyn noticed something slightly unusual about their handshake. A masonic bond.

The manager nodded towards the street and the men in suits standing by the cars. 'Yours?' he asked.

'Ours,' said Gaynor. 'I should've told you.'

'They look a bit edgy,' the manager said.

When the armed officers saw them leaving the Angel, they opened the car doors. One of them was talking into a portable phone.

'If you'd sign here,' the car delivery man from Customs told

Rosslyn. 'There's a full tank. The keys are in the ignition.' He handed over an envelope. 'The cash. If you'd sign again.'

It was approaching 3 p.m. when the cars went their separate ways from Rotherhithe, away from the Thames and its water sparkling in the sun beneath the cloudless sky.

34

In Amersham, Davina Wesley's garden was empty. The dogs and cats were inside the house. So was their mistress. She was upstairs in the darkness of her bedroom where heavy curtains shut out the afternoon sun.

Her arms, stretched above her head, were tied to the flex of the ceiling light over her bed. Her ankles, like her arms, had been bound with industrial adhesive tape and were tied to the left and right feet of the bed. A length of blue silk torn from her dressing gown had been knotted around her mouth and then taped over. Space had been left for her to breathe through her nose. She wondered how much longer she would be kept prisoner on the rack, in her own home, on her own bed.

Her shoulders, so painful from the struggle with the intruder an hour or two before, had by now gone numb. Pain, perhaps from a trapped nerve in her shoulder blade, throbbed down the length of one arm to her fingertips. At first she tried to lower her weight into the mattress to pull the flex from the ceiling fixture. But the attempt proved futile. It was less painful when she lay completely still. She knew there was no alternative but to wait for the armed intruder to set her free. If she ever was going to set her free.

She listened to the sounds below. Several times she heard doors opened, then closed. The intruder was moving through her house.

There had been the sudden wild barking of the dogs. Then silence. The dreadful combination of the silence and the intruder's impassivity intensified her fear to an unbearable pitch.

What terrified her was that she now knew the intruder was the sister of the IRA woman, Dee McKeague. 'One by one,' Anna McKeague had told her, 'you'll all go. That'll be the end of it. You know what I'm talking of.' In the silence of her bedroom Davina Wesley drew her own conclusions, alone, and in the dark. 'You're to provide me with the means,' McKeague had said with the same awful calmness, with a still certainty Davina Wesley supposed to be a hallmark of the insane: immunity from doubt or fear. There had been no point in trying to appeal to her assailant's reason; indeed, after the first whip of the gun to the side of her neck and head, the blurred vision and the aching of her skull had made thought almost impossible.

She realized the woman she was dealing with was possessed of formidable physical strength which enabled her to use the thick adhesive tape both to bind her, issuing instructions all the while, and raise her body up to the flex of the light above her bed. The intruder seemed intent on inflicting humiliation in addition to pain. Davina Wesley was familiar with the theory of the process, this aspect of applied psychological warfare which, it was believed, and not without good reason, had been used by the British in Northern Ireland in the past. The lessons had been taught to the British by American special military instructors with experience in Vietnam. Old pleasures, like old habits, die hard and the British army had learned their lessons well. No point in not using one's education, especially when it was offered by a relative in the great family of nations.

At one moment, McKeague had said, in a voice something like that of a judge passing sentence: 'You know why I'm here. We don't need to explain anything to each other, do we?' It was as if she were establishing a common bond. The Americans called it the tie of recognition. Davina Wesley had looked at her tormentor; the pinched face, the harsh eyes. McKeague continued: 'We both know about obeying orders, don't we? And the cost of disobedience. Together, we've a chance of making it. Your only chance is if you stick with me.' She went on: 'Don't squirm. Just relax. We're in this together. You and me. I'll let you go all in good time. You'll see. I keep my word. Your bloody dogs and cats, though. They've got to go. Don't worry. I'll make it painless for them. Trust me. They're only animals. Don't wet yourself.'

Soon, from the kitchen below, there was the sound of four muffled shots. Then the cats howling. And the sound of running water. Davina Wesley realized her dogs had been executed and her cats drowned.

Then interminable silence. The incessant beating of her heart. The tightening of her ribcage. Throbbing in her ears. She supposed she was to be left like this, hanging here, until McKeague decided otherwise. What was meant by the 'only chance' she was far from sure. She tried to keep her mind working. She theorized, rehearsed logical arguments in her defence and pleas for sense and reason. She thought of Alan Rosslyn and of Bryan: she willed one or both of them to turn up unexpectedly. She would explain and justify everything to them. Now she was ready to talk, to make the peace, with Alan, Bryan, with anyone who cared to listen to her. Only: *Set me free. Let me live. PLEASE.*

Strung up and marooned in the darkness of her own bedroom, she imagined the light of the afternoon lengthening outside across her garden. There was no sound, except for the occasional footsteps from below, the noise of McKeague stalking through the house; taking her time.

If only the woman downstairs would set her free: she'd consent to any deal. If only. *Set me free. Let me live. PLEASE.*

35

Rosslyn read the sign on the gate: Montbretia Cottage.

The bungalow, built of Cotswold stone, was set back from the hillside road two miles south of Winchcombe. The front garden was the sort of colour riot you see in advertisements for seed merchants in the tabloid Sunday supplements. A perfect lawn surrounded the flowerbeds. A second carefully painted sign in five languages warned BEWARE OF THE DOG. Outside the front door, tied to a trelliswork construction for rambling roses, was a makeshift flag-pole. A Union Jack dangled from it at half-mast.

He left his car on the roadside verge, adjusted the gun in the holster beneath his jacket and let himself through the garden gate. He didn't want to excite the dog, cause an alarm or set the old soldier Coker on edge, so he made his way to the front door across the lawn. When he sounded the bell a peal of electric chimes sounded inside. There was no reply to the funereal chords. No barking dog.

He took a deep breath. Perhaps Coker had gone AWOL. He waited a few minutes. He saw Montbretia Cottage was equipped with elaborate burglar alarms. There were small video cameras tucked in beneath the roof. A small red light flashed from one of them. He checked his watch. It was past 5.30 p.m. and he'd promised himself an hour or so with Coker here, then he'd drive on to Manchester to find Wesley's sons. He had given no prior warning of these visits. Instead, en route, he'd asked Harding's office to send a local police officer round to the Wesleys' student squat near Alexandra Park in Manchester as well as here, to Coker's place; and, as far as the local police could tell, the men he wanted to see would, most probably, be at their respective houses when he called. The police had been told to watch the residences discreetly without raising suspicion. Rosslyn hoped the local coppers had got it right.

'Can I help you?' a man's voice said softly behind him.

Rosslyn turned round sharply to see a small powerful man wearing a shirt of Indian cotton outside a pair of blue linen trousers. His eyes were hidden behind dark glasses. He was standing a few feet away, barefoot and holding a machete. His head was shaven and his sunburned face ended in a trim greying beard. Not what you'd expect to see in an English country garden – this bouncer with his glinting heavy slasher, with the muscles of a bodybuilder pumped full of steroids. When Rosslyn showed him his ID, the man looked at it with suspicion. 'Well now, Mr Rosslyn, what brings you to Montbretia? I didn't know the Customs performed their duties in the Cotswolds. Or are you to do with VAT?'

'No. I'd very much appreciate a few moments of your time, Mr Coker.'

He looked Rosslyn up and down. 'You must be hot in that suit of yours.' He fingered the sharp cutting edge of the machete. 'Carrying a weapon, are we? Well, well. How d'you know my name?'

'This is Mr Levy's house, isn't it?' Rosslyn asked, avoiding the issue of the gun. 'And he was your friend.'

'You could say so, yes. I'm Coker. Cokey. And correction, I'd say I was a friend to poor old Lev. That's what we called him. Lev. And you want to reminisce about Lev. Or d'you want to talk about me?'

'About Mr Levy, if it's OK with you. I don't want to intrude on you, so soon after your loss.'

'Come round the back then. We'll have a mug of tea, or something stronger if you prefer.'

The two men walked around the side of the house. From there the view stretched to the horizon, a magnificent panorama of rolling fields, streams and woodland.

'Great view,' Rosslyn said. 'Really nice.'

'Yes,' said Coker. 'More's the pity Lev never saw it. He bought this place for his dog and me. In that order.'

'And he'd go to work each day in London from so far away?'

'Yes. That's what he did, four days a week. A cab to Cheltenham, well, more a driver from GCHQ. And I stayed back here playing mother. Gardener, cook, repair man, you name it. Vet even. I was into dogs in the army. Pull up the canvas chair. That was Lev's.'

On the wooden table outside the open kitchen door there was a large jug of orange juice and a bottle of vodka. Beside the jug Rosslyn noticed a tape recorder and a pile of some half-dozen unmarked tapes. There were also several used glasses and a bucket of melted ice.

'You'd do better with a cold drink, Mr Ross.'

'Rosslyn.'

'Welsh?'

'Maybe, way back,' Rosslyn answered vaguely.

'Not Irish?'

'Not to my knowledge. We're all a little Irish, aren't we?'

'Micks don't usually agree with me,' Coker said darkly. He set the machete on the table. 'You'll do better with a Cokey special. Vod and orange.' He poured orange juice into the glasses with the same large quantity of vodka. His hands were shaking. He pushed a glass across the table to Rosslyn, then slumped down into a deckchair, raising his sunglasses to his shining forehead. Rosslyn noticed Coker's eyes were bloodshot and watery, an alcoholic's eyes. He might have been weeping. He raised his tumbler.

'To Lev,' he said. 'Old Lev. Wherever he may be.'

'To Lev,' said Rosslyn. 'Absent friends.'

'Old Lev who's discovered more friends in death than he ever had in life. That's the beauty of it. If you'd call them friends, trooping the colour out here with an "I'm from Special Branch. I'm from the Security Service. I'm from GCHQ. I'm an intelligence officer." I count them in and I count them out like that bloke in the

Falklands. I've even had the bloody Foreign Office out here. All for Lev. Lev for all. Lev was born in the dark. He wasn't afraid of anyone. Not even me. I don't frighten you, do I?'

'No,' said Rosslyn untruthfully.

'That's good. We know where we stand. Dare say I'll be getting more visitors out here in jolly old Montbretia. TV. Journalists. I watch a lot of TV. Must be funny to see yourself on it.'

We have a windbag here. May open up on his own accord. With no prompting. Or maybe he's another time-wasting barrack-room lawyer who's on a binge, bleeding inside for old Lev.

'You must be pleased to get visitors then?' Rosslyn asked.

'Don't get me wrong. I'm not lonely. Graduate of the university of hard knocks, that's Cokey. Not much you can tell me.'

'And these people from the Security Service, what did they have to say?'

Coker stretched his massive arms above his head. 'That's just what they said. They all wanted to know what I'd told everyone else. All more interested in that and not what I *could* say, right. I thought, fuck 'em. Told them nothing.' He heaved himself forward in the deckchair to tap the tape recorder. 'I said, "I don't talk about my private life unless it's for cash. Up front. On the table. No cheques. No credit cards. Cash." And I tell them everything must be taped by me. That shuts the buggers up.' He slumped back in the deckchair. Some of the orange and vodka slopped down his white shirt. 'Shit.'

'I've come to say I'm sad about what happened.'

Coker laughed. 'You knew Lev, then?'

'Not really.'

'How can you be sorry, then?'

Rosslyn stared into his glass. Coker wasn't going to move. He had cash. Even if he offered whatever Coker asked, he reckoned the man wasn't going to talk.

'I've made it a rule,' Coker said. 'A rule.' He refilled his glass, this time from the vodka bottle alone. 'Never to do a favour unless I've had one in return. I don't mean words, promises. I mean actions. As in the army. You get medals for actions, not words. You want to know what I mean?'

'Tell me. I'd like to hear.'

'Take these ponces who've come out here to see Cokey – all

expenses paid. Not one did a thing for Lev. Not bloody one of them. Know something?'

'What's that?' Rosslyn asked with a friendly smile.

'I'll tell you something. One person visited me here like yesterday, could have been the day before. I was, you know, a bit pissed. Fact, very pissed. Odd thing is this woman, she's quiet, soft-spoken, a Mick. Irish. Wears this crucifix around her neck. She's a nurse. Know what, she's come out here from London. Why? Because she was the one who scraped up Lev's remains, with Montgomery's too.'

'Who's Montgomery?'

'Monty Montbretia was Lev's guide dog. He never harmed a soul.' Here he removed a tape from the recorder. 'The nurse sang along with me. Here, with me, from where you're sitting. In that very chair. "Danny Boy". And I recorded it. On this.' He lifted the tape to his lips and kissed it. 'She was really lovely. One of us.' He flicked at the tape with his forefinger, then gently tossed it on to the pile of others.

Rosslyn kept his eyes on it.

'So sweet, this nurse,' Coker went on. 'I thought, you know, someone's got to say the truth. So I told her this and that. No names, mind – no pack drill. Well, let's say, no pack drill but a few names, not that they'd mean anything to her. She was impressed with what Lev and me had made of Montbretia. How did we manage on Lev's salary? What were the perks? So I explained how Lev was good with money. Not that he wasn't tight-fisted. "Mother must prepare for the rainy days," he used to say. "Old Mother Lev who lives in a shoe."' Tears started from his eyes. 'Yep, they were good days we had. And the nurse knew what real grief means. She had a sister she loved who was arrested on suspicion of terrorist charges.'

Rosslyn flinched.

'The cops or someone did for the sister,' Coker continued. 'The bastards didn't have the balls to admit they were out of order. But they wouldn't, would they? They beat her up in custody. This nurse, Angela, Angie, she was never allowed to give her sister a decent burial. It's the same with me and Lev. The bastards won't let me have his remains because it's suicide. Until they're satisfied there wasn't any foul play. And Angie says she knows there wasn't. Lev wasn't well. He'll have blacked out and fallen. There was always the chance it'd end like this. We all die alone in the end, don't we? Well, I believe *they* had it in for Lev. *They* wanted to see him done in, didn't they?'

'I don't see why they should,' Rosslyn said.

'What's it to do with the Customs?'

'I think Mr Levy may not have died accidentally. That he was murdered by someone we're trying to trace. Didn't any of your previous visitors suggest that to you?'

'Yes, they did. But I didn't believe it.'

'Why not?' Rosslyn asked.

'Because Lev was too useful to the authorities.'

'You mean he had enemies?' Rosslyn suggested.

'Don't we all have enemies?'

'Most of us do, yes. But not the sort who set out to murder us. You see, I think there's every possibility Lev was conned into meeting someone in the underground at Camden Town. Someone who deliberately planned to push him beneath that train and make it look like suicide.'

'Angie said that's not what happened,' Coker said.

'Yes. But she hasn't had the benefit of seeing the forensic scientists' reports. They're beginning to tell a different story. They point to the person we want to find.'

'Who is it?'

'A person who's already killed three people,' Rosslyn said. 'And tried to kill a fourth, maybe even a fifth. And Lev could've been victim number six, along the way.'

Rosslyn ached to shout it out. *The nurse: she isn't Angie. She's Insect.* He wanted, here and now, to reel off the roll-call of dead and injured. *You drunken freak: she's been sitting here. It's Dee McKeague's sister. So she has a sister.* He remembered the interview at Paddington Green. She was going to trade in her nearest and dearest. *Who's protecting this sister?*

'I don't like being told Lev was involved in anything like this.'

'I don't like it either,' Rosslyn said. 'You don't know this, but one of those who died was my girlfriend. So I know a little bit how you're feeling. To me this is personal as well as professional. But I'm seeing you on a professional basis. I promise you, it's in everyone's interest that you tell me if you can think of anything,

anything which could explain why someone wanted to kill Lev. Don't you want to see Lev's killer caught?'

Coker looked into the distance like someone seeing a change in the weather. He was about to say something, then thought better of it.

What's he holding back? Rosslyn wondered. *He's thinking up a deal, like Dee McKeague's; he wants to save his own bloody skin. Maybe he's the heir to whatever little fortune Lev's stashed away. The bungalow and garden could be worth a quarter of a million – enough to see him out with vodka and orange for the rest of his days. Given the quantity he puts down, there may not be too many days left to him. Or has he already done some deal with the previous visitors, spilled the beans and got immunity from prosecution? Coker has form. He's known to SIS. He's a player too, like everyone else.*

Coker got to his feet unsteadily. 'I don't want to talk any more, Mr Rosslyn. I've seen a lot of trouble. I learned my lessons in the army and I got a lawyer to put my case. And that's what I've got to do now. I need someone on my side.' He walked a few steps across the lawn and continued talking with his back to Rosslyn.

This was the moment when Rosslyn palmed the tape from the table and slipped it into his jacket pocket.

'I've already said too much,' Coker said. He fell silent.

'I think you would be wise to talk to a lawyer,' Rosslyn said. 'That's what I'd do if I were you.'

'Are you leaving now?'

Rosslyn was on his feet. 'Yes.'

They walked together around the house. 'It'll be a help to you to find a good solicitor,' Rosslyn said. 'He'll advise you on your rights. Tell him everything you can. It'll be best not to talk to anyone else in the meantime.'

'That's what the others said. That's why I liked talking to the nurse. She's the only one who seemed to care. You too. You've got to appreciate I don't like the police. It's in the blood. I'm sorry you lost your girl. You didn't tell me what happened.' He leaned across the roof of Rosslyn's car.

'Some other day, perhaps, Mr Coker.'

He drove away as fast as the twisting road allowed. Minutes later he got through to Harding on the car phone: 'Deirdre McKeague's sister. Who is she? Where is she? What's her full name? It could be

Angela or Angie or not. She could be a nurse, or have disguised herself as a nurse. And don't forget there was a nurse seen in England's Lane just before the bomb went off.'

'It'll take time,' Harding said.

'It can't wait. Hold on.'

He shoved the tape into the slot below the car radio. He heard a woman's voice, flat and plaintive, singing 'Danny Boy'.

'Stay on the line,' he told Harding. He fast-forwarded.

It was Coker's voice he heard next:

They provided Lev with this thing, gear called an Apollo speech system. It's a voice synthesizer for the blind. You tap the keys, it speaks the words. Brilliant. You can tune the voice up and down, like it could be a man's, a woman's, a kid's. You can't tell who's talking because it's a machine. He'd do the business sometimes for people in the intelligence game. Act as go-between. This woman would use the same kind of system so he never knew her voice. That way everyone's identity was scrambled. You're talking big-time, I mean Lev was talking with the IRA, the bombers, hit-men, you name it. He took his orders and obeyed instructions and got paid in cash. So what did he do wrong? He ends up under the bloody tube train. All because he did what he was asked, soldiering on, one blind sod doing his bit for good old England.

'Can you hear this?'

'Some of it,' Harding said. 'You'd better call me back when you've heard the rest. We'll put the call out on McKeague's sister. And I hope you're right about her.'

'So do I,' Rosslyn said. He pulled down the sun flap against the glare of the sun, lowering behind the Cotswolds. He looked at his watch. With luck, before nightfall, he'd be in Manchester.

36

Davina Wesley winced when the industrial adhesive tape was peeled from her face. Still worse was the pain as feeling returned to her shoulders.

'The two of us alone,' McKeague said. 'Now we're going to keep very calm, right?' She drummed her fingernails against the handgun. 'We're in this together. You need me, don't forget.' She seemed very cool. 'Everyone's compromised now, aren't they? And your problems are soon going to be over, right?'

Davina Wesley tried to speak. Her mouth was completely dry and she found the words wouldn't come.

Her silence must have seemed to McKeague to be a provocation. Suddenly McKeague hit her in the face.

She covered her stinging mouth with her hands thinking: *I am dealing with a psychopath*.

'We're going over to Beaconsfield together,' McKeague said. 'There's no hurry.'

'You may not get in,' Davina Wesley said, trying to placate her. 'They may not let you in.'

'But you're going to take me there – with you.'

'What are you going to do?'

'What am I going to do? Once we get inside, you'll see. Unless you want to end up in your deep-freeze with your cats and dogs.'

'I . . . I'll have to call the security people. If we're to make an unexpected visit. We can't just turn up at the barrier unannounced. They don't know you.'

'That's your problem.'

'You want me to drive you into Beaconsfield, then into the unit, tonight?'

'Yes.'

Here was a moment of hope. *Good. Play for time*. The guards knew every member of staff. Any visitor needed a pass and McKeague didn't have one.

'You're going to pull rank,' McKeague was saying. She seemed to be reading Davina Wesley's thoughts. 'There won't be a search. If you fuck up, or let the guards think there's anything wrong, I'll blow your head off and theirs too.'

'What is it you want?'

'I'll tell you when we get inside.'

'Is this to do with my work?'

'What d'you think?'

'But you don't know what my work is.'

'Don't I? I'll have you know I've done your dirty work for you. I've worked both sides. The army, RUC, Special Branch, MI5. They all trust me. So do my own people. I know about your fucking work because the army told me about Beaconsfield way back when. I know what precautions they took in the Falklands too. What the fucking RAF knew about Saddam's nerve gases. I know what scares the Brits shitless. So do you. Because the fucking Brits manufactured the gas along with the Japs.'

'Is it the gas you want?'

'You'll see.'

'Or some other device?'

'You'll see. I wouldn't be here if it was possible to bomb Thames House. It's impossible, isn't it? You know that. It's built of steel and stone and concrete.'

'It's the gas, isn't it?' Davina Wesley persisted.

'Whatever it takes to wipe them out. The whole lot. Maximum of three minutes once the gas is in the air supply. There's one man I want to die in there. The bastard who murdered my sister. The Customs shit. He's got away with it once. This time he won't. Count yourself lucky. Now you're going to clean yourself up. Do something with that face of yours. And wear this gear.'

McKeague tossed her a pair of trainers and a tracksuit she'd taken from the wardrobe. 'I know whose voice has been on the phone to me. The same fucking voice that told me where to get the fee. Out of your husband's safe. Who arranged for me to get the tape from the man in the tube station. What about the bastard, the Customs man, Rosslyn?'

'I don't know what you're talking about,' Davina whispered.

McKeague was smiling now. 'Christ, I thought you'd be devious. But you're very devious, Davina. I almost admire you. You're really bent. Now I know your name too, do you know something? I feel a whole lot better. I never did like the feeling of not knowing everything about you. Now I do, and it feels good. Much better.' She opened the curtains a few inches. 'We'll wait until it's dark,' she said. 'Tidy yourself up. You've got a reputation to preserve.'

37

Rosslyn had Coker's taped voice for company in his car on the way north to Manchester. He listened to the poor and sometimes indistinct recording with a new feeling of lightheadedness. Like when a child finds a fifty-pound note on the pavement and the local copper says, 'I'd keep it, laddie' – or when you watch some sweating Arab open up his bags and his designer talc can is stuffed with cocaine and you've got him. Possession is nine-tenths of the game. Here was Coker, the worse for wear, talking to the sweet and sympathetic 'Angie' in the peace of the sunny Cotswolds:

Lev was what you'd call the 'Statutory Crip' – you know, the poor disabled bastard you have to employ. Mind you, there was nothing wrong with his brain. He was a bloody genius with money and technology. Only thing was he couldn't see, could he? So the Security Service Commission treat him like a bit of a pet, along with Monty.

Now, on the whole, Lev never asked questions about the jobs they gave him. He trusts the SCC people to be kosher, above board. It's secret work. And much of it he doesn't piece together. Interdepartmental disputes, office politics, confidential complaints.

Then this department head in MI5 comes to him with the instruction he act as conduit between her and this IRA double agent. This woman is giving Lev her instructions, already processed – she's used a compatible system – and he's being asked to forward them on, so there can be no trace. None.

Then there's 'Angie' asking: 'He gave all the instructions?' And Coker says:

I don't know. She used the same system. Listen, I'm saying Lev was only a conduit. He did what he was told. He got paid a bonus in cash. Always cash. Here, I think, that's odd. Cash. Not a bonus cheque. Cash. And old Lev, he thinks, maybe this isn't right. So he puts a trace on the phone numbers. And he comes up with the number of this person in Amersham. Her name's Davina Wesley.

Rosslyn shuddered. Four times he replayed this section of the tape: 'the number of this person in Amersham. Her name's Davina Wesley.'

Then 'Angie' is asking: 'What's the number?' And Coker says he doesn't remember whether Lev ever mentioned the number itself. If he did, well, he's forgotten it. 'It's only for emergencies. Strictly business – official.'

*

Rosslyn hunched over the steering wheel trying to concentrate on the traffic, listening to the tape of Coker's meandering gravelly voice. He hated having to believe Davina had betrayed him and that she too, like Mary, had concealed the truth.

He pulled out into the fast lane, slamming the horn at a lumbering container truck. Its klaxon deafened him. Davina had opened his wounds of grief.

She got her teeth into me. She has betrayed me. She's made me bleed. She's a liar. And last night, Jesus knows, last night I was in bed with her. I allowed myself to be seduced by her. Totally abandoned myself to her, let her try to heal me with her sex. He thought of his letter to her, travelling with a million others, like his thoughts, in as many different directions.

I have betrayed myself. I've been conned by a one-night stand.

What has she done? he asked himself.

He replayed the tape. Coker's voice sickened him and the sensation it produced seemed horribly similar to the nausea he had felt when reading Mary's diary.

What has she done?

His imagination failed to produce a coherent answer.

Headlights from a bus close behind flashed into his driving mirror. He swerved into the centre lane. The bus overtook him at over ninety. Some German tourist group from Bremen. In the rear window he glimpsed three laughing girls with shaven heads. He caught sight of their blackened teeth and their faces painted white like circus clowns from a nightmare. They were sticking their tongues out at him blowing him obscene kisses, mocking him. He felt he was now the circus clown. He was tempted to leave the motorway, to return to Davina.

No point in going back to hear more lies. She'll keep. I want straight answers.

He felt his fury getting the better of him. Let's try her kids. They won't tell the truth about themselves but they'll grass everybody else up.

38

It was barely light when he reached the 1960s tower blocks beyond Manchester's Alexandra Park Road. Arlington House was the block he had to find, where the Wesley sons hung out in a student squat. Most of the street signs had been obliterated by spray paint; and the prostitutes, white, black and under age, leered at him from the pavements. He found himself in a line of cars also being driven by single men glancing furtively at the sad parade of women. Then he saw the notice ARLINGTON HOUSE. Someone had altered it to FARTING HOUSE STINKS.

He parked his car between two wrecked vans. A gust of warm wind threw dust in his eyes and there was the beat of reggae pumping from the windows of the tower block. Most of the ground-floor windows had been boarded up. They too had been painted over with obscenities. In a doorway across the street he saw two dark figures and glimpsed the passing of a package wrapped in silver foil. Any other night he'd have nicked them for possession of illegal substances. They too, like the prostitutes, looked little more than fourteen years old. He decided to take his bag with him from the car and instinctively he felt the bulge of his gun and holster.

Two flights of concrete stairs, reeking of urine, led to the door of the flat where the police had said the sons of Wesley squatted. There was no bell, so he thumped the door.

No answer.

A black girl stuck her head out of a window in the next door flat.

'Jonathan and Felix Wesley live here?'

'Yeah.'

'Do you know, are they at home?'

'Yeah.'

'Thanks.' He beat on the door again.

The girl said: 'Like sex, yeah?'

'Not tonight, thanks.'

'You don't like me, yeah?'

Rosslyn shrugged.

The door to the flat opened suddenly. 'Hello,' Rosslyn said. 'Are Jonathan and Felix Wesley at home?'

'So?' The man's voice was almost drowned out by the stereo.

'I'd like to talk to them,' Rosslyn shouted above the din.

The man yelled into the flat for the volume to be turned down. He sniffed. 'Why?'

Rosslyn saw a girl in a T-shirt, nothing else, peering at him from the gloomy hallway. The place seemed filled with a dozen cats. 'Christ,' she said, 'don't let the fucker in.'

'Don't worry,' Rosslyn said. 'No one's in any trouble.'

'Like what trouble?' the man said. There were open sores around his mouth.

'I'm a friend of their mother's,' Rosslyn said. 'It's a family thing. She's asked me to bring them some cash.'

'Are you buying or selling?'

'No.'

'You're a cop?'

'No I'm not. If I was, would I be here alone?'

'You have smack?'

'I've told you. I just want to give some cash to Felix and Jonathan and I'm in a hurry.'

The black girl next door was shouting: 'OK, OK, Johnnie. Show him in, yeah.'

'Felix is next door,' the man said, touching his mouth sores. 'She'll let you in, won't you Claret?'

'That's her name, Claret?'

'Claretta. She's known as Claret. Claret Glass – the one with the honey arse.'

'Thanks for the introduction.'

Claretta showed him into the flat. Once she'd closed the door and set the safety chain in place, she grinned. Rosslyn saw she was holding an open flick knife. 'If you're a cop, I'll say you raped me and I opened you up in self-defence, yeah?'

'Fortunately, for both of us, Claretta – '

'Ms Glass,' she threatened.

'Fortunately, Ms Glass, I'm not a cop. Just a friend of the family.'

'A fucking spook,' said a man's voice behind Rosslyn. 'What's your name?'

'Alan Rosslyn.'

He was tall, a little over six feet, unmistakably his mother's son and, strangely, thought Rosslyn, dressed in a pale blue silk dressing gown just like hers.

'You're a friend, a spook, one of the enemy too, Mr Alan Rosslyn.' His left ear lobe was missing and Rosslyn could tell from the punctured swollen forearm that whichever son this was had a long-term problem with dirty needles. 'Who are you? How do you know I live here?'

'Your mother told me.'

'She doesn't know where I live.'

Jesus. I've blown it. Claretta's fist clenched round the handle of the flick knife. 'She does. Who else could have told me?'

'The cops, Mr Alan Rosslyn. The cops. I don't like them. They don't like me. I don't like my mother. And she doesn't like me.'

It wasn't difficult to see why. Rosslyn held his ground. 'Well, Felix – or is it Jonathan? Which?'

'He's Filo,' said Claretta. 'As in pastry, yeah.'

'Well, Filo, your mother Davina, she's very anxious to hear from you. So much so that I've got five hundred quid for you.' He glanced at Claretta in time to see her eyes widen.

'What's the catch?' the man said.

'She wants you to phone her. Tell her you've got the cash.'

The man looked at Rosslyn quickly. 'I haven't got it yet.'

'For fuck's sake, Felix,' Claretta snapped. 'Christ, what am I hearing?'

'Fuck off, Claret,' Felix shouted. He breathed out sharply, his lips flapping. 'Mum wants me to phone her?'

'That's what she'd like.'

'Tough shit. I haven't got a phone.'

Rosslyn took out his wallet. He thumbed through ten fifty-pound notes, took them out, and folded them into a wedge. 'I have a car phone. You can use that.'

'I don't want to talk to her.'

'OK, fine, why don't we talk to her together?'

Claretta was seized with greater determination. 'Do it, Filo.'

'But I don't know who you are.'

Rosslyn began to fabricate: 'Sometimes I visit Manchester, right. I'm in the printing trade. I travel. Some friend of your mother's told her I could use my line of chat to give you the money. I'm supposed to be persuasive. That's my game. Getting people to use our printing facilities. I'm just doing a goddamn favour.' He looked at his watch. 'I have an appointment at Ringway – so if we can make the call, you get the cash, I've done the favour, and that's about your lot.' He sniffed the air. 'And if I was a cop I'd have arrested you two already, wouldn't I?'

Claretta folded the blade back into the handle of the knife.

'I've got to find Mum's numbers,' Felix said. 'Or do you have them?'

'No, I don't. You get the numbers, whatever, and we'll call her.'

Felix disappeared further inside the flat. Rosslyn watched Claretta fingering the leaves of a yucca tree.

'What's his mother like?' she asked.

'I hear she's really nice,' Rosslyn said.

'That's not what I hear, yeah.'

'What do you hear, then?'

Claretta grinned. 'I'll tell you what I heard.'

'Go on.'

'I heard she likes women too.'

'I don't follow you.'

She was looking at him with mock pity. 'Where have you *been* for the last ten years?'

'Well, well, well,' Rosslyn said.

'You're not very bright, are you?'

'I was always a slow reader at my school.'

'I'm surprised you ever got to school.'

'Tell me what you heard.'

'You want it on a plate, then?'

'If that's the way it has to be, yes.'

'I heard she got about the women members of staff.'

'I don't deal in gossip.'

'And you don't seem to deal in much else, either.'

'All right, let's have it your way, then. What's the gossip?'

'I heard she had at least *two* affairs.'

'Who with?'

'You are uphill work, aren't you? Frances someone. And this Frances, she dumped Davina for younger meat. Some fem called Serena. And the rows. *Jesus*. This woman, Serena, comes up to see Filo and Jonathan, and she raves and rants, screaming at the boys to tell their mother to get fucked. "Your mother's a jealous bitch. Nothing she won't stoop to. Even murder." It was terrible. Like, awful.'

209

Felix was shouting: 'I can't find the *fucking* thing.'

'Then fucking *look* in the grass drawer.'

Rosslyn felt the warmth of her breath. 'It totally bust Jonathan. You know, he's in hospital. Clinical depression. He's totally fucked out. Yeah. Couldn't handle it. I mean. Could you?'

'You say she threatened to murder Frances and Serena?'

'Sure – she's *disturbed*. Doesn't know who she is. Crazy. Bisexual. Like physically and emotionally she fucks everything in sight. Mentally, well, I mean, either you are sane, or you aren't, yeah?'

'Felix knows all of this?'

'You aren't bright, are you? I've *fucking* told you. He hates MI *fucking* Five. Hot-house. Whored-ing boarding school. They cover up everything, don't they? Including murder.'

Her look. Her frown. The large wide eyes. The intensity. The extent to which she seemed to pity Felix told him she was like a traveller making the truthful declaration. 'What does his old man think?' he asked her.

'*Think*? How would I know? He's on the game too. Ask Felix. Those people are bent. They're all the same. *Twisted*. So fucking screwed up you wonder they can stand up in the morning.'

'You've met the father?'

'If you call it meeting, yeah. I mean, I'm black. His son's girl. You can't think he's ever going to love me much. He's not your average *Guardian* reader.'

'But he has been here?'

'Sure. To throw money at the mental home in the hopes the shrinks would unscramble Jonathan's brains. He throws money at Jonathan too. "If you talk to me, I'll give you a fiver for every word." He's trying to buy his son off like a rent-boy. It's really evil. He tries Felix too. Showers him with cash to move out of here. Get the fuck away from me. "You can't seriously think, old man, that it's a good idea to sleep with a black girl." Then he realizes Felix is a junkie and blames me for that.'

'That's where he's wrong.' Felix was standing in the gloom at the far end of the corridor. 'You can't buy people off,' he added. 'Even Mum wouldn't try that. That's why I don't get this move of hers. To send me this five hundred quid.'

'I suppose she wants to make the peace,' Rosslyn said. 'After all that's happened in her life.' After a pause, he added gently: 'Did you hear what Claret was telling me?'

'Yeah, it's all true. Don't you believe her?'

Rosslyn shrugged. 'It's none of my business.'

'What do you know about our business?' Felix asked.

'Nothing,' Rosslyn said. 'I heard you and your brother are students . . .'

In his mind he saw Davina's garden. For a second it was *her* voice telling him how she'd been in Manchester the week before the deaths of Monro and Watson. Hadn't she been here to see Jonathan's theatre production? He was 'the actor in the family' and she'd wanted to take the k d lang compact disc to him. 'That was when I heard the awful news' – that Monro and Watson had been blown to kingdom come.

He heard his own voice adding: '. . . and I heard something about Jonathan being an actor.'

'He's for real,' Felix said bitterly. 'How can he fucking act? He hasn't spoken a word for months – for eighteen months. He sits in front of TV with the other nutters nodding and moaning. It's horrific.'

'All because your mother's gay?' Rosslyn said. 'What do you – ?'

'Look,' Felix interrupted sharply. 'I don't give a shit about gays. People's sex lives. What they do in bed. That's their business. I'm not even jealous of Claret, am I?'

Claret gave a sanguine nod.

'My mother doesn't need me to pity her. Am I supposed to feel sorry for her? I feel sorry for myself.' He showed Rosslyn the mess of his inside arm. 'See?'

The bruised and swollen veins filled Rosslyn with disgust.

'So she's been dumped. What do you want me to do about it? I reckon the woman did my mum a favour. I just wish – *I just wish* my mother would stay out of my life.'

'You'll take her money, won't you?' Rosslyn said.

Felix looked over Rosslyn's shoulder. 'Yeah. Sure. Let's get it over with, right?' He pushed past Rosslyn out of the door.

'It's been nice meeting you,' Claret said with a limp and dismissive flick of her hand.

'You too,' Rosslyn lied and hurried down the flight of concrete stairs.

'Aren't you scared?' Felix asked while Rosslyn unlocked the car.

'Of this place?' Rosslyn said.

'I mean, you look nervous.'

'So do you.'

They got into the front of the car side by side. Rosslyn kept the doors and windows closed in spite of the septic smell of Felix's body. He noticed there were bloodstains on the blue silk dressing gown. 'Tell me her number,' Rosslyn said. 'And I'll dial.'

'I have four numbers for her. One at home, one for her personal fax, one for her office, and one . . . an emergency number.'

'Read them out.'

Felix obeyed. Rosslyn scribbled the four numbers down on the inside page of his road atlas. Then he dialled the home number and turned up the speaker's volume so they could both listen.

After a few rings they heard Davina's voice: 'I am sorry there is no one available to take your call right now. But if you will leave your name, number and the time you called I will get back to you as soon as possible. Please speak after the tone.'

Rosslyn handed the telephone to Felix with the wedge of notes.

'Hi . . . er, this is Felix. Mr Rosslyn here has given me the cash. It's a lot . . . er, thanks a lot too. See you one of these days soon. Hope you're fine . . . er, that's it, thanks.'

Felix was breathing heavily. 'Makes me feel weird, that. Hearing her voice. Sounds no different.' He turned his face to Rosslyn. 'Level with me,' he said. 'You are a spook, aren't you?'

'No.'

But Rosslyn had undone his jacket. He was too late to stop Felix reaching over to touch the gun in its holster. 'Then what's the gun for?' There was a wild expression in his eyes. 'Why are you so jumpy?'

Rosslyn said: 'In my line of business you have to travel a lot alone. All sorts of places. You don't know what sort of people you'll meet. It's best to be prepared.'

'Are you a private eye?'

'No.'

'But you know my mother better than you've let on?'

'Maybe. Maybe not.'

'I want to know, is she in trouble?'

'Not as far as I know, Felix. What makes you think she might be?'

'Only what I read in the newspapers. When was it? March, the end of March. There was that bomb in England's Lane. Two civil servants, what were they, like, Home Office or something? They were killed by a bomb.'

'I know. I read about it.'

'And England's Lane was where Frances lived with Serena Watson. What you don't know is that I went down to London, King's Cross, to score some smack. And while I was about it I checked out England's Lane. And I spoke to this local newsagent and asked him, could he tell me where those two women were. He said, it wasn't any secret.'

'Why were you so interested?' Rosslyn asked.

'For Christ's sake.' Felix gazed ahead through the windscreen. 'You ask me why was I so interested? I've told you they were involved with my mother. She wanted them dealt with. If necessary, totally. You're a spook. You should know the form.'

'For the last time, I'm not a spook.'

'Then why are you so bloody interested?'

Rosslyn felt acid in his stomach. He tasted it in his mouth. And Felix's presence nauseated him. It was bad enough that he met pieces of filth like Felix day in and day out. But the fact that this was Davina's son filling his car with his body's stale stench made matters even worse. His nearness was repulsive. *Let's do the business and get out and as far away from you as possible.*

'And why are you giving me the fucking money? It isn't from my mother. That's just a front. You're covering up. You're no different from the other bastards who've been trying to question me.'

Rosslyn avoided the paranoid stare. He smiled painfully into the distance, aware of lights going on in the windows of the tower block.

'Those people from the Foreign Office, Special Branch, Home Office, or whatever Micky Mouse outfits they come from.' Felix laughed. 'You should've seen them. The suits. The official cars. The Bill have been nosing around only today. Asking if I'm at home. Some prat said yes.'

'What did you tell these people who came to see you?'

'Sweet fuck-all. You seriously think I'm going to tell them any fucking thing?'

Rosslyn thought: *For God's sake. Go ahead, arrest him. Bang him up.*

As far away from me *as possible. Give him all he wants of his beloved smack. Give it to him. Take it away from him. He'll talk.* His mind went into overdrive: something in him refused to accept – he was refusing to believe – what Felix and the girl had told him. He was a thousand miles from the quiet cubicles and the strip and search; even the safety of the basement cells at Paddington Green; the havens where the despair and fury was in the eyes of others and not his. He'd try a different tack.

He looked into Felix's bloodshot eyes. They were watching Rosslyn's fingers taking out another wad of notes. 'Listen to me, Felix. We don't know each other. We're not going to meet again. I'd understand, if one single word of what you and your girl have told me tonight is true, you'd have a big reason to hate your mother. But I think your story is total bullshit. You have a drug problem –'

'Just a minute,' Felix interrupted.

'No, you wait. I'm talking. You listen to me. No one gives a shit about gay women's antics. I don't, you don't, the law doesn't. So let's cut out all that crap.'

'I care.'

'There's only one thing you care about. And that's you. See this – ' He was holding the notes between his thumb and forefinger beneath Felix's nose. 'I'm giving you this cash from your mother.'

'Does anyone else know about this?'

'You do. Claret does. I do. And your mother. So do the people who monitor her calls. You've said nothing to the Security Service people who've tried to question you.'

Felix shivered.

'I can help you,' Rosslyn continued. 'I can get you a brief. I can call one here and now. Of course, the problem we have is that you are not going to make much of a witness. Juries tend to disbelieve addicts.'

'I can't testify against my mother.'

'Any trial will be *in camera*. That's not a problem. They can do what they like. It may not get that far if you answer just one very important question to me. Now. In words of one syllable. Was your mother responsible, in any way whatsoever, for murder? Now, Felix, go ahead. Answer me.'

'Yes,' Felix said hoarsely.

'Not on her own, though?' Rosslyn asked. 'She got someone else to set the bomb?'

Felix was staring out of the car. *He can't be far off his next fix.* 'Those two blokes. They have my smack. Please. Can I go?'

Rosslyn saw the two figures in the shadows of a broken doorway.

'I've got to go,' Felix was saying. He tried to get out of the car but Rosslyn touched the button to lock the doors. Then he pressed the button to lower the window of the passenger door.

'Tell them to wait for you.'

Felix sniffed. 'No. They haven't clocked me. They won't hang around if they see you with me.'

'OK, Felix. You tell me. Did your mother pay someone?'

'Yes.'

'Who?' asked Rosslyn, torn between disbelief and suspicion.

'I don't know.'

'Did she tell you it was down to her?'

'No.'

'Then how the hell do you know it was? You said "Yes", she fixed someone to do it. What is it you're *not* telling me? Come on, Felix.' He waved the money beneath Felix's nose. 'Think. What is this going to buy you. Lots of lovely smack. *Think.* What have you got at your end?'

'My father.'

'*He* paid the killer?'

'No. Ask his cleaning woman. Gloria. The Filipino.'

'Why? Were they involved?'

'Involved with Mum? No. I was involved with Gloria.'

'*You* were?'

'I've just told you.'

'What did she tell you?'

'Look, I've got to go.'

'You can. Once you've told me what Gloria told you.'

'She's clean.'

'We're all clean, Felix. Now, what the fuck did she tell you?'

'My father's flat was turned over. Right? Twenty-sixth of March. Gloria was there when it happened. This Irish woman forces Gloria to open the door. She, this woman, knows when Gloria appears, right? Someone's told her in advance. They must have. How else would she have known? No one knows my father's routines.' He fell silent.

'Go on.'

215

'I can't. Look. They're leaving.'

'OK, I'll come with you,' Rosslyn said.

'No, you fucking well won't.'

'Get out, Felix.'

They left the car. Rosslyn walked a few paces behind with Felix between him and the figures in the shadows.

'Hi!' Felix called. 'It's OK. This is Alan. He's my friend. We're together.'

They neared the shadows. The two dealers were dressed in black leather jackets, jeans and trainers.

'Cheap bastard,' one of the figures whispered.

Rosslyn saw the flurry of leather. The two men's knives.

'You're under arrest.' He drew his gun.

He saw the gold wrist bracelets. The edge of the broken bottle. Felix sinking to his knees.

Rosslyn fired into the first man's knees. Then, a second shot into the shoulder of the other, who spun round crazily. Rosslyn saw the man's gold teeth, the wide eyes.

'Don't kill me,' the man with the shattered knee whimpered.

'Get the hell out of here,' Rosslyn said.

'I can't,' said the man through his clenched gold teeth. 'I'm dying.'

'No, you aren't,' Rosslyn said. 'You'll live.'

'You'd better get a doctor,' Felix said, clutching his bleeding hands.

Rosslyn stooped over the man with wrist bracelets. He yanked a flat package out of the leather jacket. 'Here,' he said to Felix. 'It's yours. Once you've finished.'

'I'm hurt,' Felix said.

'I don't care,' Rosslyn said. He saw the two figures trying to crawl away. *'Don't move!'*

They lay on the ground, moaning.

'Felix. Just get back to the car.'

The blue dressing gown was drenched in blood.

For a moment, getting into the car, Rosslyn listened. The stereos blasting out the reggae; some news programme on TV. The noise had covered the sound of the gun.

He turned on the headlights. Across the street the lights showed the two men struggling to crawl away. Rosslyn drove the car up to them and kept them in the beam of light. The figures crawled on: Rosslyn advanced. Two snails, one tortoise.

'This woman was in your father's flat.'

'Yes.'

Rosslyn kept his eyes on the crawling leather. 'And?'

'She tied up Gloria. She made my father – he was naked, in his bath – she made him get out, go to his safe, open it, and give her what was in it.'

'What was in it?'

'Gloria said she heard the sum of two hundred thousand pounds in foreign currency.'

'What was your father doing with that much?'

'He used it to pay agents.'

'All of it?'

'I don't know what he did with it.'

'Who else knew about this cash in the safe?'

'I didn't, did I? I wasn't there.'

'But Gloria was,' Rosslyn said.

'Yes. And I guess my mother knew too. She must have known. She knows everything about my father. That's why she's left him.'

'And this woman takes the money leaving Gloria behind?'

'Yes. Tied up. And my father. Gloria's sister finds them like that.'

'Why didn't she call the police, or did she?'

'They're illegal immigrants, aren't they? My father threatened to report them if they said anything. So they didn't. They're frightened of my father.'

'Does he know you were involved with Gloria?'

'No.'

'Is it still going on?'

'No. And I'd rather you didn't say anything about it.'

'Who to?'

'Claret.'

'No, I won't say anything.' The two figures had given up the struggle. One of them had apparently lost consciousness. 'OK, Felix, take the rest of this.' He handed over the money. 'If I were you I'd clear out of Manchester right now. Those two are going to say you shot them for the smack. I'd disappear for a time. Until all this is over. Right now you're in trouble. So is your mother, so is your father.'

217

'So are you,' Felix said.

'Me? I'm not in any trouble. Now get lost, Felix.'

Rosslyn watched Felix shamble across to the entrance to the tower block. He was clutching his arm, the cash and the heroin. Rosslyn drove round the two men huddled in the gutter. One of them yelled out: 'Fuck you!'

Same to you, Rosslyn thought, and thanks for being there when I needed you. Unlike policemen, there's always a heroin dealer around just when you need one most.

Now Davina: will you be there when I want *you* most? Where are you now? In the garden, under the moon, with the dogs, the fancy wine, the heady perfume? You are going to take me straight to Insect. No more gentleness, no more feeling sorry. It's open warfare now. You're under siege. You're taking me straight to the scum who murdered Mary and I'm going to feed you to your *fugu* fish.

He left Manchester for the south and Amersham.

39

At 11.25 p.m. Davina Wesley stands in the clutter of her study. McKeague releases the safety catch on her handgun. Click. She's growing impatient with Davina's nervousness. They've come to the study to telephone the security guards on gate duty at the STR Unit in Beaconsfield. McKeague has prepared the text of the brief message Davina will give them. Davina's word perfect. That's fine. But each time she rehearses her delivery of the text she sounds tense and agitated.

Now McKeague has her try again: 'Davina Wesley. I've got to collect some papers from my office some time before midnight. I'll be unaccompanied and staying about half an hour. Thank you.'

She tries to concentrate on how to please McKeague with her delivery. She's perplexed by McKeague's avowed intentions. What did she say? 'Whatever it takes to wipe them out. The whole lot . . . There's one man I want to die in there . . . The Customs shit' – Alan – and the raving about the nerve gas.

True, there are supplies of it in deep storage at STRU. But McKeague isn't a scientist-technician, trained in the use of the apparatus required to initiate a controlled release of the lethal tetrodotoxin. She guesses: *McKeague has in mind some longer-term offensive. Put yourself in her position. Supply tetrodotoxin to her Dublin masters for eventual distribution to the IRA's active UK mainland units. Announce they're in possession of the most lethal weapons of nerve gas warfare known to man. It represents a bargaining counter of formidable proportions.* What scares Davina, and diverts her concentration from the casual warning message to the duty guards, is McKeague's evasiveness.

She imagines the worst: *This calm and extraordinarily self-possessed woman is obviously enjoying herself. Each move she makes seems governed by an unusual, almost military precision. It's what you'd expect from the experienced bomber, the street operator, the planter of devices: but the complete lack of anxiety she shows shortly before her penetration of STRU is uncanny. More, she reveals no apparent fear of the tetrodotoxin. You only need to think of men, women and children suffering instant death as they inhale the minutest quantity of the poison. Death from a weapon spreading through the air none can see.*

Now, the call to the security guards on duty at the gate has to be made. When Davina stands in her study, about to make the call, she grows still more nervous.

She notices the telephone bells have been switched off. That, at least, is one good sign. She is always in at night; if she intends to go out then she has to follow the rule to tell the duty guards of her whereabouts. There is the chance they might have tried to telephone her earlier. Indeed, to her temporary relief, she sees the small red light on her answering machine is flashing.

Someone has called her.

There might be another, much more welcome caller to her house whose suspicions will surely be alerted to the unanswered doorbell. She wishes she'd given her numbers to Alan. *To hell with the Thames House monitors of the landlines. Alan isn't stupid*, she tells herself, *it can't be beyond the wit of a Customs officer to find a way of obtaining my numbers.* Now her concentration switches to something else: she's received a fax on the direct link with Thames House. The line is only used in emergency. Otherwise they communicate direct with her office at STRU. The machine has spewed out the single sheet of paper at an awkward angle. It lies upside down, on the carpet.

'It's going to look suspicious,' she says, 'if my telephones are turned off.'

'They'll think you're out.'

'That's what I've been telling you. I don't go out unless I've told the unit beforehand. See. The machine's flashing. Someone's called.'

'Then play it.'

Davina touches the play button. 'And I've got a fax,' she says.

McKeague retrieves the sheet of fax paper from the floor. Before she can read it, the message on the answering machine begins: 'Hi . . . er, this is Felix. Mr Rosslyn here has given me the cash. It's a lot . . . er, thanks a lot too. See you one of these days. Hope you're fine . . . er, that's it, thanks.'

'That's my son,' Davina says defensively. 'From Manchester. I don't know what it means.'

McKeague hesitates. 'What's this about you giving Rosslyn money to give to him? Jesus Christ.' She seems to be losing her nerve. 'What's it mean?'

'I honestly don't know what he's talking about.'

McKeague is unconvinced. 'What's it mean?' she asks again. She's waving the fax about.

'We'll keep calm,' Davina says with a voice of increased confidence. Her tone infuriates McKeague.

'Does Felix know?' she hisses.

Davina shrugs. 'Know what? He knows nothing.'

'Your husband tell him?'

'Bryan knows nothing either.'

'Like hell, he's in the same boat as you are.'

'Not quite.'

'And Rosslyn. What is Rosslyn doing with your son in Manchester?'

'I've told you. I have absolutely no idea.'

'I think you do.'

'Then you tell me. There's nothing more to say. Alan Rosslyn isn't responsible to me, or to MI5.'

'Bullshit.'

Davina says nothing. The message from Felix confuses her too. So does the thought that Rosslyn is with him. At length she says: 'There's nothing we can do about it, is there? What difference does it make?'

'You tell me.'

Davina shrugs. This is good. Time's being wasted.

'This fax,' McKeague says. 'What's it say? Here.' She hands it to Davina who reads it.

DG/DDGS
TO *IRO/CTI/CTIR/CECP/CS/PTS/STRU/SS/LIAISON*
MBS INS STATVS STAR ONE OP INS MIN ATT
1800 HRS 16 JUNE
CONF REPT ACCEPT BY 2400 15 JUNE
END

'What is it?' McKeague asks.

'There's to be an emergency meeting of department heads at Thames House, tomorrow at six p.m. I have to confirm I'll be there. See – STRU, my unit. And if I don't answer they'll send someone over from Beaconsfield to bang on the door. You'd better let me reply to it.'

McKeague says nothing. She is biting her lip.

'I've got to fax my reply to my chiefs,' Davina says. 'DG/DDGS. Say CONFIRMED STRU. It's simple to do.'

'This meeting,' McKeague says. 'Why a meeting?'

'You want to know what it's about? OP INS. The search for you. You can think about it. Either I don't go, in which case, well, they'll know something's seriously amiss. Or I do go and, who knows, I could be of use to you.' She seems to see the sense of it. *Now she really needs me*, Davina thinks.

'I think I should be there,' Davina adds. 'There's no other choice, is there? You're looking at the notice of the sort of meeting all the senior officers attend. This time, the home secretary will be there. And, in the past, I've known the prime minister to attend as well. That's what MIN ATT means. And that's what it says.'

McKeague shrugs. 'You'd better reply.' She smiles. 'Tell them you'll be there.'

'Are you sure that's what you want?' Davina asks.

'Makes no difference to me,' McKeague replies.

'I suppose it doesn't.' Davina reckons McKeague sees she has no choice but to let her go to Thames House. It seems to be a signpost to her release. Eighteen hours. Time to negotiate with her captor, to breathe, to think. To limit the damage. 'I don't even have to fax my reply,' she adds. 'I can modem it. My computer. Direct access.'

'Do it,' McKeague tells her. 'Say you'll be there.' She watches in silence. Davina taps the keyboard with her acceptance. When she's finished McKeague seems to have relaxed. 'Feel better?' she asks lightly. 'We'd better call the unit.'

'You drive,' McKeague says, 'until we reach the lay-by near the gates. Then I get into the back, in the boot. After that you know what to do. You smile, you wave, you drive straight through. Not too fast. Not too slow. If there's a second's hesitation, I'll blow their heads apart, the car goes up and you with it. Take a look at this.'

Davina sees McKeague's conversion of the boot. She sees the neat arrangement of the high explosive, the detonator and timer. A slit has been cut right through from the boot and rear seat to enable McKeague to keep her handgun aimed at the back of Davina's head while she's driving.

'We're going now,' McKeague says. She waves at Davina to get in. Davina pauses. She thinks: *If they don't search us on the way in, they will on the way out. She hasn't worked out an exit strategy.*

'Cool,' McKeague says, 'stay cool. Get in. Drive steadily.'

They turn out of Davina's drive. She drives steadily, as she's been told, with McKeague in the front passenger seat, the gun in her hands.

'What will you do when you've got what you want?' Davina asks.

'What will *we* do? I have air tickets to Madrid. *We* get a plane to Cuba.'

'I haven't got my passport.'

'I've got one for you. Dublin isn't stupid.'

'Cuba?' Davina says, then falls silent. Oncoming headlights dazzle her. There are others, behind her, reflected in the driving mirror. 'Tell me what it is you're looking for. It's the gas, isn't it?'

'Look,' McKeague says sharply, 'we're both in the same boat. We've both worked both sides. Why don't you see it? Your lot – you – get me to clear up your mess. I do my job. I get paid. I don't ask why. I count the money. I get supplied with weapons. I do it. Now no one, I mean *no one* told me my sister would be murdered. You're looking at someone who's giving her sister a tribute. You're going to provide me with the means.'

'What are the ends?' Davina asks lamely.

'I don't give a shit for ends. I'm interested in me. If you can't see that, then fuck you. If you do, you'll live. If not . . .'

The lay-by shows in the beam of the headlights.

'To hell with it, if not . . .' McKeague says. 'Slow down, we're here.'

40

Arc lights illuminated the sign headed WARNING with the declaration that the STR Unit is a prohibited place. The guards were expecting their chief administrative officer and gave her a cursory wave.

She waited for a moment until the gates were opened. Her hands, now damp, gripped the steering wheel tightly. Fear churned her stomach. She seemed to have lost the sense of feeling in her feet. Her toes were numb. Behind her she could hear a faint metallic tapping in the boot. *McKeague's reminder of the gun. The high explosive. I mustn't disturb the equilibrium.*

She drove towards the car park space marked RESERVED CAO. McKeague's voice said: 'Keep the engine turning. Reverse and park with the rear of the car against the entrance door. Now, get out. Remove my case. Shield me from the video cameras. Open the door. Your card.'

'It's difficult in the dark,' said Davina, but the door opened.

'There are surveillance cameras,' McKeague said. 'You'll have to feel the way to the lift. Don't touch the light switches.'

'You can't turn the lights off in the lift.'

'I'm not going to,' McKeague said.

'They'll see you,' Davina insisted.

'I've thought of that,' she said drily. 'I'll tell you what to do. Now, move inside.'

The handgun jabbed her side. She walked close to the wall of the corridor with McKeague holding the hood of her tracksuit top. There was no sound except for McKeague's trainers against the rubberized floor tiles. As they reached the lift doors McKeague jerked Davina's tracksuit top. 'When the lift gets here, you smear this.'

Davina felt her fingers pressed into a small tin of Vaseline.

'Smear it on the camera lens. Ready?'

'Yes.'

'Call the lift.'

Davina pressed the button. The lift arrived.

'Go ahead,' McKeague whispered.

Davina once more followed her instructions, reached up to the lens, smeared it, keeping a foot in the doors to prevent them closing. 'OK.'

McKeague got in the lift and pressed the button for Floor 4. 'You do the same to the camera in your office and beyond it. Remember, if you make a single move to the alarms, there's this.' The gun jabbed Davina's ribs. 'Don't think about the car. It's shit full of HE. Primed to go off if anyone touches it.'

'Suppose the guards – ?'

'Too bad.'

They came out of the lift into the darkness. The corridor led to the laboratory. There was the hum of the air-conditioning. A water cooler rattled in the darkness. Small pinpricks of green and red light showed from small fascias. Now they were at the door to her office, the familiar cold touch of the glass partition.

'Where's the camera lens?' McKeague was asking.

'There isn't one in my office.'

'You said there was.'

'I didn't.'

'God help you if there is.'

'There isn't.'

'OK, open the door.'

They went inside the office. McKeague walked around the desk. She lowered the shaded desk lamp. When she turned it on it gave a dim greenish light. 'Get a pen. You're going to write a note. Hurry.'

Davina watched her take a Biro from the plastic container on her desk and tear a piece of paper from the pad next to the desk lamp.

'Write this,' McKeague said. She dictated: 'I am responsible for the murders of Deirdre McKeague, fighter in the cause of freedom. Martyr. Mary Walker. Frances Monro. Serena Watson. Patrick Levy. I commissioned these five killings using a recognized agent of MI5. These deaths are my sole responsibility. May God have mercy on my soul. Davina Wesley.'

The one scenario she dreaded constructed itself in her mind. She realized why she'd been brought here. She saw the horror facing her only a few short steps along the corridor in the deep storage vaults.

41

Hearsay's what it is, thought Rosslyn; *hearsay and conjecture from the wino Coker with a record, and from Davina's offspring with a very heavy drug problem*. He was five minutes from her house, driving too fast in the early hours for Amersham, non-stop from Manchester, and angry that neither Davina nor Gaynor had answered his calls. He had thought carefully about the two unreliable witnesses and had tried to sift the possible facts from the probable fantasies. Now it would be Davina's turn.

He parked his car some distance from her house. The silence and the darkness seemed to carry a warning. Fear and anticipation set his nerves on edge. He was in no doubt the confrontation was going to be unpleasant, the explanations lengthy; it would be hard to avoid the accusatory tone.

Outside her house he hesitated. The curtains were drawn, but he could see there were lights on in every room. He stood still and listened. The heavy breathing was his own. And there were other sounds. The dull hum of men's voices. One of the upstairs windows was partly open. The men's voices were coming from her study. Davina was not alone.

He moved nearer to the house, to where the darkness was deeper, to collect his thoughts. He'd seen no car parked near by. *Have these visitors, like me last night, arrived by train? Are they guests, or those faceless visitors in suits who'd got to Coker first and tried to question the awful Felix?* He drew his gun. Were they friends of Anna McKeague? Legitimate investigation officers would not have come here alone in the early hours. They'd have posted watchers who would have seen him arrive. By now they'd have asked him to identify himself. He shifted uneasily in the dark, then decided to check the windows from the garden.

The passage led beside her house to the garden. He could make out the steel rubbish bins. But as he skirted round them his foot collided with a plastic bag filled with bottles. The rattling broke the silence. He froze, sure he would have alerted the dogs. There was no noise, however, and no longer the quiet drone of the men's voices inside the house. He looked about in the stillness. His eyes caught the glint of a window in the garage wall. As far as he could tell, her car was not in the garage. And there was no sign of her either from his garden viewpoint and still not a sound from the dogs.

To his surprise he found the door from the garden into her kitchen was unlocked. He tried the handle carefully, easing the door open, willing the dogs to keep their peace. A small stone was caught beneath the door. It scratched the stone floor. With the door a few inches wide he eased himself in and didn't bother to close it behind him.

The first thing that struck him as odd was the kitchen freezer. Its lid was open and leaning against the wall. Treading carefully, step by step, he made for the door to the hallway. When he passed the freezer he glanced inside it and then stared.

The dead eyes of her dogs stared back at him. He stepped away, nauseated by what he'd seen, his foot colliding noisily with a pair of shoes on the floor. The dead dogs. Her empty shoes. He'd heard of women who commit suicide, who kill their pets, then for some unholy reason remove their shoes before they blow their brains out. She too? He leaned heavily against the sink and listened. The door to the hall was closed. Now he heard footsteps from the other side.

He took his gun in both hands and aimed it, chest high, at the door.

Then the lights went out.

There was a second's silence. The door was opening and there was another sound behind him. The scratch of stone on stone from the door to the garden.

'Don't move.' It was a woman's voice. 'Put your gun down. On the sink. Slowly.'

A second later, the lights went on and the door ahead of him was kicked open. He saw Gaynor standing in the doorway with his gun in his hand. 'Jesus,' he said. 'Alan.' He turned to call upstairs. 'Rosslyn.'

The woman was Cavallero.

'You might have told us in advance,' Gaynor said.

'You didn't answer your phone,' Rosslyn said. His voice was shaking with anger. 'Christ. Who's upstairs?'

'Harding.'

'Where's your bloody car?' Rosslyn said.

'Up the street,' Gaynor said. 'Don't get shirty with me, Alan.'

'You didn't see it?' Cavallero asked.

'I came the other way,' Rosslyn retorted angrily. 'From Manchester.'

'Time spent in reconnaissance is –' Gaynor began.

'I know,' Rosslyn interrupted. 'You could've killed me.'

'We'll go upstairs. Harding wants to talk to you.'

Harding, frail, with an overcoat over his pyjamas, his legs in splints, was on Davina's bed in an ugly mood. 'This time,' he told Cavallero, 'you stand by the window. No more balls-ups, please.'

Rosslyn could see he was in pain. 'Where is she?' he asked.

'We were hoping you could tell us, Alan.' Harding was taking an envelope from his overcoat pocket. It was Rosslyn's letter to Davina. 'You can thank Verity for this.'

Rosslyn was numb.

'She's had Mrs Wesley's mail intercepted. This is yours?'

'Yes,' Rosslyn replied bluntly.

'Well, Alan,' Harding said very slowly, 'I'm keeping this. In the circumstances I'd rather no one else saw it. Do you feel the same? Well, I'll spare you the answer. Do you know where she is?'

'No,' said Rosslyn.

'You're compromised,' Cavallero said. 'Your letter could sink us. It could destroy our case against her.'

'You think?' said Rosslyn.

'I know,' replied Cavallero.

'I'm not allowing your private life to get in the way,' Harding said. 'You've pissed in the wind. What I want you to tell me is where the hell is she? Her car's gone. She was at the STR Unit in Beaconsfield at midnight. She stayed there for an hour. Then she left. The guards saw her arrive and they saw her leave. It's on the video tapes. I think you know where she is.'

'You have to believe me. I don't.'

227

'I hope you're telling me the truth.' Harding looked at the letter with contempt. 'God help us all. You've seen Levy's boyfriend and the sons?'

'Levy's pal, Coker, yes. And the son, Felix. The other one's in a mental hospital. Letter or no letter, Davina was behind it. She set the plan in motion to kill Monro and Watson.'

'Her son told you?'

'In so many words, yes – '

'Hearsay,' Harding muttered.

'I know.'

'And Coker? What did he tell you?'

'She was behind Levy's murder too. The sister of Dee McKeague shoved Levy beneath the tube at Camden Town.' Rosslyn produced Coker's tape. 'It's on here. Coker poured his heart out to someone posing as a nurse. This damns Levy. It damns Davina Wesley.' He gave Harding an awkward smile. 'That letter of mine to her – hearsay, conjecture, call it what you like – it doesn't prove I slept with her in here, in the bed you're lying on, in those sheets.'

'I wouldn't enter into that, if I were you,' said Cavallero.

'Put yourself in her shoes,' Rosslyn said. 'If you were to set out to prove to me you're not a lesbian, there has to be one convincing way of doing it. That's what she did here. In this bed. Lesbian, what the hell. She's bisexual, if it matters. You said "check her". Well, so maybe I did, maybe I didn't. Believe what you like.' He glanced at Gaynor, then at Cavallero. 'You tell me how the money passed from SIS to MI5, on to Bryan Wesley, then to McKeague's sister?'

'Anna McKeague,' said Cavallero. 'She was told how to steal it.'

'Of course she was,' Rosslyn replied with growing impatience. 'Is that a statement, or a question?'

'A statement,' Gaynor said. 'The Filipino maid saw the robbery. She cracked. At some point on the twenty-sixth of March, Anna McKeague takes the money to the Chinese, Leung. Leung shifts it from one account to another, Basel and Milan. But she gets caught with a whole load of bogus Deutschmarks and Swiss Francs. The Triads do her in.'

'Then where is she?' Rosslyn asked. He glared at Cavallero.

'No use asking me,' she said. 'Anna McKeague's a long-standing double agent registered with the military and MI5. They won't admit to it.'

'When did you ask them?' Rosslyn said.

'I didn't *ask* them. I found out myself. We have our own trace on her. She's the one, her sister, the one you interrogated at Paddington Green, who was commissioned to kill Monro and Watson. The same freelance who shot Mary Walker. You saw it happen.'

'I saw it,' said Rosslyn. 'But I didn't see McKeague.'

'You know why?' asked Harding.

Rosslyn shrugged.

'Because MI5 arranged for her to dump a bomb on their bloody doorstep. Why? To make her look good in the eyes of Dublin. It was Mary's tragedy she blundered on the scene. Then McKeague shot her. And MI5 realized the shit they were in. They couldn't admit it. They couldn't deny it. They landed themselves in it. So, our friend – your friend' – he thumped a clenched fist down on the bed – 'she exploits the situation for whatever brain-damaged reasons she has. God alone knows, maybe they *wanted* Monro and Watson murdered. Nobody is going to say outright that MI5 eliminated two of their own because they're gay. I seriously doubt it. It's not against the law. But you can't legislate for nutters.'

'I did tell you,' Cavallero offered, 'that Davina Wesley is a highly complicated woman.'

'Disturbed,' said Rosslyn. '"Disturbed" was the word you used.'

'Disturbed all right,' said Harding. 'I'd be disturbed if I were her right now. Specially because McKeague's been here too. Today.'

Gaynor was holding up two polythene bags containing the remnants of industrial adhesive tape, short bits of red and yellow wire. 'And there's the usual collection of hair fibre. She's been here. And there are the dogs. Davina Wesley doesn't carry a weapon. McKeague must have disposed of the dogs. Either she, or Wesley, has driven off in Wesley's car.'

Rosslyn watched Harding shift his body into a more comfortable position on the bed. 'Do you mind telling me who your source is?'

'Don't push it,' Gaynor said.

'Someone on the level,' said Harding.

'Or do you mean on the square?' Rosslyn asked making a heavy hint at masonry.

'Alan,' Gaynor said sharply.

'I'm right?'

'I said don't push it, Alan. Please.'

'Alan,' said Harding quietly. 'You said "on the square" brother. Your words not mine. That make you happy enough? Don't concern yourself. Leave me to protect my sources. You protect yours. Concentrate your mind on finding Davina Wesley and McKeague. I'll tell you why nothing matters more. Because, Alan, tomorrow, there's a final meeting taking place at Thames House. Tomorrow evening – this evening – at six. We're all to be congratulated.' He looked at Cavellero who smiled briefly. 'Even the bloody home secretary will be there. Operation Insect's at an end. MI5 will tidy up the loose bits. We're all to be there, except me. I'm in hospital. Or supposed to be. McKeague stays in place. Davina Wesley, who knows?'

'If there's been anything untoward,' Cavellero chimed in, 'they'll hold their own inquiry.'

'Right,' said Harding. 'With or without Davina Wesley they'll hold their inquiry. I dare say no one will miss her much. Not even you, Alan. Not now.'

'You accept this?' Rosslyn asked. 'We let them close it?'

'No,' said Harding. 'No, I don't. What do you think?'

'I think she will hit Thames House – with Davina Wesley, or without her,' Rosslyn said. He was looking at Gaynor. 'The plans. The structure. She knows the access.'

'What's she going to hit them *with*?' asked Harding.

'What would you use if HE's no good? I'd use gas. How would I get it? From MI5's STR Unit. They've got tetrodotoxin.'

He gave a brief outline of his first visit to the STR Unit and his identification of the fish in the tanks.

'They won't admit they've got it,' said Cavellero. 'It's in breach of every war convention in existence.'

'I want to see if any of it's gone missing,' Harding said. He turned to Gaynor. 'Fetch your car. You,' he said to Cavellero, 'you help me downstairs. And mind the dogs.' He seemed to relish his own black joke.

Outside, Gaynor and Rosslyn set off to fetch the car.

'The old man's very pleased with you,' Gaynor said. 'He actually thought your letter was quite amusing.'

'He did? Fuck that. It's not how I saw it.'

'He's made of the same stuff as you,' Gaynor said. 'In his way. What he's burning for is a conviction. If that means sleeping the night in this place, well, you do what it takes. Seems you did.'

'He said that?'

'In so many words,' Gaynor laughed. 'You got her.'

'Maybe,' said Rosslyn. 'It isn't over yet. Not by a long chalk.'

'I know,' Gaynor said. 'I meant "you got her" – not "we've got her".'

Rosslyn shrugged. 'Let's not quarrel about it. We're on the same side.' Then he muttered, 'A few minutes ago I was beginning to think otherwise.'

'It was a possible cock-up,' Gaynor said. 'Don't let Harding get to you. None of us is immune from the Great British cock-up. The art is to keep it inside your trousers.'

'Very funny,' Rosslyn said bitterly.

But he was grateful for Gaynor's stab at humour.

'Park your car off the road,' Gaynor told him. 'Leave it out of sight.'

42

Gaynor drove fast along the deserted road to Beaconsfield with Harding seated awkwardly in the front seat and Rosslyn next to Cavallero in the back.

'We have to assume one of four things will happen when we get there,' Harding explained. 'Either the guards will let us in without a murmur – which I doubt. Or they will call Thames House to get authorization for us to go in. Or they will say they have to speak to Mrs Wesley. If that happens, we can ask them to find her for us. Or they'll say "Get stuffed." The odds are three to one against our getting in without a row. If I'm right, and they make trouble, Dickie, you show them your gun inside whatever guardhouse they have. Keep them covered inside and have them open the barrier. Then you drive this in, Alan. Park. You and Verity go to Wesley's office.'

'How do we handle the locking systems?' Rosslyn asked.

'They use the new system we have at Vauxhall Cross,' Cavallero explained. 'It's a part of the precautions against bomb attack. I know the system. Except for the main gates. They change the codes every shift. Once we're inside there isn't a problem.'

'Are they armed?' asked Rosslyn.

'Only the senior officers,' Cavallero said.

'When you get to Wesley's office,' Harding continued, 'you're looking for two things. One: signs of what she was doing there. If you find any material evidence should be removed then remove it. Make your own mind up. Two: you take the place apart for any sign that safes, strongrooms or vaults have been tampered with. From start to finish, we have twenty, maybe thirty minutes at the outside. Count yourself lucky if you get that long. Then we return to London. After that, we have until six p.m. tomorrow to compose and print our report for the Thames House whitewash.' He hesitated.

The WARNING sign was illuminated.

'Good,' Harding said. 'They've seen us.'

The guard came over to the car. 'Can I help you?'

Gaynor lowered his window. He showed his ID to the guard. 'I'm Gaynor, Customs & Excise. This is Commander Harding, anti-terrorist squad, Scotland Yard. Ms Cavallero, Foreign Service and Alan Rosslyn, Customs & Excise.'

'And what can I do to help, sir?'

'We want to take a look inside,' Harding said.

'Do you have authorization, sir?'

'Yes.'

The guard looked doubtful. 'Can I see it, sir, please?'

Harding showed his ID. 'This is it. Are you the senior guard?'

'Yes. And I'm sorry, sir. Even the prime minister has to obtain prior authorization to gain access. Except in emergency.'

'This is an emergency,' Harding said.

'We're not on Red Alert, sir.'

'That's good,' Harding said. 'You come round my side of the car, if you please.'

The guard looked behind him to the lights in the window of the guardhouse. Rosslyn saw the flickering of a TV and the broad back of a man in shirtsleeves hunched in front of the screen. The shape of a thinner man appeared in the window. He was also peering at the TV and was silhouetted against the bright light. Then Rosslyn saw him step out of view. As the man did so the car window next to Harding's face lowered with a hum.

'See this?' Harding said to the guard, pleasantly. 'Look at this.'
The man leaned into the car.

Suddenly, Gaynor heaved himself over Harding, his arms outstretched, his big hands wrenching at the guard's ears and hair, yanking his head further through the open window into the car.

Harding leaned backwards. His left hand pressed the button by the door handle to raise the window. Up it went, humming and straining, until the guard's head was trapped and held. With his other hand, Harding smothered the man's open mouth. The guard's eyes closed tight in pain.

Gaynor was already out of the car, his hand inside the guard's jacket. He removed the handgun. Then Cavallero, who had the rear window down now, took it from him.

'Get them to open the gates,' Harding said quietly.

The figure Rosslyn had seen a moment before silhouetted against the window was coming down the short flight of steps at the entrance to the guardhouse. He began to speak: 'Can I help?'

'Raise your hands,' Rosslyn snapped. 'Don't speak.'

The man's mouth fell open.

'Take six steps to your left.'

Cavallero made a rush for the open doorway. Out of the corner of his eye, Rosslyn saw the TV watcher look at her, appalled.

Rosslyn said to the man he was covering: 'Tell your friend to open the gate. Lift your arms up.'

As he added 'higher', he heard the shot from inside the guardhouse. A moan. Then 'Bastard bitch.' God, he thought, Cavallero's killed him. Then he heard her shrill voice: 'Want one in the other knee? Open the gates. Now.'

Rosslyn glanced at the high solid steel gates. Either side stretched the continuous brick wall and on top of it the electrified and barbed wire. There was no sign of the Alsatians and their handlers he'd seen on his previous visit.

Still, the gates didn't open.

His heart was thumping. The entry wasn't going according to Harding's plan. It was Cavallero who was inside the guardhouse, not Gaynor.

'You're fucked,' said the guard a few feet from Rosslyn.

'Fuck you,' Rosslyn said. 'Keep your arms raised.'

'You're crazy.'

'Yes,' said Rosslyn. He moved a fraction sideways. He heard the car door slam and hurried footsteps. Gaynor passed him and strode into the guardhouse. 'You!' he shouted. 'Alan, bring him in here.'

'Move,' Rosslyn said. 'Don't turn round. Walk backwards. Up the steps.'

Gaynor pulled at the man's shirt collar. 'Get in here.'

Inside, Cavallero was standing over the man on the floor. His right knee was oozing blood. He'd passed out.

Gaynor pressed his face up to the guard Rosslyn had covered. 'The console. Release the gates in ten seconds or you are dead, right?'

'You won't get in,' the man said.

'Do it,' Gaynor demanded. 'Or we fucking blow them apart, and you too, mate.'

The guard stood staring at the console. It must have been the one moment he dreaded. Out here in the peace of the countryside, the endless safe routine so suddenly shattered. Rosslyn could smell the man's nervous breath.

Gaynor said: 'Wife and family?' The man nodded. 'That's nice. You've got seconds, my friend. Or you'll never see them again. Open them. They stay open. You touch an alarm, the bomb goes off. Ten seconds. We're counting. The gates.'

Rosslyn saw the man's hand touch a square green button and two numbered white ones. Then Gaynor brought the side of his handgun down across the man's neck. He hit him twice with tremendous force and the man collapsed sideways against Rosslyn, then down to the floor.

'Go,' Gaynor said.

On the way out Cavallero was saying: 'They've already set off one alarm.'

'Forget it,' Gaynor shouted, suddenly short of breath. 'Go. You're on your own.'

The sound of Rosslyn and Cavallero's footsteps filled the compound. Then there was silence except for the click of Cavallero's plastic card in the slit of the black steel door and the quick buzz of the lock's release mechanism.

The narrow corridor to the lift was as he'd remembered it. So was the terribly slow lift down to Floor 4. He stretched his neck, his eyes open at the lens of the video camera.

234

'Gaynor can see us,' Cavallero said, following Rosslyn's stare.

'I'm not sure he can,' Rosslyn said. His fingertip touched the surface of the camera lens. 'See – Vaseline. Last time that happened was when McKeague did the same thing to the camera in the car park and got Harding.'

'Anyone could've done it.'

'In here?' Rosslyn said. 'I don't think so.'

The lift doors opened. A short passage led to the forensic laboratory filled with the hum of the air-conditioning. Then they entered Davina's office.

'Let's do this one first,' Rosslyn said.

They were thinking alike: both coming to the reconstruction from different schools of training; both with very little time to retrace Davina's actions. Daylight, says the book, daylight is the investigator's best friend. No friendly daylight had lit Davina's office down here. They walked carefully around the desk examining the floor.

The desk drawers were locked. So were the filing cabinets, one marked red, the other green.

'No sign,' Cavallero said.

'She's been here,' Rosslyn said. 'Definitely. I can smell her perfume.'

Cavallero sniffed. 'What is it?'

'Chanel's Coco.'

'You're the Customs man. Duty Free's not my line. Perfume lingers.'

Rosslyn shone the desk light on a blank pad of paper. 'Look. Hard pressure marks on the table. A note written in a hurry.'

'By her?'

'I can't tell.'

'Maybe she never came in here. We're wasting time. Where's the vault? Hurry.'

Rosslyn saw her shiver violently.

'Fuck, this place is cold,' she said. 'Where's the vault?'

'Something like two, maybe three doors down the corridor.'

They read the notices on the doors. Coded signs. XD3 GAMMA, XD3 DELTA. They were massive bright white enamel doors with elaborate locks. Set into each of them there was a narrow observation slit of very thick glass.

235

'I can't unlock these locks,' Cavallero said. 'I don't recognize them.'

'We've seen enough already,' said Rosslyn.

'We can't tell if she *has* definitely been here,' said Cavallero. 'Let's get out of this hell-hole. If she was here, she came and went.'

'Wait,' said Rosslyn suddenly.

The third door was marked XD3 EPSILON. Beneath the legend was a red stencilled skull and crossbones. Next to the stencilled message was a single sheet of paper taped to the door. He recognized Davina's handwriting.

I am responsible for the murders of Deirdre McKeague, fighter in the cause of freedom. Martyr. Mary Walker. Frances Monro. Serena Watson. Patrick Levy. I commissioned these five killings using a recognized agent of MI5. These deaths are my responsibility. May God have mercy on my soul. Davina Wesley.

Cavallero was already peering through the observation slit. 'God. Look.'

For a second Rosslyn saw his own features reflected in the glass. Then he peered inside the vault. No more than a small hygienic chamber, it was lit by a dim and even light. His eyes were drawn to other distant lights at the far side. He saw the tanks of swimming *fugu* fish, the salamanders and Costa Rican toads.

On the floor, in the centre of the vault, grotesque and rigid, lay the naked body of Davina. Her eyes were completely white. It was as if they had been frozen in their sockets.

Cavallero held on to his arm tightly. 'We're getting out of here, Alan. *Now.*'

43

Verity Cavallero's eyes had not deceived her. The guard had triggered the alarm. 'We should've done it differently,' she said to Rosslyn. 'We blew it.'

They were walking across the compound to the gates where the approach road to the STR Unit was jammed with police cars, ambulances and Fire Service vehicles. Blue and yellow lights flicked round and round. Sirens drowned the crackle of the radios. Police officers were shouting to make themselves heard above the din. An ambulance had backed up to the guardhouse doors. Paramedics were lifting a stretcher into it. Its doors were closed and the ambulance siren began to wail as it steered an awkward course through the jam of emergency vehicles and away into the night.

Rosslyn's thoughts were in turmoil. The conclusion that Davina had died by her own hand was somehow out of his reach. It seemed impossible to believe, moreover, that it had been her rigid corpse inside the vault. His mind refused to form a connection between the horror of it and the living woman he'd touched and smelled and more besides less than a day and night before. Yet there she lay. Cavallero took the awful evidence at face value. There was the suicide note. The victim's corpse. She'd had a motive and the opportunity. 'And someone else has the same,' Rosslyn said. 'As well as the opportunity to cover up.'

They had left the way they had come. Up in the lift. Out into the cleaner air. Now this. And then a figure detached itself from the crowd of police officers near the guardhouse.

It was Gaynor. 'Harding's waiting for you. It depends on what you two found.'

'She's dead,' said Rosslyn.

'Who is?' Gaynor asked.

'Davina Wesley,' said Cavallero. 'Suicide.'

'You're sure?'

'See for yourself,' Rosslyn replied. 'She left a note.'

'Where is it?'

'We left it where we found it,' Rosslyn said. 'Fixed to the door of the toxic gas vault.'

Gaynor glanced to where his car stood, next to a police patrol car. 'We'd better tell Harding. There's an inspector with him in a rough mood. You saw the body, but had anything been stolen?'

'Not as far as we could see,' Rosslyn said.

'Pity,' Gaynor said. 'The inspector won't let us leave.'

'Why not?' Cavallero said.

'You should know,' Gaynor replied. 'You shot one of the guards.'

'In self-defence.'

237

'Try to sound more convincing if they question you,' Gaynor said flatly. 'Let Harding do the talking.'

Harding was sitting stretched back in the passenger seat of Gaynor's car. Instead of one police inspector in an angry mood, Rosslyn saw two. Harding began the introduction with his school-boyish look of innocence. 'Both these officers have been acting on my instructions.'

'On whose authorization?' asked the inspector who seemed to be the senior of the two.

'Mine,' said Harding. 'They report to me.'

'If anyone's reporting,' the inspector said shortly, 'I am.'

'What did you find?' Harding asked.

'You answer to me!' the inspector shouted. 'What the hell were you looking for?' He glared at Harding. 'Don't you answer.'

'*Sir*,' said Harding.

The inspector had abandoned respect and ignored Harding's request for it. 'You tell me,' he hissed at Rosslyn.

'There's the body of a woman in a top security vault. Attached to the door is a suicide note in her own hand.'

'How d'you know?' the inspector demanded.

'Know what?'

'That she wrote it,' the inspector shouted.

'No need to answer,' Harding said.

'Who is she?'

'No need to answer,' repeated Harding. Quietly, he added: 'You'd better get your men down there now. But I'm warning you it may be very dangerous.'

'You mean a bomb?' the inspector asked, open-eyed.

'No,' Harding said coldly. 'If there was a bomb these two officers wouldn't be here now.'

The inspector was still more infuriated. 'What are you talking about?'

'Highly toxic nerve gas,' Harding said. 'If I were you, I'd wait until you get a scientist or a doctor out here who knows what he's doing. If you know how to handle the sort of nasty weaponry that's stored down there, fine, go on in. As your senior officer, I'd advise against it.' He turned his head to Rosslyn. 'You know about these things.'

'Yes,' Rosslyn said for the inspector's benefit. 'I'd wait until the experts show up.'

238

'You've been down there before? You know this place?'

'Yes, I have been here before,' Rosslyn said. 'And I'm telling you, if I were you, I'd close the gates and seal the place off right now. No one, and I mean no one, should be allowed in.'

The inspector looked at Harding. 'You told him to say this?'

'For God's sake, I did not. Use your common sense. More than that.' He lowered his voice. 'I don't want your junior officers to hear this.'

'I'm not taking threats from you, commander.'

'This is not a threat. It's a bit of advice.'

'No.'

'You listen to me,' Harding said viciously. 'If I'm suspended for breaking and entering some Ministry of Defence secret shithole, that's good. Look at my fucking legs, see, huh? A bomb, right? I'm supposed to be in hospital. I'm not swanning around out here for fun. I'm here, inspector, because it's my lousy job to arrest known terrorists. That's why I'm here with two Customs officers and a member of the Security Service. From Six, not Five. We were obstructed, by violence, by those pig-thick toe-rag guards from entry. We acted in self-defence. You haven't got a chance in hell of nailing me, or them. Your job –'

'You don't have to tell me what my job is, sir.'

'I don't give a suck of a monkey's cock for your job,' Harding blazed. 'I think that you are obstructing a fellow police officer in carrying out his duty.'

'I've a good mind to arrest you, sir.'

'And the same to you, inspector. And you can't, can you?'

The other officers who had listened in silence were staring at Harding, then at the ground. One was fidgeting; another was looking at his watch. They knew Harding was right and the inspector knew Harding was right, but he was answerable also to MI5. The STR Unit was on his patch. The number one place for protection at all costs. And he had a line to the army if needs be.

At length the inspector said: 'There needs to be a full report.'

'There will be,' Harding said. 'There'll be a very full report. And if, right now, you'll clear a way for us to leave to continue our job, we'll leave you here to continue yours.' He waved at Rosslyn to get in the car. The others followed suit. 'Thank you, inspector.'

'Commander,' the inspector said blankly.

'In your shoes,' Harding said with a chilling smile, 'I'd have done the same thing.'

Gaynor turned the key in the ignition.

44

The new headquarters of MI6, formally known as the Secret Intelligence Service (SIS), is the £85 million post-modernist pile on the south bank of the Thames at Vauxhall Cross. Bugproof. Bombproof. With wet and dry moats. The windows are impregnated with metal. The rooms are lined with lead. You can see out. But you can't see in. The fortress at Vauxhall Cross has earned its sobriquet – Babylon-on-Thames. Across the river, downstream, stands the sister building Thames House, by Lambeth Bridge.

Rosslyn watched the sun through the tinted windows, drinking coffee, listening to Gaynor's three-finger tapping at the word processor. Cavallero had said it would be 'in the interests of security' for them to stay put in Vauxhall Cross for the twelve or so hours until the meeting across the river at Thames House.

Now she returned to her fourth-floor office suite with another word processor on a trolley. 'If there's anything else you want . . .' She smiled. Rosslyn wanted sleep but he wanted McKeague even more. He was looking at Lambeth Bridge, the very spot where he'd stood with Mary last winter. Yes, he wanted McKeague even more.

'Why don't you try and get some sleep?' Cavallero asked.

Rosslyn smiled wearily. 'Later.'

'There's a couch next to Harding's,' she offered.

He noticed traces of blood on her white shirt. 'You OK?'

'Not my blood. I keep a change of clothing in my filing cabinet. You should start your report now.'

He sat at a desk by the window. Like a schoolboy in detention, with his fellow truant, Gaynor, tapping at another desk, he dredged his memory for the tell-tale details of the stories, tying the threads together like the strands of an academic's thesis. From the arrest of Deirdre McKeague way back, to her interview at Paddington Green, cross-referencing days and times, statements and events and evidence. Evidence seen, heard and retrieved. He lost himself in the webs of it, commenting on loose arguments based on the issues still unresolved: the fabrication of the interview tape, the whereabouts of the police car at England's Lane.

Some things seemed unmeasurable. What do psychologists finally mean by bisexual? Was Davina bent at the heart of it – or had she acted upon someone else's order to have Monro and Watson murdered? Were their deaths some deliberate sacrifice made to gain sympathy for the Security Service? If so, who had ordered it? To whom were they answerable – the home secretary and the prime minister?

These preparations for the 6 p.m. meeting were interrupted several times by deliveries and telephone calls fielded by Cavallero.

They came from Customs & Excise. First the printed transcripts of Rosslyn's interview with McKeague. Version one: the true one. Version two: the fake.

Others came from New Scotland Yard: the forensic reports in full and the more recent, now fully expanded report outlined in the memorandum he'd read at the Angel in Rotherhithe the previous day.

Shortly after 1 p.m. Cavallero brought in a salad lunch and a report of a different kind.

'I thought you'd like to know the status of the Thames House meeting,' she said casually. 'The home secretary's bringing the prime minister. Or the other way round. It's a full turn-out.'

'Why?' asked Rosslyn.

'Search me,' Cavallero said. 'All part of open government,' she added. 'There's a lot of it about.'

'Good,' said Rosslyn. 'Who told you?'

'The Home Office. Lucas. Sniffing Jules. Don't underestimate him. The poodle has a nasty bite. He's got Bryan Wesley on his back. Trying to find Davina.'

'Doesn't he know about her?'

'He can't. For some reason no one's said a thing about it.'

'Won't be long before they do,' Rosslyn said.

'It won't,' said Cavallero, and the way she spoke made Rosslyn stiffen. 'They've found Davina's car abandoned behind White City. Burned out. No traces, except the registration plates. Our friend is being very careful. White City. The west. Heathrow. Perhaps she's got away.'

'I doubt it,' Rosslyn said. 'I feel I've got to know her now. She's got unfinished business. Harding. Me.'

'By tonight she'll be on her own,' Gaynor said. 'Disowned by MI5. I love the idea of the prime minister being there. Prat.'

For almost an hour they speculated on why the prime minister was coming to Thames House. As if there weren't more important things to do in Downing Street. The beggars, the homeless, an economy in terminal decline, a country on the skids. Eventually, it was time to return to the reports.

Rosslyn wrote up Coker and the Wesley son. Then Davina. This was the toughest.

I am writing about myself. It felt like a betrayal. Then, a final conclusion. The summary. He tried to avoid the rhetoric. 'In my view, it is what the report does *not* say, rather than what it *does* say, upon which the findings of this investigation must turn. These gaps, I submit, can only be filled by a full, frank and open statement of operational evidence by the Directorate of the Security Service (MI5).'

The rhetoric stayed. He couldn't find a better way of putting it.

Open the curtains on the life of Anna McKeague.

At 4 p.m., like an invigilator, Cavallero collected the printouts for duplication.

It was finished and Rosslyn felt the tiredness in his body. Cavallero showed him to the bathroom next to the room where Harding was still sleeping.

Rosslyn took his bag with him and, waiting for the bath to fill, he turned to the end of Mary's diary. He was ready, he felt, to read the final day.

2 inches of snow covers London. Visibility almost zero. Temperature 2 degrees below freezing . . .

She was shouting at him: *MI5 will change my life tonight.* [Tonight it will change mine.]

He read it again. Look at the comparisons; select the quotes.

I hear him say, 'The truth, the whole truth, nothing but the truth.' Why? 'Because they know it already.' Well, they don't.

[And here again is THUG who still wants her in his bed.]

This is what I'd do as a terrorist. Plan long-term infiltration. Get an informer in place. The sympathetic weasel. Get the geography of the MI5 headquarters right. Then I'd find a disaffected soul who needs the cash. Some government scientist with lethal knowledge. Not of bombs. Forget the bombs. Too old-fashioned. I'd up the stakes. Use chemicals to poison the water, poison the air, fuck up the air-conditioning. Gas the spooks. Wipe out the lot of them in one fell swoop. Far-fetched? Not at all. Still with me?

Alan . . . underestimates himself and how much I love him. Always have, always will.

He set the diary on the floor. As he straightened up he saw himself reflected in the wall mirror; then reflected again in another glass above the washbasin. He stood: the reflections stood. He felt that curious sense of meaninglessness when you repeat a word so often that all you hear is the sound of it, when the word is separated from its sense. It was a feeling of acute dislocation. Likewise he sensed the *déjà vu*, some trick brought on by the mind's exhaustion, a flash dream, a dream of a dream. The moment of acute anxiety when the real is unreal. The final diary entry struck him like this. For here was the twist of circumstance tying the knot together with a fearful sense of inevitability.

He lay in the bath, weary to his bones.

Now there was a voice at the door: 'Hurry up.' It was Gaynor. 'We have to leave in twenty minutes.'

45

The unmarked car, a black Rover driven by Gaynor, took under ten minutes to complete the short journey from Vauxhall Cross to Thames House door to door. Three large cardboard boxes were on the front seat containing the printed copies of the reports. Rosslyn and Harding were in the back of the car with a collapsible wheelchair for Harding. Cavallero had already gone ahead.

'She's provided you two with this,' said Harding. He opened a slim flat metal case.

Rosslyn leaned over and saw a set of dull metallic tubes. 'Skeleton Heckler & Koch. MP5KA6. Magazine fits in here, at the front of the barrel, fifty yards effective killing range. You won't have seen one like this before, I suppose.'

'We didn't use them at Lippitts Hill.'

'No. That's because the skeleton version isn't in manufacture yet. The feed is here. A thirty-round box. Cyclic rate 700 r.p.m. Moderated bursts, or single rounds and restricted to five rounds per burst.'

'Whose idea is this?'

'Mine,' Harding grunted.

'Why?'

'Because you've convinced me. I've seen your reports. And Dickie's, and Cavallero's. Either we've got it right, or we're disappearing up our own arses. Either McKeague will hit Thames House – bullseye. Bingo. Or we've lost her and we look thick as shit and MI5 say, "Nothing to do with us." Either way, it's going to be nasty. But if McKeague shows up, then you have the weapon. Dickie waits on the bridge. I'm taking this gun in with me. If and when you need it I'll slip it to you. Otherwise it's the meeting we concentrate on. We hear what they have to say. We listen. They make whatever first move they've dreamed up. Watch Bryan bloody Wesley. And Lucas. Their diversionary tactics. Lucas will go for Cavallero. Cavallero will go for Wesley. They will either go for each other's throats, or they will get each other's scalps. My money's on Cavallero.'

Gaynor steered a steady course over the ramp, then down the ramp into Thorney Road car park. There he said: 'Good luck. I'll be waiting on the bridge.'

'Shoot to kill,' Harding said. 'When and if. It's your blood they want, Alan. Our money's on zero. The whole lot of it. Let's see McKeague do her job.'

Rosslyn's watch said five minutes to six.

46

TOP SECRET

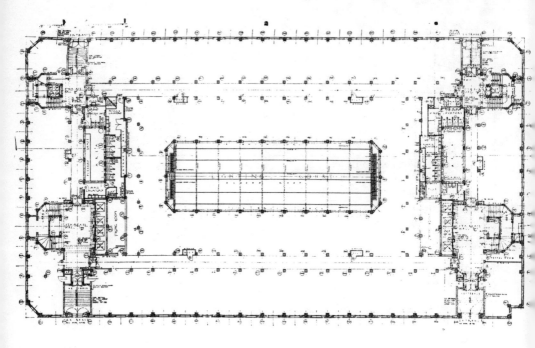

Plans of the ground floor.

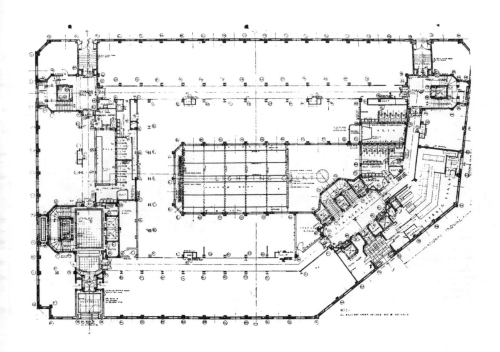

THAMES　HOUSE
Grosvenor　Road,　London.
Sir Frank Baines - *Architect.*

47

The Agenda is on a single sheet of paper.

Thursday 16 June, 18.00 Hours

In Attendance:

Prime Minister, First Lord of the Treasury and Minister for the Civil
Service
Secretary of State for Northern Ireland
Secretary of State for the Home Department

Staff:

DG
DDG (Ops)
DDG (Admin)
Directors Int. Branches
Directors: Pro. Sec., Pers. and Suppt, STRU
Branches
Leg. Adv.
Counsellor
Supernumeraries (SIS, Home Dept.)

Observers:

Commander T. Harding, Metropolitan Police
Mr A. Rosslyn, HM Customs & Excise

1. Prime Minister's Introductory Remarks

2. Secretary of State for the Home Department's Introductory Remarks

3. DG's Address and Closing Remarks

Close of meeting 20.00 hours
Refreshments in DG's suite 20.05 hours onwards.

Rosslyn's eyes watch the director general escort the prime minister, home secretary and the secretary of state for Northern Ireland to their places at the table.

The prime minister smiles. 'Good evening, ladies and gentlemen.'

It's the first time Rosslyn's seen the prime minister in the flesh. He looks larger than he appears on TV and in the papers. There's a pleasantness about the face. The lines at the edges of the eyes are more marked. The eyes twinkle. The aura is one of friendliness, familiarity.

Here's someone I know, I think.

For a moment the prime minister's eyes seem to catch Rosslyn's. Rosslyn returns the smile. The others, the home secretary, the secretary of state for Northern Ireland seem, somehow, to be lesser people. Functionaries almost. They look somehow creased; weary, suspicious, edgy. *I wouldn't trust them in the Nothing to Declare section. They're hiding something somewhere. Definitely suss. Would you mind stepping this way, please.* Rosslyn can't quite put his finger on it.

The director general starts: 'May I first of all welcome you prime minister and secretaries of state. I speak on behalf of all my staff in warmly welcoming you here at what, we know, is an especially difficult period.'

You'd better believe it.

'We continue to value your support and interest as the threats to security become increasingly complex. We are, sir, keenly interested in the content of the introductory remarks you wish to make.'

The prime minister speaks without notes: 'Director general, ladies and gentlemen. Thank you, director general, for your kind remarks. I speak on behalf of all of us when I say that all right-thinking people believe in the efficacy of the Service. We are sure in the knowledge that you here remain most profoundly committed to the standards of dependability and professionalism required to meet the most considerable threats to national security. Indeed, as you say, director general, these are, in the highest degree, complex.'

Rosslyn notices Harding is as usual doodling. A caricature of the PM seated on the toilet. Not a bad likeness. Harding's crutches are propped against the back of his chair.

The prime minister warms to his theme. *Blah-blah-blah.* 'I am not, I think, exceeding my brief in disclosing a secret to you here this evening. The government's policy, to be as open as we possibly can be about the Service, was recommended to me by Her Majesty the Queen. I agree with Her Majesty.'

You'd hardly stand there arguing with her.

The prime minister gives a self-effacing smile, almost mischievous. 'We are each, in our different ways, opening the doors, granting public access to government and palaces.'

Only under duress you are.

'We have embarked upon a level of interservice co-operation that is rare among civilized nations. But there are risks. I know them. You know them. Today I am pleased, personally, that representatives of all services fighting terrorism are here present. This, for me, is a personal landmark, to be here and because I do *wunt* to acknowledge the new spirit of co-operation you have achieved. I sometimes wish it might spread among the rows of my own backbenchers.'

There is a ripple of sycophantic laughter around the table. Lucas from the Home Office apparently hugely enjoys the joke. So does the prime minister. Rosslyn and Harding remain impassive.

'Secretary of state,' says the director general to the home secretary.

'Prime minister, director general, staff,' begins the home secretary.

His voice is silky, the accent artificial – *crème fraîche*. A hint of sourness. The pronunciation of English diverts you from its meaning. 'To' = 't-er', 'people' = 'peeperl'. Most diverting, 'individuals' = 'eendeeveeduerls'. The delivery is peppered up with references to 'service', 'the interests of the United Kingdom and its citizens'; 'accountability to Parliament', 'flexibility', 'the need for change', 'principles', 'aims', 'a safe world for future generations'. Blah-blah-blah.

If bullshit was music we'd have a brass band.

The director general gives thanks for his 'insights and support'.

Harding throws a disgruntled glance at the wall clock. 6.20 p.m.

'It falls to me,' the director general opens, 'to meet my responsibilities. To follow those clearly defined procedures laid down by the Security Service Act and to report accordingly on a matter of substance to the Service. If you could circularize Paper A, STR Unit Beaconsfield?'

Copies are passed round the table. There are a few moments of silence. The scratching of a pen. A bronchial cough. A digital watch beep.

The director general continues: 'You will see that in the early hours of this morning various officers, all of whom, with one exception, are present, contrived to enter the STR Unit at Beaconsfield. The account of this unauthorized entry, inspection, break-in, call it what we may, is set before you.' She pauses. The broad fingers shuffle the papers in front of her. 'I cannot say that this behaviour reflects other than extremely seriously upon those who are responsible for it. I will deal with this in a moment.'

Another hesitation. Rosslyn looks across the table at Wesley. The normally florid face has paled. He is fidgeting with his cufflinks.

The director general goes on: 'Davina Wesley died some time last night. There is no suspicion of foul play. STRU's most experienced team of forensic scientists has established the time of death and its cause and that Mrs Wesley took her own life.' She turns to Bryan Wesley. 'On behalf of us all, I wish to convey to her husband Bryan, their two sons Felix and Jonathan, our heart-felt condolence and sympathy. It is enough for me to say that Davina had been under great strain from pressure of work. She was a fine colleague, dear friend, devoted mother.' She lets the emotion of her tribute hang a moment. 'I know, as a professional, she would wish us to continue our work.'

Rosslyn tries to read Wesley's mind. But the face is bland. The cheeks puffy. The eyes a little swollen. It is impossible to gauge what Wesley is feeling. His eyes return to Harding. He's about to speak.

Davina was seen leaving the unit – that was McKeague. Don't they see it? What are these lies?

Harding nods at him. *Don't speak.*

The home secretary raises a hand, looking at Harding. 'If I may say, off the record, one is aware, Commander Harding, of your efforts. I realize the considerable courage it took to absent yourself from hospital, against the advice of your doctors, in pursuit of a suspect you had some, if I may say, *general* reason to believe had entered the vicinity of the STR Unit. I am also aware of the somewhat hasty, possibly rash action' – he has turned to Cavallero – 'taken by an officer of SIS. But I must emphasize it will jeopardize operational matters should some disciplinary action be taken. I have made it clear, with the prime minister's agreement' – the prime minister nods gravely – 'that no such disciplinary action will be forthcoming.'

Rosslyn bows his head. *Christ. They're closing ranks. I don't believe this.*

Now he's forced to believe it as the home secretary continues: 'The past few weeks have seen an unprecedented degree of co-operative investigation in the extensive search for the killers of the two distinguished officers on the twenty-sixth of March last. We have decided, upon the advice of the director general, to place the investigation solely in the hands of MI5.' The sweet and sour smile beams at Harding. 'In the circumstances, we feel it right and proper, commander, that the scars of the terrible injuries you have sustained so very recently be allowed to heal. I know we can rely on your experience and judgement to tell us you should relinquish the duties you've carried out with such conspicuous gallantry.'

Voices mutter 'Hear, hear'.

'May I add my thanks and congratulations,' says the prime minister. 'I can confirm your service, commander, will not go unrecognized. I am happy to report we will seek to honour you in the customary manner. I speak in great confidence.'

The meeting has relaxed. It's good news time. Only Rosslyn, Harding and Cavallero have grim faces.

What are we looking at? Rosslyn asks himself. *Sir Thomas Harding, Knight of the Velcro Garter. Another knee-bending arse-licker?*

The prime minister smiles pleasantly.

The bastard's going to cut Harding's balls off. With a fucking knighthood. A biscuit for the old dog. He's going to cut his balls off.

Harding says quietly: 'May I say a few words, director general?'

There are victory smiles and nods.

'I'd like to thank you, prime minister, home secretary, for the generous things you've said. And I'd like also to convey to you, director general, and most of all to you, Mr Wesley, my sympathy at the untimely loss of your wife. As this investigation is at a close I would like to place a few brief items on the record by way of conclusion.'

The prime minister smiles and glances at the wall clock. A blink at

6.55 p.m. It's a warning smile. Better keep it short, commander.

Who continues: 'With two of my colleagues, Mr Rosslyn here, and Mr Gaynor, who unfortunately cannot be present, and with the co-operation of Ms Cavallero, I have overseen the preparation of a comprehensive report and analysis of what we have come to know as Operation Insect. These documents are extensive. We don't, I realize, have time to study them here and now. But the conclusions my experienced colleagues and I have drawn reinforce the good sense of all that has been said by you, prime minister, and you, secretary of state, fully endorsed by you, director general.'

Harding's voice now assumes a darker tone. 'I hope you will hear me out, prime minister.'

The prime minister nods. His face wears a keen expression.

'We accept the operation is now closed.'

You don't have any choice.

'We don't seek to question why. We are, after all, servants of government. But, of course, we are, also, servants of the facts. I hope I may be excused if, during my long service, I've occasionally got facts wrong. Last night I may have done. Perhaps, very tragically, Mrs Wesley took her own life.' Here he pauses. 'But, in my judgement, the facts are open to a very different interpretation.'

Christ. Here we go.

All at once: the director general wants to speak; so does Wesley; so does Lucas.

Cavallero has pushed her chair right back from the table. Her left hand rests on the stack of printed reports. The prime minister seems ready to pour oil on troubled waters. He wears a mask of concern, genuine or counterfeit it's hard to tell.

And then, suddenly, Harding is out-manoeuvred by an invisible hand. A senior woman clerk has appeared with a note for the director general. 'Commander, there's a telephone call for you. Apparently it can't wait.'

Harding is extraordinarily calm. 'I'd ask you to listen carefully to Ms Cavallero's summaries.' He stands up painfully. He is deathly pale. 'Help me out of here,' he says to Rosslyn. He makes slow progress in his wheelchair around the table to the exit. His voice is strong. 'You will hear that an agent of the Security Service, commissioned by Mrs Wesley herself, murdered WPC Mary Walker, Monro, Watson, Levy and finally Mrs Wesley.'

Wesley's eyes are closed.

'This is wholly unacceptable,' the director general blurts out.

'It's not for me to decide if it's unacceptable,' says Harding. 'What I'm telling you is that the agent is a known IRA terrorist. You've been sailing too close to a nasty wind and you've capsized.' He's behind Bryan Wesley. 'Mr Wesley here can explain the financing of the operation.'

'May I say – ?' Wesley asks.

He's overridden by the director general. 'This is not on record.'

The home secretary slowly lays a pen down on the surface of the table.

In the sudden silence, the prime minister says: 'Go and take your phone call, commander.' The face wears the expression: What one hand can give the other can take away. 'And when you return I want you to substantiate your allegations.'

That's your knighthood down the slot, commander.

The telephone is in an adjoining room. Harding takes the call. Within seconds his hand is reaching inside his jacket. 'Take it.' He passes the Heckler & Koch to Rosslyn. 'Gaynor's standing by at the bridge. She's here.' Then, to the senior woman clerk: 'Get in there NOW. Tell the fuckers to get out on the roof. DO NOT, REPEAT NOT, LET THEM STAY INSIDE.'

The prime minister's protection officers are in the doorway.

'You heard me. Get in there NOW. Get them out of the building and anyone else you can.' Then he pushes his wheelchair away from the desk backwards to the window.

Far below, Rosslyn sees Gaynor in the street to the right and then, to the left, a small white police patrol car. And hears those endless questions to the nurse at the bomb site in England's Lane.

There is a bomb squad Land Rover down there too. All the paraphernalia.

And those markings on the roof:

a large   V
then   P   O
then, at the bottom, a large orange circle:
         O
and the familiar red and orange strip around the doors.

The bluff has failed. Why? Simply because she's parked on a

double yellow line on Millbank and even at the worst of times, coppers have instructions that you can't park here.

'Alan – go for it!'

Harding wheels himself through the door. He sees the notice: IN CASE OF EMERGENCY DO NOT USE THE LIFTS.

The meeting must have dispersed in some other direction to find the fire stairs to the roof. He wheels his way along the corridor, listening to the dull hum of the air-conditioning. He supposes death will be very sudden. What had Rosslyn told him? It only takes a second.

Then there is the scream of sirens and the violent roaring of the klaxon horns. Thames House is under siege.

48

Dressed in the WPC's uniform, neat and smart, Anna McKeague is out of sight crouched at the barred and bolted entrance to the derelict toilet on the riverside at the northern end of Lambeth Bridge. She has allowed herself a maximum of thirty seconds for cutting through the rusted lock and chains and opening the steel doors to gain entry to these disused toilets. Thirty seconds only during which, she knows full well, she is vulnerable to some chance observation from the police officers in the street above her. She has calculated her position carefully though. If she crouches, twisted, at an angle, her enemies' line of vision will be very narrow. If she keeps strictly to her schedule the odds are that she will gain entry to the abandoned toilets without being seen. Once inside, unseen, she will deal with the brick wall to gain entry to the tunnel beneath Millbank which, according to the plans, leads below the street into the deepest basements of Thames House. It is, of course, a calculated risk which entails keeping a very cool head. So she hums the song from the good old days. The song she had sung with her sister at their last meeting in the bar way back when in Andersonstown: the sisters' duet in passable imitation of a tune by a singer called Tanita Tikaram:

Tell me if you want to see
A world outside your window.

And adding in muddled recomposed verse from Yeats:

Remember all those generations,
They left their bodies to fatten wolves,
Left their homesteads to fatten foxes,
Fled to far countries, or sheltered
In cavern, crevice, or hole,
DEFENDING IRELAND'S SOUL.

The sisters had loved the song and had endured accusations from their cousins of being 'stuck in the groove in the middle of the road'.

Out of Ireland have we come.
Great hatred, little room,
Maimed us at the starts,
We carry from our Mama's womb,
Fanatic hearts.

Overhead, as Anna McKeague correctly reckons, opposite Thames House, the police car is now the object of intense scrutiny by the bomb squad teams new on the scene. *Touch it, you bastards, you fucking maggots, and the vehicle explodes in your faces. Go on,* she wills them. *Rock my baby, plods. Go blow you bastards. Touch my baby with your shaking fingertips. Be scared. Gently rock my virgin vehicle carelessly and kill yourselves.* She's dizzy with her feelings of impending triumph. 'Go for gold,' she whispers. 'For gold and Dee.'

She hums and sings beneath her breath. Overhead the sirens wail to the dirty London evening sky. Twice she applies heavy pressure with the metal clippers and it takes her three powerful squeezes to snap the rusted chains and open the door. Now she is inside the deserted toilets. The doors to the cubicles are all open. The bowls and seats have been smashed and the tiled floor is also broken as if someone sometime had tried and failed to steal the blue and white tiles. A film of slippery green slime, the colour of institutional linoleum, covers the floor.

She walks quickly past the cubicles and the row of urinals opposite broken washbasins to the furthest wall and here, in one corner, she finds the gap in the patch of wall which has been filled in with bricks. Her hands are steady. She prepares the explosive device, just powerful enough to blow a gap in the bricks for her to squeeze through. She has calculated that it will not be large enough, when it goes off, to attract the attention of the swarm of police officers overhead. Again, she has calculated that the massive foundations of the bridge next to the toilets, and the depth of the building will adequately soundproof the *thunk* of the explosion. There is, of course, a risk that the sound will travel; but there is no alternative way into the tunnel beneath the road. The risk has to be taken. She is sure her route into Thames House will not yet have been discovered by the enemy. And she is now at least fifteen seconds ahead of schedule. She rolls her shoulders like a sprinter on the start line for the hundred metres, full of confidence in her ability to win.

The timer is set for thirty seconds. The countdown starts. She steps back through a broken doorway by the thick supporting wall. Thirty seconds. Twenty-nine. Twenty-eight. And on. The other song Dee loved was:

> All good children need travelling shoes
> Drive your problem from here
> All good people read good books
> Now your conscience is clear
> Now your conscience is clear.

Down here there's a slow demonic rumble. Heavy police vehicles pass by overhead. *Look your love has drawn red from my hands.* Ten. Nine. Eight. *Come down after me you bastard fucker Rosslyn. Be the first to die the death from the gases squeezed from the fugu fish. God Almighty, send the fucker down here to me so I can see him die.*

She kneels on the floor. The green slime seeps through the knees of her black policewoman's trousers. Three. Two. One and – *thunk.* The perfect small explosion opens up the hole to the tunnel. Even before the dust clears, she's holding her breath with her eyes shut tight, groping her way through the dust and into the tunnel, carrying with her the tetrotodoxin canisters, her flashlight, her handgun and her equipment bag.

The flashlight beam shows the way downwards to the foul dark water. Its smell is rotten like milk soured during a thunderstorm. It worsens like the stench of meat maggots bred by the fishermen cousins on the maternal side of the family across the Irish Sea. The beam of light cuts the dark and the tunnel seems longer and narrower than she had expected and she has gross sewer rats for company. Fat and sleek and poisonous. The light shows a mouth bared. The rat lisps and hisses.

'I feel good,' she says. 'Good.' But the stink is nauseous. *The blood-dimmed tide is loosed, and everywhere the ceremony of innocence is drowned; the falcon cannot hear the falconer; things fall apart; the centre cannot hold.* Deeper into the tunnel the water rises to her waist. She holds the canisters, the gun, the flashlight and the bag above her head. Her feet feel sucked down into the thickening slime. *Not night but death. God of mercy, these tunnels have been sent to save my soul. Now faster. These are the plans of Your subterranean world no one knows. Just me. Keep going to the end. Show me the light. Your Light. A terrible beauty is born.*

She pushes deeper into the tunnel. Ahead is the noise of rushing water and, miracle, the plans are right, the sewer floor is rising at a tilt. Closer to the wall the water is sluggish and turbid. A rat slithers across her shoulder. 'Fuck you, Ratty. Gerroff!' She twists her neck away and too far sideways near the wall, so the rusted steel wire, cut and twisted and sharp as a butcher's meathook cuts into her neck beneath her ear. She winces. Bites her lips in pain. Squeezes her chin sideways to her shoulder and feels the gout of blood. Her fists clench the gun, the canisters and the flashlight and her equipment bag strap. *God Almighty have mercy. Mother of mercy. I'm bleeding bad. I hear you say, Dee, I love you girl do this for me not night but death.* She prays to the Almighty that the car above will soon explode. *Please God kill them now. Start the chaos. Give me turmoil. Now.* In her mind she conjures a genuflection to bring her luck.

49

Alarm bells smashed the calm of Thames House. Most of its two thousand or so staff supposed a fire drill practice was underway. The fire practice, so they reasonably reckoned, must have been arranged for the visiting prime minister's benefit. Here was the perfect chance to demonstrate the formidable protection afforded to the world's most modern working repository of secrets. The hidden pumping of the heart of government, the guardhouse keeping the Kingdom United: here is proof that Thames House is invincible.

Therefore, according to the fire notices on the walls of every room in the flamboyant building, the staff 'processed in an orderly fashion'. WALK AND DO NOT RUN TO THE DESIGNATED EMERGENCY ASSEMBLY POINTS. A few senior officers stayed behind on each floor level to make quite sure that the most sensitive offices were secure. God help anyone who had failed to lock their document safes and computer programmes against attack by fire, by flood or bomb.

Then, everything checked, the senior officers made their various ways to the EAPs, the emergency assembly points. There, once they had checked their staffs were all present and correct, they waited for the all clear. Throughout the building they stood in waiting groups, chattering, vaguely amused, pleased as schoolchildren gathered to satisfy the visiting officers from the schools inspectorate. Many of them clutched bottles of mineral water: Perrier, Badoit, Volvic, Strathmore; defence against the efficiency of the air-conditioning system that dried their skin, their lungs and probably their brain cells too. Many were irritated by this practice show of safety precaution. Others were resentful when they found smoking prohibited in the DSAs, the designated smoking areas. And then the alarm bells stopped for a moment and the silence was interrupted by the voice of the chief safety officer over the loudspeakers.

This was no practice. It was for real.

'All personnel will proceed to Group Two EAPs and report to DFOs.' (Translation: Go to the most secure emergency assembly points and show yourself to the duty fire officers.)

It was a new and serious twist. No longer a practice. Jesus Christ. A bomb alert. They made their way, like insects, hundreds of them on each floor, to the interior of Thames House where the vast protective walls, massively reinforced against bomb attack from any angle, afforded maximum security.

Once they reached the safe areas, they waited, more anxious than before, for further announcements from the chief safety officer, the former major in the Corps of Royal Engineers, whose droning drawl had so often steered them through the emergency procedures he had personally contrived. This evening the major had a packed house under his command. Staff had been told to remain fully operational until 20.30 hours; to be at home to the prime minister and the home secretary.

Crowded together, perturbed, they waited for the major's orders, which were not long in coming. Once again, the major changed his mind. Older hands at interrogation detected a quiver in his voice hinting at fear: hesitation, the beginnings of a stammer.

'The building will now be evacuated. Floors: basement levels, ground floor to floor four to evacuate by the north and south exits.' And suddenly the major's voice had to compete against the renewed ringing of the alarms. 'Floors five and upwards including telecommunications and satellite stations to the roof area ... I repeat: in the event of signal failure requests for direction will be made to senior fire officers.' The rushed orders inspired new confusion in his listeners. 'This is the CSO speaking. I repeat. Are you receiving me? ... What? ... Wilco. Out.' New sounds, klaxons, hooting, wailing, powerful sirens, drowned his awful warning.

Amusement turned to unease; to anxiety; to growing panic in the corridors and passageways and the emergency stairwells. And when the first of the men and women tripped and fell, those behind them, like a drunken stadium crowd hell-bent on escape, were wholly incapable of preventing themselves from falling over the sprawling and falling bodies.

When the screaming started the panic had taken hold.

Rosslyn shoved and barged his way through the desperate crowd jammed into the entrance area.

Why evacuate, for Christ's sake? Don't you know there's a bloody suss car parked on your fucking doorstep? The two thousand of you will flee the building. Hopelessly exposed. Head on into the fury of the bomb blast. Do you WANT to die? He could sense their fear. He could smell it on their breath. The sickening smell of fear. He saw the wide eyes, like a pen full of sheep in fear of herdsmen rounding them up for the final ride to the abbatoir. The smell seemed almost tangible. This smell of rottenness, the aura of helplessness surrounding the condemned prisoner in the dock.

Don't you know, you brain-dead clowns? You will run out of here. Be ripped to shreds. The bomb squad is out there with their howling sirens. The warning lights. The roaring motorbikes. The bullhorns. Can't you see the trap?

Too late. The howls of panic were beginning.

'GAS!'

'Get out of the fucking way. Get outside! NERVE GAS!'

And the screaming rising to full pitch and the major's voice rising from the ceiling speakers in hysteria like a toff horserace commentator's.

He jabbed a guard in the kidneys with his fist, then threw himself through the exit doors. Outside.

Here he stopped.

Armed police had the road sealed off. He saw officers running from Rover 827s carrying carbines. They wore black overalls and black slit-eyed masks and carried gas masks. Some pointed their guns at the staff leaving the building.

Through the bullhorns: 'Get back. There is a bomb. This is the police!'

Men and women were trampled underfoot. A briefcase broke open in the road, its contents, dozens of sheets of paper, scattered. He glimpsed a woman police officer fiddling uncertainly with a Webley gas grenade launcher. He saw several women run from the building with blood streaming down their faces like innocent victims of a pub brawl. One of them screamed: 'Can't you see I'm pregnant!'

With his gun in his hand Rosslyn jumped the police cordon of plastic tape. Gaynor stood at the end of Lambeth Bridge by the roundabout. 'She left the car,' he said. 'She's carrying gear.'

'Where's she gone?'

'I don't know. She's wearing black trousers. White shirt. Police uniform of sorts. It's her. That's the car.'

'Why didn't you stop her?'

'I saw this woman cop get out. I didn't see where she went. One minute she's by that car, the next she's gone. Called the bomb squad. Then Harding. The routine drill. She has to have gone round the back. The only route's from the river. It's a rising tide. Enough water to prevent her getting in via that route, if there is one.'

High above, figures appeared on the parapet of Thames House. More and more of them stood silhouetted against the sky. An SO 19 helicopter was hovering a few hundred feet above the roof.

'She can't have got round to the rear,' Rosslyn said. 'It's totally blocked.'

Gaynor shrugged. 'Best put your gun away.'

It was no use asking the police officers if they'd seen a WPC who didn't quite fit. The place was swarming with them. And one of them screamed at Rosslyn and Gaynor to clear off. 'Take cover!'

Then Rosslyn saw it.

Round the corner of Lambeth Bridge at the western side.

The steps down to the riverside pathway.

To his left, the river.

To his right: the single-storey disused public toilets.

'Take cover!' The shouting was even more insistent.

And in his mind he saw *those plans again. These toilets.*

The steel doors had been put there years ago, welded and bolted, fortified against tramps and beggars. The protective chains of the side entrance, the attendant's door, had been clipped apart. Rosslyn touched the naked steel, then went inside and saw the derelict urinals, the row of basins and recent marks in the slime on the broken floor tiles. He pointed towards a brick wall. A hole had been blown in the wall, large enough to crawl through. 'This is her. She's gone through this. She's here somewhere. She has to be. Give me your flashlight.' Gaynor's was a small metallic pocket torch with a powerful narrow beam. Turning it on, Rosslyn edged himself through the hole in the bricks. Gaynor followed.

'Service duct,' Rosslyn said. 'Look.'

They were barely able to stand up. After a few paces the narrow beam of the flashlight showed the tunnel sloping downwards to some steps. Rosslyn trod carefully. The rubber soles of his shoes hardly gripped the thick slime. There was a sudden movement to his side. He flinched. The beam illuminated the wet and twitching body of an escaping rat.

At the base of the steps they stood in the putrid water. It was almost completely black except for the torchlight and some other much weaker shafts of light filtering through overhead drain covers. Rosslyn kept close to the soaking wall. He thought he could sense the rising of the tide. Reeking of faeces, the water seemed to get thicker and slimier as it grew deeper.

'There's no way back,' Gaynor whispered. 'It's filling up. Shit, I can't see fuck all. Point the light. Jesus, the stink.'

The odour was overwhelming. 'We're going on,' Rosslyn said. He heard Gaynor retch.

The hoarse raw choke and the splash of his vomit.

Fuck it.

'Keep moving.'

Ahead there was a louder sound: rushing water, like the emptying of a massive pipe. A new shaft of thin watery light from above showed a curve in the tunnel. Rosslyn cursed.

Pig-thick engineers – or were they architects? – must have reckoned the tide would keep any sane human out of this fetid tunnel. They hadn't reckoned on an Insect.

Up to his waist in the cold and filthy water he urged Gaynor on. 'Or do you want to go back?'

'No,' Gaynor said. 'Go on.' But his voice was lost in a sudden roar from above. The tunnel heaved. A tide of wet dust, a flying paste like concentrated wet manure, fell through the darkness. Then old masonry flopped and splashed into the water.

The car bomb had exploded overhead.

The timing was perfect. The decoy bomb. More dust. More flying glass. Splinters slicing flesh. More mutilation. The searing pain of fragments in the eyes. The burning plastic. The living wounded and the dead.

Gaynor said: 'I can't see.'

'Here.' Rosslyn grabbed the outstretched hand and lost hold of his handgun. 'Gun.' He only just managed to hold on to the flashlight. He lowered himself in the water up to his neck. 'Christ.' His foot touched the gun. He held his breath and submerged, his hands finding the weapon. 'Christ. It's no bloody use now.'

'Let's go back,' Gaynor said.

'No.'

'She's fucking armed, Alan.'

'We're going on.'

Faint light ahead showed a fork in the passage. To the right was the source of the noise of running water. The torch beam showed faces of rats and their wet bodies darting along the ledges. To the left was a short flight of steps. When they reached them the ooze and mud was thinner and Rosslyn's feet squelched on drier stone. Ten more steps and they were both up in a different, narrower passage where a layer of damp waste across the stone floor concealed a network of rusted twisted cables. Other useless cables, long since severed, protruded from the walls at either side: remnants of building works carried out more than half a century before. This was an old access passage, a pre-war sealed conduit, a route on a forgotten map. The passage twisted sharply left, then right, then left twice more. Gradually the air, still and cold, grew drier and the stink was more like that of sickly poison fungi.

Rosslyn's wet shoes clanged against a heavy metal object. Possibly some abandoned generator. They were standing in a dry room. Then a corridor. A mesh of spiders' webs stuck to his mouth. As he wiped his lips his narrowed stinging eyes could just make out another steel door. It stood slightly open. First Rosslyn, then Gaynor, squeezed through it. Across a space, large as some disused garage, the floor thick with grease, was another wall. This one seemed to be of relatively recent construction. And the gap in the broken masonry showed all the signs of a small and controlled explosion. From above, he could just hear the sirens wailing. Again, the timing to perfection. This perfect plot. Rosslyn stared into the gloom, his mouth shut, breathing slowly through his nose. *She's blasted in under cover of MI5's crazy sirens, the strident hooting of the klaxons. And she won't have dropped her weapon.*

'She's in here somewhere,' Rosslyn whispered. 'We'll move in without the light.' Here in the darkness, he had the feeling he was being drawn unarmed and defenceless towards her, that she'd drawn him, as she wanted, into her slime, her subterranean territory; that finally she had won.

A hum grew in his ears. It was electric and powerful like a warning. *She is taunting me. Come and get me if you fucking dare. And you haven't even got a gun that works.* He felt a warm stickiness on his head. *What would I do if I were her?* In here. In the impenetrable darkness. His mouth was full of the taste of the dead water. *What would I do? Bank on chaos, invest in it. Then, after the first alerts, in the panic, wait for the bomb. Then let them come and get me.*

Overhead, he heard a strange wheezing and sucking. Close by him in the blackness, Gaynor's voice was saying: 'Where the fuck is she?'

Rosslyn made no reply. He was touching the stickiness on his head, in his hair, but when he lifted his hand to his nose he could only smell the Thames mud.

And more of the new warm liquid dripped on to him. It was running down his face. Now, when he caught some of it on his tongue, it tasted sweet and he realized it was blood. *I am tasting blood.* He spat.

Stepping back, he pushed Gaynor against the wall. Gaynor seemed to be on the verge of saying something. He caught his breath. Rosslyn turned the flashlight on, pointing it upwards, so its beam shone straight into McKeague's face.

His eyes took in the lacerated face, probably slashed by the old rusted wire protruding from the walls like spikes in a torture cell. Her arms were soaked and bloody and folded across two canisters, a length of piping and a vacuum pump. She was wedged up above him between the wall and crumbling masonry near a broken air-duct pipe. This was the source of the wheezing and sucking noise.

'Rosslyn.'

The blood poured out of her neck beneath her ear.

'The canisters,' she said. 'If you shoot.'

'Hand them down to me, McKeague. Slowly.'

It seemed she hadn't heard him. 'We'll kill a thousand of the fuckers,' she said. 'Right here, and, Christ, the prime minister, the fucker's here, Rosslyn, with us.'

'Let's do a deal, McKeague. Very calm, OK?'

'Fuck you, Rosslyn.'

'You want to die?' he said. 'I don't think so.'

Suddenly he saw her hand rise, and the gun pointing at him. Turning off the flashlight, he threw himself against the wall.

The shots hit the stonework above him.

'You bastard, Rosslyn,' she said and fired again. The shots whined away. Then silence for a few seconds.

Very slowly he edged himself towards the buttress of crumbling masonry, his useless gun in one hand, the torch in the other. Then in one arching movement he threw the gun with all his force to where he calculated she'd wedged herself. At the same time he turned on the flashlight to blind her. He jumped, a foot, perhaps two, grabbing her left shoe. And then pulled her, his weight sinking against the floor, so she fell sideways on top of him, a knee in his solar plexus. He felt her blood in his eyes.

The canisters and her gun fell near Gaynor who took up her gun and the torch, pointing both at McKeague who was holding a pointed chisel. She lunged with it at Rosslyn's throat. But it sliced instead through his sodden jacket sleeve.

Rosslyn saw the gun in Gaynor's hand. He was pointing it at McKeague's head.

'No!' Rosslyn shouted.

He swallowed blood; saw her roll over and grab the chisel. At the same moment Rosslyn snatched the gun from Gaynor's hand.

The chisel was raised, curving round towards his face –

Rosslyn fired between her eyes and her head seemed to freeze. Explode. Flying hair and hot blood caught in the beam of the flashlight held in Gaynor's shaking hands.

For the second time that evening Gaynor threw up. This time he retched drily. Nothing came. The air was red and black.

Rosslyn retrieved the torch and gathered up the pair of canisters. He spat more blood from his mouth. Then choked and swallowed.

The torch beam picked out McKeague's broken corpse. She lay twisted and still.

Her body seemed strangely fragile.

Her blood flowed from the back of her blasted skull.

50

I remember the ugly fury in the faces of the security guards, the wall of men and women like gaolers advancing with guns and truncheons. One of them stands with his hands in his crotch like a footballer protecting his balls against the penalty taker.

'Drop your guns,' shouts a man who turns out to be Major Someone. 'Theart's 'n order,' he says nasally. A woman covers her mouth with her hand as if to say 'You stink.'

'They've shot a police officer. Look, her uniform!'

We do stink. Gaynor and I are soaking wet, our clothes black with mud and the slime and grease. My hair and face are running with blood,

McKeague's blood, and here I am, carrying a gun. I am the enemy.

'Layer yer weppens darn vewy slerlearh indid,' says the shaky major. 'On the fleur.'

Another voice says: 'You're under arrest.'

God in hell, I think. This is it. The spooks are making out we're the terrorists. This is our doing. They're saying we did the bomb. We were in this with the dead woman.

I set the gun down in the dirt on the floor.

'Gerd,' the major sneers. 'Anything you may sayer –' he begins, but doesn't finish, because I lose my bottle, step forward and drive an uppercut to his jaw.

For a moment it's a mob scene. They want their revenge, these guards, and a truncheon thumps my neck and shoulder. The pain's excruciating. More blows. Black.

The rest is a blur. As though I'm coming round after major surgery. I see Harding's face, drawn and very worried. Maybe he's looking down on me before I'm lifted inside the ambulance. Maybe afterwards. There are jostling onlookers with their angry and frightened faces.

'It's over now,' Harding's saying. 'Don't say anything. Leave it to me.' He doesn't mention McKeague. Then he's thanking Dickie Gaynor. I hear Gaynor say: 'Thank Alan. It's down to him. Incredible. In-bloody-credible.'

51

For the third – or is it now the fourth? – time, I'm back in the King Edward VII Hospital for Officers. I have a blurred impression of suits and guns and ID cards and short-wave radios. An Australian nurse whistles 'Waltzing Matilda'.

My collarbone is apparently smashed to bits and there's a lump, feels the size of a melon, on the right side of my face. I can taste blood.

A black guy shaves my beard. 'Soon be home,' he says sweetly.

Somewhere, far off, there are muffled news bulletins. The Millbank bomb in the street outside Thames House. I fancy a woman's saying: 'If it hadn't been for advance intelligence gathering and the swift action of police officers, the loss of life would have been catastrophic.' Later, the prime minister delivers the usual speech along the lines of 'we'll never surrender'.

It has a misplaced Churchillian ring – spirit of the Blitz, that sort of jazz. No mention of the meeting, Insect or McKeague. 'We may thank God there were no casualties,' says a bishop on the BBC. TV or radio I don't know. I'm having difficulty with my sight. Like conjunctivitis I had when I was a kid and I'd wake up with my eyelids stuck together and panic.

It takes only three to four days for a bomb blast to become stale news.

A week later, when they remove the bandages from my eyes, the Millbank incident is forgotten. The bomb failed to break even a single pane of glass in Thames House. The strength of the bulletproofing is proven.

Comes the day when Harding asks for me to be brought to his bedside. He doesn't need to tell me he's taken a downward spiral. His eyes are hollower, his cheeks drawn.

'I'm fighting back,' he says. I can see he's losing. 'They've closed it down.'

'There has to be an inquiry.'

'There should be,' he says. 'There isn't going to be one, though.'

I tell him I've appreciated all he's done for me, how much his trust meant, how sad it is the truth will never come out.

He says something about being in the right place at the right time. Unlike Bryan Wesley, who's been given early retirement. 'Last I heard,' says Harding, 'they had a whip-round to buy him a one-way ticket to Manila. He can satisfy his taste for rice flesh.'

He looks so very weary. I feel sorry for him. Sad and very sorry.

He says: 'You know the best way to keep secrets, the best way's to forget them.'

'But,' I say, 'I think they could at least apologize.'

'It isn't in their nature,' Harding says. 'Their trade is lying. They seek out lies with lies. Their doors are closed. There's no such thing as accountability. By definition, they're accountable to themselves. How can liars account to themselves? How? With what? Definitely not with the truth. Why? Because they deceive themselves. They have no mission, only this idea of accountability.

'But the terrorists, they have a mission. They know where they're heading. I'm bloody sure of it. And you think accountability – this openness will beat the terrorists?'

He pauses. 'Think about it some time. I have. I do. And I'm telling you, the terrorists will win if they're up against the present mob. I hate the thought, I really hate it – but they'll win. In a way, I'm glad I won't be here to see it.'

He's exhausted. It seems unfair to let him talk like this. I offer a silent prayer that he'll survive.

Then he says: 'Put it behind you now, Alan. Go back to Gaynor and your crowd. Do what you do best.'

I stay silent. He smiles at me. I smile back. At that moment I feel great affection for him.

AUTUMN FALL

Just when we are safest, there's a sunset-touch,
A fancy from a flower-bell, some one's death.

Robert Browning, *Bishop Blougram's Apology*

52

The continued absence of Mary's diary had prompted him to start one himself. It began with the description of the final moments beneath Thames House. He had left Mary's diary in Cavallero's offices at Vauxhall Cross and she swore blind there was no sign of it. The handgun with which he'd shot the hapless drug pushers in Manchester had been sent back to New Scotland Yard. The Coker tape had been destroyed as well as the stacks of reports left on the table of the meeting room at Thames House. Cavallero had collected them and had them shredded. She sent Mary's kimono and the photograph of her to his flat in Pimlico. More than three times during the following weeks he called Cavallero with the request the diary be returned. She affected to know nothing about it.

53

He took Gaynor's advice and went to see a therapist in Harley Street.

How do you feel?

Same as before.

Do you dream?

No.

The woman you shot – what do you feel about her?

Nothing.

Nothing?

It wasn't nice.

I sympathize, you feel dead.

What?

Do you feel a sense of deadness?

No.

And – er, Davina, you loved her?

No.

And your girl, Mary, what about her?

What about her?

Do you think about her?

Yes.

What do you think?

She's dead.

They didn't get anywhere. After two sessions he chucked it in.

<h1 style="text-align:center">54</h1>

Gaynor encouraged him to return to work.

They talked in Gaynor's office of Harding, whose condition had apparently stabilized. It seemed a sort of reconciliation had been achieved between Harding and his wife. Now the writing was on the wall, she'd come back to him.

'His pension's the incentive,' Gaynor said cynically. 'He won't see anyone else. Just his wife. Not even his children.'

Rosslyn wished he'd thought to ask Harding more about his children. Now, he supposed, it was too late. He ventured to ask Gaynor about Mary's diary and Gaynor seemed to have anticipated his question.

'You left it at Vauxhall Cross,' he said. 'You were pressed for time. We all were, weren't we? Harding called me to one side. He told me: "Have Cavallero destroy this. It's very dangerous. It implicates Alan's girl."'

Rosslyn looked round Gaynor's office. Anywhere but at Gaynor's face. 'It was only her diary,' Rosslyn said. 'Her life with me.'

'I know. I'm sorry.'

'You're sorry. How do you think I feel?'

'Alan, calm down. Harding was right. It was all down there – on the last page. The gas. The whole thing.'

'She had nothing to do with it.'

'No one's saying she had. Know why? Because no one read the diary.'

'Harding did. Must have.'

'There wasn't time. He skimmed it. Saw enough.'

'And Cavallero, did she read it?'

'No.'

'But she destroyed it. She must have looked at it.'

'She didn't. I destroyed it, Alan. In this shredder. Blame me, not Harding. Not Cavallero. I'm very sorry. I had to do it.'

'You should never have done it,' Rosslyn said, shaking his head. 'Not without asking me.'

'You would've stopped me, wouldn't you? I don't blame you for feeling pissed off. What you have to understand is, it would have looked very bad if MI5 had got hold of it. Suppose we'd never caught up with McKeague. Suppose . . . you can't hide, what, fifteen hundred, two thousand dead. MI5 staff. Christ, and we're talking of the prime minister and the home secretary and the secretary of state for Northern Ireland. Come on, Alan, us too.'

'It didn't happen.'

'I know. Suppose though, MI5 had got McKeague first, instead of us.'

'They didn't.'

Gaynor said: 'Suppose McKeague had made it to Dublin, Cuba, whatever route she intended to take. Then Mary's diary had turned up. Listen, Harding was protecting you. He always did. You owe it to him not to be angry. Right?'

'Maybe.'

Maybe not.

'Right, Alan. We did the right thing. For you. Don't forget that.'

Forget?

'Well, you may have done. If so you must have been the only ones. Somebody knows who killed Dee McKeague and somebody knows who doctored and planted the tape.'

Gaynor scratched the palm of his hand. 'Alan, look, a bit of advice. Don't start a crusade. Don't come on the righteous man. Don't rock the boat. You are not going to get the truth. You know and I know that MI5 are behind this. So accept it. Leave it alone. Let sleeping dogs lie. And they aren't going to write the history of Davina Wesley either. She was a sad case, a very sad case. Crazy, don't you think? You should know.'

He's warming to his theme. Twisting the blade.

'People kill for many different reasons,' Gaynor continued.

'There she was. Carrying on the outwardly normal life. Intelligent. Trusted. Respected. All of that. Someone like her doesn't dance around advertising the fact she is bloody certifiable. You don't have to be crazy to kill. That's the sad fact, Alan. Case closed. I've told you. You did the right thing. Don't torment yourself any more.'

'I'd like to hear this from Harding. I mean, I wish he had told me himself. That diary, it kept me going on. A sort of talisman. Her voice from the dead.'

'I know you loved her. You have to put it behind you now. Don't bother Harding. He's dying. Let's get back to routine, Alan. Try to put it out of your mind.'

Put it out of mind. Like where?

55

Today is Friday. A beautiful autumn day. A perfect blue sky over London. The leaves of the trees copper, bronze, crimson. A nip in the air. The evenings growing shorter.

My other diary – my appointment diary – is filling up. So is this. You write it down, you forget it. You close the book on it.

Tomorrow's my birthday. So Gaynor's invited a few people down to the Angel at Rotherhithe. It's supposed to be a surprise party. Ironic – but it's Verity Cavallero who blew the gaffe. She calls me to say she'll be late out of work at Vauxhall Cross. 'There are no shops around here,' she says. 'My present to you is dinner for two at the White Tower. You and me. After the party. There's something I need to tell you, ask you.'

I accept. In another world I could fancy Verity.

I went to the Angel with Gaynor. Upstairs. 'Better than the last time,' he said.
I agreed. 'Damn right.'
The doors opened. The room was dark. Then the lights came on. Everyone was there. A smuggler's nightmare. Packed with HM Customs & Excise officers. And a big banner: HAPPY BIRTHDAY ALAN!

'Aaah, aaahh, A.R. Ha. Ha. Ha. Happy birthday to you!'

And the rest: champagne, streamers; 'Why Was He Born So Beautiful?' It was a great party.

Cavallero arrived, done up to the nines. 'Fuck me,' a bloke said. 'Madonna.' And: 'We're in the wrong game. Alan's a dark horse. Where does he find them?'

She kissed me on the lips. A taste of lip salve. 'Tonight's on me, darl,' she said. 'My bleeper's off. Is yours?'

'I don't have one.'

'That's not what I hear,' she said, and floated off to work the room.

The Angel's food was great. More champagne. The best.

Gaynor stood on a chair. There were shouts of: 'Open your bags. Vatman. Body search. Strip!'

He raised his hands for hush: 'I don't make speeches.'

'Good!' his secretary shouted. 'Liar!'

Lots of laughs.

'This is a special party. To celebrate Alan's birthday, his recovery from that mugging in Westminster. His return to duty. That's it. Raise your glasses. Alan.'

'Alan! Alan! Alan! Speech! Speech!' Feet were stamping, fists pounding the tables. A glass broke.

I stood on a chair. 'Thanks. Thank you and this is a great party. I'm really pleased to be back. Here's to Dickie and you!'

They all cheered. Long, long cheers. I had the feeling many of them knew it wasn't a mugging. If so, they weren't saying. It was a secret to be forgotten.

56

At the White Tower, Verity Cavallero spares no expense.

She tells him: 'I'm being posted to the Far East. Bangkok.' She leans closer. 'What do you think?'

'Bangkok. Never been there.'

'Me neither,' she says. She looks at him intently. 'Alan, tonight you're staying with me. That's the good news.'

He smiles.

'Will you stay with me tonight, please, in my bed?'

'What's the bad news? There's a bolster down the middle?'

'No.' She speaks softly. 'Alan. I'm sorry. Tom Harding died this morning. Dickie asked me to tell you tonight once the party was over.'

He freezes.

'His wife and children were with him when he went. It was very peaceful. No pain. He died with the dignity you'd expect.'

Tears form in his eyes.

'He made it up with his wife at the very end,' Cavallero says. 'She's a brave woman. She put up with more than most wives.'

'I never knew her.'

'Here.' She hands him her handkerchief. 'Don't cry, Alan.'

He can't stop the tears.

She fills his glass.

He gets up to go.

She reaches for his hand. 'Alan.'

She opens her bag.

'His wife contacted me a couple of days ago. Harding asked her to. Here.'

She hands him something wrapped inside a folded black cotton handkerchief.

'Open it,' she says. 'It's for you. What's inside.'

He unfolds the handkerchief.

'This,' he says. 'This handkerchief. It was Harding's?'

'Yes.'

Inside he finds a wristwatch.

'Tom Harding's watch,' he says.

'Yes,' she says. 'His wife, his widow, told me to be sure to explain the inscription on the back to you. To tell you his family name was actually Uglow. Harding was his second name. Thomas, Tom, his first. He asked that you forgive him. His wife knew about Mary. She had forgiven him. But, most of all, he wanted your forgiveness. I can see why he changed his name before he joined the cops, can't you?'

He turns the watch over, face down on the table.

It is a fine Swiss watch.

On its back is a handwritten engraving:

TO MY BELOVED THUG
MY LOVE ALWAYS
MARY

280